Praise for
Hell Comes To Hollywood

"*Hell Comes To Hollywood* is all-encompassing, featuring stories that span from wonderfully gratuitous, over-the-top gorefests...to tales that are genuinely haunting and linger in your mind long afterward..."
—Vivienne Vaughn, *Fangoria*

"Gorier than any PG-13 horror flick you'll see, and written better (by a mile) than any SyFy schlockfest, *Hell Comes To Hollywood* is worth a look."
—Blu Gilliand, *Aint It Cool News Horror*

"A cool collection of stories. Fun, gory, and scary in equal measure—and a sick look at the way Hollywood might *really* work..."
—Michael Davis, Writer/Director, *Shoot 'Em Up, Monster Man*

"If you're a fan of horror, delivered in any medium, this is a must-read."
—Matt Molgaard, Horror Novel Reviews

"...a badass book of short tales of terror..."
—Brett Pierce, co-Director/Writer/Producer of *Deadheads*

"*Hell Comes To Hollywood* puts that extra special chill up your spine that you've been craving. Do yourself a favor and pick up a copy."
—Little Doll Claudia, *Darkest Radio*

Hell Comes To Hollywood I
was nominated for a Bram Stoker Award

HELL COMES TO HOLLYWOOD II

Twenty-Two More Tales Of Tinseltown Terror

Produced, Directed And
EDITED BY ERIC MILLER

Big Time Books™
Los Angeles, California
www.BigTimeBooks.com

CONTENTS

ACKNOWLEDGMENTS

What is Hollywood's favorite thing, other than billion dollar grosses, plastic surgery, and shiny golden statues, that is? Why, a sequel, of course!

Hellywood is no exception, so here we are with the bigger and badder *Hell Comes To Hollywood II*. After the first book had a sold-out signing at Dark Delicacies, got lots of great reviews, and was nominated for a Bram Stoker Award, what else could I do but bring you more blood, guts, and cinema-based madness?

As with the first book, I could not have done this alone. So again many thanks are due. In no particular order, I'd like to thank the Academy, and:

The writers of the first book. Your pioneering visions set a high bar for the second batch of twisted storytellers I rounded up, and I know we did you proud.

The fans of the *Hell* series—readers, reviewers, groupies—these books would be nothing without you. I hope this volume will thrill and chill you as much as the first one did.

Del and Sue Howison. The signing they hosted for *Hell Comes To Hollywood* was a smash and got us off to a great start, and all the advice on editing, book selling, and all things horror is much appreciated.

Hollywood. If you weren't such a wonderfully screwed up place, we wouldn't have such a rich source for material.

Shane Bitterling, again for all the behind the scenes work and sugar cream pie recipes.

John Palisano, Eric Guignard, Tim Chizmar, and the many others who helped and inspired me in various meaningful ways.

Patrick Shiffrar, not just for helping in the typo hunt, but for story notes, moral support, and doggie day care as well.

Graydon Schlichter and Jennifer Knighton for their kick-ass voice work on the *Hell* Audio Books, as well as Graydon's audio production skills and laser-eyed typo blasting.

Drew Pierce for another amazing cover.

Cecil "Helly" Hellington for letting me raise you from the dead (again) and use your likeness for the cover. Modern Hollywood is the perfect place for a killer director like you—get hacking.

And Wendy, again and always.

Trilogy, anyone?

Eric Miller
Los Angeles, California
July, 2014

FOREWORD

When Eric Miller first told me about his plans to create another horror anthology set in Hollywood, I thought it was a great idea. I mean, the stories just write themselves. The illusion of this town we call Tinsel looks like a fairy tale from afar. TV and magazines shower us with pictures of beautiful, rich celebrities living glamorous lives that we either envy, or long to have.

But that's all smoke and mirrors.

The reality, the underbelly, is rife for terrifying tales. There are the true-life murders that have been tabloid fodder for decades. And stories of innocents taken advantage of by lecherous power players to satisfy their twisted desires. And a studio system that often operates like a meat grinder, sucking in talent and spitting out cookie-cutter banality. Some say Hollywood is a place where dreams die, souls are crushed and morals shed like a molting snake. And they would be right.

But it's not all doom and gloom. Many people find success when their movies open at a multiplex, come out on DVD, or appear on the internet. Sometimes success is just finishing that script that has been scratching at your skull, desperate to emerge, for years. All of that is awesome, but the forbidding stuff makes better material for horror stories.

And horror stories are something I love.

One thing that many screenwriters have in common is they started off reading scary tales. Before I watched horror films, my youth was filled with Greek and Roman mythology. Tales of gods and monsters. Until that one fateful day, I'm sure many horror fans can relate to, when I discovered the wonderful, and terrifying, worlds that lived on the shelves of the local bookstore and my school library. There were the creepy stories of dread woven by Lois Duncan, John Saul and Peter Straub. The twisted tales, both novels and short stories, told by the master of the macabre; Stephen King. And the fantastical imaginings of the amazing Clive Barker. These authors, and so many others, built the foundation and fortified my love of horror. Just as they did for so many others.

As the years went by, and I got caught up in the whirlwind of Hollywood, the novels and short stories I read dropped dramatically. When focusing on screenwriting, your mind is conditioned to think about a three act structure. How to write a story in 100 pages that's all about action, visuals and dialogue. And like a kid who lived in Neverland for too long, I forgot where I—or rather, my love of horror—began. It was in the dark, under the covers with a flashlight, reading one of "those books" that my mom didn't want me to read. A scary story that frightened me, but also touched me in a profound way. A way that allowed me to excise some of my own demons and youthful fears. While also creating new ones.

That's why I feel honored to write the forward to this second edition of *Hell Comes To Hollywood*. Like the previous anthology, Eric is doing two things. One, he is giving screenwriters like me, who've seen our writing, and reading, relegated to scripts or websites about movies, a chance to get back to our roots and in touch with the fiction that helped mold us. And two, I believe he'll introduce a whole new generation of readers to tantalizing tales of terror that will create new fans, and reignite the passion of old fans, to a genre that will never die.

Jeffrey Reddick
Screenwriter/Producer/Actor

FADE IN:

Richard Christian Matheson is an acclaimed author and screenwriter/producer for television and film. He has worked with Steven Spielberg, Stephen King, Brian Singer and many others on Emmy winning miniseries, films and hit TV series. Matheson has a cutting-edge voice in surreal, psychological horror fiction and is considered a master of the short story. His work has appeared in 125 major anthologies including many Years' Best *volumes. Sixty stories are collected in* Scars And Other Distinguishing Marks *and* Dystopia. *His mystery novella,* The Ritual Of Illusion, *is a sinister love letter to the movies. A professional drummer, he studied with legendary* Cream *drummer Ginger Baker. He is president of* Matheson Entertainment. *The story included here is an excerpt from Matheson's terror novel,* Created By, *a fiercely funny, scathing glimpse of network television.*

SETTING

Richard Christian Matheson

THE HOUSE DROWSED ABOVE SEA, groggy perfection.

It had been built in the fifties and the real estate agent, a blond bayonet, bloused in Claiborne, told Alan previous owners had included a neurosurgeon, a famous mystery novelist, a feminist lawyer who once punched Dick Cavett in the nuts, and a witless, top-forty-hit-derrick who wrote a song called *Sunshine Lady*.

The current owner had been aboard the brain trust that invented those big cardboard things you put in your windshield to block the sun. He was currently in the T-shirt racket and worth over twenty million give or take a cotton blend.

Alan walked around admiring the breathtaking view, hearing waves sledge shore. He passed leather sofas, carved African masks and framed T-shirt business awards. Started humming

Sunshine Lady, a cloying, kindergarten melody he'd always hated. It was about a perfect girl, with a perfect "sunrise smile" and how she was mysteriously abducted by an exquisite sunset that just couldn't resist her shiny teeth. It had made the top ten in '82 but got bumped by Melanie's *I've Got a Brand New Pair of Roller Skates*—a more complex achievement.

The place was exactly what Alan was looking for. Big, airy rooms, light-flooded, accented with white-washed trim. Huge decks off the living room and master, overlooking blueberry sea. There was a fireplace you could look through from both the living and dining rooms, a sandblasted ceiling. Glass blocks that stacked sunlight. It was tasteful, easy to be in. Almost a million. But the way things could go with the pilot, the new deal at Universal, money was coming fast. And he wanted a new place. A new atmosphere. Something different.

Something he couldn't put his finger on.

"You like?" she was following Alan around. Lifting big sunglasses.

He didn't answer, starting to remember something. An article he'd read, years ago. An item that evaded detail, tucked away in the back of *Variety*. About the...but it couldn't've been this house. This house was too cheerful. If something like that had happened in a place, you'd still feel it. There would be a feeling; a nausea. The white walls would have a telltale pinkness here and there where the paint didn't quite—

"Nice."

"Gorgeous." She had a lung-cancer laugh; struggling for sufficient oxygen. Lit a Virginia Slim, took out her calculator, and opened the sliding door, seeking deck sun. A refuge to do math.

Alan followed, leaned on the deck railing, instinctively smiled at the view. A family of porpoises was doing a smiley, slo-mo cruise through waves, yards off shore. As they traveled north, Alan kept staring, eyes losing focus. His mouth went dry as he imagined them being harpooned, silver skin bleeding, mouths screaming. The ocean turned to blood in his mind, an awful burgundy, crashing on the sand.

"There may be another offer coming in this afternoon. Just so you know." Her right foot tapped air.

Alan watched the dolphins writhing as the whalers laughed pulling them closer to small boats. The young dolphins tried to stay with their parents, though the older ones frantically nosed them away to save them. The men had no faces, just smooth flat skin; slits for mouths. The mouths grinned, as arm muscles pulled harpoon ropes, and the porpoises were dragged through plasma, clubbed on the head. They struggled, making a horrible noise, and the sea churned, red foam.

Alan turned to her. Looked back at the perfect blue Pacific. A windsurfer scalpeling currents.

"The one who was a song writer…"

She looked up, sharply. Down again at her calculator. Flicked an ash into a potted cactus.

"Did he live here in the seventies?"

Then, all at once, he remembered. The article, buried deep. The murders. The man and his wife tortured in a two-hour attack by a former band member he'd fired when *Sunshine Lady* hit. Alan remembered hearing about the details at a party, where the host, a famous TV star, was tight with the LAPD.

The guy described detectives saying the couple was beaten, stripped naked, and nailed by ankles and palms to the bleached, wooden floor. The killer had taken two hours to crush their heads, ball-peening the skulls progressively harder until bone under bruised skin began to give.

The murderer later admitted that while they were still alive, begging him to call an ambulance, he'd found an electric knife in the kitchen.

He'd sawed all the way down the man's sternum, slitting open skin and muscle, making crude scrimshaw on bone before moving the humming blade across to her. As her head shook from side to side, nipples were circled; cut off.

Then, more cutting and sectioning, finally sledding to legs, thighs, and tendons which were sawed into ruin. The murderer had testified later that it took half an hour to trash both bodies. The screaming had slowed things until he realized by cutting their larynxes he could work in relative peace.

When he was done, he took the desecrated bodies, placed them side-by-side on the master bed, resting on Ralph Lauren pillow shams, staring forward, waiting for the police.

"A murder…"

She said nothing.

She was lying; could tell Alan knew it. She looked at the sun doing cut-crystal on ocean. "I think someone in the office mentioned there was a break-in at one point but that's all I know. I got the impression it was years ago." She smiled useless comfort. "Anyway, in L.A. it's hard to buy a nice house that hasn't had something. That's why they invented alarms, right?"

Alan watched the porpoises steer around the small peninsula, continue north toward Malibu pier.

"I have a feeling they'll let this go for nine twenty-five. The owner just bought in New York and he needs to be there full-time for business."

He looked through the dining room window, at the wood floor. Tried to detect nail marks: holes or nicks, spaced far enough apart; spread-eagled scars on hardwood.

"I remember hearing about a murder," he said, not looking at her. Drawn once again to the floor; the sacrificial trauma sponged in cracks and grooves.

"Would you rather look at something else? I have a couple listings up on Broad Beach that are to die for."

To die for. He folded the phrase into smaller and smaller sizes until it disappeared.

"But I remember you saying anything beyond Zuma was too far north."

He went back inside, trying to decide if he could live in a house where something so ghastly has happened. His mind saw things; that was always the danger. His feelings and perceptions could shift for no reason and inexplicably imagine terrible prospects in anything.

A mother pushing her baby on a sunny park day could suddenly change, in his mind, to a crying woman whose selfish husband was leaving to take the baby to another state, where it would be molested; murdered.

A smiling cashier at McDonald's would become a crumpled statistic, victim of a gang drive-by which would strike exactly at the moment Alan was being handed his McNuggets. Exploding blood would puddle on the shiny metal counter.

The times he imagined people pulling alongside his own Porsche and shooting him. Or the times a windy night sounded like footsteps. Or the moment a neutral face at a mall became an abhorring glare that would follow him out to the parking lot and beat the shit out of him until he was bloody; begging for his life.

It was everywhere.

A voice on the phone, soliciting for Vets of Nam, who didn't like him saying no, he "already gave six months ago." The way he could see the voice break in to his apartment and wait, and he would open a closet late one night and it would plunge a knife into him.

The mention of his mother making him imagine her alone, inside her casket, pounding to get out, ripping at puffy satin, screaming helplessly, nails torn off as she struggled to claw free.

"Broad Beach is too far," he said.

"Well, we can keep looking. There's always new stuff coming out in listings." She was looking at Alan like he scared her a little. Like something about him was changing. She was studiously measuring what he needed to hear, watching carefully for reaction.

He looked at her.

Saw her getting old. More desperate than she already was. Saw diseases rooting. Saw all those who ever cared about her, pulling away and despising her frantic demands as she sat alone in a corridor in a depressing nursing home. Saw the sheet being pulled over her face, covering carefully bleached hair.

"Can I tell you something...don't buy if it doesn't feel right." She smiled, teeth pressing brown lipstick. "We'll find you something you'll love."

Alan watched waves spread champagne on sand, as the sun passed out. He felt overwhelmed, knew somehow, despite the house's nightmare history, this was home.

Where he could create.

The wind came up, strumming chimes that hung on the deck, and he told her he wanted the house. It was the right atmosphere. He could be himself here. Was somehow even fascinated by residues of terror and helplessness that stared up at him from the floor. He didn't know why. But he imagined himself kneeling on the wood, staring at it until blood seeped from the peg and groove; surfacing welcome. He imagined placing an ear to the dented wood, hearing tiny pleas.

She seemed surprised Alan wanted to go ahead with it and smiled quickly. "That's wonderful," she said. "I'm sure we can get this." She touched his arm; financial foreplay. "We better write this before someone beats us to it."

He said nothing, moving onto the deck, sounds of torture drenching his mind.

After attending the private Christian college John Brown University *with thoughts of entering the ministry, Del Howison dropped out and backslid all the way to starting, with his wife Sue, the most famous horror store in America,* Dark Delicacies. *"I felt a need to be in a field with less hypocrisy." He has been awarded the* Bram Stoker Award *from the* Horror Writers Association *and the* Il Posto Nero Award *from Italy.*

THE LAST GREAT MONSTER

Del Howison

Did you really run into a monster on your path, or just a mirror?
~Terri Guillemets

EARLY SATURDAY MORNING Shelley Cherwinski killed the last great monster. She was on her way home from an 18-hour production day at the film studio, going over the continuity from the day's script in her head, when she hit the beast. The impact sent her little white foreign sports car sliding to the left, the steering wheel spinning through her hands, a glimpse of large teeth and wide eyes as the car crossed the road and bounced down into the ditch. The horn, just like in a Hollywood production, was stuck bleating out a continuous sheepish tone as steam rose up from underneath.

When the snowflakes of reality slowly fluttered back into her brain and she gradually awoke from the nightmarish accident, her eyes began to focus and in her headlights she thought she saw the back of some large animal lumbering into the woods and disappearing from sight. She was still suffering from accident shock or the emotional trauma of seeing a monster for a split second before ramming into it. Either of which made her doubt her sanity. Her next thought was wondering if she had monster coverage. Finally the constant horn began to give her a headache and, pissed off, she slammed the palm of her hand against the steering until it quit making noise. The silence was deafening.

There were sounds. Things moved in the brush away from her, animals that had probably seen the accident and were trying to escape before they too became speed bumps. There were clinks and pops from the car, some were the hot engine cooling and some were the car trying to unfold itself from its crinkled condition. There was dripping and there was hissing as liquids dropped on to something hot under the hood. She moved her body parts slowly knowing something could be brok... Wait! Liquid hissing as it hit something under the hood! She had to get out before she went up in flames with the car. She pulled the handle but the door wouldn't open. Jammed! She leaned as far as she could towards the passenger side and then, with all the strength she could muster, slammed her shoulder into the driver's door. It popped open and she rolled out into the ditch... mostly.

As she dangled face down into the cattails and long grasses, her hair hanging into the muddy trough, the seatbelt held her firmly in place. Ass up and face down she had to get herself unbuckled. Later Shelley would remember seeing under the car from where she hung and noticed no evidence of any fire. But just one of those drips could be gasoline and then it would be all over. She twisted her body and reached up, grabbing the steering wheel. That was when she heard something moving through the woods. Only this time it was headed toward her.

Bad words passed through her mind and she struggled to pull herself upright. With her left hand Shelley clamped onto the steering wheel while she dug frantically at the seatbelt clasp with her right. Finally it popped and she slid out backwards and dropped down into the muck. Wasting no time she crab-walked in reverse, away from the car, knowing it was going to blow up in her face at any moment. It was only when her back struck a large rock that she was able to climb to her feet. She scaled the bank to the asphalt and waited for somebody to come down the road. It really wasn't all that well traveled at 2:30 in the morning.

As she stood there she remembered the large animal and the sound of something moving toward her in the brush. Her cell phone was in her car where she had set it on one of those sticky pads on the dashboard. There was no telling if it was still there. She assumed that what she had hit and what she had heard in the woods were animals, maybe one and the same. In her mind all animals could see in darkness. With the blinding headache she was cultivating she wasn't even sure she could see in the daylight. There were blue and green dashlights she could see from where she was standing and headlights lit the woods directly in front of the car. The residual light from those helped her to see the area immediately around her.

As she began stumbling towards her car a sound came out of the trees that dropped Shelley to her knees. She grimaced as her bones smacked the pavement but the noise, which could only be described as a wailing moan, so frightened her that she became nauseous with a set of the dry heaves that doubled her over. It was either from the noise, as she told it, or the trauma from the accident, which is what the cop who wrote up the report two hours later thought, but something made her sick. Take your choice.

Nothing came out of the darkness to attack her and the car didn't blow up in her face. When Shelley was finally able to get to her wreck, the phone was jammed in that joint where the windshield meets the dash. Jammed so tight that she had to strike at it with the handle of a plastic hairbrush to crack it loose.

She speed dialed her director, who told her to call the cops and then went promptly back to sleep after reminding her of her call time in six hours. Then she called the cops.

Now she was being rolled into the ambulance after repeating her story three times, twice to the same cop and once to an insurance accident investigator who luckily got the call as he was returning home from a party and a late night breakfast. He assured her with a smirk that he would check out the monster insurance angle but said she was probably covered even if it was a deer. Her cracked ribs were starting to hurt as the adrenaline began to wear off and she was painfully starting to discover areas of her body she'd never thought of before.

The cop stood with his hands in his pockets watching the red lights of Shelley's ambulance drive away and then turned to the insurance man next to him.

"Well?" he asked.

"She hit something alright. That something seems to have crawled off somewhere into the woods."

The cop shined his flashlight quickly up and down the boundary of trees. He turned his head and spit a stringer into the ditch.

"It will be light in another hour and I'm waiting until then before I look around. I already stepped in the filthy ditch water trying to take photos of her car."

Then he hiked up his leg to show the water line on the material.

"Hmm," the insurance man said looking at the wet shoe.

"Don't like it," said the cop. "I've already got some sort of foot rot and a big toenail the color of a school bus. I'm waiting until I can see."

"What do you think about her monster story?"

"Could have been a coyote," the cop said.

"Hmmm."

"Or a bear," he added.

"Had she been drinkin'?" the insurance man asked.

"Nah," the cop said. "I didn't smell anything. Just tired I think. Slow reflexes."

"Still," the insurance man said. "That monster story is a doozy."

"That it is," said the cop.

"First time for me," said the insurance man.

"Hmmm," the cop answered.

Daylight crept in with the arrival of the tow truck. It was all clinking chains and groaning metal while the cop stood in front of the truck waving the occasional automobile around the scene. The insurance man walked out to where the cop was yelling at somebody slowly passing in a car to *quit gawking and drive.*

"Well the truck's got it so I'm outta here," the insurance man said.

The cop turned back to him.

"I heard from University Hospital. She'll be alright," he said.

"Well that's one good thing."

"Maybe," the cop added.

"What do you mean?"

"She's seems to be sticking with the monster story."

"Maybe she bumped her head when she fell out of the car. Maybe she's a little traumatized," the insurance man said.

"Either way I'm going to poke around a little in the woods. See what I can see."

The insurance man walked back towards his car.

"Thanks for your help, officer. I may be speaking with you later."

He climbed into his car, swung it around on the asphalt and headed back to the city. The cop watched his car shrink in the distance and then turned to the woods. It was time to find out what Shelley had hit. Whatever it was, it was big and it had left the accident scene. There could be trouble and he might have to write a citation. He inadvertently touched his holster and then jumped the ditch and walked to the edge of the woods. He wandered up the wood line one way and then back the other until he found where the monster had gone in. It seemed like a starting point.

It was wide or at least it cut a wide swath through the weeds and underbrush. At about twenty feet in it appeared to be dragging its leg or some part of its body. One strong footmark dragging the other from what he could tell. Blood began to show up on the ground and vegetation. What started as drips and drabs became smears and finally splashes. Then there it was, matted fur crusted with dried blood and dirt, limbs bent in an odd direction, body crumpled to the ground. It's head and chest was rolled towards its knees in a semi-fetal position, probably from the pain. Evidently the dead weight became too much to drag anymore and it had to drop.

The cop knelt down noting the smell of the wild beast. He had been next to elephants at a circus and they smelled just about as bad. He couldn't tell if it was dead or alive but either way the carcass hadn't had time to ripen yet so this was its natural smell. Black bears carried a similar odor with them. He had no idea what he was looking at with it all curled up. Mammalian, certainly. Outside of the smell the only thing that resembled a bear were the claws. The legs were more amazing in that they had the backwards shaped knee of a chicken but without any other avian quality. Full and thick like an ape it was a joke on the Bigfoot myth with an air of danger about it.

He stopped looking. He needed something else. He needed a camera crew. The cop smelled something along with the stench of the beast. He smelled money. In his report Shelley had given him the name of her director. He would have access to a crew. He needed to document his find.

The cop stood up to leave when something moved in the brush behind him. He turned slowly and could make out an eye and the end of a snout through the bushes. It was watching him. Another beast partner was watching him? His heart raced and he began to slowly back away from the body at his feet. Death was close at hand but his sweat came from the anticipation of a living beast, a monster of the woods. There was a huff of air from the thing in the bushes. It was deep and rumbling and suddenly the cop was afraid of not ever leaving the woods. He took his phone from his pocket and snapped a couple of quick out-of-focus pictures of the dead creature. At least he had proof. Now he needed to leave.

He backed away from the monster corpse, gun drawn, trying to keep an eye on where he was walking and an eye back in the woods where the other creature rumbled about in the bushes. If what was in the bushes was anywhere near as big as what lay dead on the ground he could be in big trouble. With each step backwards the cop felt better and better. Once he was out of sight of the beast he turned and ran for his squad car.

He slammed and locked the door. Turning the key he got the A/C cranking. He'd sweat through the uniform. The cold air helped him steady his breathing. On the passenger seat lay his notes for the accident report. He looked through them until he found the name and number of Shelley Cherwinski's director. He dialed the number and listened to the ring. It was really sounding like a cash register ringing up a sale.

"They went in right along here," the cop said.

He led the three men along the woods line looking for the spot where the weeds had been trampled down. He was off work and on his own at this point after having pulled the graveyard shift that brought him here the first time. The three men with him were trudging behind on the uneven ground hoping he'd find the entrance soon. One of them had taco stand morning gas but kept putting it off on the monster.

"I can smell the carcass from here," said the soundman.

The cameraman shook his head.

"Smells more like *Big Breakfast Burrito #3* to me," he said.

"Here it is," the cop beamed with a smile as big as being the first man on the North Pole.

He started in when the director grabbed him and pulled him back.

"Wait. We need a shot of this."

The cop looked at him strangely.

"This ain't the monster," he said. "It's only where they headed into the woods."

The director smiled at him as if he were a young child without knowledge.

"I know. It's for dramatic effect when we put the entire piece together. I mean, for all we know, Shelley Cherwinski could have killed the last great monster last night."

"Oh."

"Now back out of the shot please."

The cameraman stepped up and slowly brought the shot up from the ground, ending on the dark wall of woods. He kept it there a moment so the viewers would be able to take in the denseness.

"Cut!"

The director turned back to the cop and waved him on.

"Lead on, McDuff," he said.

"Stamper," the cop said. "Kenneth Stamper, not McDuff."

"Great, but not what I was referring to."

"Oh, I thought you wanted me to lead you into..."

"Go! Go!" the director said, motioning Cop Kenneth forward with a sweep of his hands.

Stamper turned and rattled his way into the woods followed by the cameraman, the soundman and the director. The entourage threw him off a little and he would turn now and then to smile at the camera and make sure they were still with him. Each time the director would point forward like signaling a first down and the cop would turn and continue on with his trek through the underbrush. After a couple of minutes he stopped and turned back to the camera.

"What?"

The director pushed up past the crew.

"Just ahead is where I found the beast. I had been following the drag marks and with my head down had almost tripped over the body. It was right up there about fifty feet ahead."

He pointed towards a clearing. The cameraman followed the cop's hand with the shot and continued on towards the spot in the woods. Then he zoomed in, very dramatically, on the bushes and brush blocking the clearing.

"Cut!" yelled the director. "Now let's think this through first. I don't want us to just go plunging into the spot."

"Do we have to do that first part again without the talking?" he asked.

"It's okay," the director said. "We were shooting MOS."

Stamper frowned. "What does that mean?'

"Without sound."

The cop chuckled to himself. Hollywood sure did throw away its money on directors who didn't even know how to spell. He hoped the director at least knew what he was doing directing.

The director looked around the area and then back at the cameraman.

"Murray, I want you and Becker here, to go up on that rise behind and above the clearing. Once the two of you are set, wave at me. I'd like the shot of McDougall coming up on the body. Now get going. The light is bad enough as it is and I don't know how many takes this will be."

"Stamper," the cop said. "You mean sort of like reenact the first time?"

The director slapped him on the shoulder.

"You're a pretty bright guy, McDonald. You may even have a future in show business."

"Stampe... You think so! Wow, that's great."

"Yeah, yeah great. Now once Speed gives us the signal I'll call 'Action' and you go through to the spot just like you did the first time. Don't be too sure of yourself. Remember, you're pretending you've never been here before. Not too fast."

"No problem," Stamper said and rubbed his hands together in anticipation.

He thought about how he was going to play out his upcoming *discovery scene.* Not too big, he told himself. That looks corny. He knew to keep his out-turned hand away from his forehead. Too silent movie. Don't look at the camera. He had to remember it wasn't here. This was real. This was reality. Suddenly Murray's voice crackled over the radio.

"Once we give the signal and see the copper come into view we can walk and slide down this little hillside so that the camera moves toward him as he is moving toward us with the beast body somewhere in between."

"What's the point?" the director shot back.

"We can't actually see the ground where he is going. We really need to see the beast and him at the same moment. This will work, trust me. We'll stay upright and the little slippin' and sliding we do on the way down will just add tension to the scene. Becker, grab my belt as I balance this camera going down. I want you behind me anyways. Hot air rises."

With a crackle the radio shut off. The director looked at Stamper. He knew he was going to need all the help he could get to make this look half-assed real.

"Alright," he said. "Let's try one like that. We can always change if we don't like it. Are you ready up there?"

"Let it rip," the cameraman said and waved.

The director looked at Stamper.

"Get ready. When I say action start walking."

Stamper shook his head yes and took a deep breath.

Oh brother, the director thought. "Camera?"

"Rolling," the reply came back.

"Sound?"

"Speed," the soundman answered.

"There's no slate so fake it."

Stamper could hear somebody clap their hands and say "take one."

The director looked at Stamper and pointed the direction he was to walk in.

"Annnnd Action!"

Stamper stared at him. The director shushed at him with his hands.

"Go! Go!"

Stamper shook his head and gave the director a wink to let him know he was an old pro at this. He straightened his uniform shirt and started walking. As Stamper rounded the trees he could see the cameraman and sound guy starting down the hillside towards him. He knew he was on camera and suddenly didn't know what to do with his hands or how to swing his arms. So he smiled a big goofy smile and started walking like a little kid at an amusement park.

The revelation stopped him cold in his tracks. Murray slid to a stop on the hillside and was rear-ended by Becker forcing out another round of wind-breakers.

"I didn't ask for a tableau," the director shouted. "What?"

The camera panned from Stamper's face slowly down to the spot where the monster lay in the field. Except that the monster wasn't laying there. The grass was all matted down like a deer bed but there was no monster. Stamper was dumbfounded and stood frozen at the spot. The camera crew continued to move down off the slope and close in towards Stamper. The director pushed him in the back.

"Let's go. Get in there and investigate. We'll cut this footage in later and fix it in post."

"Looks like something was drug off over this way," Becker pointed out. "Maybe he was dragging himself."

Stamper shuffled towards the site of his failing fortunes until all four of them met in the middle. Reaching down he pulled up a tuft of odd looking fur and pointed out some bloodied grass to the camera. They all stared down at the big spot of nothing when a noise in the bushes made them turn.

As the found footage shown later on the *Unexplained Questions* tabloid show revealed there was a lot of screaming, a flash of teeth, odd growls, wide eyes, a splash of blood, and spinning camera that dropped to the ground continuing to run. A blur that appeared to be the foot of some fur-covered animal briefly filled the frame. The show kept freezing that frame, having *experts* explain what it was the home audience was seeing. Since the program was syndicated many people did not watch it at the odd hours it was played. Yet for those few cryptozoology lovers who watched, the commentator earnestly and quite dramatically told the unbelievable story of how on that fateful Saturday, driving home from an 18-hour production day at the film studio, Shelley Cherwinski had killed the second to last great monster.

Assembled from body parts stolen from the Los Angeles Coroner's dumpster, R.B. Payne lives in hope of becoming human. Meanwhile...he writes. Recent work can be found in All American Horror of the 21st Century: The First Decade *and* Times of Trouble. *For* Butcher Knives and Body Counts, *he analyzed three 1930's slasher films. Upcoming stories will be featured in* Expiration Date *and* Unspeakable Horror 2: Abominations Of Desire. *Richard has written multiple screenplays and two have been optioned. Currently he is writing a comic for* Island Tales *and will complete his first novel later this year. He and his wife (a film editor) divide their time between Laurel Canyon and Honolulu. More at* www.rbpayne.com.

MEXICAN CLOWN HANDS

R.B. Payne

THE DEAD LAWYER'S EYES BULGED, his tongue protruded sloppily across his lower lip, and mottled bruises encircled his neck in the shape of massive thumbs and fingers.

"Mexican clown hands," said Rodriquez.

"Jeez, you think?" Trang said, pointing at the mahogany desk until his sergeant made the *fuck-I'm-an-idiot* face. The clown hands lay next to a spilled cup of coffee.

The killer always left them behind.

Ignoring the plush office and trophy wall of celebrity photos, Trang studied the clown hands. Typically, they were oversized gloves made of cheap rubber, a novelty costume accessory for fiestas. The bony fingers sported blood red nails and thick purple veins bulged on pale white skin. The grotesque hands would scare the shit out of peasant kids south of Juarez or Tijuana. Here in Hollywood, they'd be a party gag or sex toy. But as a tool of murder, they obliterated a hell of a lot of evidence.

The problem was these Mexican clown hands weren't rubber. They were *papier-mâché*, too fragile to be used for strangulation. The rigid fingers had no flexibility. Yet, forensics had matched each pair to their corresponding victim.

Three unsolved murders.

Now four.

The forensics team unpacked their gear. Trang called to them.

"Tear those freaking clown hands apart. I need to know how they were made."

"No *problem-o*," said one of the techs.

Trang flinched. The hair on his neck electrified as ethereal strands of something like spider webs crossed his face. He tensed even though he knew nothing was there.

Nothing was *ever* there.

A twitchy nerve, perhaps.

A tic.

His throat tightened and he couldn't breathe. A bead of sweat ran into his eye as he finally sucked a lungful of air. His eye stung from the sweat and he wiped it clear. Shaking the odd feelings off, he signaled Rodriquez. "Let's grab some breakfast."

"Pass. I'm gonna hang with the body snatchers."

"You won't learn crapola here. The perps are back in Mexico already."

"No way, boss. It's a serial killer."

"Bullshit. This shyster defended Eduardo Gonzales last year. Probably pissed off the *El Diablos*. It's got the markings of a gang hit."

"Yeah, right," said Rodriquez. "Like gangs use clown hands."

In the hall, Trang punched the button for the elevator.

What a fucking mess.

Pausing outside the tower of steel and glass rising to the smoggy sky, Trang lit a cheap cigar.

Maybe this time they'd get a break.

Trang pinned a morgue photo of the lawyer to the evidence wall. Now, *four* faces stared lifelessly at him, each face trapped in a death mask of strangulation. What had they seen? Did they know their attacker? Were they aware of their impending death or had they been rendered unconscious? There'd been no trace of sedation or other drugs. Still, the victims were clearly looking at someone when they drew their last breath.

Trang chewed his unlit cigar butt.

Something had to tie these victims together. Darcy Hyde, a hair cutter at an upscale Beverly Hills Salon was found in a dumpster behind a Sunset Boulevard after-hours club. Hector Garcia lay on the concrete ramparts of the Lake Hollywood dam, three spray paint cans beside him. Werner Hannemann floated facedown in his swimming pool in Laurel Canyon. Jeff Reynolds, Esq. was pulling an all-nighter on some legal briefs when someone yanked his plug.

Strangled.

The Mexican clown hands were the only clue. But no DNA inside the gloves. Not a hair. Not a drop of perspiration. Not a fucking cancerous freckle.

Trang scanned the latest forensic report. The water in the gloves had been untreated, the mush was newsprint, and the paste was flour and salt. The colors were from cheap Mexican paint contaminated with lead.

Sure seemed South of the Border.

Had to be a gang hit.

Footsteps preceded a rap at his door. Rodriquez hustled into the office.

"Hey boss."

Trang rested on the edge of his desk and said, "How's the hunt for Hannibal Lecter?"

"I swear it's a serial killer," said Rodriquez. "Listen to this." Rodriquez read aloud from a photocopied news article. *"Beautician to the Stars Murdered.* The body of a young woman was discovered in the alley behind The Pink Flamingo Club at 3:22 AM by the Los Angeles Police Department. A victim of foul play, the woman was identified as Miss Darleen Hyde, of 1024 Crescent Heights Avenue..."

"Pink Flamingo Club?" interrupted Trang. "Can't those morons at the Times get their facts straight? That club has been closed for years. *And* they've screwed up her name."

"The facts are straight, boss. This," he waved the photocopy in the air, "is from 1987. *Darleen* Hyde, get it? Not Darcy."

"Listen. Any cop can find related names. But those cold cases have nothing to do with us. Jesus, ever since you put in for promotion you're chasing too many loose ends."

"Routine investigative police work. Similar name and location. It's what they teach at the academy."

"Screw the academy. If you want to get promoted learn to trust your gut."

Trang leaned to his computer and moused. "See?" said Trang. "Ten female D. Hyde's since 1907 if you include ours. Now get the hell out and don't come back until you've got something meaningful."

"I tell you, boss, it's a serial killer."

"Yeah, and he's ninety years old. Try and explain that to the D.A. Besides, Miss 1987 was crushed. She wasn't strangled."

Rodriquez slammed the door as he left.

Trang shifted the cigar butt to the opposite corner of his mouth. Could Rodriquez be right? He entered another query into the police records system.

H. Garcia.

Thirty-three Garcia deaths since 1907, the oldest year of records in the system. Well, it was a common name. Like Trang.

The next one was easy. Werner Hannemann, one hit. Rare name. That squashed Rodriquez's theory of a serial killer honing in on like names.

One more.

Nineteen J. Reynolds. No pattern, just the ebb and flow of murders in L.A. over the decades. Sure, there were thousands of unsolved cases. So what? L.A. was a big city with a history. Still, something-somewhere-somehow had to link these murders.

Grabbing his car keys, he headed out of the precinct. Maybe a bowl of Pho noodle would help him think things through.

"No way, *vato*," said Rodriquez. "I'm way more Hispanic than you are Thai."

"How do you figure? You're as Mexican as a Taco Bell burrito."

"Hispanic. Not Mexican."

Trang accelerated the unmarked police car up the concrete ramp onto the 101. One thing the crimes did have in common was geographic co-location. Proximity. All of the deaths had been in Hollywood.

Near the studios.

Rodriquez rolled his window down. "Have *you* ever even been to Thailand?"

"Screw you. I was born there."

"Yeah. And you moved here when you were six months old. Do you speak Thai?"

"Good enough. Do you speak Spanish?"

"Good enough."

"When's the last time you were in Spain?"

"The wife and kids and I went to Cabo last summer."

"Shit, Cabo's not Spain. It's Mexico."

"Yeah? Well, Thai Town's not Thailand, either."

The two men rode in silence as Trang navigated the traffic and the Hollywood sign came into view. The final wisps of morning fog were dissipating and bright sunlight glinted off the massive white letters.

"Let's face it," mused Trang. "We're Angelenos."

Rodriquez popped a fresh stick of gum into his mouth. "You got that right, boss."

Trang exited on Hollywood Boulevard and passed the old Grauman's Chinese Theatre where wannabe actors in costume were staging a fight between Darth Vader and Spiderman while Marilyn Monroe's dress fluttered on cue to entertain a busload of Japanese tourists.

"A goddamn freak show," said Rodriquez.

Trang navigated to Sunset Boulevard and the alley where Darcy Hyde had been someone's good time.

But not hers.

Trang and Rodriquez relaxed in a Koreatown bar.

"We're looking at this the wrong way," said Trang, leaning back into the cushions of a worn leather booth. What a freaking waste of time the day had been.

"Maybe," said Rodriquez, sipping a beer, "we ought to be looking at the M.O. Fetish strangulation?"

"I already checked that. I went through your same-name cases. Not one mention of Mexican clown hands and very few unsolved strangulations compared to gunshot or knife wounds."

"So that leaves us a serial killer, right?" Rodriquez said, a smug look on his face. "And there is no known gang of Mexican clowns. I checked the Gang Registry. I mean, seriously, *vato*, what kind of gang targets a hair dresser?"

"Have you seen the prices for a Beverly Hills blow-n-go?"

Rodriquez laughed.

"Any leads on the gloves?" asked Trang.

Rodriquez scrolled through e-mails on his smartphone. "I got hundreds of manufacturers from South Central to Rio de Janeiro."

"And?"

"Shit. I could spend a lifetime interviewing these Mom and Poppers. Besides, we're looking for *papier-mâché* hands. Nobody *manufactures* them. They're all hand-made by old *abuelas* living in backwater Mexican villages."

Trang rubbed a cool beer bottle on his forehead.

"But I gotta admit somebody is custom-making clown hands for these murders," continued Rodriquez. "Still, I don't see how you can strangle anybody with *papier-mâché hands.*"

The chorus from *One Night in Bangkok* filled the booth and Trang answered his phone.

"Yeah, yeah, I got it."

Hanging up, he said, "Call your wife and make pretty talk. We got another stiff."

As the moon rose over the Hollywood Hills, Trang studied the contorted face of the film director dead in his media room and said, "Jesus, I know this one."

The contorted body sprawled on a divan, arms and legs askew. A spilled cocktail dampened the carpet. Rodriquez, on hands and knees, examined the Mexican clown hands.

Papier-mâché clown hands.

"You busted him before, boss?"

Trang stepped closer to the corpse. Purple and black ringed the victim's neck in a neat circle of deep finger marks.

"No. Does he look like a perp? His name's Stewart MacAdam. Back in the day I did weekend security at the studios. He was like a Second Assistant Director or something on *Road Kill Pussycats II*."

Trang motioned to the forensics crew to start but he didn't step away. "My gut is sure telling me something."

"Yeah," laughed Rodriquez. "You're hungry. I can hear your stomach growling from here."

"Shut up. I'm getting a hunch."

The spider web came first. Of course, nothing was on his skin even though his nerves said something lingered. The spider thread sharpened like the touch of a razor blade.

He shivered and rubbed his cheek.

His throat constricted. Phlegm formed and for a split second he couldn't breathe. He swallowed the wad as an acrid film coated his tongue.

"Okay," rasped Trang. "I want a history dig on the victims. You might be right Rodriquez; it could be a film freak. It is Hollywood, after all. Now let's get the fuck out of here."

Birthplaces, schools, friends, marriages, divorces, jobs. Arrests and affiliations; country clubs, churches, street gangs. Sexual preferences, perversions, drug use.

Rodriquez threw down a handful of scribbled notes. "Jesus, I don't care even if they are dead. There's not one of these people I'd invite into my house."

"Get used to dealing with John Q. Public," said Trang. "People are born innocent. After that, it's a crapshoot. You can't scratch anybody too deep without finding ugly."

Trang shifted papers. "So what have we got?"

"*Bupkis.*"

"*Bupkis*? You call that Spanish?"

"Yiddish. I picked it up when I worked vice in the Fairfax Division. I can say *nada* if you want me to live up to my cultural stereotype."

"*Oy vey*," laughed Trang. A chime sounded, and he opened an e-mail. "Sonofabitch. Looks like every victim drew wages from Optassia Studios. Those boys in I.T. are occasionally helpful."

"And?"

"So get the car. We're gonna visit Optassia. But first, I've got a hankering for a brisket of beef sandwich."

Rodriquez grabbed his jacket. "Greenblatt's. It's on the way."

Even Hollywood has seedy neighborhoods, and Trang hung a right off of Melrose into one of them. The stucco gate over the entrance to Optassia Studios fluttered with a cheap vinyl banner announcing *A Galaxy of Stars for 100 Years*. Trang stopped at the security gate and flashed his badge to the guard who went to make the requisite phone call.

While they waited, Trang surveyed the studio grounds. The sound stages and offices sure showed their age. Built during the heyday of silent movies, they'd recently been painted a beige color.

If beige was a color.

"Seen better days," observed Rodriquez.

"Cheap paint. Like putting a new dress on an old whore," said Trang. "You know, teen sex and trucker movies saved Optassia in the Seventies. I could pick up a grand over the weekend just keeping morons away from the starlets."

"I sure don't know how they hang on now."

"Me neither. They made some pretty great Westerns way back in the day. I loved those when I was a kid. You remember Big Jim Spencer and his horse Loco?"

"Can't say that I do."

The guard waved them in and they parked.

Inside the Admin building, Trang shook hands with the Head of Production; a wrinkled man named Hank Harrison that looked like he'd started at the studio before Clark Gable heard of *Gone With The Wind*. Trang knew him from the old days and fifteen minutes later a report whirred out of a laser printer.

Trang scanned the pages.

"Let me get this straight," he said. "You're saying my five stiffs all worked for the studio, but never on the same project? Darcy Hyde did hair for *Dance Your Ass Off* eight years ago. Hector Garcia did set painting three years ago. Werner Hannemann was a working cinematographer decades ago. Jeff Reynolds was handling litigation and MacAdam is one of your working Directors?"

Harrison grimaced. "Bottom line is like most studios we lose a handful or so of our *extended family* every year. Sometimes it's a big deal. Most of the time it's just production staff and day help. My secretary sends flowers but I can't tell you their names. We do lose a few important people on a regular basis. We lost a director in the '70s and it nearly took the studio down. That really hurt."

"When was that?"

Harrison scanned the report. "'73. We lost six associates that year."

"Names?"

Harrison read them off as Rodriquez jotted them down.

"Six, boss. No name matches."

Trang said, "Yeah, I figured that out," but his thoughts leapt forward. "What did they do?"

Harrison consulted the list. "Hairdresser, set designer, camera operator, legal clerk, director, security."

"Jesus, all our victims worked at those jobs," said Trang to Rodriquez.

"I knew it, boss! A serial killer."

"Cool your jets, Columbo."

Trang turned to Harrison. "We're going to need a list of all your security staff, all the way back to when the studio began."

Back at the precinct, Trang and Rodriquez poured over the list of security staff. More than a thousand names. Every production team hired their own crew and the studio had been making movies for a hundred years.

They narrowed the list to the living and reduced the potential victim list to about four hundred. More than half had moved away, so they weren't a priority. Still, that left more than two hundred, an overwhelming number.

"We got to go public," said Rodriquez, marking names on the list. "There's no way we can protect them all."

Rodriquez checked another name.

"Hey, boss. Is your first name Khajee?"

"Yep."

"You're on the list."

Trang swallowed, passing an imaginary lump. The pieces were adding up. "I already knew that, dumbshit."

"Don't worry, boss. I got your back."

"Here's something interesting," said Trang, putting down a stack of police reports. "All of the '70s victims were crushed and none of the cases were solved."

Rodriquez looked up from his computer.

"I've checked the victims against IMDB. I can't find any project those six worked on. But here's the weird. On the very first picture ever made by Optassia Pictures in 1912 there was a Dorothy Perkins listed as a costumer. Back in the day costumers did hair. Therefore, a hairdresser, get it? And the following year she was mauled to death in her Hollywood Hills home. So I ran a query through Records and guess what? Including her, there were six maulings that summer. All fatal."

"You're suggesting those deaths have a bearing on our case?"

"Not enough info in IMDB. We only know about Dorothy Perkins since she was working on a Griffith picture when she died and the obit mentioned the Optassia film."

"Have I ever heard of this masterpiece?" asked Trang, already knowing he hadn't. He'd never paid any attention to the old two-reel silents.

"*Showdown at Robber's Roost*?" asked the docent at the UCLA Film Archives. "Yes, we have a digitized copy. The original is far too valuable to be viewed."

Fifteen minutes later Trang and Rodriquez were seated in a viewing room.

"Gum?"

"No thanks."

Jangling piano music overlaid the titles, and silvery images opened on a frontier town. The story was simple. A virginal girl loved the town's sheriff. The townsfolk thought the sheriff was cowardly. Between chasing cattle rustlers and drunken cowboys, not much happened until a circus came to town.

Unknown to the local citizens, the performers were a notorious gang planning to rob the town's bank and escape back to Mexico. During a sequence of the circus performers entertaining the townsfolk, a clown did gags in the center ring wearing Mexican clown hands.

"What does it mean?" whispered Rodriquez, even though they were alone.

"It means I hate coincidences."

Later in the film, a bank robbery was thwarted; the sheriff won the heart of the virgin, and a posse burnt the circus tent to the ground. Thus, in a fiery hell, the robbers perished. The End.

Standing outside the viewing room, Trang chewed his cigar stub. His cell phone rang and he listened to a voice mail.

Hanging up, Trang said. "The boys in Forensics reassembled the paper mush. Put it back together like a jigsaw puzzle. Most was unreadable but they determined it's the L.A. Times, October 1912. There's a partial headline on a story with the letters T-A-S-S in the title."

"It's Optassia, right boss? There's no such thing as two coincidences on one case."

"Bingo. Contact the archives at the Times and find that article. Meanwhile, let's rattle the cage at Optassia."

Hank Harrison was deader than the proverbial doornail.

Natural causes at his home in Beverly Hills.

Nothing suspicious except he'd left an unfinished note he'd been writing when his heart gave out or a blood clot hit his brain.

A single word.

Furnace.

Over the next two days, Trang, Rodriquez, and a crew of forensics scoured every furnace on the lot at Optassia. Other than a few charred rat bones, there was no evidence of the crimes.

"It's just like Orson Wells in that movie," said Rodriquez.

"What are you talking about?"

"You know. *Rosebud.*"

The lights were low at the Formosa Cafe, the bar was busy and the chatter was loud.

Trang scanned the menu. Not exactly Chinese anymore, the offerings were Pan-Pacific Asian classics with a California flair.

But the miso salmon sounded good.

Saturday night was date night for Rodriquez and Mrs. Rodriquez. Private time. Being a cop's wife wasn't easy. There'd been a Mrs. Trang once but that had been a long time ago.

Trang sipped a beer and ordered salmon for one.

Signed movie star photos and memorabilia covered every square inch of the restaurant walls. Classic to contemporary Hollywood. Humphrey Bogart. Lauren Bacall. Johnny Depp. Warren Beatty. Vanna White. James Dean. Hell, there was even a photo of Big Jim Spencer with his horse Loco in some Old West frontier town.

Trang leapt from the booth. "Furnace..." he said. "By God, that's it."

Now it all made sense.

Trang's flashlight illuminated a faded *Do Not Trespass* sign posted on a gate where a dirt road ended four miles past the middle of nowhere. He rubbed his cheek to remove the prickle of cobwebs on his face.

Nothing was there.

Nothing ever was.

He cleared his throat and sucked a lungful of air. His throat tightened. Heaving a shovel over the barbed wire, he hopped the fence.

If he wasn't right, he was dead.

Well, he might be dead anyway.

About fifty-odd miles northeast of Hollywood, the suburbs ended and in the desert sat the long-abandoned Furnace Rocks, a film location known to movie buffs as the place where classics such as *Winchester Justice* and *Robbin' Hood* had been filmed. The Old West set had long since been torn down and everyone lost interest decades ago. Trang remembered hearing about this place as a kid, but it was Google that connected the dots.

Google and Big Jim Spencer.

Trang's flashlight sprayed a cone of light across red boulders the size of houses, separated by narrow canyons filled with sagebrush. The moon had set but the Milky Way eerily lit the landscape. A warm breeze kicked up a steady swirl of dust.

He moved quietly. If his deductions were correct, he was looking for something...not quite human.

In the distance, a glimmer lit the horizon. A mile later, Trang crested a rocky knoll and skidded to a halt.

In a deep hollow, a circus tent floated—an apparition where ropes were no longer needed to tether canvas to the material world. Pale figures materialized and entered through an open flap.

The spider web came and his throat tightened. Somewhere a Mariachi band played and their music drifted to him on the desert breeze.

More ghosts materialized.

What the hell was going on? This kind of shit just didn't happen except on fake reality shows.

Yet, here was proof.

Trang touched the gun in his pocket.

What good would it do?

His throat was nearly closed now. He slid down the hillside until he stood near the entrance. Each labored gasp brought only a trickle of air. A spark ran up his spine as he recognized a face from a photo.

"Darcy!" Trang hissed. "Darcy Hyde?"

The wisp of her ghostly form turned to him, a confused look crossed her face.

Trang followed her into the tent.

In the center ring, a lion tamer cracked a whip as a big cat ran through its tricks. Over the barrel. Through the hoop. Roar.

He searched the ground for any remnant of the past.

Where was it?

He didn't have much time.

It had to be here.

Somewhere was a grave.

Spectator stands encompassed the interior of the tent, filled with ghostly patrons. Old men and women. Children. Modern folk, flappers, WWII soldiers in uniform, Depression-era bums, Fifties housewives. On the far side, were two Goths and a punk rocker.

The lion roared.

That explained the maulings in the Hollywood Hills in 1913.

Trang swallowed the imaginary lump. Jesus, he was light-headed now. He didn't have much time.

With the sound of an unseen cannon, a Strong Man ran into the center ring, and bent a metal bar into a figure eight.

Of course, it was the Strong Man that had crushed the victims in 1973.

With a roll of unseen drums, a clown appeared. The crowd laughed as he struggled to open a trunk.

The clown was disappointed. The audience groaned. The trunk was empty. Then, in a swirl of light, a pair of Mexican clown gloves floated in mid-air.

Papier-mâché clown hands.

The clown slid his hands into them.

Squeals of laughter and terror filled the tent as the clown ran the perimeter of the ring and threatened the audience.

The clown slipped to a stop in front of Trang, the Mexican clown hands locking on his throat. The clown smiled, no, it was only a painted smile. His eyes were filled with grief. And anger.

All the strength in Trang's legs disappeared as the clown's fingers tightened. The world grew dim as the ghosts in the audience grew brighter and brighter.

This was it, then.

He was the policeman.

The sixth victim.

He had failed to prevent his own murder.

A poor excuse for a detective.

He had taken his last breath.

"*Alto*," cried a voice, and Trang strained to open his eyes. Rodriquez stood in the tent's entrance waving a flashlight.

The hands tightened about his neck as Rodriquez was spewing words in Spanish.

A spider web crept across Trang's face.

Razor sharp.

The clown was luminous and bright.

Trang's chest ached.

There was no more air.

Then, the Mexican clown hands released. Trang collapsed to the dirt. Boots appeared in his blurred vision and Rodriquez's hand touched his shoulder

"Stay down," Rodriquez said, picking up the shovel. "We still got company."

The clown, the strongman, the lion tamer, and the lion encircled Trang, floating a few feet away. Their attention was focused on Rodriquez.

"What...what are you doing here?" Trang whispered.

"I tailed you. I told you, I got your back. Now where should I dig, boss?"

"Anywhere in the ring. Everywhere."

Rodriquez took a few steps and pressed the shovel into the dirt.

A dozen quick scoops.

Nothing.

He probed to the left.

Nothing.

Then to the right.

"Got to be here," Trang said, as he crawled on his hands on knees to stay close to Rodriquez. He couldn't stand up yet, and who knew what the spirits would do if he tried to rise.

A few yards further on, Rodriquez shoved the shovel blade into the dirt again. *Thump*, a splinter of wood emerged from the soil. Ten minutes later, Rodriquez had cleared the dirt from a grave. He lifted a rotted plank of wood revealing a dark hole.

A cloud of dust and rot drifted out.

Gagging, Trang reached into the pit, searched. Bones. Dirt. Cloth. Something smooth. He pulled out a skull, remnants of leathery skin and hair flapping on one side.

Then another.

And a third.

Lastly came the lion's skull, a grisly mane still attached.

Trang spoke to the clown, his voice more a rasp than anything else. "The bones will be returned to your families."

Rodriquez squatted and whispered. "I don't think they speak English, boss. I'll translate."

"No need. They know what I mean," said Trang.

The mariachi music stopped.

A clap of dry desert thunder echoed through the desolate canyons and a tornado of dust and light encircled the detectives. Fragment by fragment, piece by piece, atom by atom, the ghosts dissipated into the swirl.

A pair of Mexican clown hands appeared in the air above their heads and dropped to Trang's feet.

His Mexican Clown Hands.

The wind abruptly stopped. The tent, its audience and the performers had vanished.

"You alright, boss?" asked Rodriquez.

Trang nodded his head *yes*. "Where do you think spirits go?" he asked.

"I don't know, boss. Somewhere happy, I hope."

Rodriquez focused his flashlight and flipped open his notebook. "Serial killers, boss. I told you. This afternoon, I located the old Times article on microfilm. Once upon a time, a fire killed three men and a lion from a Mexican circus after *Showdown at Robber's Roost* wrapped production in 1911. Right here in Furnace Ranch. Four witnesses did nothing to save them—a hairdresser, a set painter, a cameraman, and a director. Just watched them burn. Later, a lawyer and a policeman covered up the case at City Hall. The relatives inquired but the studio buried the story. Literally. Nobody cared about Mexicans in 1911.”

“I figured it was something like that when I saw a picture of Big Jim Spencer out here at Furnace Rocks.” Trang coughed hard and spat into the dirt. “You saved my life. What did you say to them?”

“I promised their story would be told.”

“How the hell are you going to do that? We just saw something straight out *The X-Files*. Who’s going to buy that shit?”

“Well, maybe…I’ll write a book.”

“Like the Captain will let you do that. No way.”

“So, I’ll leak it to the Times.”

“That *might* work. Still, we did solve eighteen murders, Rodriquez. That’s got to be a Hollywood record. Maybe we *can* write a book.”

“More like six hundred, boss.”

“How do you figure?”

Rodriquez unfolded a sheet of paper and lit it with the beam of his flashlight.

Hundreds of scribbled names.

“The circus comes to town every year. Every kid knows that. Six murders a year for a century. All connected to Optassia Pictures. Same M.O. Crush. Strangle. Maul.”

Trang nodded. “We’re screwed though. We’ll never be able to clear all those crimes off the books. Who’ll believe us?”

Trang rose unsteadily to his feet and slung his arm over Rodriquez’s shoulder for support. “I thought Saturday night was date night, pal.”

“It is. The missus is waiting in the car and she’s mad as hell.”

Trang looked back over his shoulder towards the dark hole in the ground. “Jesus. Six hundred innocent people.”

“Nobody’s innocent in Hollywood, boss. You taught me that.”

Anthony C. Ferrante made his feature writing and directing debut with the cult ghost movie Boo *starring Dee Wallace. However, that film is not nearly as ironic as his latest directorial efforts, the pop culture sensations* Sharknado *and* Sharknado 2: The Second One. *In addition to directing* Headless Horseman *and* Hansel & Gretel, *Ferrante has also written or co-written numerous horror films including* House of Bones, Scream of the Banshee *and* Red Clover. The Crimson Marquee *is Ferrante's first published short story and was inspired by the movie theatres he grew up with (and practically lived at) in his small Northern California hometown. This story had to be pried out of his cold, clammy rewriting hands in order to make it into this collection.*

THE CRIMSON MARQUEE

Anthony C. Ferrante

THE POPCORN MACHINE BARELY WORKED, the soda dispenser never had the correct carbonated water to syrup ratio and the candy counter was filled with boxes of chocolaty goodness that probably had more "ness" than "good" shaking around inside.

None of this mattered though at the El Mira Cinema in Hollywood. It was one of the last remaining revival theatres in the city and people came for the classic double features. Not for the odd-tasting popcorn, not for the stale candy and definitely not for the uncomfortable, questionably sticky seats. It was a place where time stood still, with the clock turned back to whatever decade or era the theatre programmer had concocted for the evening.

Reese Waldon had been a fixture here. Just shy of 21, he spent the last two and half years selling tickets, changing the iconographic marquee and cleaning up the confetti and water bottles after the weekly midnight showings of *The Rocky Horror Picture Show*. It was a good job, not perfect, but tolerable especially since he was attending UCLA film school and the job allowed him to bone up on his movie history.

In some ways, it was an honor, not a chore, because the El Mira used to be the premiere movie house in Los Angeles. The theatre opened as a glorious 1000 seat movie palace in 1941 with state-of-the-art projection and sound for its time. All the now classics had made their debut here with star-studded premieres—*Casablanca, Citizen Kane, The Wolf Man, Sullivan's Travels* and the list went on.

The theatre was gorgeous during its heyday, with hand-painted murals decorating the sides of the walls of fully-naked women romping in an Adam and Eve-esque jungle garden (minus an Adam) and large velvet curtains which hung from solid iron rings.

What made the theatre unique, though, was the crimson marquee. Outside, the unique red paint encased the marquee as the lights mixed perfectly with the color to give it a majestic, grandiose feeling. Tourists would travel to the theatre just to take a picture in front of it. The neighboring Grauman's Chinese Theatre couldn't hold a candle to it, except of course by location. The Grauman Theatre survived because it was in the heart of Hollywood. The El Mira was further down the boulevard and in time the location did it in, as did the nature of movie exhibition.

Like all movie palaces, the multiplexes destroyed most of these singular destination spots. Why show one movie when you could offer customers 24 different options? Not surprisingly, the El Mira was chipped and stripped away of its character and identity as it slowly became a casualty of progress. Initially, the owners in the 1980's split the 1000-seater into three separate screens. The loge seating upstairs was turned into two 250-seaters, while the bottom half served as the 500 seat main attraction.

Adequate, but certainly no longer majestic.

Political correctness also resulted in the biggest crime of all as the naked murals found those curvaceous figures covered up by newly, and sadly, poorly painted fig leafs.

All this renovation couldn't salvage the theatre from second run status. The studios moved their premieres to the brand new multiplexes with their state of the art sound and pristine seats and the El Mira couldn't keep up. There were only so many options for theatres with rich histories like that. Scale back, show second run movies or shut down completely.

The El Mira chose the first two. In the early '90s, the two smaller screens closed down, and the owners renovated the space, serving as shop space to the occasional lawyer, real estate agents and during election years, political headquarters for budding (and questionable) mayoral and city council candidates. Soon, those tenants exited and the space ultimately was converted into storage space for the owners. Meanwhile, the theatre was turned into a revival house showing double bills of new and classic movies. Pick the right double bill and the theatre was routinely packed. Pick a dud, and it played to empty seats.

Over time, there was less interest from the public in classic 1940's screwball comedies or 1950's film noir. What sold tickets were horror movies, exploitation and grindhouse cinema. The more screams that echoed through the auditorium, the more tickets sold. It's as if the theatre wanted it that way. You'd get your film students, your horror fans and that small rat pack of wannabe Tarantinos sucking up pop culture like dirty old sponges.

Reese preferred when the theatre mixed up its selection of films and dug deeper into the past. Deep down he knew if the theatre didn't put people into the seats, there would be no theatre and he was out of a job.

Still, the El Mira miraculously survived in spite of itself. There was no way the foot traffic could support the operation, but the owners were reluctant to sell and with the theatre granted historical status in the late 1990s, the city couldn't tear it down even though the homeless mainstays and the junkies were relocated to downtown as the buildings surrounding it were all given million dollar corporate facelifts with trendy shops and criminally over-priced parking meters (with one hour limits) occupied the space. Then again, even when there was interest from outsiders to buy the property, there was one thing that routinely kept buyers away.

The place was haunted.

Few saw the ghosts, but those that worked there knew they existed.

The manager and projectionist was Big Joe Barton. He'd been threading 35mm film at the theatre for over twenty years and had stories to tell.

There was the time one of the ghosts took a liking to an employee. Her name was Vanessa and it was said that the ghost left her presents. Some were innocuous, like the candy boxes lined up on the counter to form a heart. Another was one of those big rings that the curtains hung from. What made it so strange was the rings were solid. The only way to remove one, was to cut through it and that was impossible. It was a fun joke—whether it was real or an actual spirit, but the time Vanessa was accidentally locked in a closet overnight to the sounds of moaning and groaning in the supposedly empty lobby, she quit the next day.

Other ghosts rumored to be at this place were a custodian whose presence could always be felt by the mysterious chemical smells that came out of nowhere, the Lady in Green (who many thought was a former starlet who committed suicide) and the El Mira's original owner George Bridgehead whose body was supposedly buried in the theatre's basement.

But one thing Big Joe had learned—it was better to stay out of their way. He did his job, the ghosts did theirs—whatever that was.

Big Joe was a talker, but he prided himself on his work. In fact, with so many digital cinemas now, he was the last of a dying breed. The El Mira's current owners refused to convert to a digital projector, so time stood still at this theatre. Movies from the new millennium had less 35mm prints available, if any at all, so there was a clear dividing line of what the El Mira could show and what it couldn't.

Big Joe was always generous in threading up an unofficial late night showing for Reese, especially if he brought a six-pack or if it was Saturday, a Cuban cigar to the projectionist. They would talk for hours about everything: movies, music and even the best places to buy ice cream. Big Joe had been an ice cream truck driver until society became more cautious about big beefy guys with tattoos in white vans selling Big Sticks and Bomb Pops to toddlers.

The other thing that made time go quicker in the ticket booth was the endless succession of candy counter girls who came and went as fast as the one-night-only double features. Chances are if you landed a part-time job here to sell concessions, you were either desperate, running from something, or not trying hard enough to find a real job.

Big Joe always preferred to have attractive women staffing the concession counter. Put a pretty face on a damaged product— even if the person selling it was damaged themselves—and you could sell anything. And it worked. Big Joe called the constant turnaround of girls "runners."

Reese preferred to call them "temps."

The list of runners was too numerous to count. Some were nice, others quiet, and some didn't last a week because face it, working a concession stand in a musty, slightly seedy, run down theatre was not the ideal dream job especially when a Hot Topic was two doors down. Heck, Vanessa lasted two months, only because she found the "ghosts" attention to her endearing, until it turned sour that one night in the maintenance closet.

Twenty year-old Emmy Rosen was only on the job for two days, but Reese was smitten from the moment she walked in. She kept her brunette hair tied up in a ponytail, revealing an impeccably perfect face unburdened by minimal make-up. She was naturally beautiful, but unlike girls who used their flawless looks as weapons, she either had an incredible sense of humility or had no idea how attractive she really was. And it was her smile that melted Reese every time he saw her. It was a beacon in an otherwise drab and rundown place. If there was only one drawback, she didn't seem too interested in the movies, but she was eager to please and always courteous with customers.

When the crowds came in, it became very difficult to engage in idle chat, but as people pushed their way through or rolled their eyes as they waited in line to get a bag of stale popcorn, she always made sure to give Reese an "oh well" smile.

Emmy didn't seem to fit the profile of a runner. She didn't end up here as a way station to a better job or was forced into working somewhere because of overbearing parents trying to teach their kid a lesson in working for a living. She clearly just needed a place to go and get away from things.

As the crowds died down from that night's Dario Argento double feature, Reese finally got the nerve to strike up small talk.

"So, do you go to college?" Reese asked, fishing.

"Community college, well, sort of, I was enrolled last year, but I had to take care of my mother, she hasn't been feeling very well," said Emmy, fumbling with a butterfly pin she had attached to her shirt.

"She okay now?"

"Uh-huh, but, by the time school started up again it was too late to get any classes," Emmy said. "So I'm sitting things out this semester and sorting through things."

"About what you want to do?"

"You could say that," she smiled.

The last patron exited as Reese locked the door.

Emmy offered a half smile and quickly changed the subject. "So what about you?" she asked. "Clearly, film nerd."

"And proud of it," Reese smiled back.

Emmy took her time card and punched out as Reese unlocked the door that lead into the basement.

"I know your shift is over, but if you're not doing anything, I could use some help changing the marquee," he asked. "Big Joe believes in safety in numbers."

Emmy paused. She looked at her phone for a second, considering it.

"Waiting for somebody?" he asked.

Emmy set her phone down. "No," she replied. "I've got nothing better to do. Besides, my bus won't be here for another thirty minutes."

The staircase leading to the basement was narrow, but long. The crimson paint on the walls was chipped and peeling. And the musty smell emanating from the bowels of the place probably was not healthy for anyone.

As Reese and Emmy descended, Reese counted out the steps aloud. Finally, he reached step number 24—which creaked loudly.

"Why the counting?" she asked.

"So I don't miss a step," said Reese. "The staircase is very deceiving. And take it slow—no running. It's easy to trip down here." He began to count the remaining steps out loud. "36...37...38," said Reese as he finally took the final step at the bottom and pushed open an age-spotted door.

Emmy followed, but stumbled into the shadowy basement, clearly missing the last step, before regaining her composure.

"That's why I count," Reese smiled as the door creaked shut behind them.

Compared to the cramped lobby, the basement revealed a whole other world. It was the place time forgot.

Posters and cardboard cut-outs from the entire 70-year plus history of cinema were spread all over the basement. It was organized for the most part by year. And there were doors leading to rooms too numerous to count.

"That's a lot of doors?" said Emmy.

"Dressing rooms, left over from when the theatre first opened," said Reese. "During premieres, the stars would get ready downstairs before they came up to greet the public. You can actually find some pretty amazing signatures written on the walls if you take the time to look around."

"Like who?" Emmy asked.

"Walter Brennan, Gene Tierney, Barbara Stanwyck," said Reese. "Sally Rand, she was a famous fan dancer. There's a poem of hers written on a wall somewhere."

Emmy looked confused. She didn't know any of them. Reese noticed her lack of film history, and fumbled for a name she might recognize.

"You have to know Humphrey Bogart," Reese said, with a hint of desperation.

"Sort of sounds familiar," Emmy said.

"Bogart!" Reese said, exasperated like the film nerd he was. "*Casablanca, The Maltese Falcon, The African Queen.* His famous line was 'here's looking at you, kid.'"

Finally recognition. "Okay, I know that line," said Emmy, smiling at how worked up Reese had gotten.

Reese was pleased, for a moment, but then realized the truth. "You don't know the line, do you."

Emmy smiled. They both laughed.

"You'll pick up a few nerd IQ points if you stick around long enough," said Reese. He headed over to the far left corner where all the supplies were. Letter bins, a ladder, and a suction pole to take the letters on and off the outside marquee were neatly organized and he began to set aside the letters that he needed.

A strong odor suddenly wafted through the basement.

Emmy grabbed her nose. "What is that smell?"

"The custodian," replied Reese. "Sometimes he leaves his supplies behind."

"He's not here now is he?"

Reese shrugged and smiled. "The custodian is the last person you should be worried about."

Emmy moved closer to the stairwell door, clearly a little spooked by the basement.

"What's the matter?" Reese asked.

"Nothing," she responded. She propped the door open and stepped back onto the stair.

"The basement give you the creeps?"

"No, I just..." She tried to be strong, but Reese could see right through her.

"Well, it should a little bit," he said. "The place is haunted."

"Now you're just trying to scare me."

Reese collected all the remaining letters into a bucket, then grabbed the ladder and suction device. "Yes, haunted. You don't believe me?" he said.

"I think you just want me to get scared so I'll come over there and grab your shoulder until we go back upstairs," Emmy said, flirting, but a little serious about it too.

Then—*CLICK!*

Out went the lights. Emmy, tumbled from the one step on the stair she was standing on. Despite the darkness, she rushed over to Reese's direction and grabbed his shoulder.

"Easy. It's probably just a fuse or something," he said, smiling in the darkness.

In the far corner, a woman emerged. Her skin was pale, her face terrifying and her green dress flowing as if a draft was blowing it around.

Emmy screamed, turned Reese toward the woman in green's direction, but she was no longer there.

"What are you—" he started.

And then another creak! The loud sound was unmistakable. The 24th step.

Emmy swung around looking at the stairwell leading upstairs. A shadow appeared. "Who is that?" she said.

As the shadow descended, Emmy grabbed Reese's shoulder tight, unsure of what new manifestation might appear.

As the shadow got closer, the light hit the face of the cherub-looking Big Joe, who peered down below. "Hey, I shut things down, lock up when you're done," he announced.

As he got a better look, he spied Emmy clinging to Reese. "Oh, I didn't know you were still here, saw you were clocked out." He then looked at Reese. "You told her, right?"

Emmy backed away from Reese, embarrassed.

"What is this?" Emmy said, a bit peeved. "Is this some kind of geek initiation—trick the new girl by making her think the place is haunted, get her scared and then Big Joe shows up for the super scary finale?"

"No tricks, the place is haunted," said Big Joe. "You have to watch yourself. Safety in numbers. And always count the steps."

"I heard," said Emmy and then she let out a big "hmph" and stormed up the stairs.

Big Joe looked back at Reese and shrugged.

"Good goin' Joe," said Reese.

"Sorry kid," said Big Joe. "You should know better—runners."

"Temps."

"Same difference—neither one stick around."

"She's different."

"Reese, they're all runners, but, for your sake, I hope she's not. Now come on, you know it's not a good idea to be down here alone."

Reese and Big Joe ascended the stairs, counting, as the shadows in the basement began to shift and move.

Something was down there with them.

؃

The next day, Reese waited for Emmy to show up. She was late. He had butterflies in his stomach—an aching pain that he gave Emmy the wrong impression the night before—that he and Big

Joe were playing some kind of trick on her, giving her enough reason to get the hell out of Dodge and never come back again, fulfilling Big Joe's prophecy that she was a runner. Reese was heartbroken. He didn't mean to upset her, he just wanted to talk to her. It was rare that any of the candy counter girls had anything interesting to say, let alone an interest in interacting with him. Maybe Big Joe was right—they were all runners. Their days at the theatre were always terminally numbered.

After people were let into the first showing, the doors swung open and there was Emmy.

"I'm so, so, so sorry I was late, I just—" Emmy was scattered, her eyes puffy as if she had been crying. "My bus was late, and, well, I'm sorry."

She grabbed her time card and was about to clock in when she saw it was already done for her. She looked at Reese, confused. "I clocked you in, just in case."

Emmy smiled, a genuine smile and very quiet, appreciative "Thank you." It was obvious she wasn't used to people doing nice things for her.

"Something came up with my mom, I'm so sorry, I—" Emmy started to say before Reese cut her off.

"You should have at least called, you could have been fired," Reese said.

"Really," said Emmy, half smiling. "I thought this was the kind of place where they couldn't afford to do that."

"Well, you have a point," said Reese.

As the final showing began in the theatre, a classic 1980's slasher film played in the background. Those movies were all the same to Reese. Maybe it was *Labor Day Massacre, Veteran's Day Vivisection* or some ridiculous thing like that. It didn't matter, it was crap and he knew it and refused to give some of the lesser exploitation films the time of day by remembering their actual titles.

Reese closed down the ticket booth as Emmy cashed out the concession stand and clocked out.

"Were you kidding, about this place being haunted?" Emmy asked, very curious.

"It's haunted."

"How do you know, have you seen anything?"

"Heard, not necessarily seen," said Reese. "Strange things happen all the time. Some have seen the Lady in Green, there's also this weird smell of dirty soap water. We think it had something to do with a custodian that died here. I think he was downstairs with us last night."

"And you didn't bother to tell me?"

"I told you. That smell came from the custodian."

Emmy tried to process all of this information and then realized the most important thing Reese said: "Someone died here?" Emmy asked, concerned.

"We think he died."

"What does that mean?"

"This place has been around since the 1940's, someone was bound to keel over at one point or another," said Reese. "I'm surprised more guests don't take a dirt nap after eating the popcorn here. Even the grease stains have grease stains on that old machine."

"How many?" Emmy asked, a little concerned.

"I haven't seen anyone die, and I don't know how many, but, strange things do happen, so, the ghosts had to end up here somehow,"

"I want to see one of them, I want to know if they're real."

"I've never seen one, just felt their presence. Don't think I would want to either."

Emmy thought about it for a moment, but Reese could tell she was serious.

"You don't want to see them, do you?" Reese asked.

"Yes, I do," she said, adamant. "What do we have to do?" She eagerly grabbed a flashlight.

Reese stared at her for a moment. There was something different about her today. She wasn't clingy and scared by the darkness below. She was curious, interested and adventurous. You could probably add foolish to the list, but he would never say that out loud to her.

"Bad idea," Reese responded. "So why do you want to see a ghost anyway? Last night, you didn't have any interest whatsoever."

"I want to know if there's something else out there," said Emmy. "I want to believe."

"There are things here that even Big Joe and I don't mess with," Reese pushed back.

Emmy paused, not sure if she wanted to confide in Reese, then tears rolled down her cheeks. "My mom," Emmy said, tears welling up.

Emmy regained her composure.

"She passed away," Emmy said matter-of-factly, trying to fight off emotions.

Reese wasn't sure what to say. This was a big thing for her to confide in him, but they weren't close enough for him to comfort her.

"Please," Emmy pleaded.

Reese paused for a moment. "Let me ask Big Joe first," he said turning toward the projection booth. Then a scream from the movie playing on the big screen echoed into the lobby followed by a door slamming behind him.

He turned around—Emmy had descended into the basement alone.

Reese ran to the door, tried to open it, but it was jammed. As he pulled on the handle, a terrible thought crept up on him. Maybe something didn't want him to help her...

Emmy counted the steps on the way down and on step 24, the loud creak sounded. She continued down and then started counting like Reese. "36...37...38..." she said, pushing the door open and taking one last step into the basement—this time not stumbling like she had before.

As the door shut behind her she walked into the center and looked around. A draft made a small whirring sound, which startled Emmy and then—

CLICK.

The lights went out.

It was pitch black as the sounds of the movie upstairs slowly faded away. Then there was silence—the eerie kind.

"Reese? Emmy asked nervously.

No answer.

Heavy breathing broke the silence. The sound came closer to Emmy.

"Reese," she screamed out.

No response. The breathing was louder.

Emmy fumbled with the flashlight and clicked it on. She shined the light in the direction of the sound.

No one there.

"Reese, why are you doing this?" Emmy called out.

Still, no response.

And just as her flashlight died on her, the lights clicked back on all on their own.

However, the area looked different—no longer the same basement she just walked through. Dirty water dripped from the ceiling. All the paint was chipped away from the walls. It was as if the basement had aged 100 years with a click of the switch.

She looked at the floor—a full sized door with the initials "GB" carved into it was embedded dead center into the ground. The door was weathered by age; cracks, splintered wood and dust gave the impression of a coffin of sorts.

Emmy reached for the handle, unsure it this was a good idea or not. She twisted the handle and jerked the door open. Behind it—dark crimson dirt. Emmy wasn't sure what to make of it. She dug her hands around and held up the red earth, then glanced down below—the dirt was moving and then she noticed thick, pinkish worms moving underneath. She looked at the soil in her hands—more worms.

She dropped the crimson dirt and wiped off her hands frantically and backed away. Then something pushed through the dirt—it was two hands that were formed by the writhing worms.

That was more than enough for Emmy to get the hell out of there. Panicked, she slammed the door over the worms and frantically searched around for a doorway that lead back upstairs, but nothing looked familiar. She quickly retraced her steps and came to a door hanging off its hinges. She went toward it and saw that a weird symbol was carved into it. There were stairs on the other side of it. It was a good start.

Emmy shined her flashlight up the stairwell, it looked different too. Noises emanated from above. The movie? Reese and Big Joe laughing at their cruel joke of terrifying her? None of it mattered though. Getting out of there and this place for good was the only thing that raced through her mind.

She pushed the crooked door aside and ascended the stairs, but then remembered what Reese said: *38 steps.*

She went back to the bottom and began to count as she went up. "38, 37, 36..." she said out loud.

When she got to the 24th step, the wood didn't creak like before. She took two steps back, stomped on the step to see if she missed one. Nothing. She did the same thing on step 23. The creak was not there. Looking back down at the spooky basement, it just didn't matter so she continued anyway.

She shined the flashlight around. Her breathing getting heavy. She continued, "22, 21, 20," and then the steps stopped, a door blocking her way. She was at the top of the stairs. Emmy was confused. There was a door to potential freedom, but there were only 18 steps.

She reached out to the handle, unsure what was on the other side, but risked it anyway. She twisted the handle carefully and opened the door, shining the flashlight inside. It appeared to be an attic. She waved the light around the room and all the walls had wood splintered everywhere. It was as if something trapped had been trying to get out and finally gave up.

And then she saw it. The light illuminated a terrifying woman, her face mangled and scratched as strips of flesh clung to it. Her fingernails were ripped off, her fingertips bloodied as the shredded flesh revealed bone. On her dress was a faded name tag: *VANESSA*.

The woman let out a blood-curdling wail and rushed toward Emmy. She fell backwards as the bloody creature came face to face with her. The woman's breath was heavy; she tilted her head as she looked at Emmy, as if unsure what to make of the terrified girl.

Then the woman reached out to Emmy, ready to claw at her with what remained of her fingers. Emmy closed her eyes, knowing her time was up, but then—nothing.

Emmy opened her eyes and the woman was gone.

The door Emmy entered was still there, she ran toward it, but the screaming woman appeared again. Now she was mad. She wailed again, but Emmy was fearless and ran right at her—and *through her*. There were no physical properties to the disfigured woman, at least that Emmy could tell and she slammed the door shut.

A pounding on the door began. The woman wanted out. She continued to cry out, but Emmy didn't wait for the woman to escape from her supernatural prison.

The wood around the door frame began to splinter as Emmy was about to run down the stairs, but whispered "no running" to herself. She still moved fast on her trip down. On the last step though, she fell down and landed in the basement.

CRACK!

Her arm bent backwards, a bone sticking out as she cried out in pain. As Emmy writhed around on the floor, sobbing in agony and holding her shattered limb, she could only think of one thing: *I have to get out of here. I have to get help.*

Choking back tears, she fumbled around and found the flashlight with her good hand. As she stood up, she shined her flashlight at all the doorways and began frantically counting to herself.

Thirty-eight doorways including the one on the floor.

Thirty-eight steps.

She saw a ghost. She got her wish, but now she had to find a way back. She stumbled to different doors and opened them, shining the flashlight in each one. All of them led to stairways, but they were all different. The size of the steps changed. The coloring of the inside stairwell walls were all unique, but none were crimson like the stair to the lobby.

Her mind reeled through the pain and panic. Where was the door that led to the theatre, the one with 38 steps? Did each stairwell lead to a different ghost?

Finally Emmy found a stairwell that looked vaguely familiar. Some peeling red paint, but only five steps up, there was a door. She reached for the handle, curious, but stopped.

Then she heard a voice.

"Emmy?" the weak voiced called out.

Emmy was confused, but the voice was familiar.

"Emmy, open the door," the voice cried out. "I need your help."

Emmy teared up. "Mom?"

"Just open the door sweetie," the voice on the other side encouraged her.

Emmy looked relieved, and she opened the door fast, but behind it was not her mother. It was a completely different apparition—this one solid white—less monstrous, but terrifying nonetheless. The creature had a large, Cheshire Cat grin across its face with rows of sharp teeth glistening with saliva. Its eyes burned red. Demonic, angry, it didn't matter. Its interest was solely on the living flesh of Emmy and lunged toward her.

She slammed the door shut and hurried down the stairs, still careful not to run. Reese warned her about running. He was right about counting steps, so he must be right about that.

Emmy cried out, "Reese. Please help."

Then, pounding on an upstairs door. Then pounding from another direction. All she could hear was incessant pounding—all the doors at the top of the stairwells were crumbling with supernatural force. And then there was a crashing sound that spread down the hallway as doors shattered one by one. Steps revealed themselves behind each open door frame, and the terrifying wails of ghostly prisoners emanated from each stairwell.

Emmy stood in the center of the room and shined her flashlight.

Ghosts of various men and women stood in each doorway, some of them missing limbs, other missing their faces, others 100 percent demonic and some merely spectral white and scary as hell. They all smiled as they slowly walked toward the one living thing in their presence.

Then the ghosts parted as the first door she had opened, with the crimson dirt in the floor, was revealed. A body emerged from the muck, but like the hands, it too was made from a mass of interlocking writhing worms. The aberration opened its ragged mouth, releasing a horrifying moan as more worms fell from its maw. The worm corpse opened its arms wide as if to welcome her. Emmy wanted nothing to do with it or any of the other ghastly apparitions that surrounded her. She backed up even more terrified at what she released.

Emmy looked around. Trying to find an empty door—the one door that would lead to safety—to the theatre lobby. And she found it. The one door a ghost didn't come from. As the ghostly entities cornered her, she ran up the stairs.

The other ghosts followed and faster than she anticipated. Hovering, floating, and dripping with spectral goo, they advanced on her.

She ascended the stairwell and cried in relief as she saw the familiar red paint peeling from the theatre stairs. She counted backwards, and was getting close. There still wasn't a creak on the 24th step, but, the panic kept her going and going, "Ten, nine, eight, seven, six, five, four, three, two, one..."

But the last step did not lead to the theatre door. There was a missing step and an unfinished door at the top with no handle.

Something was wrong.

Emmy shined her flashlight where the step should be—and saw only a blackness that led down to a deep dark abyss. It was a large enough chasm that she could barely reach the door, but even if she could reach it there was no handle.

She started to run down the steps again, but the other ghosts filled the hallway, with their sinister smiles and disturbing wails. They were drawn to her life—like moths to light.

Wormface led the charge, still coming toward her, arms outstretched wide looking for the embrace Emmy would never give it. She backed up as they got closer. She only had one choice.

The abyss.

It was her only way out.

As the ghosts came face to face with her, she looked at them. "Reese?" Emmy asked one last time.

As she stared at the ghosts around her she noticed that the apparitions were not as terrifying as they were moments before. There was a sadness; their wails more like cries. In that moment, she sensed a similar pain beneath their scary veneer.

Still, it felt like a trick and she only had one way out.

"Leave me alone!" she screamed and then defiantly jumped into the black abyss where the missing step was. Her scream echoed the entire way down.

Upstairs there was another scream from the movie theatre and it blended with Emmy's scream below, almost in unison, until Emmy's scream was no more than a fragile whisper in the wind.

Reese continued to pound furiously on the door. One last powerful punch and the door creaked open. "Emmy," he called out. "Emmy?"

Reese headed to the basement. As he walked down the stairs quickly, he continued to count the steps, finally it was "36, 37, 38" and then he took one more confused step—"39?" Reese's face went ashen. He opened the basement door, hoping Emmy would be standing there.

She wasn't.

He looked at all the doorways and then he saw something different. There was a new door where the letters for the marquee were stored. He walked up to it. He nervously opened it and looked up the stairwell. A shadow outlined on the wall with a shape that was distinctly Emmy.

"Emmy, is that you?" he said. "It's okay, you can come down now."

Then he saw something carved into the door frame. It was a butterfly, similar to the pin Emmy wore. He looked back up the stairs, and the shadow was gone, followed by the sound of a slamming door.

Gone.

Emmy was lost, but she always had been.

❦

The final patrons left the theatre as Reese locked the door. He clocked himself out.

Big Joe appeared. "I know you liked her," said Big Joe. "Maybe one day, you'll find the one that doesn't get away."

Reese was devastated. "She didn't have to go down there, she would have been okay."

"She would have went down there eventually," said Big Joe. "You know this place is like that. It has needs."

"The police, they'll ask questions."

"She punched the clock, she took the bus to and from work. If anyone asks, she left for the evening and we never saw her again. There's nothing but the truth there."

Reese realized Big Joe was right, even if he didn't agree with him. He went into the ticket booth, and grabbed a sign from the drawer, his actions almost ritualistic in nature. As he closed the drawer, a solid iron ring from one of the curtains rested on the counter. He picked it up, looked at it. Clearly, it was a gift for him. He set it back down, a sad look on his face.

Reese called out to Big Joe. "You were right."

"About what?"

"She was a runner."

"They always are," said Big Joe, and he walked away.

"Here's looking at you, kid," Reese spoke softly to himself, an homage to his brief time with Emmy.

As the timeless, shining crimson marquee glowed in the night, Reese stared out the window, almost a ghost himself as the lights turned off, sending him and the theatre back into the shadows again. Before he closed the door, he took the faded, dog-eared sign he had grabbed and put it in the window.

It read: HELP WANTED.

Lisa Morton is a screenwriter, author of non-fiction books, award-winning prose writer, and Halloween expert whose work was described by the American Library Association's Readers' Advisory Guide to Horror *as "consistently dark, unsettling, and frightening." In 2012, she won the* Bram Stoker Award *for both Non-fiction* (Trick or Treat: A History of Halloween) *and Graphic Novel* (Witch Hunts: A Graphic History of the Burning Times, *co-written with Rocky Wood and illustrated by Greg Chapman). Her most recent books are the novels* Malediction *from* Evil Jester Press, Netherworld *from* JournalStone, *and* Zombie Apocalypse! Washington Deceased *set in Stephen Jones'* Zombie Apocalypse! *universe. She lives in North Hollywood, California, and online at* www.lisamorton. com.

SHE-DEVIL A-GO-GO

Lisa Morton

"C'MON, BABY, SHAKE THOSE big beautiful titties for daddy!" Ross shouted from behind the camera.

Loni obliged, grinning into the camera Ross held below her knees and doing a shimmy that caused her size 44DD breasts to jiggle back and forth behind her tight halter top.

"Yeah! That just sold another dozen tickets right there," Ross told her. He checked the shot through the viewfinder one last time, then called, "Cut!"

Loni's grin fell faster than a cheerleader's dress on prom night as she stepped back, feeling beads of sweat trying to push through the skin of her forehead. "Ross, honey, can we take a break? It's so hot out here," she whined.

"Sure, Loni, we gotta change mags anyway and check the gate." Ross slapped the young camera assistant until he stopped goggling, then handed the finished magazine to him and waited for a new one.

Loni wandered over to the cooler, sitting in the shade of the porch, and got another diet soda. As she pulled the ring from the top, she looked around, frowning.

Yeah, right, welcome to the movies, she thought bitterly. This wasn't how she'd seen her first leading role going—slouching against the unpainted wooden wall of a rattletrap shotgun shack in the middle of the Mojave Desert, making a movie called *She-Devil A-Go-Go* that had a cast of eight and a crew of seven. Still, she was getting a hundred bucks a day for being here, and that was more than she'd made back at the club, dancing for drunks who might tip her a single, if she was lucky.

She nodded as her co-stars approached. The plot of *She-Devil A-Go-Go* centered on three strippers who get fed up with their sadistic boss one night, accidentally kill him, steal his MG convertible and the contents of the safe, and go on the lam across the desert. She played Julie, the dim-witted comic relief of the trio; her real-life best friend from the club, Maddi, played the hot-tempered Latina Chili; and an actress named Deva Braun played the tougher-than-nails leader, Wanda.

Maddi also grabbed a can from the cooler, then leaned up against Loni. "How's it going?" she asked. Then she eyed her friend again, and her eyes went wide. "Loni, are you okay? You don't look so good."

Loni did wipe sweat from her forehead this time, and knew she'd just smeared her makeup. "I don't feel so great, either."

Maddi put her hand to her friend's forehead. "Well, you don't seem to have a fever, but...you're really pale, and you look tired."

Sighing, Loni ran the icy can over her face. "It's just this miserable heat. We should be getting hazard pay for putting up with it."

"Or for putting up with Ross," Maddi added.

Loni eyed him as he finished putting a new mag on the camera. He was moderately handsome (if more than a little predatory), with thinning hair and a pencil thin mustache; it was impossible to know just how old the man was. But it wasn't his face where Loni's eyes finally came to rest. "He's not so bad."

"Yeah," Deva noted, "especially not if you're fucking him."

Maddi giggled, but Loni squinted at the other woman. "How would you know? You haven't fucked him."

"Yet, you mean," added Maddi.

Deva looked out from under her black bangs to where Ross was setting up his next shot. "Don't worry—when the time comes, I'll give Ross a fucking he'll never forget."

The snarl in her voice made Maddi and Loni exchange a long, uneasy look.

"Oh, Ross, love me...oh yeah..."

It was lunch break, and the rest of the cast and crew were seated outside around tables, feasting on Chicken-in-a-Bucket; but Loni wasn't interested in food right now.

They were in Ross' private trailer—the one he'd brought to the set himself, towed behind his station wagon—and Ross had Loni bent backwards over the trailer's built-in bed, his face buried in her exposed breasts, his mouth hungrily sucking.

Loni moaned in pleasure and her back arched, pushing more of her prodigious flesh against Ross' mouth. Ross moved one hand down to her hot pants, working the zipper.

"Oh, Rossi, I want you so bad..." Loni cried out.

Ross made his own noncommittal moan, and shifted his mouth to the other breast.

"Please, give it to me, baby, I need it—"

Ross pulled his head away from her breasts and leaned back, panting, his eyes closed in ecstasy. His breathing slowed, and for a moment Loni wondered if he'd come; he seemed sated, somehow filled...

Then he grabbed her waist and started to turn her. "Bend over, baby," he ordered.

Loni resisted, even as he tried more forcefully to pull her around. "Ross, honey, couldn't I just look at you this one time? We always do it this way—"

Ross started to pull away. "Fine. We're done then."

"No!" Loni gave in, turning over so that she was bent forward over the bed, and she even gave her bare ass with spread cheeks an enticing little wriggle. "Whatever you want, lover."

She waited, anticipating—and then gasped as she felt him enter her. He was so big that first thrust always brought a moment of pain...and then the delicious pleasure took over.

When it was done, she heard the door to the trailer open and then slam as he left. No words, no final kiss. Not even a "thank you". Nothing.

It always went like this. Ross sucked her, fucked her, and then trucked on out, while she lay on his bed, feeling drained, used. Not happy and spent, but tired, weak, and somehow much older.

In the script for *She-Devil A-Go-Go*, the characters Julie, Chili and Wanda tried to hole up in what they thought was an abandoned ranch house, only to find it inhabited by three studly cowboys and their crotchety, perverted old father. When one of the cowboys began to suspect the women, Wanda demonstrated her karate skills by dispatching him with ease, then dragging his body off to a nest of rattlesnakes.

They finished the day off shooting the big fight. Wanda/Deva chopped at the enthusiastic actor, who flailed about vigorously and finally back-flipped into the sand. The sun was sinking as they wrapped up the scene with a spectacular shot of victorious Wanda standing over the man, one high-heeled go-go boot planted in his back while the desert wind whipped her long black hair over her own considerable cleavage. Ross finished the shot, called "Cut!", and sidled up to Deva.

"That was beautiful, Deva, just beautiful. Like you, doll. Sure you don't wanna join me back in my room tonight? We could celebrate with some bubbly, just you and I..."

"What about Loni?" Deva asked.

"C'mon, it's 1966, haven't you heard of swinging?" Ross asked, practically itching as he eyed her chest.

Deva fixed him with that hard stare that had won her the role. "See, Ross, the problem with swinging is that it goes both up and down. If we swing together, I'm liable to be way up, while you're going down."

Ross stepped closer to her, so close she could feel his breath on her cheek. "Where you're concerned, Deva, I'm willing to go down."

She forced herself to stand close to him for a while, then stepped back and blew him a little kiss before turning away.

She just hoped Ross didn't see her shiver in the desert heat.

The next morning the three women arrived together at the set, where they were greeted with new script pages. Loni saw in dismay that her character, Julie, would be murdered today by the old man, who would stab her with a steak knife before sinking back into his wheelchair.

"What is this shit?" Loni roared as she saw the rewrites. "How could he change this overnight?!"

"He didn't change it overnight," Deva calmly told her. "He's had those pages ready all along."

Maddi and Loni both gaped at her for a moment. "How could you know that?" Loni finally demanded.

"Did you look in the mirror this morning, Loni?" Deva asked.

Loni was stunned into speechlessness. Yes, in fact, she had looked into the mirror—and hadn't liked what she saw.

She looked ten years older than she had yesterday.

There were new wrinkles around her eyes, the skin on her face looked doughy and was sagging in places, and her hair hung limp, without its usual youthful bounce. Her body felt slow and heavy, and her knees had actually cracked loudly as she'd staggered out of bed.

Maddi stepped forward for her friend. "Okay, spill" she said to Deva.

Deva answered, "It's Ross. He did this to you. He gave you the first draft so you'd think you had a big starring role, but he always knew this would happen, and that he'd have to write you out after he'd been fucking you for a week."

Loni gaped for another second, then barked a single sharp laugh. "That's crazy."

Deva just shrugged, and looked out over the desert vastness.

Loni and Maddi exchanged a look, then Maddi put an arm around her friend's shoulders. "C'mon, Loni, let's go talk to Ross. We sure don't need this crazy bitch right now. She can go hang with those rattlesnakes if she needs some friends."

As they stalked off, Deva watched them go, guilt and regret descending on her. She'd thought this might happen, but she hadn't known for sure...until today. Now her suspicions had all been confirmed, and she knew what she had to do. Still, it didn't make her feel any better about Loni, about what had happened to her.

Especially knowing that she might have stopped it.

The next day—after Loni had wrapped her big death scene and been sent home—Ross staged a fight between Maddi and Deva. In the script, Chili suspected Wanda set up Julie's death, and she tried to take on the bigger woman; after a few rolls in the desert sand, however, Wanda easily gained the upper hand, and swore to Chili that she had nothing to do with Julie's demise. Then Wanda convinced Chili to help plot the old man's end, so they could take the fortune he had hidden under his mattress. And, of course, avenge Julie.

After the morning's shooting, lunch was brought in (two-hour old burgers this time). As Ross loaded up his own plate, Deva suddenly cut into line in front of him, offering him a seductive smile. "Sorry. I'm just feeling like I seriously need some meat today."

Ross gaped for a second, then said, "It might taste better in my trailer."

Deva, who'd seen the trailer rock for the last week as the entire crew smirked at Loni's shrill cries, answered, "Well, Ross, it might...but it'd taste even better if it aged a few days."

"Is that a promise?" Ross asked her, his voice suddenly husky.

"Think you can wait?" she responded, then ducked away from him as quickly as she'd arrived.

She risked a look back, and saw Ross standing stock-still, his eyes locked onto her, and she felt both the beginnings of triumph and more than a little fear.

That night Maddi answered a knock at her door, half-expecting it to be Ross, but it was Deva.

"What?" Maddi asked. She didn't like Deva, didn't like her bossy confidence and the way she'd treated Loni, and she made no attempt to hide her dislike.

"We need to talk," Deva said. She had a book in her hand, with newspaper clippings sticking out from inside.

Maddi sniped back, "About what? Thinking of forming a book club? Or is that an acting book? 'Cause god knows you need it."

Deva suddenly pushed past Maddi into her hotel room, and slammed the door before Maddi could respond. Maddi stepped back, knowing that in a real fight—just as in their cinematic one—she wouldn't stand a chance against the bigger, better-muscled woman.

"Promise me you won't go to bed with Ross," Deva said, staring intently at Maddi.

Maddi gawked for an instant, then blurted out, "Why? So you can have him to yourself?"

Deva slammed the book down on the cheap hotel table, and pulled out a clipping, which she thrust out to Maddi. "Know this one?"

Maddi took the clipping and eyed it. It was a movie ad cut out of a newspaper for a film called *Myrna*. The ad showed a not-so-pretty but extraordinarily well-endowed young woman dressed in a flimsy negligee, draped over a rock beside a river. Below the photo was the line "A Ross Moore Film".

"That was Ross Moore's first film, made back in '60," she said, her voice suddenly soft.

Maddi handed the clipping back. "So?"

"So…the girl who starred in it, the one who played Myrna—she was my sister, Myrna Horner," Deva said.

"Yeah?" Maddi answered, even as she was thinking, *Guess big boobs run in the family.*

"She slept with Ross, too. She was nineteen. After the film she looked forty. She died a year later."

Maddi instantly flashed on Loni, but kept that thought to herself. "Awww, my heart's breakin'," she blurted sarcastically.

And instantly regretted it, as Deva charged her. Maddi's feet pedaled backwards until she was up against one of the hotel walls with Deva's arm across her throat, and the woman's furious face just inches from her own terrified one.

"Yeah, well, your heart *should* break, because she meant more to me than anything in the world. There was nothing I wouldn't have done for Myrna. *Nothing.* And, y'see, I think Ross killed her, and I'm gonna see to it that he pays for that."

Maddi took in a shuddering breath, then gasped out, "How'd Ross kill her?"

Deva released her and stepped back a pace. "He's not human," she finally answered.

"Hey, I don't like him much either, but—"

Deva cut her off. "I mean *really* not human."

Maddi could only blurt out, "What?!"

Deva handed her another yellowed newspaper clipping. It was headlined "Army Cameraman Miraculously Survives Four Bullets, Two Bomb Blasts". It was accompanied by a photo of Ross, grinning, in combat fatigues.

"So he's lucky," Maddi said, returning the clipping.

"According to his birth certificate," Deva added, "he's seventy-six. Does he look seventy-six to you?"

Maddi crossed her arms. "Fine. So he's a lucky dirty old man."

Deva reached back and grabbed the book, which she extended to Maddi. Maddi took it and saw the title was *An Encyclopedia of Demons and Spirits*, by one Gordon Rodgers.

"After my sister died," Deva said, "I started keeping track of Ross Moore's other films. Wanna know why he never uses the same actress twice? Because they all die within a year of making a movie with him."

"You're kidding me," Maddi replied.

"I'm not. And it's not VD, if that's what you're thinking. I started doing some research. I think he's some kind of sexual leech—he sucks energy out from women through the breasts. It keeps him young. And invulnerable."

Maddi wanted to laugh, but didn't dare antagonize Deva further. "You expect me to believe that?"

Deva nodded at the book. "Just read through that. And go visit your friend Loni. See how she looks. And ask her what Ross was like in the sack."

"What's that got to do with anything?" asked Maddi.

"Because if he's what I think he is...he won't even have a dick."

And then she left.

Maddi ran to the door and locked it, shaking her head in disbelief. She wondered if she should tell Ross.

She wondered if she should sleep with Ross, just to prove Deva was crazy.

Either way, it could wait until tomorrow. Maddi needed to get her beauty rest.

The next day was Saturday, and Ross released the crew after a shorter-than-usual day. They'd finished the first week of filming on *She-Devil A-Go-Go*, and were halfway through now. On Monday they'd resume filming at 6 AM.

Maddi had driven back to her Los Angeles apartment, her head a whirl of thoughts (which was giving her a headache). At the last minute she'd decided to take the book Deva had given her, and that night she flipped through it until she found the section on sexual predators.

She gave up after a few paragraphs. She'd never been much of a reader to begin with, and this stuff was just indecipherable, going on about *pranic* energy taken during sexual activity, and the scarcity of this type of monster, and the relationship to the *incubus*.

Far out, she thought. *That Deva is one loony bitch.*

She decided she'd tell Ross on Monday.

Then she visited Loni.

It was Sunday morning, a bright summer day, blue and cloudless, but when Maddi arrived at her friend's apartment at noon, Loni was still in bathrobe and slippers.

And she looked fifty.

Maddi didn't know what to say. She tried at first not to look at her friend, but it was like trying not to look at a big basket drawn in tight pants; she couldn't *stop* looking. Loni's face was lined, her eyes sunken, her jaw line now hung with jowls. Flesh sagged from her arms, and she looked at least 30 pounds heavier. Loni sat at her dinette table, chain-smoking Camels and sipping gin, and all she could talk about was how famous they'd all be when *She-Devil A-Go-Go* finally opened.

Maddi didn't have the heart to tell Loni that she doubted if she'd live that long.

Before she left, Maddi asked her what Ross liked to do in bed.

"He's totally a breast man," Loni answered between cigarette puffs. "Oh, yeah, and he's kinda kinky—likes it from behind."

"So did you ever see his dick?" Maddi asked.

Loni laughed, and it wasn't a healthy sound. "Who cares about seeing it? I will say this: If he isn't at least twelve inches, I'm a virgin."

On Monday morning Maddi returned to the set, reluctantly.

Today's shooting schedule called for her character Chili to seduce one of the cowpokes, and Maddi had a hard time working up much enthusiasm for the seduction. The actor playing "Rowdy" was handsome enough, and not a half-bad kisser, but she kept thinking about Ross watching her, and it was hard to act like a nympho when her skin was crawling.

After lunch they were scheduled to shoot dialogue scenes with Chili, Wanda and the old man, and for a change Maddi was happy to have very few lines. In between takes she felt Deva's gaze on her, as well as Ross', and she tried to avoid them both.

At the end of the day Ross called her to his trailer.

She entered, nervous, picking at the belt loops on her white denim hip-huggers, as Ross sat on the edge of the trailer's bed, eyeing her. "Is something wrong, Maddi?" he asked. "You seemed distracted today. You looked like you had a hard time in the kissing scene."

"Sorry, Ross," she managed, "I'm just...preoccupied. With a sick friend."

"Oh," Ross feigned sympathy, "nothing too bad, I hope."

"I'm afraid it might be. In fact it's Loni."

"Loni?" Ross stroked his mustache thoughtfully, then nodded. "I'm really sorry to hear that, but I'm not too surprised. She didn't look good her last day here. Hope she didn't catch some weird desert bug. Well, please let me know if there's anything I can do to help."

His expression of concern seemed so genuine that Maddi found herself thinking again that Deva was crazy. Of course he was human. So what if he liked women with big tits? What man didn't?

"Thanks, Ross."

She started to turn to go, and suddenly he was there, blocking her way out of the trailer, way too close. "Y'know, I've been meaning to have a little chat with you, Maddi," he said.

She didn't know what to do, or say. She tried to back away, but the trailer was narrow and two steps had her cornered between a counter and a table. "Ross, I—"

He ran a finger along her bare arm, and she felt goose pimples rise. "Y'know, Maddi, you're the prettiest of the three. And the most talented."

She warmed despite her misgivings. "Really?"

Ross nodded, and pressed up against her. "Really. You were terrific in those scenes we shot this afternoon; Jayne Mansfield's got nothin' on you. Even though Deva had most of the dialogue, you stole the scene."

"I did?" Maddi asked, pleased. She wanted to hear more.

"You sure did. In fact, I'm already thinking I'd like you to star in my next movie. How'd you like to play a manipulative young nurse who schemes her way into a fortune?"

Ross' fingers were brushing her bare waist now, and the rising goose flesh was no longer the result of fear. "That sounds great, Ross."

"It's a feminist statement," he said, and then he crushed his lips to hers.

Maddi's own heat rose instantly, and she returned the kiss, but when Ross' hands moved beneath her blouse to her breasts, she remembered what Deva had said, and tried briefly to pull away. "Shouldn't we get back to the set...?"

"Shooting's wrapped for the day," Ross murmured, his lips moving down her neck.

His fingers found a nipple, and Maddi gasped. "Ross, I... don't..."

"Don't what?" he asked. "C'mon, don't tell me a girl with a body like yours doesn't like to make love."

"Well, of course I do," she answered, inhaling sharply as his lips found the other nipple. "It's just that..."

"What?" he asked.

And then he slid a hand over her leather-clad crotch, and Maddi moaned and answered, "Nothing."

Deva saw the trailer moving in rhythm again, and she felt her heart sink.

She was there when Ross came out, looking sleek and happy. He saw her and walked up, and Deva felt her gorge rise.

"What's the matter, doll," he taunted, "jealous?"

"No," Deva answered, calling on all of her acting skills to look nonchalant, "just waiting for you to finish with the hors d'oeuvres."

That got arched eyebrows and a smile from Ross. "And I suppose you're the main course?"

"I think I might be too spicy for you," she said, cocking a hip and head in his direction.

The ploy worked, as his jaw dropped and his tongue practically hit the ground. "Deva, I could eat you and still have room for dessert."

Deva nodded at the trailer. "Only if you finish the appetizer first." Then she walked off.

Three days later, Maddi fainted in the middle of a scene.

When she regained consciousness, she found that a fake bullet hole now adorned her costume, and discovered that while she'd been out Ross had actually shot her death scene. Now she was done filming.

That night, she packed her things, and caught a glimpse of herself in the greasy hotel mirror. She had to admit she didn't look great—her eyes were pouchy, she actually had a few gray hairs, and she was starting to look like her mother.

On her way out of the hotel, she stopped at Deva's room. It took a few moments, but then Deva was there, in a bathrobe.

"I just want to know one thing," Maddi asked, "can you stop him?"

Deva nodded. "I think so."

Maddi said. "Then do it."

Then Maddi was crying while Deva held her, patting her back in sympathy. "It's okay, I'll get him...he won't do this again...I'll get him, Maddi."

Maddi let herself be comforted in Deva's strong arms, let herself sob into Deva's sturdy shoulder, until she was cried out. Then she pulled away and smiled up gratefully at the other woman. "Thank you," she said.

And turned and left before she asked Deva if she could stay the night.

On Friday they shot the grand finale of *She-Devil A-Go-Go*: Now the only one of the female characters left, Wanda finally frightened the old man into keeling over dead from a coronary, and fled with his fortune, only to be pursued by the one surviving son. They finally met in hand-to-hand combat, and although she was badly injured, Wanda came out on top, staggering off into the desert sunset with cash in hand.

Ross called, "Cut—and that's a wrap!" and the last remaining members of the cast and crew burst into tired applause. Ross waited until the gate had been checked in the camera, then strode boldly up to Deva, who was still wiping dirt from her face.

"Now, I believe we have a final scene in private," he said.

Deva smiled at him, and tossed the towel to an assistant. "Think you're up to it?" she asked.

Ross just grinned and gestured to his trailer. As she led the way, she felt his eyes on her like snails on a salt-lick.

She walked into the trailer, and he entered behind her, closing the door. The interior was dark, the only sound the crew packing up outside and the small noise of whirring fans inside.

"So," Ross began, "is dinner served?"

"If you're hungry enough," Deva answered.

Ross approached her, licking his lips. "I've waited a long time for this meal. Better be worth it."

"Dig in while it's hot," Deva purred.

He put his hands on her hips and roughly pulled her to him. A long kiss was followed by a tongue circling her ear. "You're the sexiest goddamn woman I've ever met," he whispered.

Deva laughed, a low chuckle, and then ran a hand down to his crotch. His hips jerked away, but not before she realized he not only wasn't hard, he wasn't *anything*. She'd felt nothing but the stitching around his zipper. He pulled away from her, eyeing her strangely. "Funny," she said, "but the other girls always made it sound like you were so big."

He smiled and pulled her close again. "Oh, you'll find out soon enough just how big I am, sweetheart."

He started to reach for her black leather bra top, but she pushed him gently back. "Let's do this in style: Got anything to drink?"

He looked mildly irritated, but stepped back to a small refrigerator in the trailer's kitchenette. "I've got champagne."

"Perfect," she told him.

And while he struggled to open the bottle of champagne, she pretended to sit back on the bed. What he didn't see was the hand she dangled over the side until she found the drawer built into the underside of the bed, pulled it open and found—

—the huge, realistic dildo. It really was 12 inches long.

She returned it to the drawer before he whirled, holding the bubbling bottle up victoriously. "Champagne it is."

"What about glasses?" she asked as he approached.

"I've got something better in mind," he murmured as he poured the champagne between her breasts.

Deva squealed as the cold liquid hit her skin, then Ross was on top of her, pinning her down. She struggled briefly, but he held her firmly, stronger even than she was. "Uh-uh," he told her, "no more games."

He didn't even wait to get her top off, but dove for the black leather, hiding his face in the rolls of her breasts. Her heartbeat quickened, and his hand, creeping up her bare midriff, found it.

"You aren't scared, are you, Deva?"

She didn't answer. She thought it turned him on even more. So be it.

After a few seconds of nipping at her through the leather, he finally began to fumble at the top's fastener, behind her neck. She pulled her head up to let him reach it, not caring whether her cry sounded like one of pain or pleasure. He grunted in anger when it took him a few extra seconds to undo the hook-and-eye fasteners, and then it was free, and he was tearing the top away, freeing her breasts, his breath hot and quick on her newly-bare skin.

Without hesitating he lowered his lips to one of her nipples, and Deva froze. *This is it*, she thought.

And then he was shuddering all over, his entire body convulsing, spittle flying from his gaping mouth as he rolled away from her spasmodically. His fingers cramped into claws that tore at his throat as he struggled to get air in and out.

Deva rolled away from him and huddled against a far corner of the bed, watching as he shook.

"WHAT—?" was all he could get out.

And then Deva was on her knees, laughing at him, joyously. "How does *that* taste, Ross?" she shouted down at him. "Bet you didn't expect a nice jolt of *male* energy, did you?"

Ross was turning blue, but his eyes managed to lock on hers, and she went on: "That's right, little Myrna Horner was my sister, but I was her *brother*. And when I guessed what you were, I found out there was only one way to stop you: A thing that lives by sucking female energy wouldn't deal very well with a transsexual, would it, Ross? Two years of surgery, a few rounds of auditions, and then weeks working on you until you'd do anything to have me, and by the time you realized that I'd poisoned your food it was too late, wasn't it? Still feel like desert, Ross?"

As Ross' eyes rolled up in his head, he grabbed for her in vain. "You—bitch—" he coughed out.

"I take that as the ultimate compliment," Deva said, before settling back to watch him die.

When it was finished, Deva wiped the champagne from her surgically-enhanced breasts, put her top back on, straightened her hair, then strode out of the trailer to tell the nearest production assistant that Mr. Moore wasn't doing too well, and they might want to check on him.

As she strode off into the cool desert evening, she offered a silent thought up to Myrna and all the others: *Those haloes should sit just a little bit easier now.*

Then she wondered if *She-Devil A-Go-Go* would be finished by someone else and released, and was surprised to find that she hoped so.

After all, she really thought she was quite good in it.

Having grown up in the small town of Watertown, Wisconsin, Daniel P. Coughlin often dreamed of what the world looked like outside of his bubble. Joining the Marines in 1997 allowed him this opportunity and what he saw changed his perception of the world. After being honorably discharged in 2001 he attended film school at California State University Long Beach *where he was mentored by acclaimed television writer Brian Alan Lane and interned for his favorite director Wes Craven. Coughlin is the author of the novels* Ted's Score, The Last Customer, Craven's Red, *and* The Heartland. *He's also the screenwriter of horror films* Lake Dead, Farmhouse, *and* Ditch Day Massacre. *His short fiction has appeared in magazines and anthologies such as* Strange Tales of Horror, Macabre Cadaver Magazine *and* Sex and Murder Magazine. *Coughlin lives with his wife and demonic cat in Orange County, California.*

FROM SCRIPT TO SCREAM

Daniel P. Coughlin

THE 90 PAGE SCREENPLAY cupped in my hand is the best thing I've ever written. This bundle of pulp is blood splatter art. You've seen it on late night television a million times before: Three beautiful women are lured to a cabin in the woods. They bring their boyfriends. When they arrive at their destination, a couple of brutish redneck rapists are foaming at the mouth, hungry for blood. The beautiful people do drugs and have sex. The rednecks happily slaughter them. Somehow, the least likely to survive overcomes all odds and slays said redneck. *But is he really dead?*

You've seen it. I've just described about a hundred movies. My telling of this tale is completed, printed out and set neatly on the passenger seat of my crappy little car. And I'm driving to a meeting on Sunset Boulevard to discuss the terms of purchase.

The day is sunny. No clouds. The sky is powder blue. Palm trees sway gently in the summer breeze. I stop at Sunset and Cahuenga, look out the window to the big Cineplex where all the cool movies are premiered. I wonder if my movie is going to premiere there.

Stop getting ahead of yourself.

I park my car in the structure behind the fifteen story tall building with tinted windows. A major news network resides here. And it's kind of intimidating. I can barely breathe. I grab my copy of the screenplay and stroll my happy ass up the staircase and through the back entrance. My lungs feel like they've collapsed. The perspiration beading up on my forehead is about to run and I know I'm going to look like an ass in the meeting. They're going to know I'm inexperienced. They'll know I'm easily taken advantage of and they'll eat me alive. I want to run like hell. But I cup the screenplay neatly in the palm of my hand, close my eyes, and pray that God will let this go smoothly. I want my movie to be made. I also wonder if God is able to bless such a request. My friends and family are more than concerned about my mortal soul. They can't grasp why I've written this "piece of garbage". I don't think it's garbage. I put all of my energy, talent, hard work and soul into creating these characters and then strung them along a flawless—yet very overused—storyline. I gave birth to these characters and placed them in this story. Now, someone wants to pay me money to film it.

Growing up in a small town in Iowa I spent many agonizing nights wondering if this moment would ever happen. And here it is.

I'm suddenly distracted when I see a fairly recognizable actor walking down the back steps of the building I'm now walking into. *He's really short.* Seeing him makes me wonder who will star in my movie.

Back to what I was saying, growing up in rural Middle America, you were considered a martyr if you left town. I left six years ago. And I can't wait to call the few people I keep in touch with to let them know that I've sold a screenplay. That little Chucky Milburn from Watertown, Iowa has sold his movie script. See, up until now, when I go home and tell everyone that I'm attempting a career in screenwriting, they kind of smile half-heartedly, sometimes pat me on the back and say things like "I'm sure you'll be fine" or "you know you can always come home if things don't work out." There isn't a soul I've been in contact with that believes I can actually work as a writer in Hollywood. And now I've done it. It's happening. I'm about to sell a screenplay.

I sure hope it gets made.

Selling a screenplay doesn't guarantee that the movie will get made, but it's the only step in the right direction. Sometimes the project falls apart, even after the script is sold; not enough money to make the film. Something better comes along. Anything really. Making a movie has to be a perfect storm. But I also know that low budget B-horror is a booming business. It's cheap to make and it's the only genre where you can get away with mediocrity. Just make sure the story makes sense, the girls get naked, everyone gets killed—creatively—and you're good.

The security guard at the front desk looks me over, trying not to stare as he does so. I'm pretty sure he's wondering if I'm famous or not. Around here, whenever someone enters the room, you check them out in order to see if they're famous. When the security guard realizes that I'm not, he lets out a sigh and asks me where I need to go.

I tell him, "Borman Pictures."

He directs me to the fifteenth floor. *The top, baby!*

In the elevator, I find myself wishing that my wife had wanted to come. But she didn't. She's none too excited for me. I wish she were more enthused about my chosen career. But she's not. And this is a sad fact I've come to accept. I love my wife, but she won't support my work. She hates horror movies, says she's having a hard time separating me from my work. I suspect the truth is much different than *just that*. I think she might be jealous that I've made the sale. Resentful even. *Nah, she's just a scared-e-cat,* I tell myself.

My heart pounds in my chest. I enter the Borman Pictures lobby.

A beautiful, I mean knock-out-gorgeous-blonde-with-the-fittest-body-I've-ever-seen-and-a-gleaming-white-smile, makes her way over to me and addresses me by my name. "Hey, Mr. Milburn." She shakes my hand. "Mr. Borman will be right with you. Can I get you something to drink?"

I want water badly, but I'm incredibly nervous, so I lie. "No, I'm good, thanks."

"Okay, let me know if you need anything." She goes back to her desk and begins typing something on her computer.

The lobby sofa is soft, comfortable. It kind of sucks you in and snuggles you, which is good because it simmers my nerves. I'm positive that the couch was made to do exactly what it's doing. I'm quite certain this piece of furniture is very expensive too. The etched wood and deep stain of the wood trimmings looks hand crafted. No cheap build-it-yourself job. Feeling the comfort of this couch, my racing thoughts settle. Not incredibly. Some. Ten minutes ago, I was going to have a heart attack. Now, I've downgraded to a severe panic attack.

I set my screenplay neatly on the couch when I realize that the sweat from my palms is soaking into the pages. I try to wipe the dampness off the manuscript, but I end up smudging the title and my name. A sudden shutter seems to vibrate up from the page. Tickling my fingers, the sensation courses through my veins. When it swims into my chest I feel cold, but a good cold. My heart rate slows. Silent confidence finds me. The sweat I keep wiping from my forehead subsides and I almost feel comfortable. I recognize this feeling. It's familiar. And I remember the day I began writing my screenplay. I remember putting so much care into the monster. Sure, he's the antagonist—the psychopath—

but I didn't want him to be without feelings and emotions. I wanted him to be sympathized with. Understood. I want people to be appalled when he takes a human life, but I also wanted them to understand his motives. And so I created him with heightened emotions. I filled him with rage and hate and sadness and most of all loyalty to his family of misunderstood misfits. I love the monster I created. And in this silly little dime-a-dozen screenplay, I care about him. This movie is similar to all the other slasher flicks, in many respects, except that my monster has been created with love.

I'm *almost* confident now as the beautiful receptionist stands and smiles at me. This time her gleaming smile is comforting, as opposed to intimidating.

"Mr. Borman will see you now. Follow me."

We walk down a long hallway. The carpet is navy blue and the walls are crimson. There are posters of many horror films strung along each side of the hall. Some of them are of movies I grew up watching. I'm giddy now as I walk into the office. The door is abnormally large and I find myself wondering if hanging it had been a big ordeal. A carpenter probably had to come in and cut out the drywall. The weight of the door... I lose that thought when I see Mr. Borman sitting behind his gigantic oak desk, which looks expensive and well maintained.

He stands. "Charlie Milburn. How are you?" he says, waving me in.

"It's Chucky." I immediately regret correcting him even though it was probably the right thing to do.

He smiles and says, "Like the doll?"

I laugh.

He laughs.

We sit.

He pulls out a neatly bound copy of my screenplay.

"The best thing about this script isn't the story. I've seen this story a million times. Made this story into a movie about a thousand times. Liked it about a hundred times and this kind of movie has bought me about ten houses."

I'm pretty sure he's gloating. Securing that I know who he is and what exactly he's done in regard to the horror movie business.

He continues, "But I've never read a screenplay with so much love for the monster. Bram Stoker would be proud to read this."

Bullshit. Bram Stoker would probably burn this after reading three pages.

"I put a lot of love into my monster. I love him." I don't know why I've said this.

The overly white smile shimmering from his mouth suddenly curls into a grin. I can't read his expression. He leans forward in his chair like he's going to lunge at me. "I'm gonna give you ten thousand dollars for this. And I'm gonna shoot it three months from now and you're gonna see this monster on the silver screen in less than a year. You've seen my movies. You know I'm not full of it."

I suddenly realize what agents are for when the receptionist leans forward grazing her perfect breasts across my arm as she sets a two page contract in front of me. Then she leans forward and for a moment I swear she's going to kiss me but she only whispers in my ear, "Sign at the bottom." She smiles at me as she places a pen in my hands, then shifts her gaze to Mr. Borman as she backs away and sways out of the office. Mr. Borman and I both watch her magnificent butt as she strolls out of the office.

I sign the papers before ever having a chance to *really* read the contract. Mr. Borman hands me a check for ten thousand dollars. The check is printed on blue paper. Then he asks me a few questions. Where am I from? Where did I go to school? What does my wife think of my work?

I answer every question with a quick, crisp answer before I'm finally escorted out of the office. Mr. Borman's next appointment shows up, a tall woman with icy blue eyes, platinum blonde hair, wearing a tight skirt that accentuates her muscular, toned legs.

"Lock the door on your way out!" Mr. Borman calls out to his receptionist.

She does as she's told.

As I'm walking out the door, the receptionist stops me. When I turn to look at her I see something different than just a shiny piece of woman used to intimidate clients. There's something genuine about her. She bites her lip as though she's nervous.

"I really liked your script. I love the villain. I can't wait to watch your movie."

I'm truly flattered. My cheeks redden. For the briefest moment I fantasize that we're in love, married and living the dream together. But my wife whom I adore is at home. I'm a good man, so I drop this silly thought and smile and say, "Thank you so much. It really means a lot to me. I'm pretty sure you have to do a lot of reading around here."

She holds up a stack of printed papers, probably five movie scripts. "I have to read all of these and write coverage."

"That actually sounds like a fun job," I say.

"Most of these are awful," she returns.

I don't know what to say. It seems like she doesn't want me to go, but I nod and allow the door to close.

Exiting the building, I take in an enormous breath of smoggy L.A. air. I hold the check up above my head. I block the sun with it as if I'm making an offering to the gods. Walking toward my car, I think about where I'm going to celebrate. It feels like fireworks are exploding all around me. So much excitement disburses through my veins. I can't just stand around and do nothing so I go to the Cineplex across the street and look up to the board and see what's playing. A sequel to one of my favorite horror movies is showing in an hour and half. This is great because there's a bar just down the street that's a known watering hole for writers. I'll go there and enjoy a number of malt beverages before watching the movie. This might sound boring to most, but I can't think of a better way to celebrate.

I'm half-drunk now and slumped low in my seat, toward the back of the theater. On the screen, I watch a group of criminals redeem themselves by way of torture. I'm giddy. I get to join the ranks of these screenwriters. *Am I as creative as these writers?* I wonder if someday I'll be able to write the ninth installment of this particular franchise film. That'd be great!

After the movie, I drive home to tell my wife about the meeting. Entering the apartment I find that she's standing in the kitchen. A full-bodied aroma passes through the living room and pampers my sense of smell. There's basil and some kind of vegetable sauce being cooked.

"Well, how did your day go?" she asks. Now standing in the living room, crossing her arms.

I cannot contain my smile as it stretches across my face. "I sold it."

I almost sense a look of disappointment about her. This expression only lasts for a second or two before she smiles and begins clapping. She runs to me and latches on tight. I can't help but wonder if she's actually excited for me or if she's simply going through the motions.

"How much money did you get?" She separates from me.

I dig into my pocket, pull out the check and hold it in front of her face.

Now the look of disappointment on her face is clear. "You got ripped off," she barks.

"I got paid to do what I love doing. This is my first sale," I retort.

She swats a hand in the air. "Come on. I made you dinner."

We have a nice dinner. Go through three bottles of cheap chardonnay. After dinner, we watch our favorite shows and then she goes to bed. I stay up and read my script again. I'm still unable to believe that I sold my first script today. About halfway through reading it I hear what sounds like heavy breathing from behind the couch I'm sitting on. I take a quick look. There's nothing. I keep reading. Fall asleep on the couch.

I wake up the next morning to the sound of my wife telling me to "wake up. Get off the couch." She taps her index finger on my forehead.

When I finally wake up I see that she's none too happy. I remember why: I got hungry in the middle of the night and made a sandwich. Now looking to the coffee table in front of me I see the evidence of my guilt in the form of bacon and turkey club.

"It looks like a grizzly bear made a mural out of your sandwich."

I see her point. The bread has been devoured. There are crumbs everywhere. Mayonnaise, lettuce and bits of bacon have peppered the table and even the floor. Funny thing, I don't remember eating the damn sandwich.

"Clean this up before you do anything else," she says.

"Okay," I agree. I'm still at a loss. Maybe my monster jumped out of the screenplay to take a bite of my sandwich. And now I think I have my next story idea.

⁊

A few months go by. We've cast the leads for the movie. I'm happy. A few of the actors are very recognizable if you're into horror movies. One of them was an A-list child actor before drugs knocked him back a grade. The producers have brought a director on board. I like him, although I don't know that he actually likes the script. He keeps asking if he can rewrite it and be credited as the writer. This is really annoying. I'm learning fast that even after you write your script, polish it to the best of your abilities, that someone else can rework a few things and then stamp their name on it. I personally don't agree with this method. Luckily, neither does Mr. Borman. Although, I think his stance is more along the lines of not having the time or money to allow a rewrite. Time is money. And I'm okay with that.

I decided to come in to the production office today because they're casting for the monster. On my way into the office, I pass a line of at least a hundred bulking muscular meatheads who are auditioning for the role. One man stands in the corner reading scenes. He's kind of hidden, but he stands out to me. His eyes are shut tight. He looks pained. For a brief moment I imagine that my monster is in the process of possessing this man. It doesn't surprise me that his audition goes well. The actor scared the holy hell out of everyone in the room when he picked up the table and launched it. *Did I mention that the table weighs four hundred pounds?*

I meet this gentleman in the hallway, on his way out. He's at least six foot six inches tall and very muscular. Not movie star muscular, but raw primal muscle. I explain that I'm the writer.

He opens up and tells me, "I have a connection with this monster you created. He's the best thing about the script."

I'm flattered. In an attempt to connect with him I say, "Hey, looks like you'll get to see some pretty girls naked too."

He doesn't look amused at all. In fact, he looks disappointed as if I should be ashamed of myself. I am. He shakes my hand and assures me that he'll be studying for the role, like mad.

Just before he enters the elevator, I stop him. "Hey man, I didn't mean that back there. The truth is, I know this movie is a cheap slasher to most, but I really love this stuff and the character that you're going to play means a lot to me. The hardest part about writing this movie was that character." I lower my head. "I love that character."

The actor squints. His forehead scrunches. I don't know if he's going to cry or punch me. "I feel like the character chose me. Your monster possessed me while I was reading the script. I felt another presence with me in the audition."

"I knew you were going to get the part...when I saw you concentrating in the hallway," I say.

"I wasn't concentrating. I was channeling the character," he returns. "I appreciate what you said."

He turns and walks away from me. Gets in the elevator. And just before the doors close I swear that I see the monster, not the actor, standing in the elevator. His tough, almost reptilian skin strikes my sight. His scraggly hair, matted with blood, jolts me. The hair on my arms stands tall. I try to tell myself that nothing crazy is happening. And then he's gone.

♋

We're on set now. It's the first day of shooting. I showed up with the producer who I worked with in the development stage. As we walk over a small hill I see the set on the other side. I can't help it, my eyes dampen. Below the hill, at least fifty people run around decorating the ranch, setting up lights, putting cameras together. It's almost too much. Surreal. All of this came together because of a crazy idea that came out of my head.

I look to the barn. The doors open. They're about to start filming. I see the monster. He's no longer the actor in makeup. I swear it's the monster. He looks just as I imagined him. As if on cue, he turns to me. We stare at each other for a moment before he nods and grabs the prop axe next to him. He walks with the director toward a group of cameramen. A few minutes later the director yells "action" and I watch as my monster unloads his rage into an unsuspecting teen, which is of course a dummy.

I hang around set for the remainder of the shoot. As the sun goes down I enter one of the trailers where the actors are getting ready or relaxing. I'm startled to see my monster sitting on a cheap, ratty old couch.

He looks up at me and shakes his head before saying, "I barely remember filming. It was like *I* ended and the *monster* began."

I secretly smile as I say, "Thanks."

The actor only nods.

I return to set for many of the days. Watching my movie being filmed is an experience I don't want to miss. At the end of the shoot, Mr. Borman shows up with a gang of caterers in black polo shirts. They pour cheap champagne into even cheaper clear plastic cups. The cast gathers for a toast. As I'm walking toward the group, I hear a couple of the actors talk about how scared they were to film their scenes with the monster. This also makes me smile.

When I arrive home later that night I find my wife in the bedroom on her knees praying. She doesn't even acknowledge my presence and I can tell that she's sad. I go to her. She holds a hand up, halting me. She finishes praying and then turns to me with an exhausted expression and asks, "How was your day?"

I tell her, "Amazing."

She smiles and walks past me and into the kitchen where I can smell her delicious pork dish smothered in pineapple salsa. She knows this is my favorite. She makes me a plate and I grab a bottle of wine. We toast to my movie and then talk about her day. She had a rough one at the office. Her boss is a sexist asshole and gets away with harassing all of his employees. I want to go to her work and punch this man in his face, but she can't afford to lose her job, on my account. I tell her that after a few more screenplay sales she'll be able to quit her job.

She smiles and says, "That would be nice." She doesn't believe that I'm going to make it as a writer.

This makes me sad. Frustrated. Because I *am* making it.

After dinner we watch a few shows and then head upstairs and make love. We cuddle and then finally fall asleep.

෨

A few months pass and I'm sitting in a room full of nervous people at a marketing firm. I stand behind a two-way mirror and watch them watching my movie. Very few are scared except for the parts when my monster shows up. During one of the more intense scenes I look to the screen and I swear the monster is staring at me before slamming his axe into one of the characters. It almost seems as though he's looking for a sign of approval. I nod and he tosses the axe down. Blood sprays across the dirty ground.

Toward the end of the screening, I watch as members of the focus group turn to each other. There are microphones surrounding the room and I can hear them talking about how the movie was so-so but the monster was terrifying. To this I smile. I write down on the yellow notebook pad that I really need to work on original story material.

Over the next few weeks I sit with editors as they apply the director's and producer's notes. When I see the final cut of the movie I am very pleased. I know this will not be a hit, but I'm proud anyway. This is my dream. And I am living it.

As I'm leaving the production office I overhear the receptionist talking about how they are going to be bringing in a big named writer to scribe the sequel to my movie. My stomach churns and I make my way to Mr. Borman's office. He's placing something in his desk when I enter without knocking.

"Oh hey, Chucky. What did you think of the movie?" he asks.

I say, "I thought it was great. I know I need to up my game in terms of story, but I have some ideas for the sequel."

His smile drops. He tells me about the new writer. "I think this movie will go on to have three or even four sequels. You've created a wonderful platform for my franchise."

"What does that mean?" I ask.

"Please." He motions for me to sit down.

I do.

He takes his seat and leans forward across the desk. "I bought your script because I knew the character was compelling. And the monster you created will always be the success of this franchise. I can tell just by watching the reactions of everyone that's seen the film." He frowns. "But. I have a writer who can take it from here. He's a good writer. Well, I don't know if he's good, but every time I have him write a sequel I know that the movie will bring in X-amount of dollars. This is a business, Chucky."

My stomach twists into a knot. For some reason I can hear my monster groaning in my head like one of the monsters of old. I have to shake my head when I catch a vision of my monster standing behind him. I wish the vision were real and that the monster would crush him. But then I remember that Mr. Borman is right. This is a business and we must have thick skin. Still, I can't just let my creation go like this.

"Mr. Borman, can I just write a sequel and if you don't like it then don't use it. Mine will be better, I swear."

I wait for a reaction. I get nothing. Finally, after he thinks about it for a moment, he smiles menacingly and says, "Your work here is done. Look at your contract. If you're smart you'll use your success to sell other scripts."

Rage.

"This is my story! This is my monster and I deserve to continue his journey!" I shout, unaware that I'm doing so.

Mr. Borman has probably seen this kind of a reaction before because he simply sits back and smiles. "He's my monster and this is now my journey. Read your contract."

"But I'm the one that cares," I plead.

"My bank account cares more. And I say that *my* writer will bring in more money than you. He's got a name and more experience."

I know that there's no use fighting him. He's already won. So I stand and leave.

He halts me. "Chucky! If you're going to continue acting like this I can't invite you to the premiere."

A stake through my heart.

I turn. "I don't want that, Mr. Borman. I just got a little excited because I care."

"I know," he says. "We'll see you at the premiere. Shut the door on your way out."

I do as he asks.

I drive home. Rage boiling in my guts. *My monster cries for me. I can hear him.*

When I get home and tell my wife what happened all I see is a look of contentment disguised by an expression of worry. "Well, now you can work on something more serious," she says.

"More serious?" I ask. I'm unable to believe how little she cares. I love this stuff. My escape from real life has always been horror movies. I love them. Need them. They are my drug of choice. I see the love and care in all of this so-called garbage. When I was young, I didn't quite fit in. So I would dig through my stack of horror movies—that I'd bought with money I'd earned working for my grandfather and mowing lawns—and I would pop a VHS tape into the VCR, sit back with a bowl of strawberry ice cream and let my imagination go to work. When I was infuriated because my teachers thought I was an idiot, I would grab my notebooks and write about the horrors of life. When my classmates bullied me because I was weird I would write horror stories; the kind where bullies get smashed to pieces. Horror has always been my love, my rock and my destiny. "I don't want to write fluffy serious movies. I want to create monsters and make horror movies. I love it!"

She sighs and goes into the kitchen. She doesn't understand how important these things are to me. She only knows that horror is trash and that you'll go to hell if you watch it. She's probably pompous enough to believe that her prayers are saving my eternal soul. She believes that *I'm saved* because of her.

I go to the office and begin writing a new story—the story has my monster in it. It's a different story. One in which we're at the premiere of my movie and my monster extracts himself from the screen to exact his loyalty for me. I write for what seems like ten minutes, but when I look at the clock it informs me that I've been writing for well over four hours. I've written twenty good pages of nasty, blood soaked thrills with characters that matter.

And I feel better.

∾

It's the night of the premiere, my first premiere. I'm dressed in the nicest clothes that I own—slacks and a button down shirt. My wife and I drive to the theater. We park in the structure where I see Mr. Borman chatting up some of the pretty female cast members. I see one of the girls hand him a small piece of paper. Her cheeks turn red. He smiles at her and nods, then leans in close and whispers in her ear. I shake my head and wonder if he really loves the movies or just the money, women and power.

Arriving at the ropes leading into the theater, a large security guard wearing a cheap suit places his hand on my chest and asks what my name is. I tell him and he looks at a clipboard, lifts the ropes so my wife and I can enter. There are posters for the movie everywhere and photographers take pictures of the beautiful cast members posing on the red carpet. I walk past unnoticed. One of the photographers, a woman wearing jeans and a famous horror movie T-shirt, stops me and asks if I'm the writer. I say, "Yes" and she begins snapping photos of us. I'm not very used to this type of thing so I smile the best I can although I can feel my hands starting to shake and my forehead beading with sweat. The only calm I feel is when I see the actor who played my monster. A sullen expression tapered across his face. He nods in my direction before entering the theater. I can tell he doesn't want to pose for pictures and he doesn't want to talk with anyone. When I turn around, I see Mr. Borman talking to the gossip columnists about how he believes in the picture. Disgusted, I walk into the theater.

Once inside, I grab a box of popcorn and a soda before entering the dark screening room. An usher, who somehow knows my name, escorts us to the middle of the theater and sits us in the middle of the row. I'd rather sit on the end because of my puny bladder, but this will do.

A few minutes later the director is standing up front acknowledging the cast members, producer, crew and himself. But he never addresses me. I look toward the front row. My monster nods at me. I acknowledge that he has become the monster again.

The director finishes his speech and then has a seat next to Mr. Borman and the hack writer who is to write the sequel.

The lights go out.

Complete darkness.

The low rumble of the projector cranks into gear.

The screen illuminates.

Sound surrounds us.

Hands rummage through boxes of popcorn. Plastic bags rip. Snacks crunch.

The movie begins.

The crowd knows that they're in for a low budget massacre flick so it doesn't surprise me when I hear audible laughs during scenes of bad acting. Sporadic chuckles spread through the first fifteen minutes, until the action starts. And when my monster shows up, something happens. It's almost as if the entire film-going audience takes a deep breath—in unison—and holds it. A cloud has settled over the audience. Doom. My hands are sweating. It's hard to hold back a smile. And the moment I've been waiting my whole life for happens. Again—in unison—the crowd cringes and moans. They curl up in their seats. Girls grab the arms of their dates. I am happy. Until I look across the theater and see Mr. Borman. He's smiling, laughing, shaking hands and connecting with that hack writer that "brings in a guaranteed amount of money." I can't help it. I should be feeling enlightenment. My dream has come true and I'm watching it on the big screen. But I'm filled with rage. I don't know what to do. I look to my wife who couldn't be more disgusted with the movie.

She watches my dream with her arms crossed and a scowl on her face. She turns to me and says, "Don't worry, honey. It could be a lot worse."

I don't know why, but I suddenly wonder why I married this woman.

Huh.

Between my wife insulting my work and Mr. Borman divorcing me from my heart and soul, I'm about ready to snap. Literally. I seriously consider standing up and shouting at everyone in this theater that has taken advantage of me. But I clench my fists and clamp my jaw.

The air in the theater suddenly stops flowing.

The air is stale.

No noise. Silence.

I look to the screen. My monster stares down at me. He looks gigantic on the big screen. I can't lie. This is scary. His giant hand darts forward. The silver screen seems to push outward, creating a funnel around the center. I look around to see if anyone else is catching this.

I turn right. Borman is locked into a handshake with the hack writer. Their smug smiles aren't moving. It's as if everyone in the theater has been put on pause. There's no movement. Frightened, I swing my head around the room. Everyone is still. Locked into their seats. The lead actress sits in the front row. The ugliest smile I've ever seen on a beautiful woman hangs from her mouth. The actor sitting next to her is leaning forward, holding his large soda toward his face. His lips are puckered tight. His mouth looks like an anus and his eyes are bugged outward.

What the hell is happening?

I look back to the screen. In the center of the silver rectangle my monster shoves his hand forward. He's going to rip through. But then the screen compresses around his arm. It slides forward, shrinking as he glides into reality. *Is this reality?* Next, his leg pops through, followed by his other arm. I try to shrink back, but this *is* happening. *Well, I could just be losing my mind.* That thought is very much at the forefront of my mind.

I look to my wife. Her scowl has also taken on a ridiculous form. Her face is scrunched to one side and her right eye is fully open while her left eye is semi-shut. Like she's taking a dump.

I hear a roar. Actually, it sounds more like a groan.

He's escaped the screen and stands before his frozen audience. Looking to me, he nods, marches briskly toward Mr. Borman. I can't help but notice that he's carrying the large blood-drenched axe. And when he raises it above the hack writer's head, I try to close my eyes. *I can't.* I watch as the axe severs the hand that's shaking Mr. Borman's. The stump is red and looks like it wants to bleed, but it doesn't. And his hand simply falls to the maroon carpet. When the hack writer's hand detaches from Mr. Borman, something even more peculiar happens. Mr. Borman becomes aware. He's somehow been permitted to move again. Everyone else in the theater is still frozen. And now he looks upward, to my monster. His face turns pale. The monster raises the axe. Mr. Borman shields his face with his forearm. Before the flat end of the axe hits Mr. Borman's arm, another awkward moment ensues. He looks at me. In this moment I know that he's aware that we are both on another plane of existence. He's also aware that my monster is loyal and loves blood. Terror seizes his aging face. He looks green. My monster grabs the writer's stump. He squeezes. Borman screams. And when the monster grabs the hack writer and begins choking him I silently grin. The monster glances at me as if for approval. In the silence of the theater I can hear his neck snap. Slowly, he drifts into his seat and then onto the floor. Borman stands with wobbly legs and moves toward me. I can barely hear him, but know that he's begging. My monster slowly creeps behind him. The twelve or so people in my row don't even budge when Borman kicks through their legs on his way toward me.

"I'm sorry. You can write the sequel! I'll draw up the contract tomorrow..."

I shake my head, *no.*

"Tonight, at the party... I'll have my agent and lawyer draw them up. I swear... Please, call this Neanderthal off me!"

I'm suddenly shocked. Defensively, I sit forward in my seat. The monster swats at Borman's head and he falls into the lap of one of the minor characters from the movie. Soda spills all over the girls lap and when Borman's face pops up I see that he is sorry. But sorry isn't enough. For this last comment I allow my monster to perform the task he enjoys second to murder. All inbred redneck monsters like to do this in the movies. I can't watch. Thankfully, my monster finishes quickly.

As Borman pulls himself up from the chair he's been pummeled into I ask him, "All the sequels?"

"Yes, yes, please don't let him hurt me again."

I hear a slow rush of fluid running onto the cement floor. I think it's soda from the girl's cup, but then realize that Mr. Borman has wet his pants.

He stands. The wet spot isn't *too* distinct on his charcoal slacks.

I look to my monster as if to say, "Should we let him go?"

The monster shrugs, raising his axe high above Borman's sweaty head.

I need Borman in order for my monster to live. I need this man to find financing in order to keep my creation alive and well and hungry for the blood of perverted youth.

I nod.

It all happens so fast. My head starts to spin. My monster returns to the screen. He stops. A stirring noise emanates from the seat next to me. My monster shuffles back toward me, but his eyes are focused, somewhere other than me. I turn to my left.

My wife.

"What's going on?" She looks forward. "Why isn't anyone moving?" She looks to me, then to the monster. "What's happening? *Is this supposed to happen?* Is this part of the movie?"

My monster stands in front of her, snarling and groaning. Hands outstretched. He reaches for her neck. His slobber drips from his deformed lips and onto her skirt. My wife's eyes are wide with fear. I swear her hair is standing up from her scalp.

She stutters like a nut.

I'm just a little scared, but at the same time, I'm thrilled.

She turns to me. I think she's grasped what's happening. "This is great writing! The best I've ever seen!" she screams, curling into a ball and shielding her face with flayed hands.

I smile.

Within seconds everyone is moving again. The air circulates. People are stuffing their faces with popcorn again and "oohing" and "ahing". I look down my row toward Mr. Borman who is breathing heavily. He's looking straight at me. In the seat next to him, the hack writer is red-faced and choking. Popcorn falls from his mouth. He drifts into the cushions of his seat. A woman screams as she points to the hack.

"He's choking!"

A security guard rushes to his seat, but I already know what the outcome is going to be. I secretly smile as a wave of morbid contentment swallows me.

I sink into my seat and continue enjoying my movie.

A few hours later, as we're heading across the street to a popular restaurant on Hollywood Boulevard, Mr. Borman catches up to me. I'm walking with my wife. Her hand is clamped around mine so tight that it hurts. I swear that the sweat from her palm is dripping from between our hands.

"Chucky. Wait up." He hollers. His voice is shaky.

"Yes, Mr. Borman?" I ask, smug.

He lowers his head. "It looks like you'll be writing the sequel. When can you start?"

I turn and face him. I size him up. He's scared. Probably a bit shaken from having his manhood desecrated. Another man in a very expensive suit catches up to us. I recognize this man. It's Borman's lawyer. He faces us.

The suit asks, "Is this the writer?"

I look to both of them and say, "I've already begun."

My wife's hand cinches tighter.

The sound of expensive heels hammering the asphalt draws my attention. It's the beautiful receptionist. She grabs my shoulder and smiles at me. "I loved it, Chucky. This is going to be a big hit."

Her smile lingers long enough that my wife is now even more uncomfortable. I squeeze her hand back. "Thank you."

"Is this your wife?" the receptionist asks.

I smile and look at my wife. "Yes it is."

The receptionist leans in close to my ear and whispers, "Too bad." And as she walks away I watch her perfectly fit body swagger into the restaurant.

Mr. Borman walks away. I can hear him whispering to the lawyer, "That old hack dying in the theater could make for a great story to promote the movie."

The lawyer nods and I hear him say, "I think you have a hit. And old *what's-his-name* croaking is going to be wonderful for publicity."

I pull my wife toward the restaurant. She turns to me. She's never looked more beautiful in all my life.

"I'm the luckiest girl on the planet," she says.

I can't help it. I stop and yell, "I love horror!"

William Lebeda has spent the last 23 years, 5 months, and 17 days working in and around Hollywood, most of them at Picture Mill, *designing and directing title sequences for over 200 feature films. He takes particular joy in having designed the title sequence for David Fincher's* Panic Room *and for having his face featured in the stop-motion title sequence for* House on Haunted Hill. *A lifelong fan of comic books and monster movies, he lives in beautiful downtown Burbank with his wife and their two children, where he tends to write more than he draws. For better or worse.*

CHARLIE'S ANGEL

William Lebeda

CHARLIE NEUMEYER, president of Prime World Pictures, eased his $100,000 Tesla a few more feet down the congested freeway. Directly in front of him, the god of thunder sat in the driver's seat of a dirty green minivan. The redhead riding shotgun pointed at a map on her smartphone. Earth's mightiest heroes filled the rest of the seats. One lane over, a green-skinned woman in a purple and white swimming suit waved to him through a shoe-polished window that read 'San Diego or Bust.'

Damn kids and their comic books… They've ruined the movie business.

As the traffic crawled, Charlie was tempted to pick up the overnights Meredith had left on his passenger seat. Since the daily trades had become oversized weekly 'lifestyle' magazines, his assistant had taken to printing the breaking industry news from the internet. Though this morning's batch was nothing he wanted to read. He already knew the bad news, better than anyone. His $250 million 'reimagining' of King Arthur as a sci-fi epic was box-office poison and everyone in town was sharpening their knives. Meredith had suggested the trip as a way for Charlie to distract himself from the coming barrage of calls from friend and foe. And to maybe find a new project. Instead, it gave Charlie 150 miles to stew.

Now it's all about spandex and superpowers.

With the convention center finally in sight, Charlie fumed as the gang from Earth's mightiest minivan jaywalked in front of him. A suit of red and gold armor stumbled awkwardly, unable to see through his mask. He lurched into the god of thunder and made him drop his hammer on the asphalt. The redhead in the black catsuit walked three steps behind, trying to take a selfie in the middle of the street. Charlie pulled a U-turn around the wannabe heroes and parked in a blue handicapped spot. A rent-a-cop came toward him as he grabbed his deerskin briefcase from the trunk.

"I'm sorry, Sir. You can't park here without a tag."

"This tag, you mean?"

The security guy stared dumbfounded at the $100 bill in his hand as Charlie kept walking.

Charlie stepped onto the convention floor. It was like a cross between Disneyland, Tattooine, and every war movie ever made. Thousands of homemade costumes, overstuffed backpacks, and superhero T-shirts shuffled slowly, jammed like the freeway Charlie just left. The pop-culture tourists and ironic hipsters checked out Charlie with a sidelong glance, trying to not be obvious as they whispered and pointed to their friends. He didn't belong and it showed like ink on newsprint.

Damn you Meredith.

Charlie stood and watched while the undisputed 'King of Comics' waved to jovial strangers. Like the Mayor of Comicsville, he gladly stopped for photos and gave each fan a few moments of his time, appreciating their love for comics. It annoyed the shit out of Charlie.

"Tough break, Charlie. I liked the picture."

"Thanks Stan. That means a lot. Whaddayagonnado? Win some, lose some."

Stan shook hands with Charlie and leaned close. He smelled of aftershave and soft-boiled eggs.

"Well between you and me, Citizen, you'd better win some. And soon. People are starting to talk."

Charlie smiled and gripped the old man's hand a little tighter as a fan asked to snap their picture.

Charlie avoided eye contact as he walked down the aisle of independent creators. A lot of successful source material had come out of the self-publishing world, but it was always painful. Everyone had the next big thing. And it almost never was.

A black and silver cover caught Charlie's eye. A gangly goth kid sat drawing at the table, oblivious to the convention happening around him.

"One sentence. Go."

The gothy kid almost fell out of his folding chair at the sound of Charlie's command. Then his eyes bugged out as he recognized Charlie through his greasy black bangs.

"Um. Hey. Yeah, it's a modern fantasy about a boy who meets a girl, except she's a vampire. Except she doesn't know it. And it's really great and I've drawn it myself and my sister writes it and we'd love to…"

Charlie dropped the comic like it was plutonium. "That's three sentences. And it's derivative crap."

The last trace of color left the kid's face from the brutal and accurate assessment, as Charlie walked away.

A few tables down, Charlie recognized some work from a respected working artist. "Hey Mike. Charlie Neumeyer. What are you doing over here with the indies. I thought you were over at…?"

"Trying to get off the Big Two. Start my own thing. I've got some new work and—"

"How many copies are you moving a month?"

"Uh, well, it's not about print runs, it's about impressions. We're using the internet to build—"

"Yeah, sounds great Mike. Call my office and we'll catch lunch." Charlie oozed off before Mike could reply.

Amateurs.

"Meredith." Charlie paced in a staff-access hallway, shout-talking into his cellphone.

"How's it going down there, boss?"

"Peachy. What's the word on the street?"

"Not great. We're looking at the lowest July opening. Ever."

From behind him, a squealing voice cut through the din of the convention.

"Ohmygod. You're Charlie Neumeyer…"

Charlie flinched at the sound of his own name. "Meredith, I gotta go." He hung up and turned toward the squealing. "Can I help—"

Charlie was suddenly face-to-face with the loveliest breasts money could buy. Wrapped in neon pink latex. Like a present.

"Ohmygodyou'reCharlieNeumeyerIcan'tbelieveitsyouohmy godIloveyourmoviesIcameherebecauseIwanttobeanactressand beinyourmoveswiththerobotsandthepiratesandohmygodIcan't believeI'mtalkingtoyourighthereandyou'rerighthereandIsound likealunaticohmygodIwoulddoanythingtobeinyourmoviesthat's whyIcamehere toLAnottheconventionthat'sdifferentbut anythingMisterNeumeyeranythingcanIcallyouCharlieohmygod anythingI'ddoanythingohmygodIcan'tbelieveit. Ohmygod. CanIhugyou?"

The pink latex launched itself at him. The warm saline smooshed against the raw Japanese cotton of his shirt. She sighed cool and minty in his ear.

"I'm so glad to meet you Charlie. So glad."

Charlie stepped back to view the neon pink wonder. Her thigh-high black boots really set off the neon of the bustier.

Higher up, something about her smile was even more compelling than her obvious pink-wrapped charms. Her eyes sparkled with real joy, long gone from Charlie's own. And though Charlie wasn't typically a kinky kind of guy, the Robin mask and cat ears were a nice touch.

"Nice to meet you too. Miss...?"

"Ohright. Angel. I'm Angel."

Of course you are.

"Well, Angel. It's nice to meet you too."

"I really did come to L.A. to be in your movies I'm just hereasaboothbabebutreallyIliveinLAandohnoI'mdoingitagain CharlieI'msosorryIcan'thelpitandIhavetogobacktoworkor they'llfiremeandIhavetopayrentand..."

"Angel, it's ok. Relax. When you get back to LA, I want you to call this number. Tell Meredith that we met here, and she'll set up a meeting."

Angel stroked the number on the card like it was made of diamonds and baby kittens.

"Thankyouohmygodthankyou—"

Charlie struggled to breathe under Angel's gratitude. "Just call Meredith."

And bring the boots.

Charlie stood drinking his watery Diet Coke, and glanced at the watch that cost as much as his car. He had hoped for more. The entire convention had the stench of a 3-day old carcass, and he was the last vulture. Big Comics had already sold the major properties, and now there were barely scraps. He realized that he had spent too much time with space knights, ghost pirates, and giant robots. He was too late to the spandex party.

And everyone knows it.

Charlie wandered aimlessly through the aisles. His eyes drifted past hentai bootleggers and custom swordsmiths. A gleaming replica of a familiar sword caught his eye. As Charlie stepped closer, a voice rasped.

"Mr. Neumeyer."

A withered old man sat in an electric wheelchair. His legs were wrapped with a child's Spider-Man blanket. Yellowed boxes held together with duct tape and bumper stickers threatened to collapse the rickety card table that made up his booth. His ragged face matched the weathered banner proclaiming *Cecil Cacher Comics*.

His clear eyes locked on Charlie's face. "Mr. Neumeyer."

Charlie heard the old man like he was standing a foot away.

"I know what you are looking for."

Charlie tossed his soda cup as he crossed the aisle. "So everyone says. I've heard it a dozen times today."

"What I have is different. It's unique. One of a kind, literally. Something a man in your...situation...would appreciate."

The old man unlocked his battered tin cash box, and revealed a single comic, secured in a Mylar sleeve. He held the comic in front of Charlie. "Do you know what this is, Mr. Neumeyer?"

Charlie smiled as his eyes narrowed. "I regret comics have never been my forte."

"Well now, don't be so hard on yourself. It's a trick question. Because this isn't a comic. It's a legend."

Charlie was mesmerized. The cover was spectacular. Like a movie poster, but somehow better, more real, because it was a painting instead of the typical Photoshop crap that marketing vomits out and treats like the work of the Old Masters. But this. This was something special. Charlie was stunned.

The old dealer took Charlie's silence as his cue to start the pitch. "Back in the early 90's, a comic was going to be distributed by an independent publisher. It was destined for greatness. Written and drawn by two of the brightest stars in comics, before they both lost their minds and joined Snake cults and started directing crappy movies. Something you know a little about, Mr. Neumeyer? It would have been their swan song. The greatest superhero epic ever put to paper. But the company went bankrupt before the comics could be shipped from the printer. Rumor was that the printer burned them while the publisher watched. This is the one and only copy. It was the proof, approved before printing the entire run."

Charlie's eyes drifted away toward the horizon. "Tragic. Good luck with that."

"I assure you, this is what you are looking for. Big Hero stuff. The real deal. And no one else knows about it. No one."

"And you haven't sold it, why?"

"It was my company, Mr. Neumeyer. My name on the banner. It cost me everything to get it created. And when that wasn't enough, when they burned them, this was all I had left. These are the last 24 pages of my dream. I couldn't part with it before, but meeting you here, today—this is our lucky day. We both get another chance. A second take, as you movie people say."

"And what does this opportunity cost me, Mister...Cacher?"

The faded comic dealer chuckled to himself. "Only your soul. And call me Cecil."

Charlie smiled wanly. "And how would I give you that Cecil?"

"How about an autograph? Some proof that for a moment, I was partners with Charlie Neumeyer. Simple as that."

Charlie's mouth was still smiling, but his eyes were not. "Sure. Why not, Cecil? We can be partners."

Partners my ass.

Charlie imagined Meredith dialing the lawyers when Cecil reached out a smudged backing board and a greasy permanent marker. Cecil's palsied hands shook impatiently in the air as Charlie scrawled on the board.

"To...my...future...partner...Cecil. From...your...new...friend... Charlie Neumeyer. Okay Cecil—"

Cecil violently grabbed Charlie's signature, slashing the board across Charlie's index finger. A jewel of blood grew from the worst papercut ever.

"Damn!"

Cecil went slack-jawed with anticipation.

The blood fell and smacked wetly on the white board next to Charlie's signature. "Shit. Now I have to sign another one."

"No, this is fine. Charlie. All I need…" Wiping the saliva from his mouth, Cecil stared lustfully at the red stained cardboard. Then slowly raised his widening eyes to Charlie.

"Yes, Cecil?"

"Oh no. Your signature…you don't…" Cecil looked toward Charlie, his eyes unfocused and confused.

"Can I have my comic now, *partner*?"

"It can't be…"

Charlie blinked like a man with all the time in the world. "Cecil. The comic."

Cecil pressed Charlie's blood and signature to his nose, and inhaled deeply. "You don't…"

"Have a soul, Cecil? Is that what you thought we were trading? A comic? For my soul?"

Charlie just shook his head in mock disappointment as he slowly took the comic from Cecil and put it in his briefcase.

"But…"

"Cecil, Cecil, Cecil. It's been gone for decades. You should have met me back when I was in the mailroom, Cecil. Nice try though."

Cecil coughed and choked. His eyes began to burn with fury. Literally. Intense flames burned away the old dealer's eyeballs with the smell of burning hair and sulfur. His neck and shoulders bulged unnaturally as he stretched his mouth wide. His wheelchair rocked violently as his twisted hands cracked the plastic armrests. The creaking metal of the wheelchair was a sharp counterpoint to the dull crack of splintering bone, as Cecil's skull began to deform. The skin of his face split open and peeled back when the bridge of his nose flattened and stretched forward. His lower jaw lengthened. His eye sockets contorted to the sides of his head as the last of Cecil's skin sloughed off his bloody, now-equine skull.

Cecil roared as he lurched forward on massive goat legs, his split hooves crushing the remains of the wheelchair. Razor talons shredded the Spider-Man blanket. He stood tall, his horse-head skull a dozen feet in the air. Smoke curled from his skin, charred and black as night, covered with red-hot glyphs from a long dead language. Two wickedly curved horns grew as Cecil's volcanic eyes found Charlie.

Charlie's jaw worked silently, like a fish.

"Best costume of the con, bro!" shouted a Supergirl-esque passerby as she gave them a big thumbs-up.

DemonCecil and Charlie were suddenly surrounded by dozens of cellphones and digital cameras clicking and whirring, capturing DemonCecil's transformation.

"Dude...so sick."

Charlie pushed through the crowd, fully understanding what was about to happen.

DemonCecil's talons carved a path through the attendees, spraying gore across the crowd.

"Whoa! Check out the effects!"

"Did you see that? The wheelchair dude can walk!"

DemonCecil's blazing hooves cracked the concrete floor, as he stalked toward Charlie. Charlie stumbled back into the gathering crowd.

"Demon! By the power of Odin, I command thee, stop." The god of the dirty green minivan stood before DemonCecil. His homemade hammer whirled menacingly. His smart phone-wielding redhead companion posed with martial precision. Behind them, dozens of costumed heroes gathered in the moment they had spent their entire lives waiting for. A chance to fight Evil. To be true Heroes.

Assholes.

Charlie kept moving but stopped when the screaming started. He turned in time to see the pretty redhead flung into the air, followed by the rest of her body. Charlie ran toward daylight. He knew he was going to hell. He just didn't want it to be today.

"CharlieCharliewait!" Angel grabbed at Charlie's arm as he pushed his way forward.

"What'sgoingonCharliewhyiseveryonescreamingandwhat's thatsmellitsawfulandohmygodwhatisthatCharlieohmygod Charlie—"

"It's a demon. He's pissed because he traded a comic for my soul but I don't have one."

Angel looked at him with childlike wonder. "Really?"

"Not the time. Run."

Shreds of signs, comics and humans fluttered through the air as DemonCecil charged down the aisle toward Angel and Charlie. His glowing eyes and mouth would have been spectacular if they hadn't been so terrifying. His massive claws filleted a path through those unfortunate enough to try and capture the moment for Facebook. Rent-a-cops flooded through the exit into the convention floor, blocking Charlie and Angel's obvious escape. The $100 meter-maid ran past Charlie holding his Taser like it was a 9mm.

That ain't gonna cut it, Champ.

Charlie and Angel ran back toward the concessions, toward the emergency exits. Angel stopped at the remnants of Cecil's comic stand focusing on the aftermath of his transformation. She looked carefully at the smoking piles of import DVD's and mangled leather armor.

"CharlieIhaveanidea."

"Yeah, me too. Let's get the hell out of here."

"GetaswordCharlie."

"What?"

"GetaswordIsawthisinamovieoneofyourmoviesCharliethe onewiththeghostpiratesdon'tyourememberhowtheybeat theghostsCharlie?"

"Ghost pirates? Angel, I barely read the scripts."

"Get. A. Sword. Charlie. Hurry."

Charlie dug through the charred piles until he found his prize.

Whoso pulleth the Sword...

DemonCecil carved his way through the security guards. Dozens of Taser leads twisted around his torso like barbed wire. He was burning everything in a 15-foot radius, hunting for Charlie. He watched the bright pink woman leap over the concession counter. DemonCecil's flaming roar sounded vaguely like 'Charlie Neumeyer' played on belt sanders and dental drills.

The fire alarms only added to the experience.

Angel ran the hand-crafted replica of Excalibur under the soda fountain, wetting it with a kamikaze of flavors. While Charlie held the dripping sword, Angel poured a five pound box of pretzel salt over the blade.

"Demons hate salt, because it's pure and they are not. Like slugs from Hell. You really should read the scripts, Charlie."

Charlie and Angel climbed over the counter as DemonCecil stalked toward them. Singed comic pages clung to his charcoal skin, stuck in the drying blood of the slaughtered bystanders. The steady rain of the fire sprinklers sizzled against DemonCecil's skin.

"Angel. Time to go. Right now."

DemonCecil was only a few goat-steps away. Charlie could feel the radiating heat and backed toward the emergency exits.

Sword in hand, Angel took a step closer to the demon. "I said I'd do anything Charlie."

"I don't think this is what you meant, Angel. Let's go."

"Anything, Charlie. Anything." Like Toshiro Mifune, she held the sword low, protecting the salt from the indoor rain.

DemonCecil lunged for Angel. Charlie put his hand on the emergency exit and turned to look at Angel. In that moment, everything went into super-slow motion. Angel's teeth clenched. Water sheeted off her mask. The slurry of salt and soda dripped from the edge of the deadly blade. Flames roiled from DemonCecil's unhinged jaw. His talons unfurled toward Angel. His hooves sparked impossibly as they left the wet concrete. Thousands of attendees screamed and pushed for safety. Pages of scorched comic books gathered wetly at their feet. The rain fell.

Charlie blinked, and the world ramped back into real-time. Almost faster than he could follow, Angel knelt and turned like a professional ballerina. She twisted the blade into the air as DemonCecil leapt over her head. The blade bit deeply into the monster's side. DemonCecil roared in agony as the salt and soda sizzled deep in the gouge. Black blood poured thickly from the wound, mixing like India ink with the sprinkler water.

Angel ran at DemonCecil. Slowed by the burning wound, he started to turn toward her too late. Angel dodged his razor sharp claws and hop-stepped onto one of his goat legs and climbed up onto his back. With the speed and ferocity of an MMA grappler she locked her legs around his equine neck and with no hesitation drove the blade into the base of DemonCecil's skull.

The salt burned DemonCecil from the inside out, turning his glowing charcoal skin to ash. Angel rode the collapsing demon to the ground like a rodeo champion. The sprinklers mixed the demon's ashes and soggy comic pages into a bog of sludge. Angel calmly wiped the salt from her sword as she smiled at Charlie.

And Charlie saw his next movie.

A few minutes later, Charlie walked Angel to the illegally parked electric sedan, her sword resting carefully on her shoulder. Charlie littered the ground with Meredith's printouts as Angel wiped the ashes of DemonCecil from her pink latex. He activated the touchscreen nestled in the custom teak and titanium dashboard.

"Meredith, get me the guys that wrote the ghost pirate movie..."

Meredith's voice echoed through the 24 Dolby Surround-Sound speakers hidden in the car's interior. "Charlie? What in the hell's going on down there? Twitter says there was a wild animal from the zoo loose at the convention center. Or a terrorist attack."

"Meredith. For once just do what I say and get me the writers."

"It's going to cost you. They're still pissed about the giant robot fiasco."

"Fine, whatever. Oh, and get legal started on a new talent contract."

"Sure thing, boss."

Charlie could hear Meredith's eyes roll as Angel casually put her hand on his leg.

The sound of incoming fire engines blended perfectly with the electric purr of Charlie's sedan as it peeled away from the curb.

I fucking LOVE comic books.

Carla Robinson's first produced work was in college where she wrote experimental plays, until the experiment failed and the plays bombed. Shunned but determined, Carla fled to Los Angeles, worked in film production, and in the wee hours of the night, she wrote scripts. She was selected for programs at Warner Bros. *and the* American Film Institute, *and she sold work to* ABC *daytime and* CBS *primetime. Carla hit her stride, however, when she joined the writing staff of the newly imagined* Battlestar Galactica *series. There, she won a* Peabody Award *and was nominated for a* Nebula Award, *and she was cited in* TV Guide Magazine *for penning the creepiest episode of the season. Carla later had two feature screenplays reach the final round at the* Sundance Film Festival, *and she has held staged readings of her material at* Sundance *and in Los Angeles. Carla loves to create odd but intriguing characters, and she relishes the opportunity, if only for the moment, to live within their skin. She intends to continue this work. Until they catch her at it one day.*

THE VOICE COACH COMETH

Carla Robinson

DEIRDRE HAD TROUBLE WITH DIPHTHONGS. She always had. It was the way two vowels merged into a separate, unique sound. When she was a child, a speech therapist worked with her on verbal recitations, but Deirdre found the word play only made matters worse. The therapist had her parroting phrases such as *"When two vowels go walking, the first one does the talking."* Or the annoying *"How now brown cow."*

"No one talks this way!" Deirdre would protest. In time, she came to accept her speech impediment as a product of her nomadic youth. Deirdre's father served in the Army, and every few years, she and her mother and brother would relocate to a different region of the country where she had to adapt her speech to the local vernacular. In Alabama, Deirdre developed a drawl that made her brother's name "Dave" sound more like "*Day-eve*." And later in New Jersey, Deirdre spoke in a halting dialect, using vowels never found in the alphabet. The "dog" became the "*dawg*" and when she spoke to friends it was all, "*The beach. Catch ya there.*"

Perhaps it was her peripatetic lifestyle that gave Deirdre a sense of adventure as an adult. She never felt bound by the conventions of a traditional life. *A safe life.* Add to her wanderlust, Deirdre was attractive. She had deep brown eyes that simmered warmth and wavy auburn hair with a crooked part that made it appear unkempt. Bedroom hair, the magazines called it. But it was Deirdre's magnetic quality that people most noticed. It was not unusual on the Jersey Shore, for instance, for strange men to photograph Deirdre as she posed not provocatively, but demurely as the swift Atlantic waves swirled behind her.

"You're a natural," people would tell Deirdre.

Deirdre believed them and made a decision. She packed her belongings and drove for three days straight until she reached Los Angeles. She would put her natural assets to work and make her mark as an actor in film and television.

⁊

Deirdre found work almost immediately. She was a fresh face, after all, and there was always a bit part for a woman in jeopardy who could scream on cue, or a woman scorned who would pout when a man cheated on her, or bat her eyes when he cheated with her. And of course, there were the commercial spots for women with dry eyes, restless legs, or irritable bowel syndrome. It seemed everyone in America suffered from eating too much of the wrong thing, and since diet and exercise failed to benefit the pharmaceutical companies that perched upon the economy like salivating gargoyles, the popular option was simply to take a pill. Deirdre booked commercials that sold all sorts of pills. Her warm brown eyes promised viewers they would feel better after swallowing the little blue one or two of the white ones, or upon taking a hearty swig of the reliable pink stuff. One ad man even told Deirdre that when she smiled at the camera after eating a spoonful of a particular yogurt which the voiceover claimed "Made her regular," the sale of the product tripled. Deirdre's face became an iconic image for the yogurt in a national campaign. And her speech was never an issue, because she never spoke a word in the spots. She only had to smile. Deirdre herself was the magic pill, the ad man told her. And she hated it.

☙

There are many clichés in the acting world, and many are trite, even if valid. "There are no small roles, only small actors" was one Deirdre heard most often. She joined an actors' workshop and was determined to develop her craft, in part so she would never have to hear that cliché again.

Many actors in Deirdre's class envied her success. She was one who beat the odds and was making a living in front of the camera. But Deirdre felt empty inside, and it had nothing to do with the tubs of Cranberry-Cleanse the yogurt people kept sending her. It was a perk the company felt she earned, but to Deirdre it only reminded her that she was a cog in a grand ruse against the public. She knew damn well that a person would have to eat twenty cartons of the colon-clearing yogurt for any genuine effect to take place.

"Am I committing fraud?" Deirdre asked Tamara, a way-too-thin actor in her workshop as the group began to exit the auditorium where they held their rehearsal space.

"You're acting," Tamara scoffed. "It's what we do." Tamara unwrapped a cough drop, popped it into her mouth and sucked on it for a moment, then spat it back into the wrapper. She walked away, and Deirdre frowned at the gangly backside of her as she disappeared down the hall.

A bold voice called out to Deirdre. "You should try out for this."

Deirdre turned to see a buxom woman in the hall, her finger on the events bulletin board. She approached her.

"They're casting for Lady Macbeth," the woman said. "It's just a community playhouse, but it's a role actors die for."

"I've never done live theater," Deirdre said with a visible shiver. "I'd screw up the lines."

The woman put her hands on her hips. "You're an actor. You say the fucking lines!"

Deirdre flinched and the woman stepped back.

"Sorry," the woman mumbled. "I get carried away."

"But you're right," Deirdre nodded. "I'm an actor. All I have to do is say the fucking lines."

The woman smiled and reached a hand out to Deirdre. "I'm Lucy."

"Deirdre," she replied and shook Lucy's hand.

Lucy gave a card to Deirdre. "My apartment. Tomorrow night. We'll read lines. See where things stand."

⌘

It didn't take long to find out.

"You suck." Lucy slapped the pages on the floor. She frowned at Deirdre and threw up her hands. "I mean, you're really bad. What the hell kind of an accent is that?"

"Scottish," Deirdre argued.

"Not even close," Lucy said. "You sound more like a drag queen doing Benny Hill, only without the talent."

"Well, don't give it to me gently." Deirdre slumped on the sofa and clutched a decorative pillow to her chest.

"I won't. And neither will anyone else unless you're sleeping with them. And even then, I wouldn't expect—"

"I get it, okay!" Deirdre barked. She curled her legs beneath her. "Maybe a play's a bad idea." She peered over the pillow still clenched in her arms, and waited for Lucy to respond. A moment passed. She watched as Lucy's brow furrowed, deep in thought. "

What?" Deirdre demanded.

"There's this woman," Lucy offered. "Marjorie McCann. She's a voice coach. Kind of type-A terrifying, but she's worked with some of the biggest names in the business."

"How big?" asked Deirdre, her interest piqued.

"She's discreet. Never gives names. But I know people who swear by her, and I can tell you first hand that she's real selective about whom she'll even work with."

"You've met her." Deirdre waved a finger.

"I tried to hire her, but she turned me down." Lucy rolled her eyes. "Because of this."

Lucy opened her mouth, stuck out her tongue, and revealed a gold stud that pierced its fleshy center. "Marjorie does not care for body art," Lucy warned, "especially if it's on the face or mouth."

Deirdre shrugged. "I don't even have pierced ears."

Lucy cocked an eyebrow at Deirdre and rubbed her hands together. "You should make an appointment with Marjorie."

"You really think she can help me?" asked Deirdre.

"She may be the only one who can."

Deirdre unclenched the pillow and threw it at Lucy.

℘

The drive to Marjorie McCann's home took Deirdre up a tangle of narrow roads that stretched northward into the Hollywood Hills. As her 2006 Toyota Camry squealed with every hairpin turn, Deirdre thought about what her first words to Marjorie should be. She had spoken to an assistant on the phone, and the woman took three days to get back to her. When the call was returned, the assistant gave Deirdre directions to Marjorie's home and asked her to be on time. Deirdre requested an afternoon appointment, but the woman replied that Marjorie only had one opening available, and suggested that Deirdre take it. Deirdre didn't hesitate. She agreed to meet Marjorie first thing in the morning.

"I should be gracious," Deirdre said aloud, but scowled as she heard herself pronounce it *"gra-shus."* She gripped the wheel and kept saying, *"gra-shee-us"* but the more she repeated it, the worse it sounded. Those damn vowels.

A moving van took a wide turn around a corner and Deirdre slammed on the brakes and jolted forward. The van driver glanced down from his window at her.

What does he want me to do? Deirdre wondered. The driver gestured for her to back up. She glanced in her rear view and shifted into reverse and let the car roll back a few yards on the narrow road. The moving van straightened its wheels and continued down the road, so close to Deirdre that she could have touched its driver's side door. But once the van disappeared, Deirdre could see the street sign, nearly covered by the browning palms of an uprooted tree.

"Dolly Drive," Deirdre brightened. "That's it." She shifted into gear, skidded onto the street, and peered at each home for the address. Most of the numbers were hidden by lush green ivy and red and pink bougainvillea, so Deirdre crawled along slowly, until the street came to a dead end. And that's when she saw something she had never seen before. A wooden sign stood outside the corner home. On it a white card read, *Reserved for Deirdre*. She could not contain her smile. She spun her Camry into the parking space and made every effort to angle it perfectly.

The front door opened before Deirdre could reach it.

"Welcome, Deirdre," said the petite fiftyish woman in a dark blue, somewhat matronly dress, cinched up with an oval cameo pin at its collar. "I'm Marjorie McCann."

"I'm glad you could fit me in," Deirdre said humbly. "I have to tell you, I was a little afraid to come here."

As Deirdre grew near, Marjorie put a firm hand on her shoulder. *"Screw your courage to the sticking place."*

Deirdre froze. "How's that?"

Marjorie broke into laughter, but kept her lips closed. "It's from *Macbeth*. If you are to play the Lady, you will have to recite these lines as if you are a Scottish Queen." Marjorie touched the side of Deirdre's face. "And I can instruct you, Deirdre, but it's you who must do the work."

Deirdre nodded, and Marjorie led her inside her home.

The interior of Marjorie's home was larger than Deirdre expected. This was true of many homes in the Hills. The front door often sat mere feet from the road, and tiny yards served only as a spot to stake an armed security notice to ward off undesirable passersby on their quest to find the Hollywood Sign. Still, even with the security and the ubiquitous cameras that filmed every possible angle of entry, the homes seemed vulnerable from the outside. But once inside, the reveal was impressive. Decorative rooms and fine moldings gave each home a feel from an older era.

Marjorie moved slowly through a foyer, and made a point to glance at framed photographs on both walls. The photos were headshots of smiling women, and many of them familiar. Each photo bore an autographed scrawl with words such as *Thanks, Marjorie,* or *I'm here because of you.* Deirdre stepped lightly behind Marjorie, as she was quite certain the voice coach intended for her to view the wall of fame. And why not? It was a sales ploy that worked in any business. Put the success stories on display. And as Deirdre passed those photographs, and took in the smiles of women gleaming with the thrill of success, she hoped to one day be on that wall herself. Beaming with gratitude.

Deirdre sat on a cushioned chair in Marjorie's living room and looked around at the circular area. There was a winding staircase that led to the second floor. Deirdre heard footsteps and was surprised when two women walked out of an upstairs room and made their way down the steps together. She smiled at them and they nodded in return. Deirdre wondered if one of them was Marjorie's assistant. She wanted to thank the woman for setting up the meeting, but just as she began to speak, Marjorie entered with a tray holding a teapot and two cups, and placed two doilies on a glass coffee table that smelled of freshly applied Windex.

"Have a nice lunch, ladies," Marjorie told the two women as they looked her way. Upon their exit, Marjorie poured tea into Deirdre's cup and placed it on a doily.

"Do those women work for you?" asked Deirdre.

"They're works in progress," offered Marjorie. "They studied with me awhile, but as you will learn, Deirdre, not everyone is cut out for this life. But I like to help them where I can."

Marjorie sat down, poured herself some tea, and took a sip. "So I let them live here, and they do some light housekeeping and run the occasional errand."

Deirdre nodded as Marjorie put down her cup and continued. "They're quiet and considerate, and they know the rules of the house. And right now, Deirdre, those rules concern you and only you."

"What rules are we talking?" Deirdre asked.

"We're talking about *talking*." Marjorie eyed Deirdre. "Words are my art. And my job is to share that art with you. So for the time being, the only person I will allow to speak in this home, at least during our lessons, is you."

"And you, of course," Deirdre added.

"Of course," Marjorie emitted her weird tight-lipped cackle again, and Deirdre tried to remember what sort of caged zoo animal the voice coach sounded most like.

"So, you are taking me on as a student?" Deirdre asked.

"You don't catch on fast, Deirdre. But that's okay. You will by the time we're done." Marjorie crossed her legs and let the top one swing a bit as if *she* were nervous.

Deirdre knew she was being mocked. She spent years of her life in New Jersey and was familiar with the tone. She just wasn't sure why this uptight but maternal voice coach was giving her attitude when she was there to hire *her*.

"It's just that when I spoke to your assistant, she said you only had one opening, so I wasn't sure if there were other students you were gonna interview." Deirdre loved the way she said that sentence. She felt she got her point across well. But that's when Marjorie leaned in.

"Gonna? Did you say gonna? It's two words, Deirdre. It's *going to* and the first word has two syllables."

"Oh yeah," Deirdre said softly. "But you understand my question. Your assistant told me on the phone that—"

"You didn't speak with my assistant. You spoke with me." Marjorie pursed her lips.

"O—kay." Deirdre replied, not sure how to continue.

"And yes, I had to consider whether or not you were a worthy candidate for my training regimen, but when I felt certain I could help you, that's when I called you back. And that's why you're here now." Marjorie smiled. "You don't think I give just anyone her own parking space."

"I did kinda like that," Deirdre mumbled.

"*Kinda*?" repeated Marjorie, her eyebrow arched.

"I like the parking space," Deirdre said and tried not to let Marjorie see how her jaw was clenching up on her.

Marjorie stood and Deirdre stood in return. "What you must embrace, Deirdre, is that an actor's voice is by far her greatest instrument. A powerful voice can elevate the human spirit, and connect us to the essence of the soul."

Wow, thought Deirdre. Lucy had warned her that this woman was intense, but her dedication was undeniable. Deirdre felt that if she could only get past the tea and doilies, and maybe even the cameo, she may actually learn from this woman. For the first time in her life, Deirdre began to believe that her speech impediment could be a thing of the past, and that proper training with a professional coach may just help her to speak with confidence in any situation. Her spirit soared. Deirdre knew this training was what she needed to embark on a serious acting career.

"I can't wait until we get started," Deirdre said.

"We have already begun," Marjorie replied. "But it's obvious. We have much work to do."

❧

Deirdre lay in bed that night, and thumbed through a dog-eared copy of *Macbeth*. The phone rang and Deirdre was relieved to put the play on the night stand to answer it.

"Hello?" Deirdre said, groggily.

"How did it go with the Princess of Punctuation?" It was Lucy, checking in from her sofa, a beer in her hand.

"Marjorie is everything you said. And more," Deirdre smirked.

"I hope not too much more," grumbled Lucy.

"Nah, I think she likes me, but it's hard to tell. She sure is attentive, I've gotta give her that."

"*Gotta*?" Lucy shook her head as she said it.

"Don't you start with me," warned Deirdre. "It's one thing to speak on camera or stage, but I gotta—and yeah, I said gotta—be able to speak normally with a friend."

There was a long pause.

"Lucy?" Deirdre asked, and shifted her position.

"You will never get your face on Marjorie's wall if you follow that line of thinking." Lucy sounded somber now. "Remember, Deirdre. You're working in the big leagues now."

"No shit. I'm paying this woman two hundred bucks an hour—to help me speak a language I already speak."

There was another long pause.

"From what I hear, she's worth it," Lucy stated firmly. "But I've heard some other things, too."

"What sort of things?" Deirdre stared at the receiver.

"It's probably a good thing," Lucy's voice lifted. "But I hear Marjorie takes her students' defeats as personally as their successes. In other words, if you screw up, she feels that she screwed up. So don't screw up."

Deirdre took a moment to ingest this and mumbled, "She has two women living upstairs, did you know that?"

"No, but when I had my interview, a delivery man showed up with a futon. Marjorie said she got it for a student who needed a place to stay. I guess once she takes you under her wing, she likes to keep you there."

Deirdre flipped her bed pillow over. "Maybe that's why she keeps her client list so confidential. She doesn't want the blame if one of us stinks up the place."

Lucy curled her lip and whispered into the receiver. "Speaking of that, has she had you read lines yet?"

"Shut up." Deirdre said it with a smile. "I fucked up when she did a line from *Macbeth* and I didn't recognize it, but I get the sense we're gonna—I mean *going to*—start small and work our way up to the classics. I just hope it's not a repeat of doing a bunch of nonsense sounds like I did when I was a kid, because I really hated that."

Lucy downed the rest of her beer. "If she does, and you mess it up, tell her you're half-soused. You can say, *That which hath made them drunk hath made me bold.*"

"What's that from?" asked Deirdre, confused.

"*Macbeth*, you idiot! Have you even read the play?"

"I'm reading it now. So the loud click you're about to hear is me, hanging up." Deirdre slammed the phone down with a grunt. She picked up the play, and kept reading.

❧

The next day, Marjorie and Deirdre sat at the patio in the back yard of Marjorie's house, and Deirdre experienced her first flashback to her childhood speech lessons.

"Ga-Ga-Ga," Marjorie mouthed the syllables aloud.

"Ga-Ga-Ga," muttered Deirdre in return.

"Now, try a Hard C. Ca-Ca-Ca," Marjorie sang it.

"Ca-Ca..." but Deirdre stopped before the final "*Ca.*"

"What's the matter?" Marjorie leaned forward in her patio chair, unaware that both of her fists were clenched.

"Well, Marjorie, we've been at this for twenty minutes. Don't you think it's time we speak in actual sentences? Or at least some actual words? I mean, I don't think I'm going to have to "*Ga*" or "*Ca*" unless I'm trying out for the role of a chicken or a crow or fuck—someone having a stroke."

Marjorie sank. "My mother died of a stroke."

"Oh, God." Deirdre moved to Marjorie's side. "I'm so sorry, Marjorie," she said. "I never would have—"

"My mother is alive and well and playing golf in Palm Springs." Marjorie waved a finger in Deirdre's face. "But see how effective the use of words can be when one speaks them with a clear, but provocative intonation?"

Deirdre moved away. "Actually, I think it's shitty to tell someone your mom's dead when she's out playing golf."

"Well, her golf game is most decidedly dead." Marjorie quipped with a wink. "Then, it was never really alive."

Deirdre wanted to retort, but one of the women who lived in Marjorie's house opened the back screen door and made her way out to the patio with two glasses of lemonade. The woman carried two doilies and gingerly placed them and the glasses on the table. She barely glanced at Deirdre.

"Thank you," Deirdre said to the woman. The woman nodded and walked away from them. "I'm Deirdre," she called out. "What's your name?"

On that, the woman spun on her heel and looked straight at Marjorie instead of Deirdre.

"Her name is Lauren," Marjorie replied. "The lemonade was a lovely idea, Lauren. Thank you from the both of us."

Deirdre watched Lauren's chest fill with air, then slowly deflate as she lowered her eyes and walked to the home.

"She doesn't say much," Deirdre said dryly.

"She's not supposed to." Marjorie sipped her lemonade and dribbled a few drops down her chin. "House rules, Deirdre. I work with one student at a time, and this is your time. So the only voice I want to hear is yours." Marjorie used her doily to pat the spilt lemonade on her chin. "It's what you're paying me for, don't you agree?"

Deirdre wrinkled her nose. "Are you hinting? Because I have your check in my purse. I can give it to you now."

"I never hint," Marjorie said. "Because I don't have to. I say precisely what I mean, because I use my words. And that is the lesson I intend to impart to you, Deirdre. Nothing need be left to wonder or dubious interpretation, when the person who speaks learns to use her words."

Deirdre opened her car door to leave, when something caught her eye. In an upstairs window, she saw Lauren and the woman she had seen earlier, now standing side by side. Deirdre raised a hand to wave to them, but the women only stared at Deirdre, and neither returned her wave. Then, the curtain moved, the women turned away, and a third figure appeared in shadow at the window. It wasn't Marjorie, as this woman was quite tall. The woman pulled the sheer curtain and remained in the shadows as Deirdre slid into her car and started the engine. Deirdre rolled her car forward, aware of the woman watching her. Deirdre glanced back at the parking sign, still reserved in her name, and felt a chill as she pressed the gas pedal to drive away.

⌘

Lucy stared at Deirdre over a Reuben on Rye at Canter's Deli on Fairfax and Deirdre pecked at a Cobb salad. The restaurant was filled with people of all ages and pedigrees, and the sounds of silverware clinking against flatware in the busboys' kitchen bins made Deirdre push her plate away.

"How many auditions have you had since you started work with Marjorie?" asked Lucy, as she licked her fingers.

"Marjorie doesn't want me to audition for a while." Deirdre picked up a dill pickle and took one bite after the other until the pickle was gone. "She wants me to focus only on the vocal exercises. But she did offer to double our lessons to get me ready for the *Macbeth* audition."

"Well, there you go," Lucy clasped her hands. "She believes in you. So you have to believe in yourself."

Deirdre winced a bit. "Although, Marjorie insists I refer to *Macbeth* from now on as the Scottish Play. You know about the bad luck that surrounds that particular piece."

"They don't call it a tragedy for nothing," Lucy said. "But one thing's for certain—Marjorie would never double her lessons unless she expects big things from you."

Deirdre rested her chin in her hands and looked at Lucy. "I know you said she turned you down, but if you want, I can put in a word for you with Marjorie. If you're still interested in working with a voice coach. Of course, for her, you'd definitely have to lose your tongue stud."

Lucy shook her head. "Tongue stud," she cackled. "I never noticed before how odd that sounds. Say it fast three times: Tongue stud. Tongue stud. Tongue stud."

Deirdre cringed. "Aaa! You sound like Marjorie. Just watch. She'll spend my next lesson making me repeat 'tongue stud' twenty times straight as one of her verbal exercises."

"She may indeed," Lucy waved a warning finger to Deirdre. "So watch your tongue, Stud."

❧

The lesson proved even more challenging. Verbal exercises became verbal aerobics, as Marjorie ordered Deirdre to articulate tongue twisters and alliterative phrases first while standing on her head, then while jumping rope, and finally, while peddling in circles on a unicycle. Somewhere during her fifth attempt to recite the phrase *"Fred fried fish from Fresno,"* Deirdre lost her balance and tumbled off the unicycle and fell to the ground. Marjorie shook her head, and signaled to one of the stoic women who were now so ever-present in the windows of her home.

"I hurt my knee," blurted Deirdre, holding her leg, and bending it to make sure nothing was seriously injured.

"Rebecca is on her way out," sighed Marjorie.

Deirdre perked up. She had only officially met Lauren, and she was eager to meet the other women who lived in the home and seemed so content to follow Marjorie's "rules."

"Is that her?" Deirdre asked as the tall woman whom she spotted that day behind the curtains in the upstairs window hurried outside. The tall woman carried a cloth, a bottle of rubbing alcohol, and a box of bandages.

Marjorie moved quickly to block the path of the tall woman, and took the items from her. "I'll handle it," she said.

The woman opened her mouth to speak, and Marjorie stomped her foot. "I said I'll handle it." The tall woman closed her mouth, and returned to the home.

Deirdre rolled her eyes. "So that was Rebecca," and she grimaced, as it came out *"Ru-beccah"* and carried a tone that put her right back in southern New Jersey.

"Yes," smiled Marjorie. "One of my students."

"One of your failed students?" Deirdre asked, and she gritted her teeth so much that her lips wrinkled.

"Stop that," Marjorie said, as she poured alcohol on the cloth and began to clean the scrape on Deirdre's knee.

She wiped the area and applied a bandage to it. "I said stop that!" This time Marjorie yelled.

"I shouldn't have said that about Rebecca. I don't even know her. I just wanted to make conversation. Isn't that something you want me to do for a living?"

"I'm not talking about Rebecca," Marjorie pointed at Deirdre's chin. "I'm talking about you. You're biting your lower lip," Marjorie berated her. "Your lips are the aperture to your tongue. Even a slight sore on either side of its tender lining can disrupt the manner in which the tongue vibrates to the floor and ceiling of your mouth."

Deirdre suddenly grew so aware of the position of her tongue that when she ceased the aberrant chewing and let it lie flat, she could feel her entire face relax.

"My tongue vibrates?" she asked.

"It does," Marjorie relaxed in response. "As does the full elastic musculature of your mouth's interior, from your front teeth to the back recesses of your uvula."

Deirdre swallowed hard. "I didn't mean to get angry."

"What matters is, you used your words." Marjorie patted Deirdre's knee. "Your pronunciation was lacking in tempo, pitch, and inflection, but we can work on that."

Marjorie gathered the alcohol and bandages, and in silence, she placed the items on the patio table.

Deirdre flexed her leg and stood up. She brushed off some gravel that clung to her backside and glanced at the home. The tall woman, whom she now knew as Rebecca, stood at the kitchen window and watched her. Deirdre half-smiled at her, but in return, the woman bore such a flat expression, that her mouth formed almost a straight line across her face. Deirdre examined her bandaged knee, and when she looked back up at the window, the woman had disappeared.

❧

Deirdre and Lucy sat on the floor in the rehearsal space and did a series of stretches. A few actors gathered rolled-up script pages and moved to separate corners, when Deirdre spotted the svelte Tamara and waved her over.

"I hear you got a Lifetime movie," Deirdre grinned at her. "That's fantastic, Tamara."

"Yeah," nodded the thin woman. "But I'm playing an anorectic pregnant woman, and I don't know whether I should lose weight or gain it."

Deirdre and Lucy exchanged a glance.

"Either way, you will nail it," encouraged Deirdre.

Tamara put her coat over her shoulders, and exited the rehearsal space. Deirdre leaned toward Lucy and whispered.

"I would have told her to break a leg, but I fear she may just go out and do that very thing."

"Listen to you." Lucy held out both of her palms. "If it isn't Dame Judi Dench." Lucy waved a finger. "Whatever crap that Marjorie is putting you through, I can tell you right now that it is paying off."

"I know." Deirdre's eyes dropped and she snickered. "It's in little ways that I've begun to notice it myself. Such as this morning, I spoke to my cable company and—like that—I got a late fee removed. And even better, I called Mastercard and requested a credit line increase, and I got it within a minute. That is absolutely a first for me."

"You sold them. With a shot of confidence. Could be Marjorie knows what she's doing after all." Lucy rubbed her back and stood. She offered a hand and pulled Deirdre up.

"I should tell her that," Deirdre said with her warm eyes. "Surprise her with a bottle of wine or something."

"They have that sale at the BevMo next door," Lucy said. "Buy one bottle, get one for a nickel." She reached into her pocket and pulled out a nickel. "I've got a nickel just burning a hole in my pocket, so let's do it."

Deirdre and Lucy browsed the shelves of the crowded BevMo. Lucy grabbed a Cabernet, but Deirdre kept looking.

"I have no idea what she drinks or if she drinks," Deirdre mused. "But I do know she can use a drink."

"Go with a Chardonnay," Lucy said. "She's a very white woman. Probably drinks a white wine. But make sure it's dry. I don't picture Marjorie sipping anything fruity."

Deirdre put two bottles of wine on the counter, took out her wallet, and gave her credit card to the cashier. Lucy playfully offered a nickel to Deirdre, and Deirdre playfully grabbed it out of her hand.

"How many bags would you like to purchase?" asked the cashier, as if she had been asking it her entire life.

"Oh, I forgot about the bag-thing," Deirdre muttered. "It's okay. We can carry them as is."

"You can't leave the store with alcohol unless it's in a bag." The cashier placed her palm atop both bottles, in the event the women got tempted to race out with them.

"Two bags," Deirdre said and elbowed Lucy. "But here. I have change." Deirdre searched her purse and found a couple of quarters and gave them to the cashier. She and Lucy waited as the cashier put the wine into separate bags.

Deirdre grabbed her bottle in its slim paper bag and moved to the door. She glanced back at Lucy, who had found a rack of fashion magazines and was sorting through them.

"I want to get to Marjorie's before it gets late, so I'll see you tomorrow." Deirdre waited for Lucy to respond.

"Okay," Lucy said, as she stripped a magazine of its free perfume sample and slipped it into her pocket.

Deirdre left the store, and Lucy continued to play a game of scratch and sniff with various magazines.

"Excuse me," called the cashier.

Lucy held a magazine to her nose and faced the cashier. The woman waved a wallet at her. Deirdre's wallet.

"Is this your friend's?" the woman asked with concern.

"Shit. I mean—shit." Lucy raced to the cashier and grabbed the wallet from her hand. "I'll make sure she gets it, okay? I know exactly where she's going."

Deirdre was making good time on her way to Marjorie's home. She had made the drive so many times by now that she knew all the shortcuts. Soon enough, she reached the final hairpin turn and pulled into the parking space that she was pleased to see bore her name even at night. She made an effort to close her car door quietly, so as not to disturb any neighbors who lived close to Marjorie's home.

Deirdre walked to the front door, but stopped when she heard a strange noise coming from the back yard. There were wild animals in these hills, and Deirdre even heard about a home owner who kept a flock of peacocks and emus that cawed until dawn and brought this oh-so-civilized community to petition formal bans on ever owning these cacophonous birds.

Deirdre moved around the house. Slowly. A light was on in the kitchen and its glow brightened the back patio. And it was here that Deirdre heard the horrifying gasp. She hurried to find a woman strapped down upon the patio table, her legs bound and dangling on one end. The woman's head was draped over the opposite edge of the table, out of Deirdre's view. But not for long. Deirdre moved in.

"What the hell is going on?" Deirdre could only whimper because what she saw next turned her stomach.

The woman strapped down was the tall, silent, Rebecca. The bound woman lifted her chin to see Deirdre and shook her head wildly. Blood poured from her mouth and splattered into a puddle on the patio below.

And there, kneeling beside Rebecca, was Marjorie, a serrated butcher knife grasped tightly in one of her prim hands. In the other hand, Marjorie held something long and meaty and engorged with blood.

Rebecca shook her head again and more blood spilled onto the ground. Rebecca opened her mouth as wide as she could to show Deirdre. Her mouth was empty. Because the striated piece of muscled meat that Marjorie gripped in her hand was Rebecca's own tongue.

Marjorie wiped her brow and stared at Deirdre with cold eyes. "Your appointment isn't until tomorrow, Deirdre."

Deirdre found her own mouth open now, as she panted in fear. She backed into the yard, away from the table.

"Ladies!" called Marjorie, in a mellifluous tone.

On that, Lauren and the other woman whose name Deirdre never got, bolted out of the kitchen door and stopped short when they saw Deirdre standing there.

"Deirdre forgot the house rules," Marjorie stated in a calm tone. "I need you two to help me with her."

The two women advanced into the yard, and Deirdre stared at them. She looked at Rebecca on the table, her head turned to the side now, as blood poured from her mouth. Marjorie patted Rebecca on the face and let the blood and clumps of flesh empty into a red mess of steaming ooze.

"Almost done, dear." Marjorie said softly. "Almost."

Deirdre held a fist to her mouth, and set her eyes on the two women who approached her in the yard.

"No," Deirdre pleaded. Marjorie heard her soft plea and frowned as she watched Rebecca continue to bleed.

The two women moved closer, and together, each of them grabbed Deirdre by a wrist. Deirdre's knees buckled beneath her. Marjorie glanced over at her new captive and nodded.

"I'll need another moment with Rebecca, then we can begin with Deirdre," Marjorie said as she used her hand to comb the poor woman's hair away from her bloody face.

The two women in the yard held Deirdre by her wrists, as Deirdre let her head hang downward. In the distance, one of the local wild birds cried out, and its cry echoed in the canyon. Deirdre lifted her head in response. She took a deep breath, opened her mouth, and cried out in return.

"Nooo!!!" Deirdre screamed loudly.

"Shut her up!" Marjorie scrambled across the yard, the butcher knife in her hand. She put it under Deirdre's chin.

"Bring her over. We'll dispense with this one right now."

Marjorie marched to the table. She cut the ties that bound Rebecca and rolled her onto the ground. The tall woman lay crumpled, her eyes mere inches from her severed tongue.

The sight of Rebecca lying in such obscenity awakened Deirdre. She flung both arms so strongly, the women holding her lost their grip on her. Deirdre looked at each woman, her warm brown eyes seeking humanity in their eyes.

"You're not like her," Deirdre pointed at Marjorie. "And you don't have to do what she says. Not anymore."

The two women looked at one another, and Deirdre moved to face the one she knew as Lauren. "Listen to me, Lauren. You know I'm right." Lauren pursed her lips and trembled.

Marjorie rolled her eyes, and checked her watch. She was confident the women would obey her as they always did.

"Look how she hurt Rebecca," Deirdre implored them to face the butchered woman whose raspy breath they could all hear. "We need to help Rebecca. All of us. Together."

The two women shifted their heels and exchanged a glance.

Marjorie grew anxious. She didn't like delays. She didn't like a lot of things. She wiped Rebecca's blood off the butcher knife and moved toward Deirdre and the women.

"I told you to bring her to me," Marjorie demanded and reached for Deirdre.

But the two women stepped in, and put themselves in between Marjorie and Deirdre.

"What do you think you're doing?" Marjorie snarled at them. "Who the hell else will take in a couple of dumb mutes like you?"

The woman Deirdre couldn't name punched Marjorie in the gut and made her double over. The woman she knew as Lauren struck Marjorie in the chin and let her fall on her side. She stepped on Marjorie's hand and kicked the knife away.

The guttural sound that came next made Deirdre shiver. Both women gaped open their mouths in an attempt to yell, but neither woman had a tongue anymore, and all the empty caverns of their mouths could produce was an awful, hollow groan. But they were acting in concert now, and with purpose. The women dragged Marjorie to the patio. The voice coach kicked at them, but the women subdued her and laid her across the table. They used the same bloody ties that had bound Rebecca to strap Marjorie into position.

Deirdre raced in, not sure what to do. She knelt beside Rebecca and held her head in her lap. She watched the two women arch Marjorie's head over the table to expose her throat, and gain access to her mouth. The two women gasped and grunted and seemed to understand each other. They had shared the same evil fate, and they had developed a language that allowed them to converse with one another.

"I took your tongues for a reason," Marjorie crackled in short, uneven breaths. Clearly, Marjorie never knew when to shut up.

Deirdre gently laid Rebecca's head down and moved beside the soon-to-be-silent-forever Marjorie. "What reason?" Deirdre asked. "What reason could you possibly have to butcher these women this way?"

Marjorie shook her head, and Deirdre grabbed the voice coach by the hair and forced her to look her in the eye. "Tell us," Deirdre demanded. "Use your words, Marjorie!"

Marjorie gave a smug smile to Deirdre. "I invested in them," Marjorie boasted. "My time, my energy, and my talent."

Marjorie huffed as Lauren tightened the binds around the voice coach's waist.

"And they never learned to speak as an actor speaks. With conviction!" Marjorie eyed each woman. "You lost your tongues because you failed to use them as I taught you to use them."

A bloody hand grasped the side of the table. It was Rebecca, as she struggled to stand. She was choking on her own blood and pieces of meat as she looked at Deirdre, then faced the women who hovered over Marjorie. And with a howl and an empty gasp that these women well understood, Rebecca picked up the butcher knife.

"Wait." Deirdre heard herself say the word. It lacked conviction and she knew it. She tried again. "Wait."

The three women, with eyes seething and adrenaline pumping, held still a moment.

"You're not like her," she reminded them. "Don't follow her lead. It goes nowhere but here." Deirdre indicated the hateful woman strapped to a bloody patio table. "You want to take her voice? By surviving her grotesque crimes against you, you have already done that. Your very presence will speak for you, and we will put this woman in a place where she can never hurt anyone again."

Marjorie's eyes darted back and forth as Rebecca lorded over her. Rebecca let the tip of the knife blade slip between Marjorie's lips to force her mouth open.

Deirdre held out a hand. "Rebecca. You're not her."

The terrified woman met Deirdre's eyes, stared at the butcher knife in her hand, and gently gave it to Deirdre.

"It doesn't seem like enough," said a different voice.

Deirdre spun around to see Lucy standing there.

Lucy saw the butcher knife in Deirdre's hand, and recoiled as drops of blood dribbled from it and splattered onto the ground. Lucy swallowed hard and held up Deirdre's wallet. "You forgot this."

Deirdre felt her entire body shake as she registered this rare moment of normalcy. She nodded to Lucy, as tears welled up in her eyes and watched as Lucy made her way to the bound Marjorie McCann.

"Hi, Marjorie." Lucy kneeled at Marjorie's face and stuck her tongue out to reveal her stud. "Remember me?"

In short time, police sirens neared, their red and blue lights bouncing off the hills in pursuit of their target.

Deirdre squatted to face Marjorie, sitting up now, but tied firmly to her patio chair. She held Marjorie's swollen face with one hand, and with a damp cloth wiped a few drops of blood from around the woman's mouth.

"Almost done, dear," Deirdre mocked the voice coach with her own words.

A drop of blood fell from Marjorie's lip and landed on her collar.

Deirdre used the cloth in an attempt to rub it away. "*Out, damned spot*," said Deirdre with dramatic flair, and she winked at Marjorie. "I finally read the Scottish Play," she admitted. "I know it by heart, and I realize the depth of tragedy in its every spoken line."

"You had a good teacher," Marjorie croaked.

Deirdre wanted to refute that claim, but she could not. She knew it was Marjorie's training that enabled her to master her diction. Marjorie's lessons gave Deirdre the skill to at long last find her voice, and it was with this voice that Deirdre would continue her career in acting.

Lucy moved to Deirdre. She flicked on a flashlight and aimed it at Marjorie's face. The prim woman squinted.

"Let's see it again," Lucy taunted, but Marjorie only glared at her, her nostrils beginning to flare in and out.

Deirdre hovered. "Don't make her ask twice, Marjorie. Or she'll use more than her words." She indicated the women gathered behind her. "We all will."

Marjorie glanced at the faces of Lauren, Rebecca, and the woman with no name, and she opened her mouth. And there glistened a large silver bolt pierced through her precious tongue.

"I like it," Lucy cackled.

The police sirens reached the dead end where Marjorie held her speech lessons, and two dozen police officers swarmed into the back yard with their guns drawn.

"That's her," Deirdre told the officers and pointed a finger at Marjorie. The officers looked about the ghastly scene and scattered as they retrieved the bloody knife and performed immediate aid on the badly injured Rebecca.

One officer untied Marjorie and stood her up.

"You have the right to remain silent," he said, as he grabbed her by the arm and marched her out of the yard.

Deirdre, Lucy, and the three women gathered together, and watched Marjorie McCann disappear from their lives.

"She has the right to remain silent," Lucy quipped, "but not the ability."

"It doesn't matter," replied Deirdre with confidence. "Because no one will ever listen to her again."

Kelly Kurtzhals is known in Hollywood as the comedian-turned-producer Kelly Kursten, but has finally decided to reveal her true identity. Her name (her fake name) is permanently etched on the wall of The World Famous Comedy Store, *and her comedy credits include* NBC's Later, PAX TV's Destination Stardom, *and a minor but poignant role in the film* Pauly Shore Is Dead. *She went on to write witty content for* Hollywood Squares, *witty banter for* Style's Clean House Comes Clean, *moderately droll material for* HGTV's What's With That House? *and some mostly rewritten copy for* ABC's Wipeout. *Then in 2007, she became immersed in the world of pop culture as a show producer on* E! Network's The Daily 10, *which evolved into her current role as a producer for* E! News.

BURIED!

Kelly Kurtzhals

"THE DOUCHEBAG won't even take my calls anymore," I huff into my half empty warm beer. I'm overdue on rent, now the stupid fridge is on the blink, and my agent hasn't sent me out in over two months. Not that I've booked in over twice that. Even then it was just a two-line part in a play in one of those dump theaters off Cahuenga, put on by skinny trust fund kids wearing thick horn-rimmed glasses which cost about three times my car. I'm a 37-year-old man living a 23-year-old's lifestyle and I'll tell you what, it's getting older than I am. Oh, and I haven't been laid since that play either, if I'm being honest.

"Go pay him a visit," says Chad. "My agent says the casting directors always tell you not to just show up. Don't bug 'em, they say. But you know what? The people who book, are the people who are always in their face. It's a fact."

My roommate, though it's kind of embarrassing to call him that at our age, still has that Hollywood hope. He's only 32, though he somehow managed to get IMDB to list him as 27. Moved out here five years ago into my little hovel, in the area he's since dubbed "Shitsville"—not quite Los Feliz, in the shadow of the big blue Scientology building. Not the fancy celebrity one, the one that from the back looks like a prison without bars where all those zombie robot followers walk around, right into traffic like they think they're invisible.

Oh and then there's my back, which really kills me all the time now. For a minute, I had considered asking Chad if he'd claim me as his domestic partner so I could tag onto his health insurance. We're not gay, but it would probably be way less painful. But Chad's already covered for me too much. When he first came out here from Indiana, I was living in the bedroom and he took the couch. Lately, it's become mostly the opposite. Which makes getting laid even more challenging. If I can even screw anymore with this back.

"What have you got to lose, Kyle?" Chad prods me. "Think of it that way."

"My agent, is what."

"Sounds to me like you already lost him." He points his warm beer at me in a punctuating manner. Kid gets his SAG/AFTRA card and a part-time accounting job that lets him take off whenever he wants for auditions, and suddenly he knows this town.

But that's not really what gets me into rush hour traffic on Wilshire Boulevard in the middle of the god-forsaken day. What gets me is that commercial. Smug, kiss-ass Brian Slattery and his huge pasty white face shilling burgers in a job that should've been mine, while I'm drinking swill in a too hot dump of an apartment that I can't even afford. When we were undergrads at IU, Slattery was always getting the parts that I should've had. He probably never had to go beg his agent to get him an audition. I hope he gets mad cow disease from that burger.

Barry Wills' office is air conditioned, at least. Probably to keep the tacky old headshots of people you've never heard of (and never will) from shriveling up and dying inside their frames all along the otherwise bleak walls. There's a couple people you'd recognize, by face but not by name. And then there's the group shots of Barry and some other agents posing with a big celebrity: Tom Hanks, Kurt Russell. Any famous person he met once and had his picture taken with at a party like any other slob. What really bugs me though is I've been with the guy for almost ten years now, and he's never once put my picture up on any of his office walls.

His assistant makes me wait a full 45 minutes because I don't have an appointment. Meanwhile, I'm sure the guy's in there just cruising Facebook and clicking "likes" on his mom's vacation photos to make him seem busy and important.

"You need to lose ten pounds, Kyle. Maybe 15," is the first thing he tells me once I'm allowed to sit down inside his cluttered sanctuary.

"I know, I'm gonna lose the weight. It's just, my back's been bothering me so I haven't been working out as much."

Barry sighs. He's pretty paunchy himself, not that I'd point that fact back out to him. He pushes his keyboard out of his way and folds his hands across the desk, looking me straight in the eye. "What are you doing here, Kyle?"

"What do you think? I need you to get me out on something. Anything man, I don't care. You gotta get me out."

"No, I mean, what are you still doing here? You're almost middle aged, and you've been out here what, 15 years? When you were young and hot you maybe had a shot. Maybe. Now, you're finished and you don't know when to quit. Go home, to wherever you're from. Get a decent job, marry a nice girl. Have a good life. Be happy."

My heart dips like a roller coaster. But by now, rejection is starting to feel so familiar I almost kind of welcome it like an old friend. So I just look back at him, right in the eyes. "Nothing else but this is ever gonna make me happy."

Barry heaves a huge sigh this time and turns back to his computer. "I have this one thing, but you're not going to like it. Nobody should like this, it's practically criminal."

I can't help but smile at all the hyperbole. "What is it?"

"A new reality show. On ZBN. It's called *Buried!*—with an exclamation point. Ten contestants, and they get buried alive underground without food or water. The only thing down there is an IV, a one-way camera, and a panic button. Whoever lasts the longest without pushing the panic button wins the grand prize of one million dollars." He sits back and lets that all sink in before he shrugs and remarks, "Pretty big budget for cable."

"They come get you out if you hit that panic button?"

"Right. But then, you get nothing."

"And I'd be on TV that whole time?"

"Kyle, you're not considering this. Now that I've said it all out loud I realize how outrageous it is. They make you *and* your whole family sign waivers in the event of your death. Is it really worth risking your life for a million dollars?"

"You think people will watch this thing?"

"I think if they can get enough desperate people to sign up for it to even have a show, it's going to rock everybody's world."

My agent was right about the waivers they make me sign, only they don't stop with the in-case-of-death certificate. I literally climb a mountain of paperwork before I get my first stipend. The pay is a thousand dollars a week for a month while they pre-tape you, before you go down. Let the audience get to know you. Let yourself get ready. That four grand is one of the reasons I said yes, actually. Pay off some bills and have some chump change to spare, why not? What really got me though were those Mexicans.

Driving home from Barry's office that day (he'd said, "Think about it hard," before he'd let me say yes), my car broke down on the south side of Sunset Gower Studios. I looked at the big soundstages with their little doors and their big gates, thinking about how many people go in and out of there every day. How I'm right here, so close to where Hollywood happens, but I'll never be a part of it. Those doors are locked to me. Just then these two Mexican guys in a beat up tan Toyota truck with a mattress tied to the bed drove by and honked and laughed at me and my useless Ford Escort. At my useless life. One threw out his bottle of Fanta and missed my head by like two inches. Right then I decided. I can't be some miserable loser people point and laugh and throw things at anymore. I mean, come on. How bad can this thing be if it's on TV?

And man, this pre-ground stuff, as the producer dudes call it, is sweet. I get my car fixed, buy a new fridge, move back into the bedroom. I get all kinds of doctors checking me out and one fixes my back with a quick snap crackle and pop. I'm the center of attention, these guys behind the cameras following me around asking all kinds of questions. They interview Chad who claims to be my best friend, which isn't exactly true, but I don't argue because I don't want to look bad on TV. You never know how these editors are going to revise the truth to make you look a certain way, so I am nice as pie to everybody. A round of drinks, on me. Anything you guys want. I take everybody up to the Dresden to see ol' Marty and Elaine play. Another round of drinks. Some of the girls up there recognize me from the show, which premieres two weeks after we start filming. And let's just say my strike-out streak ends big time. A blonde with dark eyeliner here, a brunette with a lip piercing there. A little, "Hey baby give me something to think about when I'm underground" and the panties are flying like hotcakes on a Sunday.

The one thing I wish though, is my Grandma was around to see it all. They interview my whole family too, back in Indiana. My mom and dad try to say nice things, but they look tired as hell and about as used up of me as always. My brother talks about how I could've stayed home at the hardware store but I chose a big fancy life in Los Angeles, and how it hasn't worked out quite so well for me. He's the one who stayed and kept the business running, that smug prick. I can tell he's pretty pissed that he's not the golden boy anymore for one moment of his life. But my Grandma, she was different. She always said she wanted to see me in something. She wrote that in the note area of the last check she ever made out to me in fact, on the night before she died last Christmas. "Someday I'll see you in something," she says. Sweet as hell. Then she passed out on the toilet and that was that for her. I ended up cashing that check, it was for $50. I wish I'd saved it, so I could look at that note again. But what can I say, I needed the money.

And I check out the competition too. There's this black kid from the projects whose mom got shot by a gang drive-by, taking care of his little sisters. A girl who could be kind of hot if she had less nose and more chin, who runs marathons and is all about the extreme endurance stuff. Personally I think people who run that much just have a lot they're trying to run away from, but that's just my opinion. There's this old lady who has like ten cats, working as an apartment building manager, reading tarot cards and still trying to get parts on things. A few more actor types that I don't think will last more than half a day. And one really buff dude who claims he needs the million dollars because his wife's dying of anal cancer and if she's able to go through as much pain as she has, he can too. It's a pretty damn good story and I really wish I'd thought of something like that. People are gonna be rooting for that guy, but it's too late for me to change my image now.

On the day of our burial, we meet our boxes and our competitors for the first time. We're up in the Nevada desert because crews and filming taxes are cheaper. I think I'm prepared but I have to admit, I get a rush of anxiety when I see my box for the first time. I realize they purposely avoided telling us what it was really going to be like, and somehow I must've managed to convince myself that it would be a nice soft comfortable coffin, like the ones you see at funeral homes. That they wouldn't really bury us all the way underground, because how could they if they needed to fix any issues?

I "meet" my box with a camera in my face and I try not to let it show but I can feel the sweat start to bead up all over me. It's a box. A solid silver steel box, six feet long for me since I'm 5'10", and about four feet wide and deep. It sits next to a hole in the ground that's already been dug for me, at least ten feet deep, with a headstone marker that has my name and date of birth in an electronic display, with a dash and an empty space for the date of death. Pretty clever, these guys. I smile bravely at the lens.

Off to the side, I notice one of the actory-type guys having a total meltdown and all the cameras rush over to him. He's hustled off and back into the RV's that brought us out here, quitting before he even begins. He's now eight grand in the hole. That was in the pile of paperwork too, if you back out early you repay the stipend times two.

So I climb inside. What else can I do at this point? I can't wimp out and embarrass myself like that. My box technician helps me lay flat and fits the IV needle into my right arm. He then wraps a tight black band around it to cover and secure it in place. "Don't worry, it will get looser," he says with an ominous grin. Of course it will. Easiest 15 pounds ever, right Barry? I'll lose it in my sleep.

The technician shows me how to open and close the trap door beneath me for all of my evacuation needs. My box will be situated atop a deeper hole, porta-potty style. He shows me how to scoot up to aim for number one, and scoot down for number two. He then lifts my lid halfway closed now so I can see there are two devices attached to the underside. One, he explains, is the camera lens underneath about five inches of impenetrable shatterproof glass. So I can't hurt myself, if it comes to that. He points to the vent on the right side of the camera, which will pipe down air to keep me from suffocating. And on what is going to be my upper left side—the panic button. The technician has me trace along the red flat button with my fingers, saying that it won't activate with a simple touch, so I'm free to touch and finger it as much as I want. He shows me how hard I have to press to make the thing activate, and we practice together a few times. He tells me that if I get to a point where I am too weak to press that hard, that I just need to press as hard as I can and repeat the word "panic" three times.

"I won't get to that point," I say. And it's the last thing I utter to another living person before I'm dropped into the ground.

I can feel myself being jostled inside as a crane lowers me down. I wonder briefly if this prone position and uncomfortable surface is going to be a problem for my back. And then I hear the dirt showering down above me.

"I feel like I'm in the mafia," I tell the camera, testing out the sound of my voice in the small hollow space. "Just when I thought I was out!" I yell, and laugh. Hamming it up. I'm going to beat that guy with the cancerous wife. She's just gonna have to keep pooping through a straw.

I laugh at that thought, and then I catch a fit of giggles and I can't stop. Nervous energy, must be. Slowly my laughter fades along with the light from the last of the Nevada sky. Darkness closing all around like a piece of paper burning up into black.

And I'm alone.

At first I think it's an effect on my eyeballs, like when you look into a light and then close your eyes but the light's still there. But after some experimenting with opening and closing my eyes, it dawns on me that it's the red light from the camera above me. A tiny pinpoint, far away in the distance behind the glass. "Hello, America," I tell it. Feeling a little silly that it took me ten minutes to realize what that was. "You're gonna be with me a long, long time."

I've always tended to get nervous in front of a camera—which is stupid, I know, since it's all I ever wanted to do. I guess that nervousness is because I want it so bad I'm afraid I'm going to mess it up. My plan was to just talk to people, when I first got down here. Knowing someone's there out there watching will keep me company, in between meditating and sleeping. I figure nobody can sleep the way I can, I can do twelve hours straight no problem. I'm going to talk until I'm tired, and then nap, then wake up and meditate, talk some more, then nap. I'm sure it'll get boring sometimes, but I can handle this. I got this.

Once I get going, it doesn't take me long to warm up to the far away red light. I talk about how I always knew I was going to be famous, ever since I was a little kid. I always knew I was special, even when nobody ever believed in me. I did everything I was supposed to do to make it happen, I sacrificed everything, my whole life. Why did it never happen?

I talk about the rejection. How even in high school I'd watch these other losers get better parts in the plays and musicals—kids who I knew, I *knew* weren't going to do anything other than lead a boring meaningless life. It wasn't until my senior year that the musical director gave me a lead role in *West Side Story*, and do you know what he told me? That I wasn't the best person for the part, but he gave it to me as a favor because he felt bad for all the years I auditioned for him. Can you believe that?

After a while, and because now I'm most likely trying to postpone the inevitable realization of my surroundings settling in, I decide to sing. I start with Billy Joel for some reason since *Pressure* pops into my head. Kind of apropos, right? I move on to *Only the Good Die Young* and *You May Be Right*, until it sort of dawns on me that they probably won't be able to purchase the rights to air these songs. Meaning I'll get less camera time than the other people. I try to think of some monologues I can remember—I get about a third of the way through Hamlet's and I can't go any farther. So I decide to go back to songs, only I just say the lyrics instead of singing them. Like a poem.

I repeat the words to *My Life* until I don't feel like talking anymore. My voice is tired now anyway. I decide it's time to sleep so I tell the camera goodnight. I planned for this too—figuring the first night would be the hardest. I stayed awake all night last night, and ate about five hamburgers too. I immediately push the hamburgers back out of my mind. I take a deep breath of the oxygen that's being piped down for me. Hoping nobody up there is asleep at the wheel.

I don't know how long I'm asleep until I jolt awake with a start. A prickling, panicky feeling flows down my chest into my arms when at first I don't know where I am and it's all blackness and confined space. Until I remember. I touch my arm where the IV band squeezes it. And for the first time since the lid closed I reach up and touch the panic button. Just until my heart stops racing, I tell myself. So I know it's there. I finger it, waiting for my heart to calm down. I press my palm up against it, feeling it comfort me against my surrounding blindness. I take a deep breath, in and out. Wrapping my fingers around the button and remembering its red color.

And suddenly I hear a little click.

I jerk my hand away as if it has just been stung, my heart racing once more. Did I just accidentally tap myself out?

"I didn't mean to do that!" I tell the camera. "I don't want to be out yet, I was just touching it. I don't want to tap out. Don't come get me yet, please."

The thought of having come this far and giving up so soon wretches me like a pit in my stomach. How could I have been so stupid? I continue to repeat to the camera that I didn't mean to tap out, I don't want to be out yet. Praying that the click I heard was just a squeak in the mechanism, and not an activation.

I'm quiet for the next couple hours, straining my ears to see if I can hear them digging above. I can't be just another loser who hit the button too soon. I have no way of knowing how many people have tapped out already. The only thing I do know—that I will ever know—is that as long as I'm down here in this box, at least one other person is still holding out too. The only way we'll know we've won is if they come get you before you ever tap out.

And that winner is going to be me. A million bucks in my hand and the whole world congratulating me? All the Brian Slatterys will finally be looking at *me* with envy for once.

By the time what my inner clock tells me has got to be close to the end of another day, with thankfully no rescue team digging me out, my hunger pains become increasingly loud. Intensely, mind-thumping loud. I thought I knew what hunger felt like before, but that was just a drop in what's now a viciously empty bucket. I know I won't die, thanks to the IV strapped around my wrist. But it is little comfort to my screaming stomach, which feels like a fist that's balling up hard enough to turn itself into stone. I feel myself sweating and panting, and I moan aloud.

"Please, can you send me down a pizza?" I ask the little red light. "Just stuff it down through these little air holes, I'll hold my breath. And I'll take a chocolate milkshake too, nice and thick. And some garlic cheese fries. Mozzarella sticks. Oh and a big plate of spaghetti, you can stick it down noodle by noodle. Please, please, please..."

I don't think I'm going to be able to sleep through this.

I've lost all sense of the passage of time. It has to have been at least five days, right? It feels more like five weeks. The vice grip in my empty stomach churns a notch tighter.

"These hunger pains never get better, by the way you stupid jerks," I accuse the red light. "I don't know who invented fasting but I would like to punch them right in their stupid face. Gandhi can suck it. This is torture, what you're doing to me right now, you do realize that right? This is insane, inhumane, and completely jack shit crazy. How can you go to bed at night and live with yourselves, doing this to us down here, for good TV? Ratings? You're abusing innocent people. That's why you made me sign all those papers, because you knew I would want to sue your asses so hard you wouldn't be able to sit down for a week. This is bullshit. Somebody get me a good attorney for when this is over, I am going to fight you two-bit cable network dicks! You people are monsters and I am going to fight you and win so help me god this is insane somebody please get me some food I am dying! Do you hear me? I am DYING!"

The red light does not respond.

I want so badly to give up. I moan and roll to my side, clutching the screaming viper that my stomach has become. How is everyone else standing this? How much longer can they hold out? I curl into a fetal ball and stretch my legs out slowly, one by one. This has become my new workout routine. The pain in my back has also resurfaced, but right now it is a mewling kitten to the dragon in my gut. But I am gunning for the back to come into its own and overthrow the stomach. Anything but this pain.

I start to feel another panic gurgling in my chest again, a low simmer. What if all this was just a plan to get rid of me? What if my agent was just tired of me and my uselessness to him, and this is actually really a snuff film? What if there is no panic button, no escape? What if that was all just lies upon lies and all along it was just an elaborate design to kill me slowly while they watched?

I turn back onto my back, reach up and touch the panic button. "Will you really come to get me if I press this?" I demand of the red light. "Will you? Or is this all fake, and nobody is ever going to come get me? Is anybody even listening to me? I'm just trapped down here until I starve to death, is that what this is?"

Tears now stream down my eyes at the thought, wet and salty, and I lick them hungrily with my tongue until I can't keep up anymore and I just sob. Why do I have to go through this when so many other people have it so easy?

Another thought bursts like a bubble through my simmering anxiety attack...what if the panic button just kills me if I press it? Can they do that, legally, if you sign your life away? I curse myself for not reading more carefully through my mountain of paperwork. How could I have been so stupid to just trust these people blindly!

I scream, banging my fists and legs against the coffin box. The noise both scares and exhilarates me—the hollow thumping of an almost-corpse. I scratch my fingernails along the surface, hoping desperately to peel something off that I can put into my mouth. I scrape so hard at the smooth metal I almost relish in the pain—anything to make this goddamn hunger less excruciating. Not getting anywhere with the scraping, I start punching. Hard. I could break my hand I punch so hard, using every last bit of strength I have with as much force as I can muster at such an awkward incline. Finally, I feel blood trickle down my right knuckle.

I put my fist up to my mouth and suck at it, as hard as I can, tasting my own sweet and sickening blood. My stomach almost breathes a sigh of relief when I do—and so I keep going. Punch and suck, punch and suck. I know without seeing it that I'm turning my fist into a bloody pulp. It's disgusting, and I don't want to think about the fact that what I'm doing now is basically eating myself alive. What if that's my only choice?

Then the worst thing ever happens. For the past—is it five days? Maybe six?—I've been experiencing the most wicked constipation in conjunction with my starving stomach. And suddenly, maybe because of the blood now in my stomach, the dam breaks.

I don't get my pants down in time before the diarrhea avalanche starts. The best I can manage is to fumble down my pants and get the trap door open in time for most of it to fall through the hole. Most, but not all. In the aftermath, I spend some time deciding when the smell is worse: with the hatch open, or closed. There is no difference, so I decide upon closed. The stench is horrific, it has a mind of its own and it is the absolute most nasty houseguest I could have ever have invited.

Nauseated, exhausted, starving. My head spins until I eventually pass out.

"Ten, ten, ten, ten, ten, ten, ten, ten..." I repeat the number incessantly. I decided ten sleeps ago that the only way I can calculate my passage of time is to count them. When I wake up, I drill the new number into my brain so I don't forget.

"Eleven, eleven, eleven, eleven..."

I'm certain that I've gone blind. I can still see that red light, but I don't believe it's real anymore. Because when I close my eyes, I see a kaleidoscope of bright colors which I decide are much better. They swirl and dance and make me feel high. The colors I soon discover become even brighter and more vivid when, if I prop myself up onto my elbows, I bang my head as hard as I can against the center of the box where I believe the red light lives. It feels good to hurt myself. The spinning feels good, too, spinning me into nothingness.

I'm ripped into consciousness by the sound of screaming. It scares me so badly I feel like my entire spinal cord is instantly transformed into a giant icicle of fear. It's the desperate high pitched wail of a tortured ghost from hell, and every hair on my body stands on end wondering who or what is down here with me. Until it occurs to me that it is me screaming. And this is a hundred times more frightening. So I scream even louder. I wake the dead and kill the living. It's a howl that comes from my own ghost who is fighting his way out of me, worming his way through each and every one of my ragged and diminishing bones. Hoping to break free.

Eventually, I feel the screaming fading away into the eternal and unforgiving darkness. I hold onto it like a man at the end of a very strong tug-of-war...me, against the sucking black hole. If only I can keep hold of the screaming man, keep his thoughts on this side of the abyss. But I lose, and the ghost leaves me with one final wispy croak.

The darkness envelops me with frigid claws into its suffocating embrace.

"Fifteen," I whisper to it. "Fifteen, fifteen, fifteen..."

At first the new idea is so brilliant and crystal clear, I can't believe I hadn't thought of it before.

"Twenty, twenty, twenty, twenty, twenty," I know it's important to keep saying this number, but this new idea threatens to hammer it away into forgetting.

"Twenty, twenty, twenty, twenty..." The number gets smaller and smaller as the idea finally overthrows my mind. The band around my right arm contains the elixir of life that's supporting me—so why not pluck the sucker out and suck on it? It's so perfect and beautiful, my broken hand shakes in anticipation as I fumble for a way to release it. My parched and shriveled throat quivers and begs.

After what feels like several hours of failure on removing the arm band, I decide to chew on the metal coil surrounding the drip tube. There's got to be a way inside this thing. I feel my teeth breaking on the metal and I decide not to swallow those, remembering my wretched experience with waste elimination and not wanting to repeat that with some indigestible large particles. But I use my broken and jagged teeth to get back to work on the arm band, chewing the metallic mesh fabric slowly until bit by bit, piece by piece, it breaks away. I'm beating you, I tell it. I'm going to beat you because I have nothing but time.

When I'm finally able to pull the strap away, I feel around my now exposed arm very slowly and carefully. There is a needle going in, I feel the slightly raised ridge where it connects to my vein. I pull the needle out carefully, trying not to break it. I feel all around it, a glass tube attached to a metal base. I twist and force trying to loosen the syringe from its housing but it won't budge. I'm so close, I think, I can do this—when the glass shatters in my hand and splatters all over.

"No!" I whimper, fumbling to get the now broken end into my mouth in time to receive whatever sustenance is inside. I suck at it hard, but there is nothing. I break away all the remaining bits of glass around the metal tube and put it up to my mouth, feeling around with my tongue. I taste a faint hint of saline and know there once was something. But now there is nothing. I keep searching with my tongue until I notice an almost imperceptible latch. Disabled, I realize. Meant to work only through the needle, but not without it. I never should have pulled it out. I never should have broken the needle.

This is when I know I'm in trouble.

"Hey!" I tell the red light urgently. Not recognizing my own dried up voice. "I didn't mean to do that, can you make this thing work again? Can somebody come down here and fix it?"

But I know in my heart that nobody is coming for me, or will ever come for me. My demise has been my own fault.

"Twenty-one, twenty-one, twenty-one..." Sleep comes easy now. It takes me down and threatens to drown me for good, each time only to release me from its grasp at just the last second, back into the harsh reality of my own deterioration.

Sometimes I still reach up and tickle the circular protrusion in my space which I vaguely recall was referred to as some kind of panic button. I couldn't push it now if I wanted to because I am just a skeleton now, a monster without any soul. I dreamed once of how to open this box, that there were words to say if I couldn't do it. That was a long time ago, when there was another vague dream of a million dollars and public notoriety. Success. It makes me feel nostalgic, though I'm not sure why.

Nobody is coming for me. Because there is nobody left.

Sleep pulls me under again.

I cry without tears. I scream without a voice. I cry because I don't remember who will miss me when I'm gone. I scream because I can't even remember who I was before I was put into this box.

"Goodbye," my crusted lips whisper to nobody in particular.

The light hurts my eyes still. It has ever since the first time I saw it again, when some men came and pulled me up out of the box. They were shouting and cheering, saying that I'd won. But I didn't know what they meant.

Now I'm in a room full of windows that face the water. It's bright, but I can't move to shut out the light. I can't move to do anything. There's a man here holding a thing that is making bright flashes at me. I don't know why he is torturing me, but I am not surprised. My life is torture.

"Hey!" says a voice behind me, that belongs to someone I've come to understand is Chad. He tells me we are friends, but I don't remember him. "Hey dude, no unauthorized pictures! I thought I made that clear when I let you in here."

"I'm sorry," says the man with the lights. "I was just snapping off a couple pre-shots. Warm up, kind of thing."

"Nothing unauthorized. I'm going to need you to delete those."

"It's fine, we won't use them. So this shoot will be of the two of you then?"

"Of course!" Chad responds, sitting down next to me. "I wouldn't go anywhere without my best bud!" He hugs me close and tickles his fingers across my ribs. More torture. I should have expected it. My face responds in a smile that my body is not feeling, much against my will. The lights continue to flash.

After the man leaves, Chad wheels me into the worst room again. There are images all over the walls in here of a man screaming in horror. This is the man I see, when I close my eyes to sleep at night. This man haunts me, he is everywhere.

"Oh come on, buddy, stop shaking! You should be proud of these posters, it's how you won a million smackaroos! You beat everybody, even after you pulled out your own IV! Alright look, I just wanted to show you something and then we can get out of here. Watch, it's me on 'The Eleanor Show' today."

Chad lights up a bigger box where a moving image of himself talking to a woman appears. "Look, the network is paying me big bucks to go on all these talk shows to tell everybody about how great you're doing. And you *are* doing great, you just need a little more time to get better. But get this, I'm going to get my own segment on 'Eleanor' now! She liked me so much she said she's going to make me her regular man on the street interviewer now. How cool is that? I'm gonna be famous!"

But I don't know what any of this means. All I can see is the screaming man all around me. I close my eyes and there he is again, only he is me and I am screaming. I am screaming.

"Nurse!" Chad calls out. "He just shit himself again!"

EPILOGUE

The agent looks at the latest picture from the cover of "In Touch" weekly of his smiling client, sitting next to his new up-and-coming one. Kyle will never be any good to anyone again, but Chad's going places, Barry thinks. Pretty soon he won't want to be tied to this lump. Barry decides that as soon as that happens, he'll change out the picture inside the frame he holds. But for now, this cover spread is getting a place of honor, right in the front lobby.

Barry calls his assistant back to take the photograph of Kyle and Chad, ignoring the woman sitting across from him. But this is on purpose. She needs to be made to feel she's the least important person here.

"Didn't two people die during the first season? That old lady, and the black kid?" The actress is still skeptical. She is long past 40, with more lines on her face than she'll ever get paid to say from a script anymore.

"Yeah, but you're stronger than that. And look at that marathon runner, Kelly Naegle. She tapped out in third place and got her own talk show."

"But she's blind now. And her talk show got cancelled."

"Joe DePerno then. Guy's down there obsessing about his wife with cancer and how he's going to leave their daughter an orphan. Taps out just minutes before Kyle starts knocking on death's door."

"It was heartbreaking."

"And great TV. So now, you go on his charity website and see, his fans have donated so much, guy's a millionaire."

"Really, a millionaire?"

"Well, at least a few hundred thousandaire," the agent quickly amends, in case she decides to whip out her phone to check.

What Barry doesn't add, of course, is that Joe actually tapped out three days before Kyle chewed off his IV. That Kyle really spent five days down there all on his own, so the producers could get the dramatic ending they needed.

But now, finally, Barry sees the gleam in the washed up woman's watery blue eyes subtly shifting from skepticism to... yes, there it is. Desperate hope. "You could be the next Kyle Prescott. Or Joe DePerno. And if you don't act on this now, I've got plenty of clients who will. You want to be famous? This is your shot."

The actress purses her lips in thought, and Barry knows he has her. "Will this get me my SAG/AFTRA card?" she asks.

"No, honey." The agent smiles sweetly. "This one's non-union."

Heather E. Ash worked as a staff writer for Stargate SG-1 *and* Glory Days. *Her one-hour original script* Square One *was chosen by* Written By *magazine (the trade publication for the* Writers Guild of America*) as one of its top five unproduced drama pilots and was a finalist in the film/television script category of the 2013* Writer's Digest *Annual Competition. She is a member of the* Writer's Guild of America, Sisters in Crime, *and serves as Secretary for the Midwest Chapter of the* Mystery Writers of America. *She teaches screenwriting and math at Chicago-area colleges, and can be heard on the occasional* Nerd Outcast Podcast *rhapsodizing (in an amusing way) about science fiction on the screen.*

METHOD

Heather E. Ash

LIKE SO MANY THINGS in Los Angeles, the rain was fake. That didn't make it any less wet as it pounded onto the heads of the children, dragging Sam's curls into his eyes. The director yelled cut and then yelled it again. He wanted scissors.

The make-up girl sprang forward, but only wielded bobby pins to secure Sam's hair with steady hands and a vacant half-smile...products, no doubt, of the pill bottle Susan had seen nestled between the lipsticks.

Sam's lips were blue. No one seemed the least concerned about hypothermia. Hell, none of the kids would have eaten lunch if Susan hadn't reminded the A.D. of work rules. The mothers of the other two boys didn't like that at all. "You can't cause trouble," Fake Blonde warned, while Fake Boobs bobble-headed agreement and added, "You want your son to work again, don't you?" Better to let their kids starve than take a chance at upsetting the D-list director of a cookie ad. They probably thought Susan was some hopeful Okie—but she knew more about this business than both of them combined. She knew people would take advantage of you only if allowed to. And everyone was out to take advantage.

Susan slipped in behind the make-up lady and caught Sam's eye. "This is the last take, baby," she told Sam. "This is ridiculous." Already twenty-six minutes over schedule.

"But Mom," he protested through chattering teeth, "this is fun!"

The McGraths did not walk into the situation blind. Before leaving their suburban Edmond driveway, Susan had registered Sam with several reputable online casting websites. His Coogan trust information was stapled to the California work permit, and she'd paid the deposit on a one-bedroom guest house within walking distance to the Disney lot. She and Mark discussed the ground rules as they attached Sam's credits to the back of full-color headshots that highlighted his round blue eyes and still-round cheeks: Three months. No roles with nudity, swearing or other inappropriate behavior for a seven year-old. They were starting a career, not making a quick buck, not chasing fame. Susan was the last person to be impressed by someone calling her kid talented, but Sam's resume was filled with local stage productions and regional commercial spots. It was a good time to explore opportunities outside of the Sooner State.

Twenty miles outside of Flagstaff, the car blew a gasket. The tow, the repair, and two nights at the Hampton Inn burned through three weeks of savings before they knocked on the door of the Burbank guest house.

A small woman with a Persian accent peered suspiciously through the door's beveled glass. "We're renting the guest house," Susan said.

The owner frowned deeper and opened the door a crack. "It's been rented."

"Yes, to us. I'm Susan McGrath."

"You didn't show up."

"Our car broke down. I called. I left messages."

"How am I to know it's not some story?" she demanded. Not once did she look at Sam, pressed up against his mother's leg. As far as she was concerned, he was part of the con, and she wasn't about to get taken in.

"Mommy, what are we going to do?" Sam whispered as they waited for the lady to return to the door with their security deposit.

"We'll find a place," she assured him. Instead of seeing this as the Universe telling her to Get Out, she chose to see it as a test of faith. "It's only an obstacle," she said.

"Bad storm last night," said Mark. "Oh, and Mrs. Collins got a new dog."

"Another Pomeranian?"

"A Samoyed. I told her to keep it inside."

Susan tried to picture their elderly neighbor walking a dog that came above the line of her support stockings. And if the plan was for a "coyote-proof" pet, then why didn't she choose a German shepherd? Not that anyone bought the claim that coyotes had snatched Mrs. Collins' previous two dogs from the safety of her Edmond subdivision's backyard. Their elderly neighbor's previous two dogs had met with coyotes. That was Mrs. Collins' claim, though Susan herself had watched the first dog nose its way out of the gate plenty of times. After his body was found in the middle of Acorn Road's dead end–broken neck, but curiously unmolested for coyote prey–Mark had repaired the fence. When Ruth Brunson's boys found Buster II floating in the community pool, they thought they were doing Mrs. Collins a favor by bringing back the sopping corpse for a proper burial. Instead, they got hysterical screams and a police officer questioning them. Mrs. Collins was still the only one who believed in coyotes, but now everyone else's pets–and children–were kept inside at night.

"You sure you can't wake him up?" asked Mark.

"He has an audition tomorrow."

"That was fast! What's it for?"

"Cookie commercial."

"Is he nervous?"

The million dollar question. If you asked him directly, Sam would say he wasn't. But worry was such a constant setting that Susan doubted he knew what the absence of it would feel like. It was a matter of degree. He hadn't had nightmares yet, not since the dog in the pool.

"How's the guest house?" he asked.

"Charming." It was brown. Brown plaid sofa, brown kitchen cabinets, brown carpet...very circa 1992. "The location's good," she added, "very close to the highway. We can walk to the library and grocery store." This was all technically true. If she opened the yellowed curtains, she would see the tops of vehicles zooming along the 101 fifty feet away. Next to the apartments were the BP Station and Food Mart where they'd stopped after a long day of house-hunting frustration. Everything they'd seen, even the studios, were too expensive, and whatever money they would save venturing into Panorama City or beyond put them in gang territory or would have them burning gas and time to get anywhere. The wall-to-wall concrete of the Laurel Place apartments wasn't aesthetically pleasing, but the unit was a one-bedroom within their price range, and they weren't going to get mugged by the guy selling oranges at the off-ramp.

She wasn't in the habit of lying to Mark. But she didn't want him arriving on the apartment doorstep with a moving van. He'd argued that he could look for electrical work in Los Angeles just as easily as OKC, because didn't film sets list all those electricians in the credits? Susan didn't even bother telling him that it didn't work that way, it was all about the relationships. To move the entire family was too huge of a gamble. Better to keep making the partial payments on the mortgage and hope that Mark continued to come through with a few days of work every so often. Better not to walk away from everything and then have nothing when it didn't work out.

But in that moment, she wanted nothing more than to have him next to her, telling Sam jokes to keep him from giving in to anxiety. Playing Scrabble or gin with Susan. Making rice and beans taste different five nights a week. Or merely serving as the six foot two reminder to any of the nineteen other households that this woman and child were not to be messed with.

Ted, the on-site landlord of Laurel Place, had unfortunately cast himself in that role. She could hear the *Everybody Loves Raymond* laugh track from the rear projection television that backed up to their shared wall. On his side of it hung a dozen signed and framed headshots of River Phoenix, an age progression stretching from *Stand By Me* to *The Thing Called Love*. Sixty-something Ted had rocked in his peach recliner, sharing vague tidbits from his days "managing River" as Susan filled out the rental agreement on a matching loveseat, Sam pressed to her side. "He was a prodigy," said Ted, tapping his hands on a round belly. Susan noted with alarm that his legs were clean-shaven despite a thick head of white hair and eyebrows that shot tendrils up from behind his glasses.

"Maybe you'll be like him, Sam."

The pen made a mark where Susan flinched.

"You want some orange juice Sam?" Ted pushed himself up from his chair and walked over to the bar across from the television. Backed by a crackled gold mirror, it held several bottles of tequila and mixers. He even had Zima, for Chrissakes. "Can I interest you in a Bahama Mama, Susan?" he asked.

"No thanks," she said, pulling out her checkbook. She felt sweat winding down her back, though the room was ice-cold from the window unit. "How much for the security deposit?"

"First month's is fine," he said, waving at her with a jar of lukewarm orange juice. "I used to work the streets, you know, so I can tell good people when I meet them. You sure I can't get you something? How about a Se—" he interrupted himself with a glance to Sam, "that thing you do on the beach?"

Susan was already shaking her head when Sam asked, "Building sand castles?"

The innocent question made Ted laugh so hard he actually wheezed, slapping his bare knee. "That's a good one, Sammy."

Ted had connections, so he'd get them a refrigerator—cheap. From the depths of a closet he came up with a queen-sized air mattress that he "kept for guests" and which Susan wouldn't inflate until she spent more precious resources on a bicycle pump and a waterproof mattress pad.

When Susan hung up with Mark, she lay down next to Sam and discovered that the bed had deflated. Nothing between her and the floor but a piece of wrinkled plastic. She ended up on the sofa, falling asleep to muffled male voices that may have been from Ted's television, and maybe not, but Sam slept through the night.

After the third boy came out from the casting room tugging at the hem of his shirt, Susan pulled aside the casting assistant. "Are they having the boys undress?" she asked.

"Oh no," the assistant chortled, his manicured eyebrows arching at the ridiculousness of it all. "He's only having them *lift up* their shirts."

"Why?"

"The character of the brother flexes his biceps in a scene."

"Without a shirt?"

"That's what he's deciding," said the assistant, turning away from her to call the next child inside.

Susan picked up her bag and took Sam's hand, leading him out of the casting office.

The cream stucco of the house lit up orange where the last rays of sunlight found open spaces within the unchecked purple bougainvillea. Sunset always arrived two hours earlier inside the canyon, so that you had to turn on all the lights before dinner, and never turn them off if the day was cloudy. The price you pay for proximity to Mulholland. And for a professional gardener... which these people obviously had decided to forego even if it meant letting the pyracantha snake inside the built-in firepit.

"This is a long shortcut, Mom," Sam spoke up from the back.

She put the car into gear and backed away from the barricade of the wrought-iron gate. Neighborhood patrol would definitely want to investigate a ten year-old Buick in one of its driveways. "Guess I made a wrong turn, buddy." She put them back on the winding road, down this time.

"Why couldn't I audition?" he asked.

"Because it wasn't an appropriate role for a boy your age."

"But all those other boys my age were there. They got to audition."

"Those other boys don't have mothers who are watching out for them," she said, merging back into rush hour traffic on Laurel Canyon.

After a moment with NPR filling the silence, Sam piped up again. "Mom?"

"Yeah?"

"I love you."

She flipped the mirror to look at him. "I love you too, buddy."

"I wish I could go to that school," Sam said, turning his head to catch a glimpse of Moorpark Elementary down the street. Susan felt conspicuous walking past the playground with Sam on her side of the fence and kids his age inside it, so every morning they detoured around it on their way to the library. "You could get a job there."

"They won't let me teach in California," she said.

"Why not? You're a teacher."

"Different states have different rules," she said. "Besides, I don't want to teach anyone but you."

This was her second year homeschooling Sam, and their daily routine carried over into their new life in California. Get up at eight, have a breakfast of oatmeal or cheap cereal, pack peanut butter sandwiches and apples for lunch and a travel mug of Folgers. Walk to the library to start the school day. Sam worked on language arts and social studies at a corner table in sight of Susan as she checked the casting notices, printed sides, and replied to emails for the hour time limit, sometimes two if the young children's librarian was on duty and no one else was waiting. Then math and science, sometimes at the gazebo in a nearby park where nannies and freelancing dads played with toddlers before walking back to the apartment to prepare for an afternoon in traffic going from audition to audition, often not arriving back until close to nine o'clock. The only parking spot left would be in the back corner against the freeway embankment, and Susan felt conspicuous and exposed walking past the curtained windows with rap music or Spanish telenovelas blaring from within. The curtains stayed closed, but she felt the eyes tracking them from their car to their front unit. Ted claimed that there were two families with young children in the building, yet she never saw or heard them.

It was a particular torture for Sam to spend afternoons in offices lined with boys his age without socializing with them. He'd tried to approach a shaggy blonde kid who was also auditioning for the role of Brother Two for a television pilot, only to have SuperTan Mom chew him out for "interfering with my son's preparation!" Sam kept to himself after that, and maybe that inhibition explained the recent dry spell. He looked five but had the vocabulary of a thirty year-old. Too young for the Disney Channel line-up, and there weren't a lot of parts written for that age because you couldn't always find one like Sam. Every casting director remarked at how "otherworldly" and "mature" Sam was, an "old soul" with the handshake of a CEO. The handshake got mentioned so much she had to train Sam in the exaggerated whole-arm kid method, and that led to a student film where he played a spelling bee contestant, and one-line in an episode of a network medical drama. Two more "daddies" and he could be eligible for SAG…if she could find something worthwhile within all the offers for Sam to play a bully, a spoiled rich kid, or a crime victim. She refused those roles, and walked out of more auditions when the casting director wouldn't do a substitution for the casual "fag" or "shit" that writers seemed to think was the lingua franca of Kindergartners these days.

"Mom, look!"

"Baby, we have to hurry." She quick-walked up Hollywood Boulevard, mentally counting down the numbers to their destination. It was still a block away and they only had ten minutes. This was a callback. She needed him centered.

"But it's your name!" Susan walked back, stepping over the pink stars of Neil Diamond and Sidney Lanfield back to where Sam had his feet planted on either side of "Susan Atwood."

"How 'bout that," she said, taking his hand.

"But that was your name, right? Before you married daddy?"

"There are a lot of Susan Atwoods in the world, honey," she said. When she looked up, a paparazzi's flashbulb went off, momentarily blinding her, and suddenly she was in the midst of too many people and it was too loud and she felt like she would have to claw her way through the crowd. No one would notice.

But it was only her and Sam, and the reflection of a car window. She put her hand to her eyes and squeezed her temples, taking deep breaths. Her headache was back.

Karen Shipton waved Susan into an empty room off the waiting area. Susan felt every eye lock on her. "I want to talk to your mom, Sam. You wait here."

Susan hated that her heart was pounding, the rush of blood and adrenaline temporarily clearing the throbbing behind her eyes. But they only talked to you privately if it was good news.

Karen cocked her head, staring at Susan. "Are you an actress?"

Susan shook her head. A preposterous question. Greying roots, thirty extra pounds around the middle, foundation and mascara and the lightest of lip glosses. "Not at all."

Karen tapped her index finger against her lips, a giveaway to her forties with the puckering from decades of smoking, then shook her head clear. "Funny. I'm usually good with faces." She laughed, "It'll come to me. Look, we're not bringing Sam back for this one."

Just like every wannabe, Susan's heart dropped. She forced her expression to stay neutral and thanked Karen as she moved for the door. But Karen called her back. "There's another film I'd like him to read for, but it...well, it skews adult."

"A horror film?" Susan asked, already disappointed.

"No. It's a drama, very indie." Karen named a director that called up an image of red carpets and a series of glamorous girlfriends. "It's his pet project," said Karen, knowing she'd hit home. "And I think Sam would be perfect."

"What kind of adult content?" asked Mark.

Wind whipped against Susan's face, pulling her hair in a line across her mouth and causing the microphone in her cell phone to roar like the seashore. The sun was too bright, searing her eyeballs and intensifying the bright pain of her headache that Ibuprofen and extra coffee could not touch. She blamed the faulty air conditioner, probably teeming with bacteria and mold throughout the night even though Sam said he felt fine. She'd left notes for Ted to please fix it. If she was going to have a headache, at least the air conditioner should blow cold air. She looked down at the sides curled in her hand, hot off the library's printer. She hadn't dared leave them at the table with Sam. "There's a lot of swearing."

"It's only words. You don't think Sam's old enough to handle that?"

She actually drew back the phone to look at it. "And the kid witnesses his father kill his mother," she continued.

"But it's got that director attached, right? He did that kid's movie... And the lead, doesn't he have kids?"

"His kids aren't pretending to dig their mother's grave." If an Oscar-nominated actor pretends to beat your child, does that make the abuse less real?

Mark sighed at the other end. She heard the scrape of his hand along his stubble, something he did whenever he was frustrated. "Sorry," he said reluctantly. "You've been gone a month without anything really happening…"

"That's why I didn't want you to come here with us," she reminded him.

"Yeah, but at least I'd be with you," he said.

Three more weeks, she reminded him. Either Sam would get parts and they could set some money aside for a visit, or they'd be on the road back. Susan couldn't decide which way she hoped it would go.

Susan headed for the table where she'd left Sam working on his book report within view of the librarians. But someone else was at the table with him—a blonde kid and a short, average-looking brunette woman. In a town of extremes, nondescript was a choice unto itself.

"Hi! We've never officially met," the brunette woman stood and held out her hand. "Wendy Walsh." Susan had an immediate flash of context, of Wendy chiding an overly-coiffed mother for allowing her child to sing the audition jingle over and over again in the room. Coiffed was a chronic offender, but no one had stood up to her until that moment.

"Mom, Caden invited me for a playdate!"

Caden's blonde spikes nodded with him, eyes sparkling. "Yeah, we're gonna skateboard, and play with my Xbox, and he can sleep over!"

Wendy held up a hand at her son. "Whoa, Caden. We need to ask Sam and his mother what their plans are." She turned back to Susan. "We would love to invite you and Sam over *when you're available.*"

Susan could already see the disappointment brewing in Sam as he stared down at his book report. This wasn't their first invitation, and every one ended the same way.

"We'd love to," she told Wendy.

They stopped at Walgreens on the way home to pick up another economy-sized bottle of Ibuprofen. She wasn't sure how Sam had come to know Caden's entire life story in the short time she'd been on the phone with Mark, but he was determined to share every detail. "Caden goes to classes with *sixth graders*," he intoned. "And they have a pool and tennis courts where he lives, and movie nights." Susan decided not to tell Sam that she knew all about the Oakwood amenities, nor that they couldn't have afforded it even when Mark was working. Not that Sam gave her enough time to respond, already on to the next factoid. "He likes Ninjago, just like me, but Cole is his favorite character. And Caden lives in Washington. The state, not the city. They have a volcano in Washington, you know. And Caden went there last year for a field trip, and they were studying the rock cycle just like me!"

Finally, as they cut through the gas station, Susan had to put a stop the Caden chronicles. "You've used up your talking for today," she declared as two police cars, sirens blaring, Dopplered past and pulled to a stop in front of Laurel Place, blocking the driveway where an ambulance and a police SUV were already parked.

Ted paced the edge of the activity, wearing a dark blue windbreaker over his omnipresent stretched T-shirt even though it was close to ninety degrees. He saw them and stepped away from the scene, holding up placating hands. "Don't you worry about a thing, little man. The police are here protecting us."

Susan got a glimpse of people moving in and out of 12A. Ricky's place. She never knew Ricky's last name, and the only reason she knew his first name was hearing it pop up from the never-ending stream of people who stopped by his apartment at all hours, staying only for a few minutes and often blocking the driveway with their idling cars, adding to the cloud of exhaust and forcing Susan to shut off the air conditioner. Too many people to think that Ted didn't know what was really happening. His expression now was somber but his eyes gleamed with excitement, so maybe the kickbacks for his silence were only in her mind. Or maybe he'd indulged in one when the cops first arrived. "They finally busted him?" she asked.

Ted shook his head. "I didn't see GSW's on the body. And I would've heard it, if there had been. My best guess is blunt force trauma, based on the mess."

"They let you in there?" she asked, gesturing to the evidence technicians who even now were wheeling out a body bag

Ted eyed her. "I'm the one who called. FedEx guy's been knocking on his door for two days, so I took the package." He shook his head and his eyes settled on a spot next to Susan. "Now don't you worry, Sammy. The police are here to help us."

Sam looked away, taking Susan's admonition not to talk to Ted to heart. Susan put her arm around him. "We have an audition."

"Oh, don't worry. I'll get them to move for you." Ted jogged up to a Sergeant, gesturing in Susan's direction. She moved Sam to her other side, to block his view of the crime scene on their way up the stairs.

"What happened, Mama?"

"I don't know."

By the time they got home, the complex was empty again. The only clue that anything had happened were the police evidence stickers and tape plastered across 12A.

At 2 AM, the screams began. She stumbled into the bedroom, still half inside the dream of sitting at a hotel bar with Mark, facing a glass backdrop with crackled gold and Jack Daniels bottles, Ted serving up drinks in his blue windbreaker. "It's a

Bahama Mama," he said, slamming down a tall glass of liquid that sloshed out and covered her in red fluid. She was almost surprised to see that her bare arms were clean as she gathered up Sam's trembling body.

"He was in the window, staring at me."

"Who was?"

"Mr. Ricky. He was covered in blood, Mama."

Involuntarily she looked up at the bedroom window that faced out to the walkway. She kept the curtains closed at all times, and had moved the heavy oak dresser in front of it on the first night. Nothing could get through except bad dreams. "It's okay, Sam. You're all right—"

A loud banging startled them both. She heard Ted's voice from outside. "Susan! Susan, is everything okay?"

She carried Sam into the living room and opened the front door a crack, enough to show only her head. "We're okay, Ted. It was just a nightmare."

Ted made a show of clutching his heart. He carried a golf driver in his other hand. "I heard the screaming and thought our killer had come back." His breath carried the thick smell of Jack and made her recoil. "Remember, Susan. I'm always next door if you need me."

She thanked him and closed the door. Locked it. And then pushed the sofa in front of it.

"Please, you're the guest." Wendy said kindly, taking the plates from Susan and scraping them into the trash can. For one delicious moment Susan pictured herself gathering up the edges of the tablecloth and hoisting the contents of the cheese board, artisan crackers and fruit salad over her shoulder. She and Sam could gorge themselves for another two days on the leftovers. She'd stopped herself to single servings for fear of seeming gluttonous—or being unable to stop—and it killed her that Sam all but ignored his food, too intent on talking non-stop to Caden.

"Are you sure I can't offer you some wine?" Wendy asked, removing the cheese.

"Tea's fine," Susan answered, swirling the ice cubes in her glass. She leaned against the tile-topped peninsula and felt a tightness unwind in her neck. She never wanted to leave the air conditioning again. "How long have you lived here?"

"This season? Three months. I've thought about doing a short-term house rental, but they do have so many amenities here." Wendy stopped, rolled her eyes. "Sorry. That sounded so pretentious."

Susan waved it off. Outside the door, she could hear Sam's excited whooping. He and Caden were skateboarding in the rear courtyard. She noted that she did not feel the slightest urge to check on him. "When will you go back to New York?"

"Another month, maybe. It all depends on the lottery, right?" Wendy wiped the table with a dishcloth. "What grade do you teach?"

"I used to teach fifth, but I don't anymore."

"No? How come?"

Susan shrugged. "I chose to stay home with Sam."

"I should pay you to teach Caden," said Wendy.

"You don't like the school here?"

"It's hard to be a good student when the girl next to you says singers don't need algebra."

Susan snorted. "As if singing careers last forever."

"Her mother's a piece of work, that one. One of those 'my special snowflake' types."

"I hate those."

"No. You don't strike me as the type," Wendy said. She stared at her a moment. Susan braced herself for The Question.

"Were you at that audition for the comedy feature? The one with the—" she mimed pulling up her shirt.

"Where the director was having them take off their shirts? Yeah, I took Sam out."

"I was there!" she squealed. "I did the same thing."

They clinked their glasses together and declared the formation of a new group: The Average Snowflake Moms.

Susan vibrated happily all the way home. She didn't mind hearing Sam tell all the details of their time outside—the way Caden could ride his skateboard off three stair steps and land on the wheels and keep going, the girl who lived upstairs from Caden who was on a TV show and called Sam a baby. "But Caden, he put his finger right in her face and said, 'You don't call my friend that' and she left, Mom!" Sam told her, as if it were the strangest outcome ever. Susan's heart broke at that. He'd never had anyone his age stand up for him before.

"Why did you change your mind?" Mark asked.

"Well, Wendy was going to let Caden audition because she's worked with the casting director before, and she won't take on a production that doesn't follow the work rules," said Susan. Wendy had given her a lot of advice during their last three lunches, even putting her in touch with Caden's agent. Sam had landed a regional ad the next day.

"She's helping you, even though her son and Sam are up for the same roles?" he asked.

"I know. It sounds weird, but she's like us, Mark. She's not an asshole and she believes in karma." She took a deep breath. "I can't wait for you to meet her."

The water in the bathroom shut off. Sam stepped out with a towel around his shoulders and saw Susan on the phone. "Is that Daddy?"

She handed over the phone. "Talk fast. We have to be on the road in twenty minutes." As he took the cell phone, she saw a red mark encircling his upper arm—like a rug burn. "What's that?"

"I scraped it on the door." Sam carried the phone into the bedroom with him. "Hi Daddy. Guess what?"

Susan hummed to herself as she put the containers of beans and rice into the insulated lunch bag. She set it by Sam's "stuff bag" next to the door when she heard the doorbell chime over the air conditioner. Ted's head bobbed outside the peephole.

"I have to talk to you," Ted slurred when she opened the door. The smell of whiskey burned her nose.

She stepped out onto the landing and pulled the door closed behind her. "I put the rent check in your mailbox," she said. She quickly squashed the little voice that piped up in her brain, *It's the last one too!* Wendy believed in karma, but Susan believed in jinxes.

"This isn't Iowa. Something could happen to a boy out that late."

There were times they got home after the sun had set, and maybe once or twice Sam had run ahead up the stairs to their apartment from the car, but if Ted were looking—and he was always looking—he would have seen Susan coming up behind. She never let Sam out of her sight.

"Ted, Sam never leaves the house without me."

"He stares in my window."

Susan straightened her spine. "No he doesn't," she said firmly, wondering which if any of the residents were watching this altercation and if any would be inclined to give statements to the police. But Ted shook his head like a dog trying to work its way out of a neck cone. "It's not safe," he said again, and retreated to his own apartment.

She locked the door behind her and rested her forehead against it. Headache back in full bloom.

"Mr. Ted's seen Mr. Ricky in his window too?" Sam asked from behind her.

Susan turned. The cell phone was open in his little hand. She wondered how much Mark had heard. She inhaled. It was time to tell him everything.

"Mark—" she began.

"Not Mark. Karen," said the casting director on the other end. "I have some good news, Susan."

Sam ran up to Caden holding his new skateboard aloft. "Look, Caden! Look what I got!" It was the cheapest version the store had, and along with the helmet and safety pads—and peach turnovers from the bakery—represented the single most irresponsible use of the California funds to date. But Susan felt like celebrating for once. It was worth it to see the joy in Sam's face, and the delight in Wendy's eyes as she bit into a pastry. She moaned. "I love turnovers." She leveled her eyes on Susan. "What happened?"

"The pastries looked good."

Wendy tilted her head and cocked her eyebrow. They'd shared too much for this lie. Susan knew all about Wendy's failing marriage, her fixation on one day walking into George Clooney's kitchen. Wendy had heard all about the dark weeks following Sam's birth, holding Susan's hand and nodding empathetically.

"He got called back?" Wendy guessed.

Susan nodded, preparing to assume a sympathetically sad expression. But Wendy threw out her arms. "So did Caden!"

Susan cheered and hugged her friend, but inwardly felt a sharp twang of disappointment. Caden had beat out Sam for three roles; Susan had seen them on the resume Wendy had asked her to proofread. Of course, as she told Sam, no one could predict what a producer was looking for, but...well, with Caden busy on the film maybe Sam would start getting more of his bookings?

"They could still both lose out," Wendy said.

"True." Susan turned and looked over the rise of the manmade hill, the splash pad on the other side victim of the drought and serving as a skate ramp. Loud thwacks and cracks reverberated in the beams of the gazebo roof.

"And if it's bad—"

Susan turned back.

"You'd pull him?"

"I don't know. He directed all those kids films." Wendy shrugged, but there was doubt. "Karen says they'll do everything they can to protect the kid."

"And remember, sight and sound. Nothing will happen to him while you're watching."

Wendy nodded. "Right." She took another bite of the turnover. "Caden wanted to ask Sam if he could sleep over. I thought I'd ask you first, in case you didn't want that."

"Why wouldn't I want that?" In fact, she wanted nothing more than to send Sam over to spend the night with Caden, to eat fruit salad and fruit roll-ups and watch cartoons and sleep without sweating through the sheets or seeing dead guys in the window. Suddenly she was crying. Suddenly she was telling Wendy everything. About Ted and the murder and no air conditioning. The constant headaches, feeling so tired that getting through every day was a chore. Everything she'd been keeping from Mark.

Wendy handed her napkin after napkin and waited for Susan's breathing to even out. "You're staying with us tonight," Wendy said.

"No."

"Yes. You need at least one good night of sleep."

Susan shook her head back and forth, but they both knew she'd do it. "Thank you."

"It's completely self-serving. I need to get someone else hooked on my favorite show before season three starts."

Susan laughed, already feeling better. She couldn't wait to tell Sam—

Wendy was looking past her. Already getting to her feet.

Susan turned. Sam stood on the top of the hill. Helmet sideways. Blood running down his face.

Where was Caden?

The ER doctor lifted Sam's shirt and looked to Susan for explanation. Raised welts covered Sam's back, already purpling. "Sam? What happened?"

Sam picked at a loose thread on the sheet and shrugged. One of his curls was caught in the bandage above his left eye.

"Samuel McGrath, answer me." She heard her voice shaking.

"Why don't you let me have a minute?" the doctor suggested, guiding her to the door. Susan knew what that meant. He had to question Sam alone. Ask if Mommy hits him and whether she uses her hands or a hairbrush.

She stepped into the hall. Wendy was coming toward her. "How's Caden?"

"His arm's broken." Wendy swallowed and took a shuddering breath. "They're taking a CT scan to check…for swelling. In his brain."

Susan folded Wendy her in my arms. "Caden's going to be okay. They're both going to be okay."

The door opened behind them. "Mrs. McGrath?"

"What do you mean he landed on you?"

"He said I should lie on the ground. To jump over."

"But why?"

"He said I had to or he wouldn't be my friend anymore. And you like Miss Wendy, so—" Sam's voice broke and he leaned his head into her arm. Susan was back in the Ingalls Elementary Principal's Office again. For the rest of her life, she would regret listening to Mrs. Davidson's account and then informing Sam he was grounded then and there. She was anxious to show Mrs. Davidson that she was not one of those parents who made excuses for her child's behavior, even though she knew Cory and Keith had bullied dozens of younger children; it was only a matter of time before one of their victims struck preemptively. She never believed it would be Sam who would punch at words. He cried but didn't argue. Sam never argued. Never stood up for himself. He accepted his punishment and stayed in his room for an hour without complaining. He threw up quietly in his trashcan. He lay silently while the doctors explained they would keep him in the hospital overnight in case the concussion was more serious than they realized.

Fourteen years of accumulated classroom supplies left behind, purchased with her own money. Sometimes she wondered which colleague was using her board games or blackline masters, if they remembered who it belonged to and how they turned a blind eye when Sam was getting his head knocked against the bricks?

At the same time, she wanted to shake him. *Why can't you stand up for yourself?* Even with his mother twenty feet away, he still had to please everyone or risk being shunned. No matter where they went, it was the same. She thought he had learned. She'd *hoped*, and believed that a door scrape was exactly as he said.

She signed the release forms. Signed the financial form that stated she had no insurance and accepted responsibility for paying the bill. Sam's safety equipment was in a drawstring plastic bag. She carried it and the skateboard, leading the way out. Behind a half-drawn curtain, Wendy leaned over Caden's bed. Susan kept walking, pulling Sam by the hand and pretending not to see them.

"Can I talk to you?" Wendy was in the hall.

"Wait over there," Susan told Sam, and took a few steps in Wendy's direction. Wendy bridged the rest of the distance, twisting the hem of her T-shirt.

"Susan, I'm just gonna come out with it. Caden says Sam pushed him off the skateboard."

Susan heard herself laugh. "Really? Did he also tell you that he made Sam lie down so he could jump on him?"

"What? That doesn't make any sense."

"He said he wouldn't be Sam's friend unless Sam let him use him as a skateboard ramp."

Wendy's confusion softened into...was that pity? "Susan," she said, using that incredulous, condescending tone she had heard enough of for the rest of her life. They never used the opposite when they were proven wrong. She was done being the one to help others feel less bad.

"You must be so proud," Susan snapped, turning and walking away.

Susan stayed awake long after Sam cried himself to sleep, watching for any sign of internal bleeding. She made herself two cups of coffee to steel herself, certain he would wake up screaming in the night, but when next she opened her eyes Sam was pouring off-brand Cheerios into a bowl. He carried the bowl to the kitchen tap and turned on a thin stream of water.

"What are you doing, baby?" she asked.

"We're out of milk," he said, sitting down at the table.

Susan opened the bathroom window above the tub to release the steam from the shower, the rattling exhaust fan ineffective. Wrapping a towel around her midsection, she said, "Try it again, honey."

"Don't fucking touch me." His throat caught on the curse. He grimaced and shifted.

He hadn't complained, and he said it didn't hurt to breathe or move, but Susan would never take his word for it again. She again offered to take him to the doctor, knowing the cost of a walk-in at the Walgreens clinic could sink them.

"It's not my stomach," he said.

"Then what is it?"

"I don't like that word," he said.

"Remember what you know about this person."

Sam nodded and stared at the script. Susan uncapped the Ibuprofen. She would have to get more. "This boy feels threatened, right? Think of a time when you were scared that something bad was going to happen. Like, when you were really nervous before the Chuck-E-Cheese audition back home and you said you wanted to throw up?"

Sam's eyes drifted into the distance as he drudged up a thought. "When the police came."

"For Ricky?"

"No. When you yelled at Mr. Lepton."

The towel fell from her hands. How could he possibly remember that? He'd been two. Mark said he slept through the whole thing. "Honey, that was just—Mr. Lepton called them because he thought I was a robber."

"Why did he think that?"

"It was just a mistake he made. He was old. Sometimes old people misunderstand things."

"Why were you yelling at the policeman?"

She inhaled. "I wasn't. But I bet it *was* scary for you, not knowing what was happening. Use that. Can you imagine what it would feel like if you were scared like that every moment of the day?"

Sam stared at her, took a deep breath, and screamed, "Get your fucking hands off me!"

Susan picked up the next line. "Don't give me no lip now..."

"No! You killed her!"

She was about to congratulate him when the bathroom door burst inward, almost clipping Susan. She heard herself scream as Ted joined them in the small bathroom, face red, panting.

"What the hell's going on?" he demanded.

Susan clutched the towel to her chest with both hands. "Sam's rehearsing," she said.

He looked them both up and down through the swirling steam, then burst out laughing. Again he slapped his knee. "I should have known. I was fixing your air conditioner and heard the commotion." A beat passed. "Well, you sounded good, kid. Just like someone was trying to kill you."

Sam beamed. Ted tipped an imaginary hat and left.

Susan stayed frozen for a long moment. Her brain was late to process the implication that Ted was not only inside her apartment, but hadn't seemed the least bit...ashamed? When she looked around the doorframe into the living room, Ted was there, hunched over the air conditioner dismantled on a pillowcase on her floor. Ted looked up for her, as if it weren't unusual for him to be working and her wearing only a towel. "I'll have this fixed up for you in about five minutes."

She pulled Sam into the bedroom and locked the door.

"What's wrong, Mama?"

"Nothing, honey," she said, pulling the suitcases from inside the closet. There wasn't time to pack everything before the audition, but they could get most of it. "We'll finish rehearsing in the car. Get all your clothes. It's laundry day."

Amir was not used to getting calls from the tenants of his "many properties." Several times he interrupted her. "You call Ted! Don't bother me with this!" When Susan threatened to make a police report, he listened to her story.

"You asked him to fix the air conditioning for you," Amir said.

"He came into the bathroom when I was taking a shower."

"I don't know anything about this."

"We're not staying there anymore."

"Fine. Okay. You leave."

"I want our deposit back. And prorated rent." There was no way to pay for a new place without it.

"Aaaahh... I have to talk to Ted first."

"Then I'll go to the police," she said.

"Fine. You call police." He hung up on her.

It had been ten minutes since Sam had entered the casting office. She'd glimpsed two men inside before she could close the door, one whom she recognized from across twenty-five years and a bar on Sunset. Back when he was the nobody with a great smile, hungry for attention, talking up all the ladies and eyeing the boys beyond.

A scream. A crash. Her body moved toward the door on its own, but Susan's mind kicked in as her hand reached the knob. It was Sam's scream, she knew it in her marrow. But was it real or part of the act?

The door opened for her. Karen led Sam out. His face was bright red, breath hitching, like he'd been crying, hard. Tears clung to his chin.

"He did great. Really well." Karen said, hugging him. "We'll be in touch." She closed the door between them, leaving Susan to mop up the emotional aftermath.

"Are you all right, baby?" Susan asked, pressing his head to her hip.

Sam offered up a weak smile. "The director said I was convincing."

They spent two hours at the Laundromat. She quizzed him on math facts and spelling words as she folded, neatly arranging everything in the suitcase and working the options in her head. No money for a motel. Amir wasn't answering her calls, so she had to assume he wouldn't be refunding their money. That left urban camping, finding a secluded spot in a parking lot or in a cul-de-sac, but Susan knew she would never be able to sleep soundly. And she desperately needed to sleep.

Her cell phone rang. 310. Susan waited until she was outside to answer.

Karen's breathless voice filled her ear with details. They would need to go to the studio for paperwork and getting Sam measured for the costume. A table read was scheduled for the day after tomorrow, with production to start in two weeks. She finished with, "Your lives will never be the same. Get ready."

Susan switched off the phone and jammed it into her jeans pocket. She stayed out in the parking lot for another minute. Their lives were already not the same.

Susan was upright before waking, disoriented because the sofa had been shoved to block the front door and had her facing the kitchen instead of the hallway. The green BP light coming through the window revealed the outline of a tiny form wedged into the corner where the refrigerator met the wall, knees to his chest. Not moving.

She approached slowly. As she neared him, she saw that his eyes were open, but unblinking. Mouth slack. "Sammy?" she whispered, reaching for him. Her heart seized at the thousand possibilities that included internal bleeding, a sudden stroke from a tiny blood clot, he'd tried to tell her but—

"Get your fucking hands off me!" he growled in a voice that was too deep and old for a small boy. Suddenly he shot upward, knocking her back against the stove, fists and feet knocking her in the ear, in the eye.

She curled up into a protective ball. "Sam, stop it!"

The assault continued. Finally, she managed to get her fingers into his arm and pull him off balance, then pin him with her body. He kept bucking and snarling.

She slapped him.

His eyes cleared, transforming from murderous into the boy she knew. He looked around wildly. "Mama?"

"It's okay now. It was a bad dream."

"Mama, you're bleeding."

Susan fingered the wet spot beneath her nose. She pulled the cuff of her shirt over her fingers to staunch it. "It's okay. We're okay." She hugged him close and waited for Ted to bang on their door, but he never did. Only when she was tossing cutlery into a bankers box next to shoes and soup cans, did she notice that there was no laugh track from the other side of the wall at 3:00 AM.

She walked Sam to the car with her. Without Ricky's customers, the driveway was empty at this hour, silent except for the windy roar of a tractor trailer on the highway above. "Where are we going, Mom?" he asked, fastening the buckles on his car seat.

"To see Daddy," she said. She parked the car next to the stairs and popped the trunk that still contained their suitcases. She brought down the crate of school books, the four bankers boxes of games and toiletries and dish towels, all the things that had failed to make the apartment more livable. It had taken thirty minutes to gather everything. She thought of doing a final sweep. How would it feel to lay in her bed in Edmond and suddenly remember a sock or a pair of Sam's Spiderman underwear accidentally forgotten, to be secreted away in someone else's drawer?

"But Mama, I have to start the movie tomorrow."

"They rescheduled it," she said, starting the car again. "Miss Karen called while you were asleep." She repositioned her mirrors, catching Sam's skeptical look, but he didn't ask any more questions.

Amazing how large the highway seemed when clear. She merged onto the 134 with the glittering buildings of Burbank and Glendale, onto the 210 past the Colorado Street Bridge and its antique lamps. The last time she'd seen that bridge, it had been from the topside. Charlie and Eric wanted to watch the Rose Bowl fireworks from a "good place" and it didn't matter that it was under construction. She would never see it again.

The sun came up as they reached Joshua Tree, and Susan drove directly into its mass instead of pulling over and waiting for it to rise so that she could drive without stretching her neck up to shield her eyes with the visor. Her headache was in full throb despite the two coffees she'd bought when she pulled over for gas. She pulled the Folgers canister into her lap, opened the lid, and poured an inch of grounds into one of the empty cups. Then she put the rim to her lips and tapped in a mouthful of instant bitterness.

At the counter, she ordered two egg and cheese biscuits for Sam and a cup of hot water to use in the car. She stole a sip of Sam's orange juice to wash down the No Doz. "What's the first thing you're going to do when you get home?"

"Play with Daddy!" he crowed, too loud for the small space. "And then see if Jimmy wants to play Angry Birds."

She sighed. Jimmy. Two black eyes and Sam still lobbied for his attention, because he was a boy, because he was across the street. Maybe losing the house to foreclosure would have a silver lining after all.

Susan took Sam with her into the women's room because a highway fast food bathroom was no place for a seven year-old. Once they were done, she gave Sam her keys and the hot water cup and told him to strap himself in. Then she turned on her phone for the first time.

The voice mailbox was full. She dialed home.

"Where have you been?" Mark demanded. "Sam's agent has been calling—"

She cut him off. "We're coming home."

"What? Susan, he got the part."

"It doesn't matter."

"Doesn't matter? It's the whole reason you went out there!"

She shook her head, though he couldn't see it. "He's seven years old, Mark. It's not a part for a seven year-old."

"Susan, what happened?" He sounded exasperated. How could she answer? Wasn't it obvious? He needed a normal life with sleepovers and cutting through yards and Little League, a first kiss hidden, not on screen for the world to see.

"Can I explain when we get there?"

"What do you mean? Where are you?"

"Needles."

"Jesus, Susan." That scratching sound again. "Are you okay? Do you want me to come meet you?"

"No. We'll be home later tonight." She felt a different kind of pressure behind her eyes and wiped away her tears. "I made a mistake."

"What do you mean?"

"Coming out here. It was the wrong decision."

"Baby, what happened?"

"I'll tell you later, okay? I have to get going." She hung up the phone and wiped her eyes.

When she opened the driver's side door, Sam had moved his backpack up to the seat next to him and unpacked several books to read. He also had another surprise. "I made your coffee, Mama!" he said proudly, gesturing to the steaming cup in the console.

She saw the tractor trailer coming up on the left but moved into the lane anyway, too late to override. The blast of the truck's air horn jolted her reflexes free. She swerved to the side of the road and braked near the sign that said *Flagstaff –10 miles.*

"Are you okay, Mama?" Sam asked.

"I'm okay, buddy. Let me take a real quick nap and we'll be on our way again."

"Mama?" he asked.

"I'm right here," she breathed, giving in to darkness. "S'okay."

White sheets. A shadow standing at the window, backlit by streetlamps in the parking lot beyond.

"Sam?"

Mark turned from the window. Haggard. Grim. Susan tried to sit up, but found her wrists tied to the bedrails.

"Sam? Where's Sam?!"

"He's all right," Mark said, and the way he said it indicated it shouldn't be a foregone conclusion. "You're in Flagstaff."

The headaches. Something must have happened. From the look on Mark's face, it was bad. A brain tumor? A stroke? Her head was throbbing even now. It was nighttime outside—was it the same day they'd stopped on the road trip? But if Mark was here...

"Sam couldn't wake you up. He called me. I called 911."

Susan imagined the terror he'd felt getting that phone call, and Sam's having to make it. She hadn't been able to protect him from that. "What's wrong with me?" she asked. "Please tell me."

"You tell me, Susan!"

Mark always got mad when he was scared. She kept her voice calm. "I've had a headache for weeks now. I couldn't stay awake." And she'd left Sam alone. "Is it a tumor?" she whispered.

"Are you kidding, Susan? You still think you can bullshit me?!"

"I'm not bullshitting you."

Mark stared at her for a long moment, then gathered himself, inhaling with his eyes closed. "There's a treatment facility here in Flagstaff that can take you."

"Treatment facility? Mark, I'm not—"

"You think they didn't do blood tests, Susan?" he yelled. He ticked off his fingers. "Alcohol. Heroin. Cocaine."

It couldn't be. She hadn't. Not for years. "I am not using drugs. You think I would get into a car with our son—"

"You've done it before."

"But that was—*I got better.*"

He covered his face again, spoke from the depths of his palms. "The studio is offering to have you transferred to Malibu so that you can be closer to Sam. I haven't given them an answer yet."

The studio. "Mark, you can't let him do that role."

"I have to get back to Sam."

"Mark!" She yanked against the restraints, lifting her shoulders off the bed. "Those people—they're not going to protect him! I'll protect him."

The look he gave her was withering. She'd never seen that look before, not even when the police had come to their door in response to Mr. Lepton's complaint that a drunk woman was breaking in to his house, thinking it was her own.

"Mark? Mark!"

The blinds covering the window out to the hallway were open. Mark crossed to the nurse's station. Susan maneuvered her hand to reach for the call button that was within fingertips' reach and pushed it. Pushed it again, over and over. There had been a mistake. They would have to listen.

A nurse came to the door. "Yes?"

"Bring my husband back in, please. I need to talk to him." She was crying now.

Sam barreled his way into the room, almost knocking the nurse over as he flew onto Susan's bed.

"Mommy!" he sobbed, climbing onto the bed.

"It's okay, baby. There's been a mistake."

He held onto her neck despite the nurse pulling, and finally she had to dash out into the hall for reinforcements.

Sam tilted his head back to look into Susan's eyes. He smiled. "Do you want some coffee, Mama? I know how much you like your coffee."

Susan went cold staring into his eyes. Empty, as if he were sleepwalking. But he wasn't. He was awake and in control of his actions. Had always been.

She watched the smile contort into a convincing mask of grief as Mark and two nurses grabbed him from behind. "No! Mommy! I want my Mommy!"

Even Susan would admit it was a masterful performance.

Lin Shaye's film career began in her bedroom at age 4, thrillingly trying on all the clothes in her closets, and creating her own comedy/dramas with Sleepyhead, her hairless doll and assorted bears, dogs and monkeys. Not much has changed—she is still completely thrilled, and still gratefully interacting with some of the best "dolls and animals" in Hollywood. Lin is best known for the early Farrelly Brothers' comedies Kingpin *and* There's Something About Mary, *but her* IMDB *credits of well over 150 films speak loud and clear of her talent for horror, drama and other genres. Her first credited film was the drama* Hester Street, *where much to her mother's chagrin, she played "Whore". And now her most recent role of "Elise" in the successful horror films* Insidious *and* Insidious: Chapter 2 *has gratefully lead to her continuing that role in* Insidious: Chapter 3. *Her mother would be proud. This is Lin's first published story. And she is thrilled again.*

CAREFUL WHAT YOU WISH FOR

Lin Shaye

I COULDN'T WAIT. I had finally made the decision. Everything seemed perfect. It was a beautiful California day; sunny, cool, and full of promise for just about anything. I had even found the perfect free parking spot right behind the store. I was ready. As silly as it seemed, as I jumped out of the car and walked into the back door of the shop I could feel my heart pounding with resolve. I had finally gotten up the nerve to do it, and have it in my life.

You see, the world seemed so full of chaos to me, that I realized I had been clinging to the things I already knew, and the people I already liked, which were not very many. Sometimes I felt like my head was going to explode with all the buttons, beeps, frigid florescent lights, LED screens, ear buds, noise and what felt like a constant hum of chaos. I knew everything was supposed to create more ease, order and information, but all it felt like to me most of the time was clattering nonsense, an indiscernible and constant blabbering sound that made my mind hurt and whatever intellect I had, freeze.

But the time had come! I was going to "take the leap!" At first when I walked into the shop I didn't see anyone. Then, quite suddenly, a head popped up from behind the counter.

In my excitement, I immediately began to babble embarrassingly, "O-K! I am ready! Wow! Finally...really, really ready! And I know exactly what I want!" I felt like a little bit like a dork, but couldn't help my own childish enthusiasm.

But the girl behind the counter, with the pierced nose and lip, wasn't listening and apparently couldn't care less. She immediately and abruptly cut me off as she pushed her way over the counter and began showing off her new tattoo—a knife gashing through a girl's angelic face that was freshly etched on her left shoulder, the gushing blood outlined in green dripping all the way around to the underside of her fleshy arm, wrapping around her wrist, finally ending in a big red puddle also outlined in green on the top of her veiny hand. Then, to make matters worse, she suddenly and unexpectedly grabbed me by the wrist with that same hand.

"Cool awesome right? It's Nancygirl," she seemed to snarl, her cracked lips curled up into her version of a smile.

I didn't know what she was talking about. I managed to pull my wrist out of her grasp, which surprisingly took some effort. What the hell was that??!! My wrist hurt.

Before I could get in one other word, she blurted out that her name was Nancy...but I should call her "Nancygirl" like her tattoo, because that was what her dead father used to call her.

Fine. I couldn't give a shit about her dead father, or *what* her name was. I just wanted her to shut up and get me what I had come there for. But "Nancygirl" was undeniable...an asshole of sorts, and probably would love that I thought so.

I was finally able to squeeze out why I was there and what I wanted. "Awwww…" She said. "We only have one left and looking at that face of yours I'm not sure you deserve it."

Surprisingly, my joy turned to wanting to smack her with the hand attached to my still-aching wrist. I did not think she was funny at all. Having finally worked up my courage to even be there, I now almost desperately wanted this "last one" and was actually afraid she would withhold it from me if I didn't kiss her ass. So I did. A big smile crossed my face as the words "awesome" and "fantastic" came floating out of my mouth. I even called her "dude" as I told her how "cool her tattoo was." I am a whore.

In this very short time, I had grown to mildly despise this girl. My excitement had completely turned into irritation. Being ignored is a real button of mine, and she was completely ignoring me…it was all about her and her freaking tattoo. All I wanted was to get what I came for, and get the hell out of there. So every little thing she did annoyed me even more. Her breath was acrid, and she was one of those people who had no sense of personal space and got way too close to you when she talked, so the smell seemed to wash over you and stay on you even after she walked away. And to make it even worse, she kept tapping her non-existent bitten-to-the-quick nails on the dirty scanner screen, leaving it even dirtier. She also had this endless string of saliva that seemed to suspend in midair when she opened her mouth, which was smeared with day-old too-red lipstick and had crumbs from some shitty sandwich she had just eaten embedded in the cracks. The shop smelled funny too, kind of like her…kind of like…rotten meat…or, you should pardon the expression, like a pussy that needed washing…and not the kind with whiskers…well maybe…and old sweat…dirty feet…kind of like what I imaged something dying might smell like.

I kept trying to get her to listen to what I wanted and why I was there, but every time I opened my mouth to speak, she would start to laugh loudly about something that I had no idea about, especially because nothing funny had just happened or been said. And every time I tried to address her, even stooping to call her "Nancygirl," she would start that hyena laugh...

I don't know how long it took me to actually realize there wasn't anyone else in the shop except the two of us. I found that somewhat odd, because when I came in, I could have sworn there was another presence.

She finally addressed me, if you could call it that. "Hey! Look at me when I'm talkin' to ya...you fucking ugly pig!"

What??? That snapped me right out of my reverie as I thought sarcastically, *Is that how a sales person is supposed to talk to a customer*?

She followed it up with "You are some fucked up bitch...ugly cunt!"

Wowwwww... OK... Enough is beyond enough! All buttons on go! I gathered myself together, heart pounding way too fast, and much to my own surprise spewed, "Who the fuck are *you* talking to me like that, you stupid whore?"

I found myself getting into her face with mine only to be met with the stench of that rancid breath. The air around me started to seem even thicker, like someone had flipped a switch and cut it off all together. Suddenly, mingling with the already putrid odor, it smelled like someone was cooking that rancid meat... what the hell? Jesus, ok I felt my breathing become shallow... Suddenly, I felt like I was going to throw up. A thought flashed across my racing mind; I had waited this long to get this, but I better get the hell out of here now before I did something I didn't really want to do. I would just have to wait a little longer.

Suddenly, as I blurted out "fuck you," and was about to turn and leave, she bolted in front of me and blocked my way with her big sweaty breasts. Her chest was heaving, and with each of her rasping smelly breaths, I thought she was going to knock me over

"Where ya goin' skank??? We're just gettin' started."

Suddenly she pulled from its box the coveted iPhone I had been desperately hoping to buy. She held it up like a forbidden trophy.

"Here ya go honey...yeah...the last fuckin one...ya wan' it??? Huh? Do ya wan it???" And using its awesome little camera she started snapping picture after picture of me, as she kept pushing me back with her breasts, shoving me and shoving me.

"You wan' it right??? Awww you wan' it hard don'cha. Up yer ass or up your pussy!?? Poor little fuckhead?!!" Click...click...click...click...

"Hey we can document the whole thing, bitch...put it on YouTube...be a star..."

Something snapped inside and I was fucking going to win. In some bizarre last ditch effort I found myself grabbing for the phone and trying to pull it from her hands. She bit me. I slapped her and grabbed at her face. I bellowed like an animal and yanked her filthy hair. If I could just get the phone and run...

But she had the element of surprise on her side. She had caught me so off guard that I didn't even see her pull something heavy out from behind the counter, or see it come crashing down on my head.

When I came to, I sat frozen for a moment...what just happened? The events of, I wasn't even sure how long, started spinning in my brain; Nancygirl, the stink of bad breath, the stench of rancid meat, suddenly the world going black...

My head was killing me. I felt something wet and sticky trickling down my face. Something seemed to be oozing from my eye; it stung and my vision was blurred no matter how hard I blinked...must be blood...did I cut myself? I tried to move my hand to my cheek to check, but it wouldn't budge even though my brain was telling it to. Then I slowly realized something; I was sitting, or rather propped upright, in the driver's seat of my own car.

As I bent my throbbing head slowly forward, I saw with horror why my hands weren't working: I was wrapped up like a bloody burrito in a filthy sheet, both arms plastered against my side, legs twisted in a painful position, all held tightly by the sheet, and the entire filthy "casing" of cotton wrapped over and over in yards of black electrician's tape. It was painful to swallow and I realized my mouth was also held shut by the same black tape. Everything hurt. Panic set in which made it even worse. All my muscles started struggling to free me, but were held mercilessly inert by the sheet and the tape. I was too confused and sore to keep struggling. And it seemed like all my blood and will had been drained out of me...

Then...what was that? I became aware that I was sitting on something, something that seemed to be vibrating with some kind of muffled sound or buzzing. And my car was running. What the hell? What was happening? I squirmed until I was able to dislodge what was under me. Whatever it was fell on the floor. And suddenly I realized—It was my coveted new iPhone... with a little note attached: "HERE YA GO BITCH! ENJOY-LOVE NANCYGIRL."

And then I noticed the infamous iPhone camera roll. Magically flipping away, from picture to picture that Miss Nancygirl-fuckhead had taken in the store, accompanied by some unfamiliar and crazed music. She had apparently documented everything that had happened to me just as she had promised, including my falling to the floor unconscious, pissing my pants, and then her rolling me onto this big dirty sheet she had laid out on the floor, stained with god knows what. She must have rolled me over and over in it until I could no longer move or have use of my arms or legs and then—then—I saw the "presence" I must have been feeling when I entered the store—a clear picture of a big slobbering bull of a guy who I certainly did not remember, wrapping me and the sheet over and over in black electricians tape. Around and around he went, so that I could no longer move at all.

I have to admit, I was transfixed by the photos. There were several other people in them as well standing around me in a semicircle, kind of a parade from hell. Like a bad version of Cirque de Soleil or Mardi Gras, but no one was wearing masks. Just horrible and disfigured faces, scared, wrinkled, with garish makeup. Men, women...there seemed to be a pack of them standing over me. I think there was even a toddler.

I must have blacked out again. And once again, I didn't know for how long...for minutes? Hours? Days? I could barely open one eye. My limbs now felt totally frozen. I was even more confused. I was no longer propped up in the driver's seat. Now I was lying down somewhere, and it was completely black. Everything was numb. I still felt the vibration of the running car, only this time it seemed like it was in motion. It rocked mercilessly and I kept hitting my throbbing head against a wall or something. Within the blackness, the air seemed even thicker, and there was less of it. And now there was that all too familiar smell...rotten meat. I found myself gagging against the black tape that painfully held my mouth shut.

I WAS IN THE TRUNK OF MY CAR! And yes, the car was moving.

I broke out into an uncontrollable sweat drenching myself and the filthy sheet, and the nausea completely overtook me. Oh god...What was happening? Please let this be a dream! Someone...please!!! I tried to scream but nothing came out and it just made the gagging worse. I think I did puke, as something vile stayed in my mouth making it impossible to swallow. Suddenly I realized all I could hear, besides the rumbling engine and the pounding of my own heart, was my brand new iPhone. It must have still been on the floor in the front seat of the car where I had last seen it.

And the GPS...or that voice...that robotic voice of Siri... saying in that special tone of hers, "Turn right 100 feet...go straight...you have reached your destination. Welcome to the Mojave Desert—Death Valley."

Doug Molitor has 200 produced TV credits, on everything from sitcom (You Can't Take It With You, Sledge Hammer), *sketch comedy* (Lohman & Barkley), *sci-fi* (Sliders), *crime drama* (F/X), *action* (Adventure, Inc.), *fantasy* (Young Hercules), *western* (Lucky Luke) *and animation* (Penguins, X-Men, Sabrina, Carmen Sandiego, Beetlejuice, Happily Ever After, Sinbad, Captain Planet, Teenage Mutant Ninja Turtles, The Wizard of Oz.) *His comic novel* Memoirs of a Time Traveler *has a blurb by comedy legend Larry Gelbart. Doug wrote script and lyrics for the Hillary-Obama duet* Anything You Can Do, I Can Do Better *which has 2.4 million views on YouTube. The following story is an excerpt from his novel* Full Moon Fever.

DOING THE LORD'S WORK

Doug Molitor

DRAKE APPROACHED HIS RENTED GUESTHOUSE. From ten yards away, he could hear the TV blaring, and see the image through the window. The screen showed a luxury high-rise in Westwood at night: Laurence Maher walked out of the building into the porte-cochere to enter his waiting limo—only to find a clutch of reporters waiting for him. Supered under Maher's beaming face was the news caption: JURY ACQUITS TELEVANGELIST LAURENCE MAHER.

The news had been playing this clip for the last twenty-four hours. Yesterday Drake had been angry about it. But this was L.A., where juries had let O.J. and Baretta walk, so you couldn't actually call him shocked. He got out his key and listened to more of the broadcast as he fumbled at the lock.

Reporter Sydney Jackson got her mic in closer than the rest, and had the loudest voice: "Mr. Maher, what are your plans now?"

"Well, the Lord told me we must raise more money, which the church will offer as a reward for the real killer of my beloved Lola."

"You lying scumbag."

Drake frowned. That kind of crudity was unprofessional from a journalist. But as he opened the door, he realized the epithet had come not from the reporter on the scene, but from the bored vampire sprawled on his couch. He dropped his keys on the hall tree.

"Hey, Nikki. Talking back to the TV, huh? Not a good sign."

"That's what I used to tell *you*. But who else did I have to talk to all evening?" She glared at him for a moment, then returned to the charlatan on TV.

The newscast cut to archival footage from Maher's long-running series, *Doing the Lord's Work*. It looked like an infomercial slapped together in a Kansas warehouse, but Drake knew the show taped right down the hill, at the one-time Monogram Studio on Sunset.

There was Maher, smug, pink and plump, with helmet-hair and a silk suit no doubt priced at a couple grand; he still looked like a hundred dollars. He was fighting back glycerin tears as he addressed the camera:

"The Lord told me if my flock doesn't tithe as He has commanded, that He will have no choice but to call me home."

Maher's fleshy wife Lola leaked mascara as she wailed to the heavens about God's fatwa on her husband. "Please, Lord, give us another chance! We need our shepherd's guidance! And folks, we need your donations!"

It was an appalling spectacle, and Drake had nothing but contempt for the way these two grifters had sheared their flock over the decades. But poor Lola hadn't deserved to have her throat slashed, and there was no doubt in Drake's mind that it was her dear hubby Laurence Maher who had sent her, butchered, to her Maker.

The TV then cut to B-roll of the blood-drenched walkway where Lola's body had been found, and then Lola's funeral, with Laurence, looking just as convincing as a bereaved husband as he had as God's intended sacrifice, delivering her eulogy:

"And since the day we married, I never have, and never will, let another woman turn my head."

Drake shook his head in disgust. "The strongest evidence that God does not exist, is that Maher has not been struck by lightning," he muttered, turning from the TV.

"Hate that asshole," said Nikki, clicking it off. Before she was bitten, Nikki had never used profanity. Now she swore like a strip-club comic. Of course, she also drank blood, slept in a coffin and nearly killed two men recently. So she and Drake were both dealing with a lot of changes.

It was well past dark. Drake felt bad that he hadn't been there when she arose in a cloud of vapor from her coffin buried under his crawlspace. "Sorry, Nikki. I had to go all the way to Norwalk for some research."

"Not another script!"

"No, no. County records. Trying to find any property Zaar might own. He has to be buried somewhere."

"Well, anyway...you're back," she smiled. She slipped her arms around him, and brushed his lips with hers.

Drake's cell rang. He picked up. "Hello? Oh, hi. Uh... tonight?"

Nikki shook her head: No!

Drake knit his brows. "Really? Okay...I'll be right down." He hung up.

"Drake, we have plans!" she protested.

"That was Lisa."

"Oh, that makes me feel *much* better."

"She's at work. Down at the morgue."

"Is there any time of day when Lisa's not at work?"

"She's a bit of a workaholic. But I did promise to help her. She said she's got a case with some kind of black magic or cult angle. I think that means she found one of Zaar's victims."

"Why did I get engaged to a guy who writes horror scripts? Why couldn't you be an expert on tax law? I bet Lisa doesn't give a shit about white-collar crime."

"Well, it's a good thing she does need me! She's my pipeline into the LAPD." He caught Nikki's look. "Not like you're thinking. She can give us info that I can't find on the Internet."

Nikki fumed. "Tell Lisa I said she has the suckiest timing."

"She was at your funeral, so she won't believe me."

"I could make her believe in about three seconds."

Drake sat down beside her. "I know you're frustrated. And it's depressing, having to hide out like this. But nobody is going to accept that Peter Zaar rose from the grave and bit you. And if you somehow managed to convince the authorities that the undead are real, they'd try to destroy *you*. That's exactly why Zaar turned you. He never swaps blood with his victims. He doesn't want any competition. But you were special—your condition is his revenge on me."

"I wish you'd stop talking about my 'condition'—like he gave me the clap."

"Look, you're different. You're no killer. But Zaar is leaving a trail of corpses, and you won't be safe until I find and stake that son of a bitch."

Nikki got up and walked away. "Yeah, I know, I *know!* I have vampirism, not amnesia."

"That's the only reason I'm helping Lisa."

Nikki didn't answer.

He came over to her, and touched her shoulder. "Are you gonna be okay?"

Nikki shrugged it off and turned away. Drake gave up and grabbed his car keys.

Relenting, Nikki reached to touch his neck. "Oh, it's oka—"

Drake gasped and stiffened.

"What?" she asked.

Drake turned back to her. "No, nothing. It's just, your hand's cold. I wasn't ready."

She walked off in a sulk. "Go. Give my love to Lisa."

"Babe, you know that…"

"I need to grab a bite anyway."

"Nikki?"

"It's an expression! I promised you on a stack of Bibles—which I can't even touch—that I wouldn't kill anyone. Right? So, okay! I'm gonna fog my way into the blood locker at Hollywood Presbyterian, like we agreed. Now, go!"

She shooed him out the door.

"Be patient, okay?" he insisted. "I'll be back by midnight! It's just, she says this case is right up my alley."

☙

Wednesday. Two nights earlier. Drake had been waiting in an alley not far from the ER entrance of Good Samaritan Hospital. Nikki had misted herself inside to take some nourishment.

As Drake waited, he heard footsteps behind him, from the north end of the alley. Silhouetted in the orange glow of a sodium streetlamp came two tall, athletic youths whose assured stride and low-slung pants immediately put him on his guard. That and the fact that one had something in his jacket pocket pointed toward Drake.

"Hey, wassup," said the taller young man.

It wasn't a question, but the answer was Drake's heart rate. He did his best to keep cool as he glanced around for possible escape routes.

To Drake, the kids looked…what, Latino? No, that wasn't it. More like Armenian. At any rate, they weren't there just to chat.

"Just waiting for my friend," rasped Drake, who figured he'd sound marginally more badass with a hoarse voice. "He's a cop. I'm on a ride-along. He just brought in a perp."

"A 'perp'?" chuckled the shorter of the two tall guys.

"Don't laugh, the kid may not make it. Not to be disloyal, but my friend's what you call a rogue cop. Bad temper. Now the

ER's gotta save the poor bastard...if they can. He lost a lot of blood."

The shorter tall guy looked a bit worried.

The taller tall guy with his hand in his pocket looked at the cars parked up and down the street. "I don't see a black-and-white. You and your cop friend walk that guy here?"

"He's an undercover cop. That's his car."

Drake pointed at the likeliest candidate, but the young man never looked.

"You a cop too?"

Drake knew he'd never pull that off. "A writer." No reaction. "I write cop shows." Well, Dexter was kind of a cop. And he'd nearly sold that spec.

The taller tall guy grinned without a trace of joy. "Shit. Bet you make some bucks."

Drake couldn't help a laugh. That ended when the taller guy whipped out a little silver automatic and jammed it in Drake's nostril.

"Shut the fuck up and gimme your wallet."

He didn't have to give it to them. They took it from his pocket. Drake was backed up to the construction site fence, smelling gunpowder, wondering if he'd ever see anyplace besides this murky little street again. The taller mugger held up a ten and two singles, as his buddy turned the wallet inside out, looking for more but finding only coupons.

"Twelve dollars? Are you shittin' me?"

"That's it, I swear."

The taller one pushed the gun harder at Drake's nose. Drake was as far back as the chain-link would stretch.

"Who walks around with twelve bucks?" snarled the angry youth.

"If I knew I was gonna get mugged..."

"Shut up!"

The shorter tall guy also had his gun out now. "You better give us something, man!"

"Okay, look, I have a bank card…"

"Yeah, and you call it in lost the minute you walk away from here."

"I promise, I won't."

"No," said the taller guy, eyes going cold. "I promise you won't."

An instant later, the gun was gone. Nikki was holding it. And the other guy's. They blinked incredulously at their empty hands, like volunteers for a particularly good magic trick. Nikki tossed the guns far over the fence, into the blackness of the construction site. Then she folded her arms, impatient.

"Where the hell did you come from?" said the taller punk.

Drake had never been happier to see anyone in his life. But he didn't quite like the look in Nikki's eyes. "Uh, guys, if you want to live…run," he advised.

The taller youth's fist shot out at Drake. The next second, Drake was on the ground, mouth stinging, tasting his own blood.

"Watch his ass, Eddie."

Eddie, the paler, less-tall guy, stood over Drake, fists knotted, all but daring him to get up.

The taller one undid his belt. "Now, bitch, we're gonna run a train on you."

Nikki glanced at his crotch. "I doubt it. I think you're more like the little engine that couldn't."

"Shut up, bitch!" he growled, backhanding her. Nikki's head turned with the blow, but immediately snapped back, with a defiant smirk.

Drake was on his feet now but Nikki put up her palm—she didn't want help. Eddie didn't even notice Drake—he was too busy gawking at Nikki.

Now the taller punk punched her in the jaw, hard. This time her head barely turned.

Eddie's eyes widened. "Artie, let's go, man."

Artie tried a few right crosses mixed with a couple of left jabs. Nothing. A body blow, then an uppercut. Nikki yawned.

"All done?" she asked.

Artie looked at his aching fists. His bruised knuckles were bleeding, but there wasn't a mark on Nikki. She smiled sweetly.

"My turn!" She seized their belt buckles in her fists and lifted both men high in the air. Their feet kicked in wild panic as they vainly tore at her hands, trying to release her grip.

"Shit!" cried Eddie.

"Yeah. It's like a nightmare, isn't it?" grinned Nikki, exposing canines like daggers.

Eddie immediately pissed his pants. "Oh God, oh God, oh God...!"

"Nikki," began Drake.

"I got this, honey," she said. "Now, where were we?" Nikki rolled her eyes sideways as if trying to recall. Then she brightened. "Oh, yeah...you two asswipes were gonna rape me!" Her tone darkened. "Except, not."

Nikki lowered the struggling men, then threw them violently against the chain-link fence. They bounced off it back into her grip. Each impact forced a groan of pain as she slammed their bodies against it over and over again, alternating—first Artie, then Eddie, then Artie again.

Ba-ching, ba-ching! went the fence, over and over. It was like a vertical trampoline, only infinitely more entertaining to the bouncer than the bouncees.

"No fun having someone slam you around, is it?" she said through gritted fangs.

A dozen more bounces and the punks' grunts got weaker, but Nikki was just warming up.

Ba-ching, ba-ching!

"Babe...you promised."

"I know," she said, giving Artie an extra bounce out of turn, just to mix it up.

Ba-ching!

"This is not you," Drake told her. "Remember who you are. You're not an avenger. You're a teacher."

"And right now two punks need to learn a lesson."

"I'm sure they have. Right, boys?"

After another rebound, she caught them. They sagged in her grip.

Eddie was whimpering in terror. "Let us go, please!"

"C'mon, babe, they've had enough."

"I think maybe Eddie has." She lifted Eddie up by his belt. "Congratulations. You've just completed Rape Diversion 101. With a pissing grade. You be good, now."

Then she cast Eddie aside. He sailed ten feet backwards through the air, caromed off the alley wall with a loud grunt and landed in a pile of trash bags. He scrambled to his feet and fled. Drake had never seen anyone limp that fast in his life.

Nikki still held Artie. She took him by his collar and pulled him in nose-to-nose. He glared back at her. "But I have a feeling Artie, here, still needs some attitude adjustment."

Suddenly, Artie pulled a switchblade knife and clicked it open. He plunged it into her right breast. No blood came out. Artie gasped.

Nikki arched an eyebrow at Drake. "See what I mean?"

Nikki slid the knife out. Her wound closed up instantly. She clamped the blade in her teeth and bit it off. She spat the blade back at the stupefied Artie. "Artie, I really can't emphasize this enough..."

Nikki began marching him backwards while pimp-slapping him to and fro with her free hand. Drake winced as the loud smacks echoed down the alley, punctuating each word:

"Don't you ever, ever, *ever*, EVER, EVER, do...this...*again*."

By this time they were at the mouth of the alley, and Artie was missing two teeth. His cheeks were purple and swollen, and blood flowed down his face from every orifice. Nikki let him go with a final smack that propelled him through a wood-back bus bench and sprawled him in the gutter.

"I hope I've made my point."

Drake stared at the mugger's limp form. After a moment, Artie emitted an agonized moan. By some miracle, he was still alive.

They were now in full view of the hospital entrance. Nikki turned and sauntered back into the alley. "Coming, honey?"

Drake hurried after her—remembering to stop and scoop up his wallet, currency and cards that Eddie had dropped.

He left the oil-change coupon.

�

Drake arrived at the County Morgue. He had to question a couple of janitors before he found his way downstairs to where Detective Lisa Chen awaited him with her homicide victim.

Lisa rolled out the steel drawer. Lying there was the bruised, battered body of Artie: his dead eyes wide, his throat ripped open with two savage punctures.

"Shit!" exclaimed Drake.

Lisa looked at him, surprised. "You know him?"

"No, no. He just...looks like shit." Drake took a step back.

"You gonna be all right?" asked Lisa. "You look a little green."

Drake nodded. The old tile-floored morgue was filled with an odor of disinfectant, which could not quite vanquish the stench of death. However, the queasy feeling in Drake's stomach had little to do with the reek in the room. Nor with any overwhelming pity for the punk who had nearly blown his head off. It was that when Drake last saw this guy, he was alive—bloodied, the daylights beaten out of him, but definitely alive.

This murder had to be Peter Zaar's work, Drake told himself. It had to be. But if so, the choice of victim was one hell of a coincidence.

"Who was he?" asked Drake, as innocently as possible.

"Artie Melikian. Not a nice guy. We had a murder warrant out on him."

So I wouldn't have been his first, thought Drake. "Guess someone saved you some paperwork," he said aloud.

"He was murdered last night, right after he was released from Good Samaritan. But the night before, someone put him in that hospital. Really worked him over, but he refused to say who. And that was Wednesday, the same night as someone stole two units of blood from the Good Sam."

Drake nodded, noncommittal. He knew exactly who beat up Artie. And who'd stolen the blood, too. He'd taken her to a movie afterward.

"Anyway, Artie here was discharged Thursday, twenty-four hours after he was admitted...at exactly seven o'clock. He was found only a few yards from the ER at 7:05 PM. Coroner says he bled to death. In five minutes."

"Wait, you said *Wednesday* was the latest blood theft? Wasn't there any blood stolen last night? I mean, like from a blood bank?" said Drake. "At any other hospital?"

Lisa looked baffled. "Uh, no. No reports. Now, look at these punctures on his jugular."

Drake swallowed hard, and stepped in close again. "Ye-eah. Animal bites, looks like."

"Animal?" she repeated. "Come on, Mr. Horror Movie! How about *vampire* fangs?"

"What is this, a test?" said Drake slowly. "Sane people like me don't believe in vampires."

Lisa took on an overly patient tone, as she might with a senile grandparent. "You once told me there are cults of vampire wannabes. Goth kids who file their teeth and drink blood? You wrote a *Dexter* spec about them?" She rolled her fingers to indicate this was his cue to supply more detail.

"Oh! Right! Yeah, probably one of those did this."

Lisa slammed the drawer shut, and frowned at Drake, exasperated. "Offhand, you can't think of any likely suspects?"

"Just two," he thought.

Lisa stared at him.

Shit, did he say that out loud? "Just too…little to go on," he added quickly. "I really, uh, gotta get back home."

Drake made a beeline for the elevator, but Lisa was right on his heels.

"There's more. We had a second killing like this. A hooker at the Marina. You want to see her?"

"Definitely not!"

"She was found at 7:10 PM last night. Also freshly killed. Same fang marks. No way her killer could get across town in five minutes."

Not even as a bat, thought Drake.

"That means we now have two murderers using the identical M.O." said Lisa. She held up a manila evidence envelope. She flexed its sides out, so he could see inside was a long black hair. "The coroner found a couple of these on Artie Melikian. The lab's running the DNA."

Drake stared at the hair, sick. It was too long for Zaar…and the same midnight shade as Nikki's. Drake punched the elevator button. The door immediately opened.

"Look, I have to be up early," he said, pretending to check his watch. He actually hadn't worn one today.

"But Drake…" she began.

The elevator doors closed and Drake was gone.

✑

It was 2 AM. The waning moon had been up for an hour. Drake had been up half the night. Then he felt a cool tickle at the top of his spine and icy hands were over his eyes. He jumped a foot.

"Jesus!"

"Guess again."

He turned to face her. "Nikki, please don't do that."

"Did I scare you, Drake? Hmm, let's see if I can really make your heart race." Seductively she slid her arms around him.

"Yeah. Just…let me get my breath."

"Whoa, I really did scare you," she said, her ear to his chest. She looked at him quizzically.

"It's just, when you mist in behind me like that, without warn—"

"Boy, there's no pleasing you. I came in as a mist 'cause you said the bat was too conspicuous. Hey, I can do a wolf. You want to see?" She put her hands out, ready to drop down on all fours.

"No, no, that's fine!"

Nikki straightened. "Something bothering you?"

"I've been home for hours. I was worried when I didn't find you here."

"I told you I was going out. I have breakfast at Hollywood Presbyterian every night now. That place is a pushover. Delicious plasma." She licked her lips. "And on the way home, I stopped down on Hollywood Boulevard. Check it out."

She opened the front door. A little black dress was hung on the knob. She shook it out, and held it up in front of her. "Like it?"

Drake nodded, wordless.

"Of course, I had to walk it home, and leave it outside—you were right, I couldn't mist it in through the door. But here it is. What do you think?"

"So you had...breakfast...at Hollywood Presbyterian tonight? And last night?"

"Yeah. Why do you keep asking about that?"

"You didn't go back to the Good Sam last night...and run into our mugger, Artie?"

"No, I told you. What's this about?"

"He's dead."

"No shit?"

"Last night, same place we saw him. Holes in his jugular. Drained of blood."

Nikki waited a moment. "Well, it must have been Zaar."

"Impossible. He was killing a hooker in Marina del Rey then."

"What are you saying?"

"That there were two vampire killings last night. At the same time."

Nikki took a second to process that. "So, you think I killed the mugger?"

"I saw you toss him through a bus bench. I got the idea you disliked him."

"Yeah, well, I may get a little violent since I crossed over, but I'm not a liar. Is that what you think?"

"I don't know what to think."

Nikki balled up her little black dress and threw it in the sink. "You know what, let's forget going out. You don't want to be seen with a bloodsucking monster."

"Nikki, I didn't say that."

"You didn't have to. Excuse me, I'm gonna turn in early." Nikki turned away.

Were those tears? He tried to take her arm but his fingers closed on mist that descended into the floor heater grate.

"Nikki, wait. Nikki!"

Drake cursed under his breath. He dragged out his toolbox, grabbed the crowbar, jammed it between the boards and started prying up the section of floor he had spent an entire afternoon sanding and sealing. It took some loud wrenching of nails—the tenant in the front house would undoubtedly hear, but screw her—and finally he got the boards up, exposing Nikki's polished oak coffin.

Drake knocked on the lid. "Nikki?"

No answer.

He knocked harder. "Nikki, come on. Open up."

From inside, he heard her muffled voice. "*Go. Away.*"

"I want to talk to you."

"*Well, I don't want to talk to you.*"

He thought he heard her sniffle. He felt like a slug. "Nikki, please, I'm sorry. I...I haven't slept in days. I don't know what the hell to believe anymore. If you say you didn't do it…then you didn't. Look, let's just forget it and go out."

"Why don't you go out with Lisa? She won't bite you! She's a real, live woman. With warm hands."

"I don't want a real live woman, I want you!"

"Go to hell, you son of a bitch!"

"Nikki, this is stupid. I love you." He banged on the lid with his fist. "Will you please open up?"

Nothing.

Drake tried to lift the lid, but it was clamped shut. Losing patience, he forced the crowbar into the crack and started to pry the lid up. Suddenly Nikki opened the lid, grabbed the bar out of his hands and slammed the lid. There was a muffled squeal of metal. Then she opened the lid again, wide enough to poke out one end of the tool. He took hold and pulled it out. She had bent his steel crowbar double. It was ruined. He threw it down on the floor, fuming.

"Okay, fine!"

Drake didn't bother to put the floorboards back. He snatched his keys and stormed out, slamming the door.

Drake must have driven around the block fifteen times. The first few he did at fifty miles an hour, but as he calmed down, he slowed down. Finally, he pulled to a halt at the base of the driveway. He didn't want to admit he was watching his own home, to see if Nikki came out. That would be stalkerish and creepy. But not as creepy as seeing her issue forth, in animal or gaseous form, headed off to commit another homicide. Fortunately, as the eastern horizon brightened, nothing emerged from the cottage.

He reran their argument in his head. Every time he went through it, he was more convinced he wasn't the least bit sure of anything…except that he had really hurt her feelings. When you love someone, you're supposed to trust them. Right?

At dawn, he pulled back up the drive, locked his car, and went inside.

He plopped his keys on the hall tree. He was bone-weary and his head was killing him. He looked over at the pried-up floorboards. She'd laid them back down and covered them with the rug. He kicked the rug aside, lifted up the boards and peered in at Nikki's coffin.

He saw a handwritten Post-It on the lid:

DO NOT DISTURB.

She had underlined it three times.

Drake winced guiltily, and laid the floorboards back down. He went to his coffee maker, which he realized he'd left on all night. He sniffed the contents, and estimated his stomach lining would survive at least one cup of this. At least he'd have all day to compose a great apology.

He found the remote and clicked on the early morning newscast, as he tried to pour in enough milk to turn the coffee a shade lighter than tar.

The image was a jiggly telephoto shot from a helicopter and judging from the long morning shadows, Drake figured this was live. His assumption was borne out a second later, as the caption appeared: LIVE—LAURENCE MAHER MURDER SCENE.

The transport team was rolling out a cadaver pouch. Sydney Jackson was narrating the scene: "Even stranger is the story of two witnesses who claim to have witnessed Laurence Maher's murder last night."

The newscast cut to B-roll: Two yups in their late twenties, standing in front of their building, badly shook-up.

Then came a close-up of the woman. The caption read: JILL STEIN—WITNESS.

She was wiping away tears. "We were watching from Jerry's apartment, across the street. I know, lock me up, I'm a voyeur. But I saw them in the window. She opened her mouth and bit him on the throat!"

There was a cut to a man identified as JERRY FLAVIN—NEIGHBOR. He looked like he had glimpsed the abyss. "She had him off the floor, shaking him like a pit bull with a rat. Then she clamped her hand on his head and just...twisted it around backwards. Like she was opening a Coke bottle. I..."

Words failed him.

"What'd she look like?" asked Sydney, off-camera.

"Uh...black hair, white dress, nice bod...fact is, she was pretty hot."

Now Sydney was speaking to the camera: "This morning, the LAPD released this artist's conception of the suspect."

The next shot on the TV was of a police sketch that could not have looked more like Nikki.

Drake's coffee mug shattered on the floorboards.

When asked to provide a short bio for this book, Ron Zwang responded: "I've been asked to write my biography and keep it to 100 words. As I think back through my life, career and all my many adventures it seems virtually impossible to sum it all up with a mere 100 words. Where would I even start? Personally? Professionally? Politically? My humanitarian work? Even as I gather my thoughts to write this bio, I can feel a resentment building. Is the publisher telling me that my life is worth no more than 100 words? Well if that's what they want—without doubt the highlight of my professional life came when Steven Spie—sorry. I'm over 100 words." The highlight of Ron Zwang's career is you reading this bio.

THE DEVIL'S FRIENDS

Ron Zwang

NOBODY LIKED FRED PINE. If he had any self-awareness he wouldn't like Fred Pine either.

To say that his films were grade "Z" would be an insult to Ed Wood. Hell. It would be an insult to film. If Pine had just spent a little more time, effort and tender loving care on them the films would be awful.

He tried his best. That was the scary part. One look at his clothes and you could tell what he had for lunch the last three weeks. Far too much starch. In his food—not his clothes. A man of slender build, he'd never be as old as he appeared. His hair looked as if it was trying to remember the last time it was washed. His wife had left him. But that was years ago. Pine figured she was jealous of him and his career. He recalled the last words he said to her as she hurried out the door: "If you think making films is so easy you try it." She did. The Ex was now one of the most successful TV directors at Paramount.

"Must have slept her way to the top," he would mutter. But he was amazed she got as far as she did for a woman who hated sex. But then again, she was doing TV. Not features.

But introspection wasn't his long suit. His long suit was plaid—and two sizes two big. Room to grow into as mother used to say.

He wore loud clothes hoping to be noticed. He was noticed, but not in the way he wanted.

In his daily ritual Pine sprinted to his mailbox hoping that his spirits would be lifted by fan mail. The closest he'd gotten was a final notice from the electric company. He wondered if anyone actually read his last letter to them explaining that he was an artist.

Pine made bitterness into an art form. Unfortunately it was the only art form he excelled at.

The Universal lot had two commissaries. One where the crews and day players ate—trays, plastic forks, paper napkins and a one-sheet of *More American Graffiti*.

Next door, 20 feet away, was the "other" commissary. This one was more Musso's than Canter's. They actually laundered the tablecloths not just wiped them down. On the walls were signed stills of Hitchcock posed with *The Birds* and Bogart from a film nobody was able to name.

It was a different time back then. We called it the '70s. So did everyone else.

Five of the best directors of the day were gathered at their table when Fred Pine walked in.

Don Siegel, looking snazzy in his ascot, spotted him first. "Look who broke away from the tram tour. Would it be rude if we all hid under the table before he sees us?"

"Rude to whom?" Sam Peckinpah slyly mumbled between bites of his Cobb salad. In contrast to Siegel, Peckinpah wore a bandana and had his mirrored shades dangling from a canasta chain. He was downing white wine in record amounts in order to kick his vodka problem.

John Frankenheimer dropped the bad news. "Too late, he spotted us."

Pine approached our table. It was a safe bet he left a trail of sweat behind him. He was beyond containing himself. "Hey, Gang. I wanted to invite my best buds to the premiere of my new motion picture event—"

"I guess we're off the hook," Bob Aldrich said out of the side of his mouth but not that softly. As usual Aldrich's tie was dangling around his neck giving the word "tie" an irony no one dared speak.

Pine gestured with his hand to simulate a marquee—"*The Rampaging Revenge of the Rampaging Robotic Robots—2.* Catchy don't you think?"

"So's influenza," Peckinpah said with a mouth full of food.

Pine couldn't be stopped. "You know my friend Grady Sutton? Well I'm bringing my 16-millimeter projector over to his place. We're showing it there 'cause he's got more chairs. Oh. It's BYOB."

Peckinpah was enjoying this too much. "Yeah, Don. Didn't you hold the world premiere for *Dirty Harry* at Grady's?"

Siegel was right there: "No I'm sure it was for *The Wild Bunch.* The opening of *Dirty Harry* was at Pinky Lee's. The after party was at Grady's."

Aldrich wouldn't be left out of the fun. "I can still taste those potato chips. What was that flavor?"

"Stale," Peckinpah drolly added. He was on a roll. "The party was going fine till Clint ate all the saltines."

Siegel: "You know he gets mean when he doesn't get his saltines."

Aldrich: "Really? How mean does he get?"

Siegel: "You don't want to know."

Aldrich: "Yes I do or I wouldn't have asked."

Peckinpah: "Didn't Grady Sutton test for the part of Harry Callahan?"

Siegel: "Yeah. But we went with Clint."

Pine dived in: "I love Grady like a step-brother but I think Eastwood was a better choice."

Siegel: "Thanks, Fred. I'm relieved you think I made the right decision."

Frankenheimer tried to repress his laughter. He was jerking around as if he were one of Jerry's kids. Or even Jerry. He was practically eating his cloth napkin to keep his laughter in.

This didn't go unnoticed by Peckinpah. He deadpanned directly to Frankenheimer, "Tell me John, who would you have gone with for Dirty Harry—Grady Sutton or Clint Eastwood?"

Frankenheimer leaped from the table heading anywhere that wasn't with us. I'd never seen him move that fast. Hell. I'd never seen him move.

But Sam wasn't done with Pine. "Sorry about Ol' Frankenheimer but he has the bladder of a 9 year old girl. He's about as much fun as Arthur Hiller at an orgy. We were thinking of kicking him out of our little group because of it. What do you think, Pine?"

"John's a good guy. I can vouch for him. I say you should let him stay in."

"OK whatever you say. I was going to invite you to join our group but now we have no openings."

"But if his bladder is really that small—"

Mid-sentence Peckinpah pointed to the other side of the commissary. "Look, there's Robert Wise. Why don't you invite him to your gala?"

Pine ran off in the direction Peckinpah pointed.

Aldrich looked in that general direction. "I don't see Wise."

"Neither do I."

Pine was outside the commissary. He barely held himself up as he clutched onto some ridiculous steel sculpture that graced the walkway. Longingly, he peered through the window. He saw the five directors drinking and laughing. They were inside. He was out.

Pine slumped down in defeat. Defeat might be putting it too strongly. Let's say self-pity.

Every snub, rejection and insult thrown his way throughout his life were all playing endlessly in his head. It overwhelmed him. Anger built as Pine got redder and redder.

He pounded the side of his fist against the building's concrete wall. Hitting. It. Repeatedly. Relentlessly. Then silence. He stopped. Pine seemed surprised when he noticed his hand was bleeding. Then came the pain. But he had bigger concerns. He took another look at the joyous director's group. Pine exhaled with a fierce determination:

"I'd sell my soul to be one the big boys."

When you first saw Fred Pine's cramped apartment you couldn't imagine how it could be any less appealing. Then the smell hit you.

Dozens of rusted 16mm film cans were casually stacked against a beat-up Moviola that was last used by D.W. Griffith as a paperweight.

This was surrounded by cheaply made one-sheets of his past endeavors thumb tacked to the wall. He autographed them himself to add "extra value". They include such cinematic achievements as *The Good, The Bad and the Monster From Neptune's Moon*, and *Space Monsters From Outer Space*.

Pine's greatest success, actually his only success, was when he sold Warners the idea for *Pet Rock—The Movie*. Can you believe the crap they were buying in the '70s? What's next? Films based on board games?

Pine was industriously engaged in picking his nose when he turned and the Devil was just there—from nowhere.

The Devil slyly spoke. "So you want to sell your soul?"

Pine was a combination of stunned and startled. "You're the Devil!"

Satan let it sink in. Then spoke: "Yeah. Every time someone offers me their soul I have to follow up. It's the only downside to the gig."

"You must get some real losers."

Satan let that thought linger.

As with any pause in conversation, Pine used it for self-promo. "You know I've got a big meeting with Francis Ford Coppola coming up?"

The Devil looked skeptical.

Pine broke the silence. "Are you familiar with my movies?"

"We have a certain place where your films play round-the-clock."

Pine sported a large grin. "You do?"

"Of course. It's Hell."

Nervously, Pine threw out the odd question that didn't involve himself. "As The Devil, what exactly do you do?"

"Wars, starvation...the usual. I've caused the impossible to happen. How else could you explain Bachman-Turner Overdrive?"

"Are you responsible for all the nasty things that happen on earth?"

"Just some of them. Never underestimate mankind. For example—I put greed out there. It's people who ran it to the end zone."

Satan flashed Pine a sly smile. "My work can be more insidious. I invented disco. When I showed it to the boys downstairs—"

"Don't you mean upstairs?"

It took Pine a few seconds. Actually many seconds. Then the dime dropped.

Satan continued. "So when I showed it to the boys downstairs they said it would never catch on. 'People dancing to music played by machines with no human emotion?! Come on'. I got great odds on that one and cleaned up big."

Pine gathered up his balls and asked the big one. "What can I do to please you, master?"

"First—don't call me 'master'. Second—if you want to please me don't ever summon me again."

"So we're in business."

"Don't call us, we'll call you."

Pine turned away for a second to give Satan his business card but when he turned back the Devil was gone.

Something extremely unusual had happened. Pine had changed his clothes. His apartment was dimly lit. Its cheap, threadbare furniture had hastily been pushed to the walls. But the real eye-catcher was a misshapen pentagram drawn on the floor in chalk. Cheap candles that surrounded the pentagram gave off an eerie glow.

Pine sweated a lot even by his standards. He quickly knelt before the pentagram. In what Pine's idea of hallowed tones must sound like, he uttered—"I summon thee the power of darkness."

He cringed in anticipation.

Nothing.

"Oh, Lucifer come see how I've done your bidding."

Pine tensed. "Please."

He anxiously awaited Satan's arrival.

Again nothing.

Pine looked more puzzled than usual. Then it hit him—

"I'll sell my soul to the devil."

He noticed The Devil was seated casually in the easy chair.

"I thought I made myself clear—"

"Just wait here a second."

Pine hauled ass to the bedroom and quickly returned dressed in a glitzy tuxedo two sizes too big. Even with the glistening of his jacket, the soup stains still showed through. From just a glance at the tux it looked as if the moths had been eating better than Pine.

He sweated even more than earlier if humanly possible. "I brought you a virgin. You still like those, don't you?"

At that Pine wheeled out a young, attractive woman tied tightly to an odd wooden gurney. A leather bag enveloped her head. Her muffled screams exploded from the sack. Her limbs wildly contorted in a hopeless attempt to break free of the ropes. As she struggled the ropes burrowed into her already bleeding wrists.

"Sir. I give thou your virgin." With much gusto Pine pulled off the bag exposing her face.

The Devil stared at the poor woman tied to the gurney. Her mouth was duct taped. Satan was stunned.

"Let me get this straight. You go to get a virgin and you bring back Maggie Chambers—the porn star? I hope you kept your receipt."

"I think I have a way of getting her to do whatever you want."

"So do I. It's called asking her."

Pine was undaunted. "I'm going to do something you'll really love."

"Stop annoying me?"

"Even better. I will prove my loyalty to you and the dark side by performing a feat of black magic on this virgin..." Pine glanced at Maggie Chambers briefly. "...Or whatever."

Pine quickly slid the side wooden panels onto the gurney. They surrounded Ms. Chambers encasing her in a coffin size box. Her limbs and head extended out of pre-existing holes.

Pine continued "I couldn't find any books about black magic at the 7-11 but I think I found something just as good."

Pine wiped dust off the edges of the instruction booklet and quickly consulted it—"How To Saw A Woman In Half."

In a corny overly theatrical way, Pine displayed his saw. He gave it a reverberating slap to prove it was real. With total confidence, Pine proceeded to saw the center of the box. By far, this was the worst thing Maggie Chambers ever had in her. Her legs kicked frantically. Her head jerked wildly. Her arms futilely gyrated as they tried to break loose of her bonds.

Her muted screams of agony were accompanied by streams of blood flying in multiple directions. Suddenly the screams stopped. Her body stopped fighting but the rush of blood continued.

A blood stream hit Pine directly in the face—temporarily blinding him. He quickly mopped Maggie's blood from his eyes. Panicked, Pine manically pawed through the instructions trying to figure out what to do next.

Pine continued to saw all the way through the center of the box. He proudly separated the two halves and stepped between them to prove his magical prowess.

"If you think that's amazing—" woodenly, he read out loud from the instruction pamphlet. "Don't start your propellers just yet. There's even more! Here's the part where I put her back together!"

With a smile on his bloody face, he put the halves of the box back together. And with a "Ta-da" he opened the box and extended his hand to Maggie. Her hand didn't arrive.

Pine looked into the box and was both shocked and horrified. He assessed the situation. "Now I'll never get my deposit back on this tuxedo. Stupid bitch."

Pine looked around for the Devil's approval but he was gone.

He sulked in self-pity.

In the dead of night in blood-free clothes, Pine stood behind the open trunk of his beat up gold '69 Ford Fairlane. His ex-wife had given him the personalized license plates as she left. *LUZR*. He could never figure out what it spelled but having personalized plates gave him a feeling of class. Maybe she hadn't been so bad after all.

Beside him, wrapped in dry cleaning bags, were two sections of what was once Maggie Chambers. The top half sat adjacent to the bottom. Pine stood frozen in thought. Should he put the top half in first then the bottom half on top or the other way around? He stood there baffled. He had never done this before.

He took out a coin and flipped it. It landed with a dull quiet sound breaking the deafening silence for a second. He bent down in search of his answer—heads or tails. Pine couldn't see the coin in the dark. Dropping down to his knees he felt around in the dirt for the coin. He then searched frantically. He was more panicked about this than the dead body lying next to him.

Finally Pine got dejected and reluctantly rose to his feet. He picked up the top half of Maggie. Surprised by how heavy she was he was thrown off balance and landed on his ass. Hard.

Maggie landed on top of him. They were face to face. With haunted eyes she peered at him through the plastic. His eyes widened. A look of sheer terror lined his face. His mouth hung open as he tried to scream but nothing came out. Through a hole in the dry cleaning bag Maggie's blood leaked out of her left eye and landed in his mouth.

Pine finally let out a pent up scream that even Maggie could hear as he struggled to push her off of him. In his panic she landed back on top of him again. Her eyes seemed to be shouting out murderer as blood streamed from her nose. Pine slid out from under her wiping off sweat. At least he hoped it was sweat. He was afraid to look. Pine quickly scrambled up as poor Maggie landed tits first with a thud. Pine muttered in absolution.

"It's not my fault you didn't know how the trick worked."

Trying to compose himself he glanced down and realized he was drenched in her blood. He grumbled, "Great. My favorite shirt. Never trust women."

This time he braced himself better and put Maggie's top half into the trunk. Then he lifted the bottom half. Unexpectedly it was heavier than the top. He paused a few seconds at her crotch. "Na. Got to keep my mind on business."

He dumped bottom Maggie on top Maggie. "I hope I'm doing this right."

Pine felt relieved. Home free. Then he noticed he was drenched in blood.

"Better change my shirt. This might look suspicious." He started to walk away but quickly doubled back, closing the trunk. "Too many weirdoes around here."

Pine was driving along listening to KJAM's Morning Zoo DJ team—"Monkey Man & Jay."

Monkey Man's voice blared out from the car's shitty speaker. "—Boy, did you see those nipples on Farrah Fawcett. I'd sure like to wet her t-shirt."

"Yeah but you'd have to do it without wetting yourself first," sidekick Jay came back with, topping his boss.

A clown horn sounded from the radio. The DJs laughed but not as loudly as Pine. If you're thinking how could this shit pass as comedy—keep in mind this was the late '70s and Chevy Chase was the top comic of the time.

"How do you think Farrah got as big as she is?"

"She's not big. 'B' cup at best."

"So who's more your type then—Randy Mantooth?"

Pine was laughing. We've never seen him laugh before. We'll never see it again.

"No. I'm being serious here."

"You mean you were being funny before?"

"How do you think Farrah got as far as she did?"

"Isn't it obvious? She sold her soul to the devil."

Fun time was over as Pine listened intently.

"Which reminds me..." And Monkey Man started in on his rant. "Coming up tomorrow I'll challenge the devil yet again to a boxing match. If he's so tough why doesn't he meet me? This is the third day of my challenge and guess what? That punk was a no show. Why? Cause the Devil's a wuss..."

"This is Monkey Man & Jay signing off. Coming up next are Jenny and her boobs playing the latest hits."

Pine left a legacy of rubber behind as the Ford screamed into a U-turn. He had a crazed look as he drove 90. Neither hairpin turns nor the thumping of a dismembered body in his trunk slowed him down.

In KJAM's parking lot Monkey Man was calmly heading toward his destination. He looked about 60 but it was hard to tell with the fat ones. He could have been 12. His comb over was practically a work of art. It looked as if it took him an hour and a half to position everything just right. The problem was even at a rumor of a breeze the whole thing went to hell.

Pine screeched into the lot, leapt out and scurried up to him. "Are you Monkey Man?"

The tightening on the man's face was a tacit admission. Monkey Man quickened his pace towards his car. He talked without a hint of slowing down. "Are you one of my moron fans? Listen, pal. I'm off the clock. Why don't you go bother your dick."

"You said some very bad things about a friend of mine today."

Monkey Man hit the brakes. "Today I busted balls on the Pope, Queen Elizabeth and Benjamin Franklin? Which one is your friend?"

"The Devil."

"So you and the Devil are friends? Then why don't you go to his place?"

"Huh?"

"Go to hell."

Monkey Man turned and continued towards his car.

Pine pulled a piano wire from his pocket. Quietly he approached Monkey Man from behind and instantly wrapped the piano wire around the DJ's neck and pulled it with all he had. Monkey Man instinctively caught the space between the piano wire and his neck.

Pine knew he was lucky that he saved a piano string from a few days earlier...

Pine stood in the parking lot of Zoetrope studios. There was a reason he looked as if he had been waiting for hours. He had been.

Then the moment arrived. The moment he had been practicing for all week. Francis Ford Coppola was heading to his car.

Pine jumped into action flagging FFC down.

"Frank!" Pine decided to call him Frank because Francis sounded too faggy.

The second time Pine yelled Frank, Coppola swung around. By that time Pine was in front of him.

"Hi. I'm Fred Pine. We're in the same business."

"You make wine?"

At first Pine was thrown off his game. But he plunged ahead.

"No. I create cinema just like you do. I'm working on my newest creation."

Pine gestured with his hand to simulate a marquee. "*Globe of the Chimps.*"

Coppola didn't know what to make of this. "Isn't that like *Planet of the Apes*?"

Pine couldn't believe Coppola didn't get it. He looked at him as if his belt size and IQ were the same. Still Pine continued with his pitch. "No. This is with chimps. A chimp lands on earth and discovers it's run by humans. The humans can talk and everything!"

Dejected from his pitch meeting, Pine headed towards the hole in the fence near Zoetrope's back gate as he tried to make sense of it all.

"How could Coppola not get it? He said he wanted to make films about the 'human condition'. What's more human than chimps? And he's supposed to be a visionary.

"I'm sure after years of working together Frank and I will laugh about this. I just know he'll make a fine assistant director. But still this can't go unpunished."

Pine snuck into Zoetrope's recording studio. After much effort he pulled out a piano string from their baby grand and shoved it into his pocket.

"That should teach him," Pine proclaimed with his own brand of smugness.

But Pine had current events to worry about. For some reason Monkey Man didn't want to die. Still behind him, Pine yanked the piano wire tighter around the DJ's neck but he didn't go down. Pine then tried to lift Monkey Man off the ground. Monkey Man had gravity on his side.

Pine never thought this would be so hard.

Monkey Man's life's trickled away as the piano wire cut into his neck. He was turning colors Pine had never seen before. What was taking so long? Pine hoped Monkey Man didn't yell for help. Then remembered he already severed his voice box.

Monkey Man's fingers were being sliced away as his blood flowed freely. Finally his life gave out. Blood drained from his face but he made up for it everywhere else.

Pine took a quick inventory of what was what. He saw he was drenched in Monkey Man's blood. Pine was truly horrified.

"Damn. My second favorite shirt." Out of breath and with all the strength he could muster, Pine dragged Monkey Man toward his car. He tried to give himself encouragement as he performed this exhaustive job.

"What else can I do but drag the body to the car?"

Pine blanked for a second. "Oh. I guess I could have brought the car to the body."

By that point he had reached his vehicle. As he opened the trunk there lay Maggie Chambers—some assembly required. Pine looked into the trunk and at the dead weight of Monkey Man's girth.

"Next car I gotta get a bigger trunk."

Pine was stumped for what to do next. "Think Fred. Think. Use your creativity. I know—Monkey Man strangled himself with piano wire. Could happen."

Pine was visibly pleased with his fine plan. He frantically went through Monkey Man's pockets. No paper to write on.

"What kind of retard doesn't have paper on them?"

Pine searched his own pockets—no paper. Almost by providence a tattered receipt blew by.

"Thank God—eh...I mean Hail Satan."

Pine bent to retrieve it as it blew out of his reach.

He reached for the paper again. And again it was blown further away. Chasing after the paper, Pine tripped over Monkey Man's body and landed in the dirt.

"What have I done to deserve this?"

As the paper landed, Pine did a full body dive and belly flopped on top of it. "You thought you could out smart me, didn't you? Well who's the smart one now?"

As Pine started to compose the suicide note on the back of the receipt he became immediately stuck. "Damn. Monkey Man can't be his real name…can it?" Pine shrugged.

"I'm sure if I just sign it Monkey Man no one will notice."

He stared at the suicide note.

Please forgive me for strangling myself and dragging myself 20 feet way. The forgiving is for the strangling part not the dragging part. It's just that as a radio DJ the music just isn't as good as it used to be and how can I live in a world like that?

All the best,
Monkey Man

Pine looked at the note with pride of authorship. "Problem solved. But it's a shame I can't sign my name to a suicide note."

Pine was all cleaned up as he stood at the edge of the Universal commissary. He stared longingly at the big time directors at their table. As usual they were laughing and enjoying themselves.

As the Devil strolled by, Pine stopped him.

"Hell's got to be better than this."

"Don't you get it? You are in hell." Satan replied with a devious smile.

With that the Devil went back to the table with Peckinpah, Frankenheimer, Siegel, Aldrich—his fellow directors.

Donny Broussard produced his first feature narrative film The Shelter *after writing and producing the short web-pilot and comic book* Vamped. *He co-directed and produced the documentary film* Little Houses, *which aired on the Documentary Channel, as well as producing the documentary* Lights Out in Blackham. He *is currently developing a feature film with his writing partner, Erin Bennett. Erin worked as Production Manager on* The Shelter, *co-wrote the comic book series* Vamped *and produced/directed the short film* Lily. *Her talents take her all over Southwest Louisiana on various commercials and industrial videos. The two are gearing up to shoot Bennett's first feature documentary* Finding Metropolis. *They are co-owners of* SM-Productions.

TIFFANY

Donny Broussard & Erin Bennett

PRODUCERS ARE A STAPLE IN HOLLYWOOD. You can't turn a corner without hearing some lackey saying, "Let me talk to the producer about that," or "The Producer is taking meetings right now." The honest truth is that producers are a dime a dozen, and only a handful legitimately care about their jobs and the productions they oversee. The rest are assholes obsessed with how much money an idea can make, without regard for artistic integrity.

I was one of those. A generic run of the mill asshole whose main ends were money and fame. I wanted to be the next Jerry Bruckheimer with every actor and actress hot on my tail to become my latest and greatest find.

Speaking of actresses, when I was working on my last blockbuster as above mentioned asshole producer, I had the pleasure of meeting Rose Kaplan. She was a solid actress with the chops to land the role, but wasn't everything the picture needed in the looks department. Rose had big thighs, thin lips, and mousy brown hair. She was not your typical Hollywood starlet. So, while I enjoyed her impassioned audition, I had passed on her for the lead in my big-budget slasher film *Death in a Red Dress*. Normally I wouldn't have given my decision a second thought, but for some reason I tucked her name away in the back of my mind, subconsciously knowing that I'd work with her in the future.

Anyway, I'll get back to Rose, and move on to the orchestration of my big-budget demise.

When the production wrapped I was on top of the world. I was spending money faster than I could make it, knowing without a doubt that the film would kill at the box office. Only, the movie going audience didn't share my enthusiasm. The film flopped and I spent months picking up the pieces.

Thankfully, Hollywood knocked the bottom out from under my over-inflated ego, and because of two back-to-back financial disasters took back the keys to the city. I say thankfully, because I was on the verge of losing everything. My marriage was falling apart, my friends were dropping like flies, and I was turning into someone I wasn't proud of. After what seemed like the end of my career, I jumped at the chance to re-examine my life and take inventory of the things that were truly important.

So, now I'm a family man and a producer of indie films. I don't make boatloads of cash anymore, but I've traded in the Ferrari for happiness.

Move ahead a few years, and I have a small indie film off the ground and have decided to not only produce, but direct. It's a small personal film written by a close friend of mine. After reading it I immediately know two things; I want to direct it myself, and Rose Kaplan is the perfect leading lady.

∽

I pick up the phone and call her as soon as I have all the pieces in place. Same girl as I remember; breathy, elegant, and confident. She is happy to hear from me. Ecstatic, actually. Her career has slowed down a little and she seems thrilled about the prospect of being able to flex her acting muscles on a feature film instead of yet another toothpaste commercial. So, as soon as I hang up the phone I email her the script and make plans to meet at an old haunt from my younger days, Tilly's, for a beer and a deal. Everything finally seems to be falling into place.

I am sitting in my usual booth, staring down at my half-drunk, perspiring beer. Rose is late, but things like that are the bread of the industry. Everyone—actors, directors, hell, even production assistants—want to make us salivate. They really want people like me to understand and feel how important they are to our films by dragging out the inevitable. It is just dragging my nerves. With a soul-deep sigh, I enjoy a slow sip from my beer and take in the surrounding patrons and atmosphere of my favorite bar from my glory days. It all still looks the same, including the people.

Hollywood doesn't truly change. Sure, appearances change according to what style is popular in the trades, but the people and places themselves rarely do. For instance, my table. I used to sit at this table every day. I'd do a large portion of my work here, and sure enough, my ode to producers that I carved into the dark wood of the table still reads, *I made a movie and you didn't!* The wooden panels covering the bar's walls are still stained with smoke, even despite the fact that smoking in bars ended years ago. The air is still thick with the stench of stale beer and pheromones.

I take out my smartphone to snap a picture of my clever table carving, when Rose walks up behind me. I don't see her as much as I feel her. After turning my startled "Ah!" into a cleverly concealed cough, the only thing that runs through my mind is the fact that she looks exactly like she did on the day we met. Like she hasn't aged a day. Her green eyes still glow with the same mischief of a twenty-something taking charge of the world.

"Hello, Ted." Rose smiles as my name slips from her lips.

"It's great to see you. How have you been?" I reply, shaking myself mentally for lingering on her boobs a tad longer than necessary.

We talk about the project for about an hour. The conversation is both lively and satisfying. By the end, I am positive I've made the right casting choice, but I don't want to give that away just yet. Us producers have to make them salivate also, work harder, reach higher. So, before giving Rose the congratulatory news, I tell her that I have a few more meetings to take, but she is in the forefront. So then, like the clumsy oaf I am, in an attempt to reach for my jacket that is hanging over the chair next to me I knock over my beer, spilling it on Rose's lap.

"Rose, I'm so sorry! I do this all the time at home." *I do this all the time at home? Who says shit like that?*

"No problem. Accidents happen." Rose says as she wipes the lukewarm malt beverage off of her leg. "Actually, it's Tiffany."

"Oh, did you change your name?"

"No. It's always been Tiffany, remember?" Rose replies in a very cold tone. I nod a little with a small smile dressed on my lips after a breath of a pause.

"Names go out of style just as fast as the clothes do, right?" I quip in reply as I take a second go at picking up my jacket. Rose and I shake hands, and go our separate ways. I just can't shake off the foreboding feeling I have after—

"Ted!"

I turn from my car as I break from my inner monologue to watch Rose running towards me, tits bouncing and dress flashing the tips of her billowing thighs. I can't help the twitch in my pants. I'm still a man.

"What's wrong, Rose—I mean Tiffany?" I stutter the word out, my tongue feeling as if it is covered in grime. Something still feels off with this girl.

"I completely forgot to ask about Pete!" Rose smiles apologetically through small huffs of breath caused by the exertion of the thirty-foot run to me.

"Who?" I ask, completely thrown.

"You're such a joker! Pete! Pete Silver?" Rose replies, all smiles and sparkling eyes.

It hits me. Pete. The exec that worked on *Death in a Red Dress* with me; someone that left me high and dry twenty years ago after the film bombed.

"Uh...I actually haven't talked to him since *Death in a Red Dress*."

"What! We were in the audition room just a week ago, Ted!" Rose laughs and shakes her head at my stupidity. She gives me a small wave and walks away, leaving me swimming in a cold river of unease. A week ago? I now suddenly understand. Tiffany. Tiffany. Tiffany.

The lead character in my shitstorm of a movie.

After my uncomfortable meeting with Rose, I head back to the office to look at more headshots and to reevaluate my decision to cast her in my passion project. After spending an hour staring at blank fake smiles and smoldering eyes, I toss the pile of photos in a manila envelope and turn off my desk lamp. This time I gracefully grab my jacket off the back of my leather chair and head out of the office towards home.

As soon as I walk through the door my two boys bombard me with a barrage of hugs, kisses, and requests. I return the hugs and kisses and settle on a little Xbox action. Not five minutes after we start stalking virtual aliens, do the boys mention that they ran into an actress from one of my films in the park after school. They don't remember her name, but describe her for me.

"Rose?" I ask with an uneasy amount of certainty pushing the question out of my knowing mouth as they describe a shapely brunette.

"Uh...nope," Danny answers distractedly, tongue hanging out in concentration. Riley nods, agreeing with his brother as he shoves a Cheeto into his mouth.

My stomach plummets and the same slimy feeling from earlier fills my mouth. "Tiffany?" I choke out through the thickness.

"Yes, Tiffany!" reply my boys as if simultaneously using one voice.

"She also mentioned that old movie you made in the dark ages. Are you filming it again or something, Dad?" Riley asks as he pauses his game to stretch.

I force a smile onto my face and ruffle his hair. "Nah, buddy. She was just joking."

I hope. I act cool and continue to blast aliens with the best two kids on the planet until my wife rings the dinner bell. The boys run to wash up, leaving me with an ache in the pit of my stomach. Is it a coincidence that my boys ran into Rose shortly after our meeting? Am I just being paranoid?

I live in Hollywood. The people here are a different brand of weird. I don't have anything to worry about.

I think.

I walk into the kitchen, my insides unclenching as I watch my wife, Lily, stir a bubbling pot on the stove, her back to me. I smile as I walk up behind her and slide my hands along the sides of her hips and pull her back towards me lightly.

A small giggle emits from her and she relaxes into me. "I missed you," Lily whispers as she cocks her head back to give me a soft kiss.

I smile against her lips and squeeze her tighter to me. My hands travel lower, exploring the outer rim of her ass.

She playfully swats me away with a wooden spoon. "The boys will be done any second now," Lily says sternly.

I continue to grope her wonderful backside, while fighting to land a kiss on her perfect lips, until I hear the sound of the boys' footsteps making their way towards the kitchen.

After dinner, the family and I sit around the table talking for a while before Lily announces that she is going to run to her mother's to bake cupcakes for the boys' friend, Chad. And will take the boys with her since she knows I have work to do.

While the boys do the dishes I retire to my home office to pull out my Rolodex and scan for other possible actresses that might fit the bill for my passion project. Yeah, I use a Rolodex. Old-school. Just saying.

As I step through the door to my office I notice an overtly strong, yet familiar smell. I call out to my wife and ask if she has started using a new perfume, but after she tells me that she hasn't, I shrug. Maybe my senses are just playing a trick on me. I convince Lily to put off the cupcakes until tomorrow since Chad's birthday isn't for a few more days, and I promise her that I'll forget about work for the night. All is well with the world.

∽

Despite the previous day's odd setback, I wake with determination and head back to my home office to peruse my trusty Rolodex. I work for a few hours, make some calls, surf the net. Then the phone rings. Much to my disgusted surprise, it's my old friend (bastard), Pete. He calls to tell me I don't have the right to remake *Death in a Red Dress*, and that he thought I had put my big budget tent pole career on hold for a more fulfilling life in indie film.

I assure him that I have no idea what he is talking about, and that I am indeed content with my new career in indie heaven. He rants for a few more minutes before finally brushing me off for another call.

"Well, then," I mutter to myself as I set my cell phone down slowly, looking at it reproachfully. This is a bit murkier than I expected. Rose has obviously been talking loud enough around town for her twisted reality to reach Pete up in Douchebaggery

Central, causing quite a ruckus for an old eighties shit fest. My phone begins ringing again.

"Hello?"

I'm only answered by silence and the slightest hint of breathing. My temper rises a notch.

"Hello!" I demand into the phone, hoping the forceful note of desperation causes whoever the fuck is on the other side to answer.

The breathing peaks a little, the quiet gasps turning into long inhales.

"What the fuck is this? If you're looking for Tony's girls it's 0-9, not 0-8."

"Ted..."

The phone call ends.

I pull the phone from my ear, fear creeping slowly into my stomach. I go to my recent calls to see if I recognize the number, but am only greeted with a 'Private Caller'. I attempt to shrug off the fear, but it settles heavily over me.

❧

A week later, having dealt with multiple production hang ups for my new flick, I decide to walk to the Drip & Sip for a cup of coffee to help ease the headache of casting calls. As I turn the corner to enter the coffee shop, focusing more on my phone than my general vicinity, I run straight into a lady, causing her to spill coffee all over herself. I quickly rush to the counter to grab a few napkins for her when she speaks.

"Is this going to be our thing? You spilling on me?"

I know that voice. I slowly turn around. I lower the napkins clenched tightly in my hands revealing Rose, covered in low-fat latte.

"Rose... Tiffany, I'm so sorry. I wasn't paying attention." I say to her as I stand there in utter disbelief that I have run into her in such close proximity to my home.

"It's no problem, really. I always have a change of clothes in the car. How's the production going? Are we still on track to start shooting after the first of the year?" Rose asks with a touch of desperation in her voice.

Before I can answer her my phone rings. I look down at the number and recognize it as a 1-800 sales line, then quickly raise the phone to my ear. "I have to take this," I tell Rose as I rapidly start mumbling to the poor sales rep on the other side of the line, while making a dash for the exit. As I hold the phone to my ear and briskly walk back towards home, I turn to look back at the coffee shop and see Rose standing in the doorway, looking at me with the coldest blank stare I've ever seen. Chills instantly overtake my body, but I keep walking in the opposite direction.

I'm starting to worry. I work in Hollywood. I deal with nut-jobs every day, but I don't really deal with *nut-jobs*, you know? As long as I've been working in this town I've never once experienced anyone as bat-shit crazy as Rose. This bitch thinks she's Tiffany. A fucking character in a piece of shit movie that no one on the planet remembers. And to top it off I'm pretty sure she is stalking me. Why would she drive all the way into my neck of the woods when she lives in the city? I head home, trying not to put too much more analytical thought into the coincidence.

With Lily and the boys at her mother's house baking, I decide it's time to put in some hours on the movie, so I head to my office, fire up the computer, and start looking at my get-shit-done list. I'm not even five minutes into procrastinating on the Internet when I notice that perfume smell again, then it hits me. Rose. That's Rose's perfume. I jump to my feet and stand there dumbfounded for a moment. Was she in my fucking house? Am I losing my mind? I pick up the phone to call the police when I hear my dog Brody barking like Cujo with a victim in his sights. Why does this happen to me when I'm in the house alone? Lily is so much tougher than I am.

I open the front door and peek outside like a twelve year old hiding from the closet monster. I don't see Brody, and his barking has suddenly stopped. I walk my chicken-shit ass over to Brody's pen and find him lying lifelessly on his side.

Fuck. Fuck, fuck, fuck. If anyone saw how fast I run back inside the house they would call the Guinness book immediately. I quickly run into the kitchen to grab one of those giant knives like the young girls clutch to in slasher films. Seems like the right thing to do.

Grasping the handle of the knife closely to me, I begin to slowly work my way through the house. I realize that lots of things go bump in the night when you're shitting your pants. I quickly dial a friend of mine that works for the local police department to send someone over to protect me from whoever killed my dog, but he tells me that neighbors poison dogs all the time, which is unfortunate and cruel, but it's probably nothing to worry about. I decide to take his advice to not panic, and file a report in the morning. But I lock all the doors just in case.

After the call, I convince myself that I am alone and it is time to head back to my office and bury myself in work. I place the knife down on the coffee table, figuring I will be fine without it against my phantom intruder. I know I should take care of the dog before the kids get home, but I'm scared. Don't judge me.

As I walk down the hallway towards my office, the smell of Rose's perfume overwhelms me. I enter the office and find her seated at my desk wearing a red dress, holding my letter opener. Why did I have to put the knife down? You never put the fucking knife down.

"Why wasn't I good enough, Ted?" Rose asks with pain in her voice.

"I—I'm...sor—wait. What?" I stumble over my words, fear gripping me like a vice. I place my back against the wall, using it to ground me in this surreal situation. Rose shifts, pushing her boobs closer together. She bites down on the tip of the letter opener, fixing me with a sultry stare.

"You told me I was the best one, Ted. You said I would become a big name in Hollywood. You said everyone would know the name Rose Kaplan. But you lied to me, Ted."

"Rose, I—"

"That's why I changed my name. I figured you would notice how dedicated I was once I took on Tiffany's role in real life." Rose smiles, baring her teeth like a wolf. She stands grasping the letter opener close to her chest. My eyes widen in disbelief as she slowly penetrates the skin of her chest with the tip of the letter opener.

"See, Ted? I bleed for this role; just like Tiffany does for her love. Anything you need me to do, I will fucking do it!"

I stand there gaping at Rose, unsure of what my next move should be. I begin to work my way back towards the doorway, but Rose stops me with a cold-blooded stare. The slightest of whimpers escape my mouth as I watch her fingers playfully smooth the blood seeping from her wound across her chest, smearing it into her skin. Moving from behind my desk, she begins to work her way towards me, fingers still splayed across her bosom.

"Anything, Ted." Rose whispers as she nears me. My breath hitches as she presses herself against me, her hands roaming across my body. The smell of iron and her flowery perfume invade my senses. My stomach churns. Her bloody hand reaches my face, and she caresses me, staining me.

"Uh, I...okay. Okay. Let's—let's go into the living room and discuss the role. We start production in a month and I'll see if I can convince Pete." I stutter, playing into her twisted game. I cringe as her face lights up like a Christmas tree, all smiles and excited giggling.

"Oh, Ted! I knew I could convince you!"

I force a smile as she gives me a bone-crushing hug, my breath wheezing out of me. I can feel the tendrils of panic beginning to overcome me. Rose turns towards the door to leave my office and walk in the direction of my living room, as if she'd done so a thousand times before. I look around my office quickly, trying to find something, anything to stop her. My eyes land on a wooden cane prop from *Death in a Red Dress.*

How poetic.

I grab the cane from its resting place in the corner of my office, and quietly gain up on Rose just as she is entering the living room. I raise the wooden cane above my head, my breathing erratic. Just as she turns towards me, I swing the cane down on top of her head as a look of understanding crosses her face.

She crumples to the ground like a *papier-mâché* decoration. Maybe I overreacted... Nah. The bitch broke into my house and cut herself with my letter opener. And she killed my fucking dog! If anything, I believe I'm *under*-reacting.

Twenty minutes later, my driveway is full of cop cars and an ambulance. I hear a chorus of three screams as I'm giving my statement to a police officer. Lily rushes into the living room with Danny and Riley trailing close behind, tears streaming down her face.

"Ted, what happened?" Lily questions, arms stretched out, looking for comfort. I ask the officer for a moment, and scoop my wife into my arms, holding her head tightly against my chest. My hands trail down her hair in a comforting manner.

"It's over now. It's over." I answer as I close my eyes, the fear finally leaving my body to allow room for exhaustion.

After calming Lily and the kids down, I walk outside to watch Rose being taken away and loaded into an ambulance on a stretcher. She looks like an angel, laying there with her face peaceful and bloodied. She seemed like such a nice girl. I turn to go back into the house when a sudden growl of my name stops me instantly.

"Ted!" Rose yells.

I turn back towards her and see only her head lift up from the stretcher.

She struggles against the restraints a little, and then says in a low, murderous tone, "I will do anything for the part."

Katarina Leigh Waters started writing at a very young age and was lucky enough to have several poems and short stories published in the children's section at her local newspaper— so being a published writer was technically her very first job. Having focused over the years mainly on her career as a performer, both as an actress and professional wrestler with WWE, Katarina is now redirecting her passion and craft towards writing and directing. She has penned several poems, short stories and recently completed her first feature script. She also wrote and directed the short film Lucille Means Light. *More information can be found at www.katarinasinfamy.com.*

ONCE UPON A TIME AT THE HORROR HOTEL

Katarina Leigh Waters

"WHERE'S THE TOMATOES for the club sandwich? Come on now, Rachel, chop chop! We're all waiting for you!"

"Raquelle, it's Raquelle, not *Rachel*," she muttered under her breath as the tomatoes squished this way and that beneath her knife. Near impossible to slice. What the hell was she supposed to do, with a knife that was totally inadequate for a job she was way overqualified for anyway? How did she even get stuck here? She should be out there, on set. Back home she had been something. Her resume stacked with plays and leads in independent films, everyone knew she had been well on her way to becoming the next big thing. Now she had come out to Los Angeles and somehow none of that mattered. And this is what she had been reduced to.

The entry level Craft Service assistant job had gotten her close to a set, but was turning her dreams into frustrated nightmares as she watched bubble-headed actresses flourish while her own talent wasted away behind a food table and trash cans. Entry level Craft Service assistant...if it wasn't so damn tragic she would laugh at how ridiculous that even sounded.

She knew the girl that had her part. Cyndi Celeste, the 'new rising star'. Bah, humbug. Raquelle could have played her part with ease and, dare she say it, a lot more grace and talent than that spoiled little brat. Just because she had a couple of fancy TV credits under her belt everyone thought Cyndi was the greatest actress on the planet. So unfair. How in the world was Raquelle supposed to get to Cyndi's level when they wouldn't even let her audition? Apparently she didn't have enough experience. It was like the Bermuda Triangle of catch 22's. Impossible to get out of. As impossible as these damn tomatoes.

Salvatore, 'chef to the stars' (or rather, the head of Craft Services at Wornsdale Studios) appeared out of nowhere. He was a pudgy, sweaty man who drank most of his salary and spent the rest of it at "Stripper Heaven" around the corner. "Rachel, what the hell are you doing back there?"

Raquelle jumped, slicing her thumb in the process. "Darn it!" she growled through clenched teeth. "Stupid knife won't cut the tomatoes, but my thumb—oh yeah, it has no problem at all cutting my thumb in half!"

"Calm down, Rach—"

"Raquelle!" she screamed. "Raquelle! My name is Raquelle! Why can't you get that? It's not that bloody difficult!!"

Salvatore studied her face. Something about the cold rage in her eyes made him understand that this was more than just a tantrum born out of a small cut. This was her breaking point. He nodded and patted her arm.

"Take a break, Rach—Raquelle. We've overworked you. We can manage without you for a bit. Come back when you're ready. They're filming one more scene before lunch, maybe you can catch it. I'm sure they won't mind you watching for a while."

Nodding gratefully, Raquelle abandoned her work station and ventured out into the studio, where they were filming the life story of H. H. Holmes, America's first serial killer. It was the fascinating story of a notorious con man who had built an entire hotel for the sole purpose of trapping and killing lodgers in its maze-like corridors and windowless 'asphyxiation rooms'.

The set was formidable. The director, Jaques Devont, took pride in demanding absolute authenticity in his period landscapes and wardrobe, transporting the viewers instantly into another time and place. Cobblestones and old-fashioned store fronts were lined with lampposts that appeared to be originals from the late 1800's. A mild breeze was created by a powerful wind machine, and the lights above the ceiling as well as inside the studio created the illusion of daylight so perfectly that for a second Raquelle wondered whether she had inadvertently stepped outside.

Raquelle looked up. The façade of the infamous 'horror hotel' and Holmes' drug store had been recreated with every little detail in place and Raquelle, who had done her research on the subject matter (just in case), wondered if the inside of the hotel was just as meticulous. She shuddered, imagining the horrors that had taken place in the real hotel.

She stepped forward, peering through light stands and people's heads towards a pretty blonde girl in a period dress. There she was. Cyndi Celeste.

A handsome gentleman with a long overcoat, top hat and whiskers was kneeling in front of Cyndi, as if to propose marriage. Raquelle presumed this was the actor playing Holmes. She giggled; whiskers—wasn't that what they called a beard in those days...? He was looking up at Cyndi from under the rim of his hat, with dark, deep eyes and the slightest hint of a smirk on his lips.

"Milady," he said as he slowly, seductively reached out his arm...

"Kind sir," Cyndi retorted, dramatically placing one hand on her chest. "Will you be attending the fair?"

Raquelle cringed. Why were they letting her get away with being so over the top? Not to mention the (very bad) British accent she was emulating. Didn't she know this took place in Chicago!?

"Cut!" yelled the director. "That's a wrap for lunch!"

The crowd dispersed, the magic evaporated. The actor was still on one knee. Cyndi was staring back at him, captivated. Suddenly, the man turned his head as if he could sense Raquelle behind him. His eyes found hers and he smiled. Cyndi turned and saw her too, frowned, then said something to the man and, with a haughty air, practically glid off stage. The actor finally got up, still smiling, bowed—yes, she could have sworn he did a little bow!—then slid off into the scenery.

Raquelle twisted her head. Where was he going? The canteen was the other way. She looked around. Cyndi was already huddled within a group of some of the other actors, laughing, tossing her blonde hair back—apparently a professional at being the center of attention. Raquelle rolled her eyes, turned away and reluctantly strolled back to the kitchen to help serve the meals.

As usual, Raquelle was one of the last ones to leave the studio at the end of the day. Cleaning up and checking for trash and glassware in the dressing rooms was just another one of her many duties. *Just like Cinderella*, she thought. *And just like Cinderella, my day will come...*

She had wistfully watched the actors come out in what they called their 'civilian clothing', laughing and joking amongst each other, an elitist group it felt like. It was unfair not to be part of that!

"My day will come," Raquelle reminded herself.

She hadn't seen the man with 'whiskers' again, although she had damn near twisted her head off her shoulders looking... She had tried to pass it off as simple curiosity at first, but finally had to admit to herself that it was more a deep womanly fascination. In short—she was attracted to this man.

By now the studio was eerily quiet. Salvatore had left her with a friendly pat on the back and a reminder to lock up after herself. Veronika, the assistant manager, had given her a list of tasks that still needed to be completed and a harsh warning that her work had been sub-par over the past week or so, and that she would need to do better if she wanted to keep her job. The bitch.

Raquelle sneered. If only she knew. One day it would be her out there, the star, standing on the dimly lit cobblestones between the high buildings under an imaginary moon...a gentleman kneeling in front of her, reaching out to her, looking up at her with that mysterious smile...drawing her in...pulling her towards him...

Raquelle opened her eyes with a start. She hadn't realized she had nodded off for a moment. She looked up and down the corridor she had been sweeping, not sure for a moment which way she needed to go. Her eyes fell upon the star right in front of her and the name beneath it in embossed lettering. *Cyndi Celeste*. Her dressing room door. Of all doors. And of course it was shut. Most actors left their doors open at night, knowing someone was going to come in and clean up after them—it was typical of Cyndi to shut hers as if to prevent unauthorized access to lesser beings than herself.

Raquelle turned the door knob. Slowly. She wasn't sure why, but she suddenly had a feeling of apprehension come over her. It was part of her job and daily routine for her to go inside Cyndi's dressing room, yet tonight she felt as though she was entering some kind of secret chamber...

She pushed the door open. Everything was as she expected. Nothing magical was happening here, no mysteries were kept; just the usual mess, a couple of plates and glasses left on the vanity, a half drunk bottle of vodka stashed behind the garbage can—a less than adequate hiding place. Raquelle poured it down the little sink and threw the bottle out.

"Sorry Cyndi, no booze allowed..." she sarcastically announced to nobody. Raquelle caught her reflection in the mirror. She really did look like Cyndi. She sighed and turned to leave, but a thought stopped her in her tracks. Behind her on the rack were Cyndi's dresses. She would look good in those. Suppose she would—no, terrible idea, she would be immediately fired. Although...no one was here...and as long as she was very careful... She shut the door quickly, feeling defiantly mischievous.

She picked up the first dress on the rack and held it up to her body. The black velvet bodice made a beautiful contrast to her blonde hair, and the maroon skirt and short, frilly sleeves really brought out her bright blue eyes.

The dress slid over her head easily and, just as she had suspected, fit like a glove. With the tight bodice snug around her waist, it looked even better than it had on the hanger. And better than it did on Cyndi, for that matter. Luckily, the costume lady had hidden an ingeniously modern zipper in the side rather than insist on the authenticity of complicated corsets and string. Looking around, Raquelle's eyes fell upon a choker—the stone the same shade of maroon, but turn it in the light, and it gave way to the illusion of deep, dark blackness. The shoes were a little loose—she felt a small stab of irrational pride, noticing that, at least, her feet were ever so slightly daintier than Cyndi's.

Opening the door just a crack, Raquelle looked out into the corridor. Who knew if perhaps the janitor was still creeping around, or if the night security watchman might have come in for a stroll, or, worse yet, one of the actors returned to pick up a forgotten item! But all was quiet and Raquelle crept undetected down the stairs, past the light stands and the giant wind machine.

Maneuvering her way over the cobblestones in the little kitten heels proved to be more difficult than expected, but she managed to stumble across them onto the dimly lit set. She looked up and around. The empty facades were lit up only by the atmospheric street lights. Someone must have forgotten to kill the switches. No matter, it worked out better for her this way. She could almost imagine she had gone back in time. That was the point of acting, wasn't it? Living an authentic experience under imaginary circumstances or something like that?

A movement between the cobblestones made her take a second look. What was that? She could have sworn she saw a small animal... There it was again! Unmistakably, flitting in and out of the shadows, then disappearing into a hole in the wall—was a rat!

The set didn't need to be quite that authentic, she thought, sarcastically. Should she let Salvatore know tomorrow? Or hope that one of the nasty black creatures ran over Cyndi's foot who was sure to panic, and see if it shut down the whole damn operation. She was wondering how it got in, when a slight breeze rustled her hair. *Ah*, she thought. *A draft.*

There had to be an open window or door somewhere. Then she remembered the wind machine and turned around. She started. Turned again. Turned more. There was no wind machine. The great big turbine that had occupied half the studio floor just a moment ago was gone. So were the light stands for that matter, the cases of electrical equipment, the studio doors, the studio walls, the ceiling...

She blinked. Had she gone further than she thought and got away from the main set up? Had she somehow ventured in between the houses and down the streets? She turned again. Which way did she come? Which way was front, and which way back? The streetlights glimmered above her. The air was foggy, moist almost—a drop fell on her cheek. She looked up at the sky. Yes, it was the sky. No more second ceiling with lights and painted clouds, this was the sky, she was outside and it was indeed raining. First drizzling, then stronger. Fighting a rising feeling of panic, she told herself that if she just walked in one straight direction she would either hit the studio wall or the entrance to the set with the lights and the doorway to the corridor...

The rain was now falling steadily. She picked up the pace, realizing she had better get out of it before the dress was ruined, or there would be big trouble! She walked faster and faster, then started running. If walking had been difficult, running was damn near impossible! She tripped a few times and finally, inevitably, her heel slipped and she fell face-first onto the wet, glistening cobblestones. Luckily, she managed to prevent her head hitting the street, but the abrasions on her arms were painful enough. Scared, frustrated and alone, she began sobbing.

A faint sound of music and laughter reached her through the mist of her tears and looking up she saw a light shining through the windows of one of the storefronts. It was apparently the front of a pub, The Gilded Keg, according to the sign dangling into the street. She got up slowly. Could it be that others had stayed behind too? What was going on in there? A night shoot? She approached the 'pub' gingerly.

As she came closer, the door opened, a little bell jingling as it went. Two men came stumbling out, in long overcoats and top hats. They stepped out onto the street and walked away, bumping into each other and laughing. Raquelle took a deep breath but couldn't muster up the courage to cry out to them. Instead, she crept further towards the pub and looked in through the window.

Inside, there was definitely a party going on. A roaring fire burned in the hearth and the pub was filled with men and women, all dressed in immaculate period costumes—corsets, top hats, ringlets. Pints of ale and short glasses with crisp liquor were being tossed back, sipped on, shared and passed around. In a distant corner a couple was drunkenly dancing and another man was using his lap to entertain a woman who, judging by her costume, appeared to be playing a 'woman of the night'.

Raquelle looked around, but could detect no cameras. Something was off. Something was distinctly off and a little too real for her liking. Was it possible that...

She shook her head and almost laughed at herself. "You are out of your mind, girl" she said quietly to herself, deciding she would just go inside, talk to someone and find out what in the world was going on. And at least she would get out of the rain which by now thankfully had become a slight drizzle.

"Oy, pretty lady!" A voice made her jump as a man in rags was hobbling towards her out of the shadows. "Ma'am I mean, ma'am..." he stumbled and almost fell, but caught himself, then broke down in a coughing fit.

Raquelle waited uncomfortably.

The man finally cleared his throat and spoke again. "Ma'am, a penny if you please, a penny..." he coughed again.

Raquelle looked at him, puzzled, then looked around. She did not know what to do. If she had indeed entered another world, this man could be dangerous. Confused, she shrugged her shoulders. "I—I don't have anything. My purse is in the dressing room, I..."

The man hobbled closer and spoke again. A whiff of cheap liquor, decay and apparently not having washed in several weeks hit her nose. "Ma'am, ma'am..." he grabbed her arm.

Raquelle tried to pull away, but the man did not let go. He and the accompanying stench moved in towards her. He was close enough now for her to see his rotting teeth, his one blind eye, the grime in his hair. The stench was becoming unbearable and his claw-like fingers were digging into her arm. Torn between a feeling of pity and pure panic, Raquelle wriggled in his vice-like grip, but in vain.

"Ma'am, just a penny...give me...give me..."

Spittle from his rotting mouth hit Raquelle in the face. While his seeing eye rolled from side to side, angrily, wildly, his blind eye stared ahead, pale blue watery and still as ice. She wanted to cry again, desperate to yell and scream, but no sound came from her lips. As much as she tried, the incredible horror of it rendered her silent. And when finally the faint gleam of a corroded knife blade in his filthy hands caught her sight, she closed her eyes, ready to surrender to her fate...

A shout cut through the darkness and the rain. A voice, in this moment the most beautiful sound she thought she had ever heard, cried out "Go! Shoo! Leave her alone!"

The words had no effect, but when a coin flew through the air and bounced off the cobblestones next to them, the man immediately scrambled for his penny, limping away into the darkness. Raquelle was finally able to take a deep breath.

She turned around. "Thank—" The words stopped in her throat. It was him, the actor that had bowed to her on set today! Halfway between immeasurable relief at seeing a familiar face and the pounding in her heart now taking over because it was him—it was him who had come to her rescue—she tried again.

"Thank you," she said, forcing her quivering lips into the semblance of a smile. The man smiled back, then stretched out his hand. Just as he had to Cyndi this morning...

Raquelle melted. She took a step towards him, then blurted out, "I am so glad it's you, oh my god, I was so scared, I totally lost my way and started to think I was crazy! Oh my, thank you so much. I'm Raquelle, by the way." She placed her hand in his, and as he brought it up to his lips for an old-fashioned gentlemanly kiss she melted again.

"My name is Henry," he said.

Raquelle started. "Henry? I thought you were *playing* Henry. Henry playing Henry?" She laughed nervously, then kicked herself inwardly for having said something so stupid sounding.

Henry just smiled and led her inside the pub, where he acquired two glasses of mulled wine and sat her down at a small table in the corner.

Out of nervousness and confusion and also, because Henry was obviously not a very talkative fellow, Raquelle started babbling again. "You know, it's just all so strange, I mean, it serves me right, you've probably noticed I'm wearing Cyndi's dress and I'm not Cyndi." She tried another nervous laugh. "And all of a sudden I'm lost on this set and can't find my way back! The lights are gone, the wind machine, for crying out loud, everything! And then here you are and all these people just hanging out in costume partying, I mean, I can't see cameras or anything, you know, for a second I totally thought I had gone back in time!" She laughed again, louder than before. "Is this some kind of weird thing you guys like to do after hours?"

Henry said nothing, just watched her with a bemused smile on his lips and after a short, awkward pause Raquelle began again. "Oh, and then that guy outside, oh my God he was so scary, if you hadn't come and saved me, I…"

Henry looked at her, his dark eyes searching hers, gently piercing her soul. "Would you like me to take you home?"

Raquelle was torn. She had been secretly dreaming of this moment, where she would be close to Henry, commanding his full attention. The pub was lively and warm, the mulled wine delicious, but… The strangeness of the evening's occurrences coupled with the other-worldly surroundings she so miraculously found herself in had fitted her with a sense of uneasiness and made her head hurt. "Yes." She nodded. "Yes, I would, actually. I am just so tired. Maybe we could do this another time?"

"Of course," he said. "I would like that." Henry smiled again, helped her up out of her seat and quietly led her through the jovial crowd to a back door at the other side of the bar.

They stepped out into the cold, foggy air. Raquelle shivered, and Henry put his coat around her. They walked in silence for a while, Raquelle out of things to say and Henry—well, he seemed to be a man of few words anyway. The silence felt not uncomfortable this time, and Raquelle almost wished she had said 'no' to the question of going home. New excitement at walking through the dark, misty streets of atmospheric 1880's Chicago next to this tall, handsome actor came over her and she looked up at Henry in silent wonder. He seemed to catch her glance and, without a word, they slowed to a halt. Henry took Raquelle's face into his hands and gently, ever so gently stroking her cheek with one finger, leaned in and kissed her on the lips…

For a moment time seemed to stand still and, like in a movie, Raquelle could imagine what it would look like, the two of them standing in the fog, between the tall buildings on the deserted cobblestone road, the camera circling above them, higher and higher, the soundtrack reaching a crescendo... But unfortunately, instead of the credits ending, the kiss did and Henry, this time taking her hand and laying it in the crease of his elbow, led Raquelle onwards, her little heels clip-clopping on the deserted streets.

After a little while, Raquelle began to see things she recognized. A store front she remembered passing whilst bringing a cameraman his vegan sandwich, and then, finally, the H. H. Holmes drugstore and opposite, the façade of his famous 'horror hotel'. Relief at being back in familiar surroundings however was immediately tinged with a slight feeling of regret that her great adventure would be over so soon. There was something magical about this night she was spending with perhaps the man of her dreams and she no longer was sure she wanted it to end.

She had barely noticed that they had come to a full stop under a street light right opposite the hotel. She found herself looking up at it with fascination and just beginning to wonder whether they had, in fact, bothered to build a full set inside, when Henry asked her quietly, "Would you like to see it?"

Feeling mischievous again, Raquelle quickly nodded. With perhaps a little apprehension but enough curiosity to silence the little voice in her stomach that said 'no' she forced her mouth to say "Yes" and towards the hotel they went.

The heavy oak door creaked as it opened. Everything inside the lobby was as to be expected. An old, empty concierge desk took up one quarter of the room, and on the other side a stairway led up to the floors above. Upon a nod from Henry, Raquelle stepped up onto the first stair and then further, step by step. He was following close behind and the sound of his breath and his footsteps, coupled with the idea that they were doing something perhaps slightly forbidden, made her heart thump and her stomach began performing little somersaults.

They started down this corridor, then that one. When they came to a very long, wide hallway, Raquelle started slowly running, then faster, Henry following her, her laughter infectious, until he caught up with her. Pushing her up against the wall they began again to kiss again, more passionately this time, with her heart caught in her throat and her head swimming.

At the end of the hall they came across a little stairway, almost hidden in a corner. Henry nodded at Raquelle's questioning look. The stairway was dark, but encouraged by a faint light up above, she started going upwards. The corridor at the top of the stairs was very small and short, and there were several doors leading away from it. More curiosity and a growing desire to show off her adventurous side in front of Henry caused Raquelle to open one of the doors and gingerly step inside.

Behind the door was another short hallway. It had a chest of drawers on one side, with a candle flickering on it. Also several doors that again led to more hallways and rooms, she imagined. It was only after the door fell shut behind her that Raquelle realized that Henry had not followed her inside. The building was so quiet that the sound of the slamming door sounded like a gunshot. Fear quickly rose up inside her when she twisted the door handle and realized that it would not open again. Bile and tears collected in her throat in equal measure.

"Henry!" she tried to cry out, but the words got stuck and she only managed a weird little cough. "Henry!" she tried again, now louder, braver at first, but the muffled sound of her voice in the empty room made her feel small, foolish and even more afraid, so she didn't attempt a third time.

She began to giggle, as if by giggling she could convince herself that Henry had simply played a silly trick on her. But in her heart she knew this was not the case and she began to sweat. The only way was onward and thinking she could find another way out, she opened the door ahead, but there was nothing but a brick wall staring back at her. Trembling, she tried the next one.

At last, a room! It looked like a normal guest room, with a bed and a vanity, and again, a flickering candle. Nonetheless, the room was still a dead end—small and windowless and so the discovery did little to quieten her fear.

She backed out again. There was one more door to try. This time she was lucky; a dusty, narrow, but longer hallway lay in flickering semi-darkness in front of her, with several more doors on either side—one of these doors had to lead somewhere, anywhere! She walked out and tried the first door. And was greeted by another brick wall. Her stomach sinking, she went along the line, faster and faster, tearing at the doors as she went. Some would not open, and there were brick walls behind the ones that did. Out of breath and sobbing she reached the very last one...

And found Henry standing in the doorway. The joy at seeing a friendly face quickly vanished when she realized that the face staring back at her, though Henry's, was indeed not friendly, and she stepped back in horror with his menacing gaze upon her.

Grabbing her with one hand he used the other to unlock one of the doors that had not opened before. He pushed her inside, all the while not saying a word. Then locked the door again behind her.

Raquelle found herself alone in almost complete darkness. She frantically began exploring the walls. There were no windows and the room was small, the candle near out of wax. She began exploring the walls—wondering if somewhere there was a crack or some kind of trap door that would allow her to escape—but found nothing. Her panic grew stronger. This couldn't be happening. Surely there was some mistake, this was a dream, or...could it be a prank? Just a stupid prank to teach her a lesson?

She started pacing around the room, banging on the walls, then the door, crying out, "Henry! Come on, Henry, stop it with the joke, let me out! It was funny, ok, hilarious, ha ha! But I've had enough now, let me out! Damn it, Henry let me the hell out! God, Henry, what are you doing, let me out...!"

But all she heard from the other side was silence.

Then, suddenly, there it was. A quiet, slow hissing noise—like air being released or—gas! Henry was letting gas into the room. She remembered the history behind the hotel and the way H. H. Holmes had used gas to murder his unsuspecting lodgers. Was it possible? Could it be that by some kind of sinister circumstances she had ended up in one of his infamous asphyxiation chambers?

She started banging louder, faster and screaming and yelling at the top of her voice: "Let me out, please! Help! Heeeeelp!!"

But the room had been sound proofed so no one could hear her cry—except for Henry. Little did she know that he was listening intently, and since there was no light in the adjoining room she could not see him looking in through a small, round hole in the wall. Nor would she comprehend the excitement and intense satisfaction that filled his chest, as he watched and listened to her gasp for air in a vain attempt to fill her lungs, claw at the walls in desperation and finally sink to the floor with a loud and irreversible thump.

Henry waited a few more moments to make sure that she was dead. He marveled at how interesting it was. How inherently fascinating to observe the struggle of her dying body, and then to see stillness where there had just before been life. Once he was certain that it was all over, he unlocked the door and walked inside. Gently stroking the hair out of her face, he marveled at her beauty. Such pale, soft skin. How beautiful her eyes had been. It was a shame that he did not have the means to preserve her just as she was, but then, what would he do with her body anyway? Plus, there would be more. More ladies with ringlets and bonnets and pretty blue eyes and whimsical smiles on their faces.

There would always be more.

With a sigh, he stood up, gathering up her body as he went. She felt surprisingly light, even with her skirts still damp from the rain. He carried her over to the trap door that was connected to a chute from here, the 3rd floor, all the way into the basement. He tossed the dead girl inside and then, whistling and humming to himself, descended his own secret staircase to the furnace below. There he would find a nice fire roaring, ready to consume the empty flesh, leaving nothing but a perfect skeleton—just like he had promised to deliver the medical department of Boston University that same week.

What perfect timing, he thought. *And what a wonderful way to get rich. Oh, what fun.*

It would be several weeks more before filming was scheduled in the replica basement of the horror hotel. If the prop master had looked carefully, he may have detected just one more perfect skeleton in the closet—but at this point he no longer remembered how many he had ordered, nor took the time to notice the difference between the ones made of slightly yellowing plastic and the crisp white human bones.

Salvatore was momentarily concerned when Raquelle failed to show up for work the next day, but then, he knew the drill. The pretty girls could never hack the job, got frustrated and left. After all, Raquelle had already shown signs of wanting to quit. Perhaps she had actually landed a gig as an actress. *She deserves it*, Salvatore thought to himself. He really hoped that was it.

He made sure that the new girl was plump, homely and had no aspirations above her station. At least that way he felt assured she would stay for a while. She did seem to develop a girlish, (unrequited) crush on the actor playing H. H. Holmes.

Poor fool, he thought. She didn't have a snowball's chance in hell with the handsome leading man. But perhaps that was all for the best.

When Tim Chizmar was a child he lost himself in evil, scary books. One day a morally righteous librarian refused to check some out. Reading about demons, be-headings, and cannibalism wasn't the norm in Linesville, Pennsylvania. Tim's mother insisted that her son be allowed to read whatever he wanted. The upset librarian said, "Your son is gonna grow up to be a great horror writer one day—OR A SERIAL KILLER." As of this writing, Tim hasn't killed anyone. Yet. But he has written and sold many screenplays in Hollywood. When he's not burying bodies, Tim is a comedian, actor, writer, director, and producer living in Los Angeles. What drives his success is knowing that somewhere in Pennsylvania, a librarian is praying for his soul.

LIBBY

Tim Chizmar

LIBBY DECIDED THAT THE NEXT SCENE would be where she would stop for the night. Often engrossed in her storytelling, it was difficult to decide where to end for the evening. She typed: *The pregnant woman stood in the kitchen and heard the ghost's voice again.* It was a spooky way to leave off on her tale written for the small screen; just the way she intended. Pushing her chair back from the computer monitor, Libby smiled with unabashed glee.

Sitting to the left of her was Squishy, a fluffy white cat who had been by her side through many tough times. In a sweet way Squishy was Libby's most loyal fan, and having him around was very comforting.

She reached out to pat Squishy on the head as he turned to his side and lightly purred. In his old age Squishy had lost most of his spunk and his purr sounded more like a groan; Libby, getting up there herself in years, could relate. There were many days when she too had no desire to purr. Still, Libby's work kept her excited; she felt like she could live forever as long as there were still stories to be told.

"Let's get ready for bed, eh Squishy?" Libby said, as she switched the computer to sleep mode. She pulled herself from the chair, and, already clothed in her nightgown, made her way to the bed where she pulled back the covers. As she settled back on the bed, Libby watched Squishy lightly paw at the covers then circle around before finally falling on the blankets with a light thud.

Libby reached across the nightstand towards her lamp that sat next to her side of the bed. She paused for a moment as her gaze fixated on a picture of herself in her younger years standing next to a man in a suit. She knew how silly she looked, being all alone in such a large bed. It had been better when Henry lay beside her, but after fifty years of marriage, he had passed away just less than a year ago. Together they had been the Hollywood power couple talked about in all the tabloid papers which Henry had called *the rag mags*. With his production contacts and her imagination they'd had a series of successful television shows and two slightly less well-received movies; always with a spooky element as that was Libby's personal touch. Besides the success in tinsel town, they had raised some good children, now grown and busy raising kids of their own. These days her life consisted of writing, talking to her family, more writing, and Squishy.

Libby's hand slipped under the lampshade as she felt for the knob. Suddenly she felt something crawl across it. She let out a startled cry and quickly drew her hand back in shock. Something was moving about under the lampshade; she could see its outline through the shade. She tossed back the covers and cursed the heavens for allowing such a terrible creature to even exist.

She knew what she had to do. She thought about how Henry would have handled the situation differently; he never killed anything intentionally. He would have happily scooped up the critter on a piece of paper and dropped it back outside with care. She had told him on many occasions that he was like a Zen master with his "I won't kill a bug" mentality. Despite his mercy for bugs, she still loved him and missed him dearly.

Alas, being a widow she knew that dealing with various insects was now solely her own problem. She knew she couldn't call her grown son and expect him to drive two hours down from the high desert just to simply kill a single spider, let alone make such a long trip this late in the night. Whether she liked it or not, Libby was on her own to deal with this despicable critter, she wouldn't be able to sleep soundly otherwise.

God, what if it crawls up my nose as I sleep? she thought to herself as she went to look for a book to squash her unwelcome guest.

Squishy watched from the bed, as Libby held a crossword puzzle dictionary in one hand and lifted the lampshade with her other. The cat made his way towards the nightstand area and watched from the safety of a pillow as Libby lifted the book. She wished not to come into contact with the insect for fear that its tiny bug legs would touch her aged skin. She shook the lampshade and dropped it onto the carpet. As she did so the small spider hurried out from its hiding spot, ran through her legs, and scurried halfway up the wall all the while passing framed awards from the world of entertainment, finally it rested in the corner near her bedroom door.

Libby raised the crossword puzzle book over her head and paused; she found herself studying the spider closely; its legs gripped the wall and, although it was still a creepy, disgusting, thing with a fat little body, there was something about it that appeared vulnerable.

It looked at her as if to say: *"Really? You're going to kill me?"*

Libby brought the book down as fast as she could, held it against the wall, and then pushed it back and forth just to ensure herself that the spider was completely dead. When she pulled the book from the wall she could not believe her eyes. Although she had properly smashed the body, tiny spiders now ran from its remains.

Suddenly, there were miniature spiders everywhere. Libby whacked at them with her book over and over while cursing in a frantic panic. She didn't stop attacking until every last one of them was smashed. Exhaling heavily, she took some toilet paper from the bathroom and wiped up the remains. The original spider must have been carrying babies; that thought instantaneously caused coldness to creep up Libby's spine. As she gave the spider a proper toilet burial, she imagined the feel of their tiny legs all over her body and experienced a second attack of chills. On her way back from the bathroom she ran her fingers through her white hair, half expecting to find that those tiny bastards had somehow embedded themselves into her scalp.

After everything had been taken care of she got back in bed, only this time she left the lampshade off with the exposed bulb glaring as she turned the knob to bring her room into darkness. She did what she could to not disturb Squishy who had fallen asleep during the chaos. As Libby lay in bed, her thoughts drifted back to that damn spider...

Libby looked left and right; how had she gotten up so high? It was as though she was on a skyscraper, and yet she was still somehow in her bedroom. Her many legs held tightly to the wall. She considered churning out a thin lace from her backside but decided against it; tonight was not the night. Her thoughts were on her hundreds of babies that would soon enter the world. They were her legacy. They would make her proud.

Suddenly Libby heard something stirring; her many eyes focused on the giant human lumbering in her direction. She had hoped it was that nice older gentleman who was always so very kind and sympathetic. Libby would certainly understand if he needed to place her back outside; often her curiosity caused her to wander. It was not the man who approached her, however.

Who was this person? Libby wondered.

She feared for herself and the lives of her unborn. She watched the white-haired woman lift the book high above her head. The look on the woman's face scared Libby; she could see it in the woman's hateful eyes that there was no chance of pleading with her.

What did I ever do to her? Libby thought as the book came down fast and hard.

Libby awoke screaming in her bed with tears streaming from her glassy eyes. She sat upright, trying to catch her breath. She felt so bad; how could she have killed that poor spider? She decided she needed a cup of tea to calm her nerves but not without Squishy. Libby shook the sleeping cat until his eyes slowly opened. He followed her out of the bedroom and down the stairs; once in the kitchen she felt herself feeling much better. This space of sanctuary always brought back memories of happy times and holidays. She recalled the smells of cinnamon and vanilla floating through the air as she got her kettle and readied it for the stove.

"Squishy, I had no reason to kill the little spider. I just had a terrible dream, actually it wasn't a dream at all; it was a horrible nightmare." Squishy curled up on a chair nearby as he licked his fur; he occasionally gazed towards her direction.

Libby continued. "It was just a spider. I'm not going to do that anymore, the next time I see something in this house that I didn't invite here I promise I'm not ever going to kill it. I'll catch it and put it outside just like Henry would have done."

Libby lowered the heat on the stove and poured a cup of scalding hot water. She had the tea bag and her sugar bowl already on the counter as she had done so many times before. She looked at her loyal companion and, feeling much better about the situation in general blurted out, *"If I kill another bug, I hope that a really big one comes and gets me!"*

She couldn't help but laugh to herself as she dipped the tea bag into her cup. Watching as it stained the water she lifted the top off the sugar bowl. For a short moment she pictured all those tiny spiders from earlier would come pouring out from under the lid and they would all attack, demanding vengeance for their mother and climbing up her arms and out from under her nightgown. Libby held her breath and scooped her sugar feeling a wave of relief that she just had an overly active imagination.

She settled back to enjoy her tea. Looking just past the kitchen area she could see the last Film and Television Awards Trophy Henry had ever accepted. She sighed and took the cup up to her lips for a sip. As she lowered it she noticed legs dangling in front of her face—another spider! One of those daddy long legs ones that Libby had always hated; it had dropped down from the ceiling directly in front of her face.

Libby screamed and spilled her tea on the countertop, scaring Squishy off in the process while the spider just hung there on its thread. It was dangling about like a skydiver's parachute caught in a tree. Libby could not believe her bad luck; she hadn't seen a single spider in the house since Henry had passed away, and now two of these wretched creatures in the very same night? It was all too much for her.

She grabbed the closest newspaper and instinctively killed the spider. When she realized what she had done Libby caught her breath and sat down. As she checked her pulse to make sure she was all right, she couldn't help but feel like a rubber band that had been stretched to its limit.

That's it for tonight. I can't take anymore. She looked at the clock in the hallway and decided that midnight was too late to be drinking tea anyway.

She did a quick search for Squishy, but shortly she gave up and walked down the hall toward the stairs. They creaked with each step as she made her way back to the bed.

Upon entering the room, Libby left the door slightly ajar for Squishy then got into bed without turning on the light. She brushed her hands under the covers hoping she wouldn't feel anything unwanted; she felt relieved to find that there was nothing there.

A few moments later, cozy in the oversized bed and nearly asleep, she heard the pitter pat of tiny feet on the steps. As her eyes adjusted to the darkness, she saw the door pushed back and a brief moment later she felt a familiar thump on the bed; it was her cat, surely pleased to finally have its master's adventure end for the night. Libby too was pleased that they could finally get their much needed rest.

Her eyes felt heavy but before she could sleep she began to wonder if she had left the stove on. Libby grumbled to herself, since she hadn't even cleaned up the spilt tea what were the odds she would have—

"Crap! Crap! Crap!" she said to herself.

Libby leapt out of bed. She noticed that strangely Squishy didn't seem to react; she reasoned that the poor old cat was probably too tuckered out to care. She reached over and gently petted him as he let out his familiar groan meow she was accustomed to, as some of his fur came off in her hand.

He must be shedding, she thought. *I'll have to brush him later.*

With little to no thought she clutched the fur in her right hand as she started down the stairs. As Libby made her way down the hallway towards the kitchen she felt light wispy filaments against her face. She was horrified to realize it was rows and rows of spider webs! Her first collected thought was to debate whether or not this was another nightmare, but it appeared as though she had not been to this part of the house in years. In her confused state she entered the kitchen and flipped on the light. Her eyes found themselves on a sight that made her blood curdle...

There was a large, tangled spider web covering the farthest wall. In the center was Squishy…at least what remained of him. He'd been wrapped up in the sticky web. His innards had been sucked dry and he was slumped over like an empty furry white sock; there was very little left of her beloved pet. Libby's brain raced for answers, trying to absorb everything; but she could only reach the chilling conclusion that this was all real. Squishy was dead and Libby, wanting to scream but unable to do so, froze and stared into the eyes of bits and pieces of her best friend.

She thought back to how she had rubbed Squishy just before coming downstairs; how his fur had come off in her hand. Libby opened her hand to see the fur she had inadvertently grasped; instead of the snow white fur Squishy had shed all over her house she was now holding thin black hairs that were toppling out from her open palm. Her breath came out in short, violent bursts.

She heard something flop off her bed; she heard the legs of whatever this was go pitter pat on the stairs. Her heart nearly burst out of her chest. It was getting closer and closer; Libby's knees buckled and she collapsed to the floor. From down the hallway she could see a distorted shadow of a giant spider with its many legs making its way slowly, very slowly towards her.

⁓

A strong breeze blew through the window and into the hotel room, finding its way from the sandy California beaches to the sleeping bodies of two newlyweds in their honeymoon suite still tired from a ravenous night of passionate lovemaking. As the chill met the curves of Libby's young nude body, she rolled over half asleep/half awake. Her eyes opened with shock.

She thought back to the dream, and oddly wasn't terrified but rather perplexed by it and its implications about the future. Next to her, still sleeping with a majority of the blankets was her new husband Henry. Both so young and full of life she snuggled next to him and thought back to the vivid dream. From the corner of her eye she saw movement on the far wall as something tiny ran and then stopped. She saw it and it saw her. There was a shared moment.

Then Libby shut her eyes and held onto Henry. Out her window the Pacific Coast Highway and the City of Angels called to her with dreams of the future.

Hal Bodner is the author of the best-selling gay vampire novel Bite Club *and the lupine sequel* The Trouble With Hairy. *Hal has been an entertainment lawyer, a scheduler for a 976 sex telephone line, a theater reviewer and the personal assistant to a television star. He has never been a waiter. Hal has also written a few erotic paranormal romances—which he refers to as "supernatural smut"— most notably* In Flesh and Stone *and* For Love of the Dead. *While his salacious imagination is unbounded, he much prefers his comedic roots and he is currently pecking away at a series of bitterly humorous gay super hero novels. He blushes to admit he recently married a man who is young enough not to know that Liza Minnelli is Judy Garland's daughter. As a result, Hal has recently discovered that the use of hair dye is rarely an adequate substitute for Viagra. Those readers who enjoy his work can send him adoring fan mail at Hal@wehovampire.com.*

HOT TUB

Hal Bodner

THE INSTANT I SAW THE POOL BOY, I knew he had to die. He was far too beautiful to live and my entire body, such as it was, tingled with anticipation.

He had exactly the kind of physique I best like to play with; a smooth expanse of broad, hard chest interrupted only by a slash of cleavage and a few tiny wisps of hair around each nipple, trunk-like thighs rippling like anacondas when he walked, and biceps which seemed to strain against their covering of spice brown skin whenever he moved his arms. When he bent to place Jason's drink on the table, the sculpted plates of his stomach slid into each other like armor that had been oiled. Even the most unaesthetic cretin of a casting director would have been able to tell that it was all natural, developed from actual labor and outdoor exercise; this youth was leagues away from the artificial steroid-pumped gym rats to which Jason was partial.

Most Los Angelenos—at least those in Jason's social set— lump anyone with brown skin into the category of "Mexican". I know better. Some years back I spent a bit of time in Mexico. I found the people there to be dull and lifeless, earthy and pale shadows of their ancestors. Not to my taste at all. Back in the day, the people of Mexico were a bloodthirsty lot, sometimes sacrificing thousands of captured enemies in a single day until the stairways of their temples were so drenched in blood that the scarlet stains can still be seen today. Then, of course, the Spanish invaded and everything went to hell. Isn't that just like the Europeans? Always mucking about with perfection until they ruin it utterly.

Anyway, the sight of this tanned and athletic young man had stirred some of my cherished memories of the New World natives. I would wager he had quite a bit of the jungles of Peru in his blood. I adored the original Peruvians, a plucky race. They fought to the death and, if pestilence hadn't wiped them out, they might even have won. I could easily picture the pool boy on a ball court, stripped naked but for a loin cloth, eyes the color of chocolate mixed with cayenne sparkling with laughter as he kicked a decapitated blond-haired Spanish head the length of the field. Better yet, I envisioned him standing framed against an impossibly blue sky, with scarlet blood staining his chalk white teeth and dripping onto the gold and jeweled plates covering his rippled chest, the strong muscles of his neck straining in relief as he chewed the tough raw heart muscle of his enemies.

Oh yes. I've always had quite the fondness for Peruvian guys.

Jason, of course, was almost completely oblivious. More accurately, he was oblivious to any needs but his own. Until he noticed the pool boy, he'd been sprawled out pool-side, face down on his chaise, floating in a mildly alcoholic haze from the combination of two Mojitos and the ninety-plus degree heat, half-arousing himself by a combination of mental fantasy, the smell of musk from his own armpits, and the pressure of the beach towel-covered chair on his dick.

Don't get me wrong. Jason's an extremely attractive man. When he was twenty-two, it was enough. But he's one of those ten percent of the lowest intelligence who *think* they're in the top one percent. Actually, I'm lucky he can at least read. When I first started mentoring him, he was dyslexic—though no one had any idea of what that was at the time. The studio had to hire a UCLA intern to teach his lines to him. The college boy doubled as a fluffer and would suck Jason off every time he was about to go on camera which, I suppose, accounts for the glassy-eyed expression that became one of Jason's trademarks. The critics called it an "otherworldly ethereal quality of mysticism and romance". Being fairly well acquainted with various otherworldly qualities myself, I fail to see how Daily Variety managed to confuse them with post-orgasmic satiation.

Jason, though, *thinks* he has taste. And the little bastard likes to test his boundaries and push me a little. Usually, I give him enough rope to hang himself and, when he comes crying back to me with a gift or two, I relent with nothing worse than a mild rebuke and a bubbling belch. Every so often, Jason goes too far and, reluctantly, I have to teach him a lesson. Most of the time, a hit to his portfolio or a few months of offers drying up is enough to bring him into line. A few times, he was out of control enough so that the punishment needed to be more severe. Unlike the plump nipples of the pool boy, both of Jason's had to be surgically re-constructed so he could go bare-chested when he starred in action pictures. The damaged testicle wasn't a problem as, if audiences were lucky, it was probably never going to be on camera anyway.

Actually, keeping Jason in Jaguars and cocaine is sometimes almost more hassle that it's worth. The guy is his own worst enemy. While he wouldn't dare thwart me in most things, in other areas he's as stubborn as an approaching-fifty actress who is convinced she can still play twenty-five. He'll have a single blockbuster hit and it'll go right to his head. It takes only a single cover story in People Magazine to convince him that he actually has talent and can do serious roles. We'll argue back and forth and, invariably, he'll come up with a few wretched pieces of tripe that he considers "serious" drama worthy of his dubious skills. Inevitably, they're dismal flops—especially if he insists on directing—and by the Tuesday after opening weekend, he's all humble and contrite, whining that he practically has to beg to be allowed back into the studio commissary or that none of his A-list buddies will play tennis with him at the Club.

That's not to say Jason's not clever. Indeed, he can be a manipulative son of a bitch. He knows exactly which of my buttons to push to wheedle himself back into my good graces. Some of the gifts he's brought me over the years have been pretty spectacular. But, as Jason gets older and fears he's losing his youth and his audience appeal, as his bankability declines with each see-saw of a major hit followed by a dismal flop or two, every parting of the ways between us becomes more violent and of longer duration. He simply cannot come to terms with the fact that *I* know best and that he is, for want of a better analogy, not much more than attractive meat.

You may wonder why I haven't just dumped him. Frankly, I wonder that myself sometimes. Part of the reason is that Jason is one of those rare individuals who are so self-centered, so absorbed with their own needs and immediate gratifications, so egoistic and focused on whatever they desire at the moment, that they have no real soul. It's pointless even to damn them; they wouldn't understand why they'd been damned nor even what damnation was all about. It's no fun poking sticks at something that can't feel the pain. Besides, Jason came along at a fortuitous time for me and I've been the force behind too many coincidences to imagine that they occur naturally without some outside help.

Jason was barely twenty when I met him. Though we were both enthralled with the movie business, our obsessions were subtly different. Jason was bowled over with the idea of power and money, glamour and fame, unrestricted sex and drugs—all in the name of Art. He wanted to be desired and worshiped and adored. As for me? Well, though I've never been one to scoff at or turn down some decent quality adoration and worship, it was something particular to Hollywood that most attracted me. The movie business is certainly not the only industry to earn a reputation as a cesspool of corruption, greed and selfishness. Hell, almost any of the Nineteenth and Early Twentieth Century manufacturing industries were worse and, very often, you had the deaths of thousands of slave laborers to sweeten the pot. But Hollywood is unique in that it thrives on the corruption of the closest held and most cherished of people's dreams.

It's easy to kill a man. Ah, but to slowly chip away at his deepest dreams, thwarting them slowly and in infinitesimally excruciating increments until he succumbs to despair, *that* is a delicious exploitation of Talent. Even better, in this town people are generally far too full of themselves to consider committing suicide to banish their crushed dreams forever. No, in Hollywood they take service jobs, or become non-pros, or get involved in support industries, trying to convince themselves—and anyone who will listen—that they really have "made it" in some minor way. Yet all the time, their failures quietly and secretly eat at their souls; they are the sources of their own agony. Delicious!

Back to my first encounter with Jason. Though I clearly remember the circumstances of my humiliation, I have no intention of sharing them. I'll say only that, no matter how big you may think your dick is, there is always someone with a bigger one who you'll want to avoid, and we'll just leave it at that. Things could have been worse, I suppose. Two thousand years ago, I might have found myself trapped in a dented brass lighting fixture and tossed into the desert. For a while, it was all the rage. Anyone who was anyone had an old oil lamp on display to be proudly shown off to honored guests accompanied by suitably fearful stories about the terrible and powerful being trapped within it. Almost all of them were empty of course, but if a visitor was foolish enough to point out to the owner that he'd purchased a fake, he was likely to have his nose slit or his right hand cut off.

In more modern times, Fate's sense of humor seems to have grown even more perverse. I know of three of my brethren who were bound into musical instruments; in one case it was a tuba played weekends in a Mariachi band. I heard of another who was trapped in a bustier owned by a stripper who was long past her prime but who still insisted on wearing the thing to perform. And there's a particularly gruesome and degrading urban legend amongst my kind which involves a shovel used by the caretakers at the Milwaukee Zoo.

In comparison, being confined to a nine foot wide circle of steaming water wasn't too terrible. But it was embarrassing. A hot tub. In Los Angeles. A red wood hot tub, no less. There were times I wanted to scream from the trite cliché of the thing but all I could do was…bubble with humiliation. At least I was located in a low-rent apartment building in the heart of Hollywood. Some of the alternatives would have been cringe-inducing. I consider myself damned lucky that I wasn't inhabiting one of those ubiquitous fat farms calling themselves "luxury" spas where, day in and day out, I'd be subjected to flabby fleshed matrons and portly businessmen just begging for a heart attack. Worse, I could have found myself in the courtyard of one of those weird ashrams out in Malibu where the sanctimonious, self-conscious spirituality of all those True Believers and whack jobs who consider themselves to be Spiritually Advanced would have quickly driven me insane.

Most of the tenants were youngish types and I am, as is already obvious, a sucker for youth and beauty—especially if it's male. The endless progression of hopeful actors, eager musicians and writers, wanna-be directors and producers and other youngsters with pie-in-the-sky fantasies were at least mildly entertaining, if monotonous and predictable after the first few years. Fortunately, there were enough bruised egos, crushed hopes, and missed opportunities to sustain me, but they were mere appetizers, preventing starvation but never satiating. I wanted, I *lusted*, for a meal. And the temptation was excruciating. Some of the youths who jumped into my hot tub were exquisitely beautiful and my incorporeal jaws virtually *ached* at the thoughts of what I wanted to do to them. Unfortunately, there are rather rigid rules for these sorts of situations and, old-fashioned traditionalist that I am, I was constrained to abide by them.

Jason, when he came along, was a less-than-perfect solution. But at least he was *a* solution. Other than his extreme beauty and marked lack of anything remotely resembling talent, intelligence or ability, there wasn't much to distinguish him from the hundreds of other young hopefuls I'd shared the water with over the years. Not at first. But as he continued to slip into the tub, night after night, to loll in the heated bubbles, I began to sense something marvelous about him, a pervasive amorality and a total lack of even the simplest human emotions as they applied to other people.

An almost perfect sociopath! In *my* hot tub! I was blessed. Truly, I was.

Then, something strange and wonderful began to happen. Slowly, Jason began to sense my presence sharing the jetting water with him. It was terribly frustrating. He knew I was there. I knew he knew it. And there was nothing I could do about it to open the door of communication. The entire responsibility fell on Jason and, as I'm sure I've already mentioned, Jason is more than a few opinion cards short of an audience survey. Even knowing that the Powers That Be intentionally arrange these bindings to inanimate objects to produce exactly the kind of frustration I was experiencing didn't make me feel any better.

I have to give Jason some credit. While most people might have thought themselves crazy, imagining a presence in a hot tub, Jason never once doubted himself. His ego is that strong and his faith in his own abilities is that misguided. He often spoke aloud to me and, when that didn't work, he even spent a ridiculous few hours trying to make contact with me by means of a second hand Ouija board he found at a swap meet. That damned Ouija board is still a bone of contention between us. Every so often, he'll drag it out and try to use it to force me to do something which he knows I have no damned intention of doing. I've told him a hundred times that the thing only works on the Dead and I am emphatically not some stupid spectre who doesn't know enough to go into the Light. But Jason has some preconceived notions that he's gotten so far into his thick skull that you'd need a sledge hammer to get them out. Believe me when I say that the sledgehammer is sometimes a mighty tempting option.

Six, seven months went by. I did what I could for the kid, which admittedly wasn't much. I was able to influence a couple of auditions that might have gone in his favor anyway as the casting folks were looking mostly for a face and they didn't need anyone to try to actually act. A few times I was able to augment the desire that an older, wealthier gent had to run his hands over Jason's nubile young, naked body. That was by far the easiest as I've always had a talent for lust. However, there were times when Jason could be even more moronic than my low expectations of him; three times when I set him up with johns so he could pay his rent, the idiot took checks! Even so, with great and exhausting effort, I was able to keep a roof over his head. Much as I was already starting to dislike him, he was my only hope and I did not want him high-tailing it back to Kansas or whatever god-forsaken place he was originally from.

The day he brought the underwear model home was the turning point. The boy was absolutely gorgeous, a bit too slender to be my ideal, but with such exquisite bone structure and an almost androgynous quality to his musculature that he would have taken even my breath away had I been in a state where breathing was possible. Jason fucked him on the lounge chairs. He fucked him on the deck surrounding the pool. He fucked him while leaning against a tree in one of the ornamental planters. He fucked him standing, sitting, laying down and in some improbably gymnastic positions that would have put any human being over thirty into instant traction. And, once he was finally all fucked out, to gild the lily so to speak, he forced the guy to blow him in the hot tub.

I'd shared my water with many other guys, and even girls, who'd had sex in the tub and nothing had happened. In this one instance, thank goodness, Jason's fixation on his own immediate needs paid off. It certainly didn't hurt that both he and the model were also already coked halfway to the tits before they got into the tub. To this day, I am amazed that his dick wasn't bitten off while he was holding the model's head under the water. Afterwards, he told me that he just assumed all the thrashing and digging-of-nails into the backs of his thighs was evidence of "passion"; it never occurred to him that it might be part and parcel of suffocation or drowning. His main concern about the tragedy, he later complained, was that he hadn't had a chance to "shoot another load", as he so graphically termed it, before the model expired.

I sensed the instant the youth died. I was still very, very weak. Even so, I summoned the strength to croak, "Get out!" and I accompanied it with a tremendous eruption of sulfurous bubbles. Even if he didn't understand my command, the stench was enough to send Jason scampering out of the tub. He stood on the deck, naked and dripping, his jaw hanging open like the classic drooling idiot, watching me as I feasted. Oh my, but Underwear Guy was delicious!

When I'd finished, a tremendous loginess came over me. Lazily, I settled onto the bottom of the tub, pausing only to send out a mental message, "Tomorrow night" before I drifted away into what passed for a contented sleep for those of my kind.

Wouldn't you know it? The ignoramus showed up with road kill!

I don't know whether it was a cat or an opossum or a rat or someone's prized Pomeranian for that matter. Whatever it was, it was bloody and disgusting and as insulting as hell. There Jason was, with the furry corpse in his hands, kneeling and holding it up to the hot tub as if it was an offering of the finest frankincense or the choicest morsels of an unbaptized infant's flesh.

"You've got to be kidding," I told him. I was still languid from my meal but I was strong enough to form some semblance of a body from the water. Even better, the range of my influence had finally expanded so that I could more easily affect things past the borders of the apartment building courtyard without getting a debilitating headache.

"It's an offering," he informed me with naive gravity.

I sighed. I'm pretty sure he missed the way I looked down my nose with disdain but, since I was still incapable of manifesting as much more than a nebulous blob of percolating water, I wasn't offended. The dubious "offering", however, was another matter.

"Dude," I began. He started, probably not expecting me to sound like a Malibu surfer. I probably could have led with the whole "Bow before your new master" routine, but I was feeling benevolent, probably because I'd found a couple of left over shreds of underwear model that had been accidentally par-boiled to exquisite tenderness. "Dude, your life is about to change."

Jason's desires were boringly predictable. Like so many others, he wanted to be a movie star. Not merely an actor. He was quite explicit about that. He wanted to be a Star. I assured him that his goals were easily within the realm of my abilities and I instructed him on what he'd have to do in order to hold up his side of the deal. To his credit, he never once balked. I let him know, in no uncertain terms, that our initial objective was to secure his future and, not incidentally mine. My first order of business was to build up my strength. Jason obliged with two street hustlers. He then found a very attractive Filipino coke dealer and we used the stash to get hold of a "full release" masseur and a Salvadoran boy who advertised naked maid services.

For my part, the auditions started coming fast and furious. Our biggest challenge in those early days was that I hadn't developed the finesse I have now. I could extend enough influence to get him the jobs, but I wasn't always able to tell in advance specifically what the jobs were for. I needed him to hire an agent or, at the very least, a manager. Jason balked and refused. According to him, he needed no one's advice on his career but his own. Evidently, he'd seen *Valley of the Dolls* or some similar crap one too many times and he thought that if he kept referring to agents as "blood sucking leeches", it would make him sound more like a knowledgeable Hollywood insider. Try as I might to talk him around, Mr. Wizard proclaimed that agents and managers had no purpose other than to suck the cream off of the talents of others though, in truth, Jason phrased it in much more graphic and far earthier words. Notwithstanding that he was fundamentally right, he still needed the help and the disagreement burgeoned into our first conflict.

It was risky for me. I won't deny that. But I took the chance. I made sure Jason's phone stopped ringing and the auditions dried up. His head shots found their way into the wrong folders. His business cards slipped into the back of the drawer or were accidentally brushed off into the garbage. It took almost a month for his predicament to register with him, and a few weeks longer before the probable reasons for it dawned over the barren field that is Jason's brain. During that time I grew famished. It's easy to resign yourself to starvation. But it's hellish to have to return to abstinence after a series of feasts. Eventually, my little Einstein capitulated. He brought me a tight-bodied little African American personal trainer. He made a surprisingly refreshing change from all of those beach boy types Jason was partial to. Even better, there was no lingering aftertaste of suntan oil.

We engaged an ancient transplanted New Yorker named Florence who was a walking stereotype, complete with fake-diamond rimmed eyeglasses dangling around her neck on a silver chain, blueish hair piled high on her head into a tight bun, far too much makeup applied as if with a trowel, a raucous voice like a hippopotamus in heat, and sturdy, sensible shoes. Florence had no idea I existed. She experienced only an overwhelming drive to make as much money for Jason as she could in the shortest possible time which, given the kind of woman she was, fell right in line with what she probably would have done even without my trying to influence her. Jason, still hesitant and abashed from the "dry" period I'd subjected him to, kept fairly quiet when I forced him to husband almost every penny. It took almost a year but, finally, I was ready.

"Buy this building," I ordered him.

At first, he bristled to argue. Why spend the hundreds of thousands of dollars he'd earned on what was, after all, a pretty run-down apartment building in Hollywood? With great patience, I explained my predicament and how fragile our arrangement was should some developer decide to tear the place down. As my words penetrated the fog, I think it may have been the first expression of fear I'd ever seen him exhibit. I don't know how he convinced Florence to go along with the plan; I only assume I'd provided some strong motivation.

There were snags. There always are when it comes to real estate in Los Angeles. It's an illusory industry. No one bedroom, nine hundred square foot, plywood deathtrap of a house is truly worth two and a half million dollars, for example. But, in LA we fight to the death to preserve our illusions; we spend far more time protecting our fantasies than we do in facing our realities. It's simply the way we are.

In this case, the snags were a muscular, hairy-chested, thirty-some year old Israeli gentleman and velvet-skinned Armenian twin brothers with the most incredible asses I'd seen in years who formed the investment consortium that owned the building. I have always had a penchant for Middle Eastern food.

Once we owned the place, evicting the tenants would have drawn too much attention. Instead, we let it become abandoned through attrition and, I will confess, a single night of over-indulgence in a trio of roommates from the second floor, wanna-be rock musicians with tattoos covering the whipcord muscles of their torsos and backs. I was sorely tempted by one of the investigating officers who came asking questions after the band vanished, a handsome blond-haired stud. But, I decided to err on the side of discretion and dignity and I let the cop go unscathed. I fancy myself a gourmet, not a gourmand.

Once the building was secure, I didn't care that Jason moved out and into his first house up in the Hills. My immediate safety was assured and I was content with the arrangement. But then, Jason started getting a little too big for his britches as the old expression goes. I honestly think it was a case of Monkey See, Monkey Do or, in Jason's case, Moron See, Moron Do.

Actors are strange beasts, blessed in spite of themselves. If you consider how far some of them get in life without having enough brains to fit into a demitasse, can you imagine what an intelligent one could pull off? He could rule the world so long as there were no mirrors to preen in and distract him, and so long as there was some poor schnook behind the scenes to write down everything he was supposed to say in public and put it on a teleprompter for him.

The first transgression that I knew about was a hitchhiker, a tawny-haired hopeful from somewhere down South. At the time, Jason had only just begun to find himself so the result was bloody, but nonetheless effective, showing not a scintilla of the finesse that my unwanted protégée would develop over the next few years.

"I'm not eating that!"

"But, but...what do I do with the body?" Jason's voice, while tailor-made for the bold and witty deep-voiced quips of the action heroes he so often plays, takes on an indescribably irritating quality when he whines or whimpers. It's a harsh, high pitched tone that combines nails on a chalkboard with hints of alley cats being roasted alive. While some of my kind might find that sort of thing pleasant, my personal tastes are more refined.

I shrugged, as if I didn't care. I didn't realize quite yet that he'd developed dark desires of his own. I thought he'd simply been unable to coax the kid into the abandoned apartment building and had assumed, insultingly, that dead was as much to my taste as fresh.

"I'm not your personal Dispose-All, Jason," I told him. "If you want to make an offering, or to bring me a gift, if you want to thank me and guarantee than my benevolence still flows in your direction, make it a proper one." I sneered deliberately, enjoying the look of misery on his handsome face. "Otherwise, don't waste my time."

"B...but..." he stammered, still unable to understand why I was rejecting the hitch hiker.

"Keep it up, kiddo. Keep working my nerves and you'll be appearing in toilet paper commercials for scale."

"I knew it," he retorted, nastily. "I knew I never should have taken the trouble to bring anything to you. I should have just dumped him in the desert with the others."

I froze as the import of his words registered. "The...others?" I asked with ominous calm which, of course, he completely missed noticing. "What...others?"

Whereupon, with blithe abandon, he began to relate the indescribable stupidity of what he'd been doing for the past several months. By the time he was done rehashing every tiny detail of each of the six murders as if I should be relishing each word, I was livid.

"Are you *insane*?" I blurted out, once he had finished and was looking to me, smugly, for approval.

"There's no reason to be huffy," he said with the arrogance that only a young actor whose last film grossed close to a hundred million can muster. "Besides, *you* do it. What makes you better than me?"

That was when I ripped his nipples off and ate them.

I apologized later, of course. Not for attacking him; he deserved that. But for risking his career by doing something that might show up on camera. Oh, he avoided me for a few months after that, not because he was afraid of my doing more damage, but rather because he was going to teach *me* a lesson. I arranged for his next job offer to be on *Dancing with the Stars* and it was almost magical to see how quickly I found him truculently standing on the redwood deck above me, looking down into the steaming water, chin set and prepared for a knock- down, drag-out rumpus.

To be honest, he made some compelling arguments in his favor. But I was adamant. I'd groomed him to be a star, not a serial killer. Even though there was some of the latter inherent in the former, we needed to keep his priorities straight. We argued for hours and it was an argument we'd have over and over again for the next few years. Each time, I'd assume I'd won and things would settle down for a while. Then, Jason would show up bearing the tortured body of an extremely handsome Vietnamese waiter from Alhambra, or a youth from the Occidental College male gymnastic team, or a young member of a construction crew who had been working on paving potholes on the 405 freeway and, within minutes, we'd be screaming at each other and hurling accusations and imprecations once again.

Physical punishment wasn't terribly persuasive; I learned that when, only a scant six weeks after I'd lost my temper and crushed his right ball, Jason brought me the body of a Ralph's stock boy that he had slowly and patiently burned alive with heated barbeque skewers. It began to dawn on me that maybe I was not as infallible as I'd thought. I realized that choosing Jason may not have been the best decision I'd ever made and that, perhaps, the compulsions he was claiming might actually be valid. Still, I was stuck with him and, after all, what healthy co-dependent relationship doesn't have a troubling wrinkle or two?

I still got on his case when he transgressed, and I urged and cautioned him to be careful. I didn't much care if *he* were caught but, as for *me*, I found myself echoing Vivian Leigh and vowing to never go hungry again. I even swallowed my pride and helped him dispose of the evidence every so often though too much Dead gives me the functional equivalent of indigestion. Fortunately, I'm much less gassy if I take the time to boil them until tender.

A few times, Jason insisted on demonstrating his technique for me. I feigned boredom but, between you and me, I was actually fascinated with how quickly he progressed and how skilled he became at inflicting pain and terror with his tortures. There was one blond boy—if memory serves, it was another personal trainer—who Jason managed to keep screaming into a gag fairly constantly for almost an entire weekend with no one in the abandoned courtyard but me and the occasional pigeon to witness. He slipped the young man into the hot tub scant seconds before he died and, in spite of myself, I had to admit it was one of the most delicious meals I've had in recent memory.

Oddly, I don't think Jason did it either to try and impress me or to make a legitimate offering. I think he did it because he was a little lonely. As his fame grew, as his extra-curricular perversions became more compelling, as his innate selfishness grew more pronounced, I think he discovered that he has difficulty relating to people. In a weird way, I think I may be his only friend. I find an odd solace in those thoughts. I'm not the friend-making type. If I did have a friend, I think I'd want him to be capable of carrying on a conversation with subject matter of more depth than box office grosses, potential projects in development and what the Kardashians were up to. But, for a time, things between us were...nice and the mental and emotional bonds between us grew stronger. Soon, while I could not force myself inside of his mind, I could often see things as if

I were gazing out of Jason's eyes and hear those of his thoughts that he wanted me to hear.

But then, the little shit started pushing again, testing his boundaries, making the mistake of thinking that merely because I'm trapped in this damned redwood cell, I can't reach out and *hurt,* or even destroy, if I need to. He'd see someone, a beautiful young man, and he'd know that I desired him. Sometimes, he'd do the wise thing and bring him to me. But, there were other times when he was convinced a director was favoring a leading lady, or when a critical review of one of his dubious performances was less than stellar or when there were too many rotten tomatoes, or when he was not immediately seated at a prime table at a trendy restaurant. At those times, he lashed out; and the one he lashed out at was me.

He sold the Hollywood Hills house in favor of a Bel Air mansion with a sound-proofed basement. There, in what used to be a recording studio, he got a perverse enjoyment out of sensing me raging and cursing at him, imprisoned several miles away in my Hollywood hot tub, while he slowly tortured some magnificent specimen of manhood to death. Other times, he'd bring them into Hollywood, right into the courtyard, where he'd play with them for hours, or even days, until they expired. Then, and only then, would he deign to gift me with the cold dead meat, unsatisfying but vital to my continued comfort.

The son of a bitch got off on teasing me, tempting me, driving me to the brink of madness, knowing that the worst I would do to him was something financial. We both knew that, as much as I lusted to do so, for me to hurt him physically to the degree he deserved would only be cutting off my own figurative nose to spite my face. We'd become symbiotic, each a parasite of the other, unable to exist without what the other half provided.

Jason became a master at pushing just far enough. Then, just when I was on the verge of abandoning all restraint and doing something drastic like ripping out his liver, he would relent and, feigning sweetness and light, he'd slide a bound, fully conscious and indescribably yummy boy into the water. I've tolerated it for a very long time, but the end of my torment is nearing.

There's a boy, you see. He's young, perhaps seventeen, a runaway, I think. He broke into the building a few months ago and has made a little nest for himself in one of the old apartment units. Cleaned up properly, I imagine he'd be quite handsome.

So far, I've been able to keep him completely ignorant of my presence. He wonders, every so often, why the hot tub in an abandoned apartment complex still works, and why it never seems to need cleaning. Fortunately, it doesn't take much effort for me to divert the lad's thoughts elsewhere. You see, he has dreams of becoming an actor, a movie star actually. This boy, however, seems to possess some actual intelligence and, for all I know, maybe even some legitimate talent.

Jason is on his way over with the pool boy, still shirtless, body glistening with sweat, bound and in the trunk of his Jaguar. He may be planning another long scene where I'm condemned only to watch or, perchance, this may be one of the times when he's feeling generous and my little Aztec will satisfy a gnawing hunger. Either way, alive or dead, I know Jason will eventually dispose of the body beneath my waters.

But Jason doesn't know about the building's new tenant. He doesn't know I've made contact with him. It's not much of a contact, not a strong connection like I've fostered with Jason. But it's enough. Jason's success has caused him to forget a fundamental fact that every newcomer to Hollywood knows. When he climbs up onto my deck with the pool boy in his arms, I'll just have to remind him.

It's a truism in Hollywood. No matter how big you are in this town, there is always someone waiting just behind you, someone wanting to get ahead, someone desperate to take your place. All it takes is the slightest...push.

John Palisano grew up the son of a fashion designer and an Emmy Award winning artist. At a young age, he often wandered around the sets of soap operas and CBS broadcast news in New York City. Later studying at Emerson College in Boston, John won the Latent Image Award *for his produced screenplay* He'd Hoped For Mars. *After moving to Hollywood, an internship with Ridley Scott led to jobs on commercials, music videos, and as an assistant on a movie where some Austrian weightlifter fights Satan. Directing his own micro-budget features was a lesson in how not to make a film. He also made music and wrote fiction, and has sold over a dozen short stories and wrote the acclaimed novel* Nerves. *John also uses his filmmaking experience to craft book trailers for publishers and authors, blending his passion for film, fiction and music. Find out more at www.johnpalisano.wordpress.com.*

WELCOME TO THE JUNGLE

John Palisano

MICHELLE REMEMBERED THE BLACK BUSINESS CARD and had a vision that it would be her way out of obscurity. "Always follow your gut," she said. She never got in trouble whenever she listened to her instincts.

She'd woken up after another anonymous day as an extra more tired than she'd felt in her entire life. Even her coffee didn't seem to do much to rouse her. She thought about calling Pam and telling her how it went. They'd both moved out to L.A. within weeks of getting out of Palmville, Texas High School. Pam settled in with a good casting company while Michelle beat the boards pursuing an acting career. She went on the occasional audition, but she never landed anything; another blonde in a sea of blondes. How would she ever stand out?

She grabbed the business card and looked it over. *Dusty Palace. Jungle Films.* There was a snake-like drawing at the bottom. He'd introduced himself the night before at the Frolic Room, her favorite neighborhood bar. He'd directed two movies she'd actually heard of, *The Longfellow* and *Hounds Of Hell.* After he left, the bartender, Mike, told her he thought the guy was sleazy. *Aren't they all?* At least she could call him…find out what he was about. So what if it was straight to home video? So what if she had to be in a horror movie? She didn't mind. Whatever the project, at least she might be seen in something that had distribution. She certainly didn't want to pantomime to invisible dance music for fourteen hours a day for the rest of her life.

She looked him up on the net. Everything he said checked out—his company website, his IMDB credits. He was legitimate.

"Wow," she said. "This could actually be something."

∽

"So glad you called." Dusty talked warm and slow.

"I just wanted to find out a little bit more about the shoot next week. I mean, what's it pay? How long will you need me for? That sort of thing?" Michelle said.

He laughed a little. "Now you sound like an actress."

"Well, I came here to act," she said. "Otherwise it's not really worth it to me to be here. I mean: I can make more at an office job back home in Texas, and work a lot less hours. It's not like I'll ever be seen doing extra work, anyway."

"I hear you," he said. "Well, look, I can't offer up too much more than two grand for the day without seeing how you act. I'm sure you'd be good enough for one of the girls in the dungeon scene, though."

"Okay. That sounds better."

"Are you good at being scared? Are you okay with nudity? Being topless? Can you scream?"

There it was. She heard Pam's voice in her head telling her not to call him. Fine. She'd test him. "I'm great at being scared.

Honestly? The other stuff? Not really. I'm not sure I want to go there just yet."

"Fair enough," he said. "I've got other girls for that, but you did say that you're okay with being scared, maybe dying onscreen, maybe a love scene, right?"

"Sure. What's a little blood and screaming?" she said.

"Right. Well, look, we're going to do that scene in two days. Here's the deal..."

⁌⁍

"Are you nuts?" Pam said. "You shouldn't be doing sleaze like that. Just stick with the extra work. It'll begin to pay off. Everyone in the industry has long hours. It's a given: The extras, the PAs, the entire crew. Heck, even those of us in the office, we all work long days. I even have to read scripts on the weekends a lot of the time."

"He's offering two grand for one day."

The line was silent.

"Really?"

"Yes."

"Get it up front."

"He's paying me as soon as I get there," Michelle said as she paced her studio. "That's rent and food for an entire month. And I don't have to wait three weeks for the check, either."

"Take it. Just be careful."

⁌⁍

Sun Valley felt like an entirely different state. There were farms and horses. Houses spread out more. It reminded her of some of the border towns she'd grown up with in Texas, so she felt immediately at home. She thought, *this is going to be great. This was a good move.* Her little Toyota Yaris pulled onto the side of the road and she patted her GPS. *Best invention ever.*

The house was larger than she expected. She saw cars lined up and down the street. She wondered where the crew vans were parked? She hadn't seen any. Where was Craft Services? Were the actors being held inside? She saw none of it and just assumed they were in another location. *Ah, so this is what indie film is like.* She proceeded to the front door. *This feels really small.*

A handmade sign taped to the door read: WELCOME TO THE JUNGLE. The bottom had the same snake logo as Dusty's card.

"Cute," Michelle said.

There was a lavender bush growing right next to the door and its smell mixed in with that of stables and horses. It reminded her so much of Texas that she shut her eyes for a moment and imagined she was home again, right on her Daddy's front porch.

The door knob rustled and she got her composure. Then she put on her bravest smile. Again, her stomach was in knots from the nerves. One day, she knew, it would all be familiar to her and she'd walk right into these situations as easy as iced tea.

Of course, it was Dusty who had opened the door. "Michelle," he said. "My Michelle. Welcome to our little place in paradise city."

The cottage seemed perfectly interior designed with all sorts of traditional southwestern themes. The walls were painted sandy with Aztec blue accents. Every surface looked fussed over. There were people sitting on the couches. One was reading a script. The others joked and laughed.

"You have perfect timing. We need to get you changed and down to set."

"Down?"

"The basement."

"Oh, right. I just don't see where this place would have a basement."

"That's why we chose it. It's rare in L.A. to find a house with any kind of basement."

Michelle met Rebecca, the wardrobe person. She had Michelle keep her jeans, but changed into a white blouse. "The blood will show up better," she said. They both laughed.

"Speaking of that? Where's all the crew trucks and stuff?" Michelle said.

"These low budgets...we have to carry everything in our trunks," Rebecca said. "Craft services is pizza. Dressing rooms are bathrooms. You get the idea. I'm doing lights, too, by the way."

"It's already a lot more fun than the other set I was on this week," Michelle said.

"Let's make it even better." Dusty reached into his pocket and gave her an envelope. She looked inside: Twenty hundred-dollar bills. It was impossible for her not to grin ear to ear.

❧

The basement was hot and unfinished, so one could see the exposed rock walls. The floor wasn't much more than a layer of sandy dirt. There was a naked woman chained to the wall. She didn't look up or respond when Michelle and Dusty entered.

"What's the name of this movie?" Michelle said. "I forgot to ask."

Dusty frowned. *"Appetite,"* he said. "Some poor fellow, played by me by the way, has a monster chained up in his basement and he has to feed it live kill every few days to keep it happy, or else."

He gestured to a huge mound about as high as their shoulders on the far side of the basement. It looked like a giant red crab coiled in on itself. Each of its claws had a shiny dagger affixed.

"That's our special effect," Dusty said and laughed.

"It looks real." Michelle said, stuttering. In fact, it looked very real. There was something about it...a presence that touched her instinct. Something about it just wasn't right. She thought that maybe it was a giant puppet, but she couldn't see any wires coming out the back. Maybe there was a guy inside to puppeteer it.

Dusty waved a hand under his nose. "It stinks in here something fierce," he said. "We better hurry up and shoot this sucker."

Dusty picked up a handheld video camera off the washer and dryer unit. "That's what we're shooting on?" Michelle said. Rebecca the wardrobe girl, and grip, apparently, walked closer to the naked woman. There was another set of cuffs hanging near her.

"You can shoot Hi-Def with this thing. It's better than what George Lucas used on *Star Wars*. If it's good enough for George, it's good enough for me."

Michelle was beginning to rethink having called him. Was she just in some terrible exploitation movie? Was this a mistake after all? Maybe she should have listened to Pam. Still, two thousand bucks to be scared of a giant crab monster is two thousand bucks, she knew, and it'd get distribution.

"We just need you to put your hands up in these cuffs," Rebecca said. "Then we can shoot."

Michelle stepped over to the cuffs and turned backward. She raised her hands, smiled, and said, "These are, like, real chains?" She had a nervous pit in her belly, just like when she rode the rollercoaster at the theme parks growing up.

Rebecca cuffed her. "These are actually cheaper than the prop ones. Don't worry: They're perfectly safe."

Dusty opened his camera, turned it on and walked over to Michelle. "Okay, so here's the scene. She's going to get eaten, and all you have to do is scream and act terrified of big old Red over here."

"Okay." Michelle said. "But once this is over I've got to see how that thing works." She nodded to the giant crab monster.

"Oh, you mean Red?" he said, then nodded with a smile. "Sometimes a magician shouldn't reveal his secrets, right?"

"I guess," she said.

"I don't want your performance to suffer. I want this to be real."

"Action." Dusty called.

Red unfolded slowly and gracefully. Michelle thought it looked like a one of those Transformers toys, or like a blooming onion, only more organic. Dusty held the camera rock solid. Red moved, creeping along the basement floor. It'd gotten almost an entire head taller since it unfolded. Four thin arms on each side closed in on the naked girl like two hands coming together.

"Farrah." Dusty said. "Wake up. Look who's here to see you. It's Red."

The naked girl looked up from her daze and saw the monstrous thing in front of her. Then she thrashed in her restraints. "Let me go. Let me out of here. Come on. Please."

Michelle did her best to keep her face looking as though she were terrified, even though she wasn't. She kept staring at the beast, studying it, recording it in her brain. The craftsmanship, she thought, was outstanding. Who'd need CG when they could make real objects look so life-like?

Farrah screamed. One of Red's hands slashed her across her belly with one of the knives. A curved slit opened and she bled profusely and quickly.

Michelle wondered how they were pulling off the effect. She thought that maybe Farrah had worn a false stomach pre-loaded with blood. Michelle thought they were quite clever. They could make it look like it was all one continuous take, and by using a handheld camera, they could tie into the whole reality TV phenomenon.

Red split in half horizontally. His eyes opened at the sides of his head: Even those seemed super realistic. It reminded Michelle of when she once swam with dolphins...she could see the intelligence in their eyes, just as she saw the intelligence in Red's. It was some magical trick.

Then Red opened his mouth, which seemed to take up the entire middle of his body. He had rows and rows of shining metal, shark-tooth-like teeth. Something else struck Michelle as funny: The smell. The air around them filled with the most rotten stench, like a hundred dead teeth, mixed with vinegar and spoiled meat. It came from Red.

She wracked her brain. Maybe they'd made him with animal parts to make him more realistic? No. She knew that wasn't it.

Red advanced toward Farrah and opened his mouth. The bottom jaw unhinged and fell to the floor. Knife-shaped teeth scraped along the dirt floor until they were just under her feet. She whimpered and screamed. "This can't be happening," she said. "No. Please. No."

In a blink, Red jerked forward and swallowed her entire bottom section. Some of the teeth gave her little slices.

Then Red clamped his mouth shut, like a giant shark. Farrah screamed and Michelle screamed, too. It was so real-looking.

Please let this be fake, she thought. *Please God let this not be happening.*

Something clicked in Michelle's head. She realized none of it was fake: Not a bit. Farrah's insides drooped from her top half. There was blood everywhere. Her head was slumped and she'd stopped moving. Her skin had gone ashen.

Red chewed on the bottom parts of Farrah. Michelle saw one foot and bit of leg before she turned away. She couldn't take any more. Tears streamed down her face and she shook uncontrollably.

Please let me live through this, she thought. *Please.*

She heard Red chewing for a few moments. *Pretend it's not real. Pretend it's just a big puppet. Don't worry about it. Act.* Then she sensed his warm breath on her. She wouldn't open her eyes...she refused to look...she refused to do anything other than what she had been hired to do, which was to act scared.

Act scared.

Then the beast's breath was away from her and she heard Dusty. "Here's where I need you most," he said. "Red here wants to copulate with you." He folded the LCD display of the camera down flush, turning it off.

"What? Someone's dead here."

He smiled. "Is she really dead or is it just a special effect? I'm not telling."

Michelle was speechless. What was he telling her? Was Farrah truly dead? She looked over to the remaining half of the woman. It was too real...the smell of the blood was real...how could it not be real? She'd seen it in front of her own eyes.

Dusty said, "Come on. You'll be fine. You'll be famous for this. It'll be unforgettable."

Red made a grumpy noise and inched closer.

"Anyone who sees this movie will never be able to forget this scene with you and Red," he said. "What do you say?"

"I...don't...want to," she said. "I don't do nudity. Is she really dead?"

Dusty got up in her face. "Do you really want to find out if she's dead or not? Why don't you just do the scene, take your money, and go home? I thought you wanted to act. Do whatever you have to do to make this moment happen for me."

Michelle felt her eyes well up. How could she have gotten herself in such a position? Did Grace Kelly really need to get choked by a telephone cord in order to become famous? "It's not really going to...?"

"We'll just make it look that way. Don't stress." Dusty's voice was very low. "You're just going to have to die in the end."

"Like Farrah?" Michelle felt sick. "I don't want to really die."

Dusty winked. "That's why they call it acting, you know?"

Michelle shut her eyes. *Can I trust him? That thing bit Farrah in half. Who says it won't do the same to me?* Michelle thought.

She said, "Just make it classy, okay?"

He laughed. "Not sure how much class is going to be involved with Red dry-humping you," Dusty said. "But I'll do my best." He unfolded the LCD on his camera and pressed a button. "Here we go. Ready?"

"Okay," she said.

Red moved closer toward Michelle. She could see that he had a much longer body than she'd originally seen. For some reason, Red reminded Michelle of a slinky as Red stretched out. He was some kind of horrific snake, she believed, like one of those fabled gigantic anacondas: Only Red was, well, red, and his head was closer to being nothing but mouth, teeth, and the six spindly red, dagger holding arms jutting from the rim of his mouth, three per side.

Dusty moved to her right side and got a different angle. She could almost see what he was shooting on the LCD. She looked at it from the corner of her eye: Michelle didn't want to ruin the shot by looking directly into the lens. The last thing she wanted to do was have to re-shoot the scene.

"Good," he said. "I'm going to be quiet now. I'll move around you two, but just be natural. Remember: pretend you're chained up in this crazy guy's basement and he's trying to feed his pet monster. If he doesn't feed the beast, it will eat him."

Michelle said, "Okay."

"Okay...so..." Dusty said. "Action."

Michelle felt Red's heaviness at her feet as it slowly crept upward. Red put his arms out. The daggers made a perfect halo shape around her face. Michelle instinctively made a whimpering sound. The daggers were so close, so sharp, and so very real. *Those are the same ones that I just watched cut Farrah. This thing could kill me in a blink.*

She shut her eyes for a moment again. Reaching down deep inside to the core of her training, she knew she had to use any acting tool available to her to make it through.

She searched her memories for something that really scared her. *You need to believe that this thing is fake. Then you need to be scared of something else...something from your past.*

What scared Michelle more than anything? A memory of a helicopter trip as a young girl flashed inside her mind. She'd been riding in the back with her father. They'd barely lifted off, and the pilot banked them to the right, when her door suddenly swung open. Her father grabbed her with both of his arms, holding her. She'd had on her seatbelt, so her father's reaction was more instinctual than lifesaving, she knew. Michelle, in that moment, looked down onto the river below them, across to the shore side landing area where they'd taken off. She was filled with dread that she was about to slip out and fall to her death. That was the feeling. She played over the helicopter moment in her head again. Her stomach tensed and she felt the exact same numbing fear.

Red slithered up and on top of her. She opened her eyes to find one of his looking right at her. He had to turn his head to his left a bit because his eyes were on the side of his head, like those of a fish. He blinked once.

She knew he was real.

No.

I'm going to fall out. Fall right down to the ground and that's the end of it. That's what I'm scared of happening. Nothing is worse...nothing is worse than that.

At her thighs she felt two nubs hardening. She looked down and saw a pair of thumb-shaped organs pushing into her. Thank God she had her clothes on.

It's all pretend. Nothing's real. Simulated.

"Okay, everyone hold on a sec," Dusty said. She looked up at him and saw Rebecca in the background quietly watching the scene. Her face was cold and expressionless.

Dusty went somewhere behind Red where Michelle couldn't see him. He returned a moment later with a plastic jug. "We'll need some blood for this one," he said.

He worked his way to her middle and poured it on her thighs, hips, and belly. It was warm. *That's human blood. From Farrah, or maybe someone else.* She tried to psych herself out of the thought. *No way. The blood's just been sitting in a hot basement for God knows how long. Maybe he just made it on the stove or something. Don't effects people make their own blood by cooking it with Karo syrup and red food coloring? It's cheaper than buying it from the supply shops, especially if you need a lot, right?*

Only problem was the blood smelled like blood, too.

Dusty said, "I'm ready," and grabbed the camera again. "Rolling."

Red's thumb-things massaged her thighs, searching for the place where they dipped downward between her legs. Michelle clamped her thighs together as hard as she could. No way was this thing going to get that close to her.

She sensed Dusty moving his camera down toward Red's thumb-things. Then he started panning the camera upward. She looked down so she wouldn't look directly in his lens again. She just let it happen without trying to force a scared face. Maybe if she kept it simple the scene would be scarier? Wasn't that what she was taught? Don't do anything. That was one of her acting teacher's voices in her head.

Then Dusty panned back down.

The blood had soaked right through her clothes and she felt numbness starting at her hips and going all the way down to her feet. It was what she'd imagined an epidural would be like.

She could still feel the thumb-things working faster and faster, but instead of hurting her, Red's weight was making her tingle. *Probably the blood rushing down from being hanged,* she thought. *There's really just a big special effects monster on top of me. That's all.*

Red moved faster. Dusty moved to the opposite side and panned up and down rapidly.

The thumb-things managed to spread her legs just a little, but not enough to get to any sensitive parts. It seemed to be working harder now that it'd gotten a small break. Michelle writhed on the chains. She wanted the scene over already.

Then the thumb-things managed to get between her legs deeper and Michelle screamed, "No."

You're going to fall out of the helicopter. That's the only thing that's real. That's the only thing to be scared of. The rest of this is just Hollywood.

The thumb-things moved quicker: It reminded her of when people would flutter their first and second fingers to simulate walking. It did not feel good at all, especially with the blood starting to dry and stick.

She looked down the length of Red's body and could see small ripples moving up and down his sections. As Red's skin moved, the circular bones stretched through. It was as though he were shivering.

Dusty kept shooting.

Then, as quickly as Red's assault started, it stopped. At least it looked that way for a brief moment. Red's face inched back away from hers. Dusty stepped back to get the whole scene.

Red opened his mouth and Michelle swore he was smiling. He moved his head from side to side, checking her out with one eye and then the other. Michelle wondered what Red was doing.

He slashed at her face with one of the daggers. She felt a hot pain flare across her right cheek, stretching from just under her eye to her chin.

She screamed, despite herself.

Red unleashed a rather giant tongue and rolled the tip. He used the tip to lick the slash he'd made top to bottom.

"No," Michelle said.

Red pulled his tongue back inside his head and shut his mouth.

Michelle looked down and could see she was still bleeding heavily. She felt as though she might pass out. *Is this what happened to Farrah right before he bit her in half? Am I about to die? How can I get out of here?*

Red backed away, slithering off her body. Michelle was relieved not to have his weight on her. She could see the nubs near his bottom, now flaccid and pale. She had an idea.

The nubs.

It had to be.

Even though she could barely feel her legs, she tried moving them. They wiggled. Her brain still worked.

Could she strike him?

No. He was too far away.

Dusty said, "All right. Take two."

Two? Hadn't he gotten what he needed with one? She'd been cut, for real. How would that edit together? Well, she didn't think continuity would be high on Dusty's priority list in the end.

The nightmare started again, with Red bulking his way toward her.

As soon as his little nubs were close enough, Michelle kicked them.

Red raised in the air with all he had. He lifted up and his back touched the ceiling. It was his turn to scream. His voice was hoarse and deep, like a sick sea lion.

"Shit." Dusty screamed.

Michelle looked down at his nubs. They were no longer pale, but red, and not from being turned on. Michelle kicked them again. The pitch of Red's scream rose. His eyes rolled back and he shoved his arms up toward the ceiling, where he stuck each dagger deep and into the woodwork.

He cried out again, his eyes locking with Michelle.

This is it. He's going to kill me for that move.

Red dropped back down, his arms whipping out from the ceiling. Chips of wood fell all over. He swung them around and violently punched them into a circle around Michelle. They were sharp enough to stick into the rock.

His mouth opened and she could see the little specks of blood in his drool. Had that been her blood?

Then Red tried to pull his daggers free. He couldn't. He pulled several times, but he was totally stuck.

"Cut." Dusty said. He hurried up toward Red. "It's enough. Stop this."

Red kept right on yanking with his arms.

Dusty said, "You're going to hurt yourself." He looked around the basement. "We'll find a way to get you free."

Michelle felt something at her wrists. She jumped. It was only Rebecca with the key to unlock her. She was so busy staring straight ahead; she hadn't even noticed Rebecca rush up to her. In a moment, Michelle was free. Her legs were so numb and she felt incredibly wobbly without the chains to hold onto.

She ducked and bent, feeling some of the blood had dried to her clothes already. She noticed she was trembling. Her heart was beating fast and her eyes were watering. Overhead, she felt Red's violent jerking ever-so-close.

Standing up on her own, and still only a few feet from Red, Dusty jumped in front of her. "You can't leave. We're not done."

"I'm done." Michelle pushed past him and made it nearly to the stairs. She hurried. In back of her, she heard Red struggling.

She heard Dusty, "We have to stop her. If she tells anyone... she's supposed to die in the end. You shouldn't have let her go."

Someone grabbed at her shoulder. Michelle spun round and Rebecca cold cocked her. "We're not through. I need this movie for my IMDB credit."

It barely registered. Maybe because of her adrenaline, or maybe because she'd grown numb, Michelle was able to shake Rebecca's punch right off. She returned the favor.

Rebecca went right down, holding her jaw, and cowered.

"Screw your credits."

Dusty was right behind her. "You." He yelled.

"Me."

Red broke free from the ceiling and dropped back to the floor with a hideous howl. His eyelids were slightly drooped. He turned to face Michelle.

She took the moment, with Dusty standing between them, and shoved him toward Red as hard as she could.

Dusty was surprised, said, "Hey." And fell toward Red.

Then he stopped moving. It took a second for Michelle to realize Dusty's back had met a handful of Red's daggers.

Dusty looked up and choked up some blood. He reached his hand out. "Please," he said.

"No," she said back, and gave him another kick. The daggers went deeper. Michelle looked down and saw Dusty's feet hovering: his entire weight was carried by Red's daggers. Dusty's eyes shut and Michelle turned and ran toward the stairs.

She didn't look back. She heard slicing sounds. She heard moans. She heard Rebecca scream.

Michelle ran up the stairs.

The scene behind her got extremely quiet.

Don't look back.

She made it through the short foyer and right to the front door. She heard some kind of scraping behind her. She grabbed the front door handle and opened it. She hurried outside. Her car wasn't far.

Do I call the cops? Do I go to the Emergency Room? What?

Michelle made it to her car. Her keys were still in her front pocket, and although they were sticky, they worked. She patted her butt and felt the envelope with her cash still intact. *Thank God for small miracles.* As she climbed in, she heard a roar coming from the house.

From behind a curtained window, she saw Red. It'd made it up the stairs. It watched her with one of its eyes. Michelle wondered if Red had killed Dusty and Rebecca, and if they'd come after her. Would Red dare come outside and expose itself? She couldn't know, and wouldn't wait to find out. *Always follow your gut. Gut's telling me to get the hell out of here.*

She did see the sign on the door, the hand-printed one that Dusty had made that read: WELCOME TO THE JUNGLE.

Michelle couldn't drive away fast enough.

❦

Later, Michelle received a text message from Pam.

"How'd the shoot go?"

Michelle looked around the room, from her head shots scattered on the desk, to the movie posters tacked to the wall, and the acting books stacked haphazardly by the couch, and sighed.

"I'm retired."

Brad C. Hodson is a novelist and screenwriter who currently hangs his hat in sunny Southern California. His short fiction can be found in dozens of anthologies alongside folks like Chuck Palahniuk and Neil Gaiman, as well as scribbled on rolls of toilet paper at random gas stations around Hollywood. He enjoys picking up heavy things made of iron, peanut butter confections, and writing about himself in the third person. Hodson's critically acclaimed novel Darling *is currently available and his upcoming novel* The Mud Angel *has been known to melt faces straight off of the skull. Which sounds awesome, but actually interferes with the reading of it quite a bit. C'est la vie. For more information, please visit www.brad-hodson.com.*

THE SCOTTISH PLAY

Brad C. Hodson

EVERY THEATER HAS A GHOST.

I've done Mamet Off-Broadway, Beckett in London's East End, and Noel Coward at a community playhouse in Alabama. From Chicago to Edinburgh, what all of those theaters had in common, other than miserable directors and bad lighting, were their ghosts. Chalk it up to throwing a group of people with overactive imaginations and penchants for drugs and alcohol into a dark building for nights on end, I suppose, but I have yet to visit a theater that wasn't reputed to house the dead.

In two thousand three, we leased a 99-seater off of Santa Monica Blvd in Los Angeles. "Theater Row," the area's called. Our building was a non-descript beige box, a chain link fence drifting from one corner and around a ten-space parking lot. From the outside, without the banners and posters and makeshift marquis, it could have been mistaken for a dentist's office. The lobby was small yet cozy, a burgundy sofa against one wall and a ticket counter against the other. Past the ticket counter, double doors painted to masquerade as cherry wood opened onto a small landing crowded with blue seats and the dry odor of old paper. The next few rows spilled downward until stopping before the stage. It was small but adequate, a simple concrete floor painted cobalt, chips here and there revealing the black underneath.

Our ghost was named Sydney. If a cool breeze kicked up some papers or someone heard a strange noise, it was blamed on him. The story was that Sydney was a silent film actor who, after failing to make the transition to "talkies," hung himself in the house that used to sit on the spot. Sydney was said to be a playful ghost, kind-hearted and happy simply to be noticed.

This story is not about Sydney.

David and I loved the place. We named it "Theatre Obscura" and planned to put rising talent to work before they were snatched up by soap operas and cat food commercials. We had a great group that first year and performed everything from *Ten West* to *Noises Off*. Opening night was always sold out.

To congratulate ourselves, David and I took a honeymoon at the end of the year. We weren't really married (this was years before that issue even hit the courts), but had been together for almost a decade and thought it deserved something special. The plan was to start in Italy and make our way north to the village in Scotland that David's grandparents were from. It was to be a calm and relaxing break from the pressures of running a business. And it was, up until we phoned the theater from Brighton to check on things.

"What do you mean, 'cease and desist'?" David scratched his scalp. "Uh-huh. And why the hell did you do that? I see." When he hung up the phone we ordered two pints of lager and took a corner booth at the pub.

"Well?"

He sighed. "James, we have been blacklisted from the Dramatist's Playbook."

"What? That's ridiculous. Why would we—"

"Because Terry, that miserable fuck, decided to cast a woman as Estragon."

"Has he ever read *Godot*?"

"It seems he has not." He sucked down half of his lager and wiped his mouth. "They received a cease and desist letter that he neglected to tell us about and which he promptly ignored. Now we have been denied access to half of all of the plays out there."

Terry was an ambitious director who, unfortunately, lacked the talent and vision that he told everyone he had. We'd left him in charge of a production of *Waiting for Godot*, the *Hamlet* of contemporary theater, while we were gone. When acquiring the rights to produce a play, the playwright often has stipulations that go along with it, things that the director is allowed to do and things that they aren't. The Samuel Beckett estate does not allow a change in gender of the characters or rewriting of any dialogue. And yet Terry, who we had spoken to before about his penchant for "stunt casting," had decided to flaunt those prescriptions and violate the contract that we had signed.

The punishment was devastating. Being blacklisted from the Dramatist's Playbook could potentially cripple the theater. It would mean the inability to stage a majority of the plays out there. Terry had pissed all over our grand little enterprise in an effort to stroke his own ego.

"We have to fly back," David said. He downed the rest of his beer and slammed the mug onto the table. "Goddamnit."

The other patrons glanced at us and went back to their business.

"I'll go," I said.

"Huh?"

"I'll go. I'll take the train to Heathrow tomorrow morning and you can head up to Scotland."

"I can't ask you to do that."

I took his hand. "I want to. I couldn't forgive myself if you came this close to seeing where your family's from and then were taken away."

"Are you sure?"

"Positive."

His smile was worth the fee the airline charged for changing my ticket.

Back in Los Angeles, my first task was to fire Terry. He didn't take it well.

"You can't fire me." Terry was a large man with arms like timber.

"I can and I have. Please leave."

"You little faggot," he said, shifting his weight between the balls of his feet and flexing his fingers. I was afraid he was going to hit me. I'm sure he would have, if the cast hadn't been there at the time.

All of the actors jumped up at the sound of the "f" word, but Terry was gay and I didn't flinch. He had always made jokes about how effeminate David and I were, as though our slight frames and fondness for musicals made us negative stereotypes. Perhaps we were stereotypes, but at least we had some kind of talent.

He stared at me, nostrils flaring, before glancing around the room at the others. He tossed his script at my face and stomped from the theater, smacking the double doors hard enough on the way out to rip one from its bottom hinge.

I spent hours over the next week groveling to the Beckett estate and to the Dramatist's Playbook. I managed to avoid a lawsuit, but wasn't able to get immediate access to the plays back. We were put on a "one year suspension," meaning that for the next twelve months we couldn't perform anything that would actually put asses in the seats.

"Fine," David said when I told him. "We can work with that."

"How?"

"We'll do Shakespeare."

"Shakespeare. In Los Angeles?"

"Why not? Shakespeare has everything. Sex, violence, the occult."

"The occult?"

"Yeah. Why don't we do *Macbeth*?"

"Shhh! Don't say that, I'm at the theater." That particular work of the Bard's is cursed. As legend goes, muttering its title inside a theater will doom the production to tragedy. Actors simply refer to it as "The Scottish Play" as a result.

David laughed. "You know, I'm only about ten miles away from his castle."

"Whose castle?"

"Macbeth's."

"Glamis Castle? Really?"

"Yeah. Listen, why don't you hold auditions and I'll direct it when I'm back."

"I don't know…" I wasn't into the idea for a number of reasons, the curse being only one of them. But David had a gift for whittling down my resolve to nothing. Before I had even agreed to it, I knew that the only way the conversation would end was with me rolling over and giving in.

We found our cast and David came home to direct. I picked him up at LAX and drove straight to the theater for the table read. He busted the doors open, threw his luggage to the ground, and leaped onto a chair with the type of energy that made me fall for him in the first place. The actors laughed and stared up at him, eyes wide, waiting for some grand speech.

David pulled a leather pouch from his pocket and tossed it onto the table.

"What's that?" Banquo asked.

"That," David said as he stepped down and sat, "is earth from Macbeth's grave."

Someone gasped, whether at the grisly trophy or mention of the name I'm not sure.

Lady Macbeth poked it with a pen. "Really?"

"Indeed it is," David said. "Or close enough to it. I just returned from Scotland where I had the misfortune of visiting Glamis Castle. While there I stole a handful of dirt from the cemetery."

This was par for the course with David. He had stolen dirt from Caesar's grave in Rome, from the amphitheater in Pompeii, and from the grounds of a thirteenth century monastery in France. It was his alternative to photographs. Pagan, in a way, but he had spent his entire life in the theater. It was impossible not to develop eccentricities.

Everyone made the prerequisite jokes about how morbid it was, about the curse, and about Terry's *Godot* ("Waiting for Godawful," one of the witches said), and then the table read started. I left them to it and went to the office to crunch numbers and plan our promotional strategy.

Our office was located behind the stage. To reach it, you had to enter through a door behind the box office and walk down a long, narrow hallway spanning the length of the theater. At the end of the hall you could take a left to go backstage, a right for the bathroom, or head straight into the office. There were two red lights hanging midway through the hall, dull bulbs that barely kept us from ricocheting off of the cramped walls. We kept the door to the office open and a lamp burning inside like a lighthouse.

This time, the hallway was dark aside from the dim red glow. The office door must have been closed. I flipped through my keys, searching for the key to the office. The booming voice of our Scottish Lord sounded through the wall.

Two heavy footsteps stomped in front of me. I looked up, expecting to see David or one of the actors.

The hallway was empty, the door to the office wide open, the lamp on.

The image of someone having been standing in front of the door, someone blocking the light, came to me. I thought of Terry and my stomach knotted.

I shrugged it off and went to work.

After the table read, when we were locking up, David asked me what I thought.

"I didn't watch it. I had too much work to do. I was in the office for most of the play."

"No you weren't."

I laughed. "I think I know where I was."

"You were sitting in the back row. I saw you."

"You didn't see me."

"I saw someone."

I mentioned the footsteps in the hallway.

David frowned. "We should give the place a once over before locking up." There are scores of homeless on Santa Monica and we've had to escort more than a few from the theater. We searched every room, every storage area and every crawlspace, but the theater was empty.

"Maybe it was someone who came with one of the actors," I said. "A boyfriend or roommate or someone."

"Must have been." He didn't sound so sure.

We locked up and went home.

That was to be my one strange experience at the theater. Two days later I slipped while walking through the rows of seats and fell down the stairs. I fractured my leg in three places and was confined to home for the bulk of the production. On the way home from the hospital I joked that it was David's fault for saying the title aloud.

Luckily, most of the work I needed to do could be accomplished from my laptop and David hired a student named Nikki to act as stage manager in my place. He was at the theater day and night. This was typical when he directed a production. He lived in the space and, while I missed him, I didn't think much of it.

"Sydney came to watch us again," he said one night while crawling into bed.

"What?"

"We saw the figure in the back row again today. I ran to see who it was but, when I got there, the seat was empty. The cast thinks it's Sydney."

This became a standard nighttime greeting during the Scottish Play. It seemed Sydney was a big fan.

As rehearsal went on, David would come in later and later, his skin ashen, his eyes circled in purple sags. Coughing fits would wake him in the middle of the night.

"You're running yourself ragged," I said over breakfast one morning. "Slow down."

"I'm fine. I've just caught a cold is all."

I wasn't so sure, but I knew David well enough to know his pattern. While the play rehearsed, his life would be consumed by it. Once it went up and no longer needed so much of his time, he'd relax and take care of everything he let slip, including his health. Doctor appointments were never made until a show was on its feet.

On the night of dress rehearsal, David never came to bed. I woke around three in the morning to find him in the living room, a bottle of Scotch in one hand and the television remote in the other. The television was on some reality show, the bare breasts of an orange skinned slut covered by a blurred bar and the volume muted. The blue glow cast harsh shadows against him and I was shocked at how horrible he looked. Seeing him every day, I hadn't noticed until that moment just how much weight he'd lost recently. He coughed.

"Are you okay?"

He turned the television off and leaned back in his chair. "I don't know."

I sat on the sofa next to him and took his hand. We were quiet for a long while.

He took a deep breath and asked, "Do you think I'm off?"

"Off?"

"Crazy."

"No. Why would I think that?"

He stared at me, eyes quivering, lips pressed together, and nodded. "Alright. Alright."

"What happened?"

He stared at our hands wrapped together. Closing his eyes, he told me what had happened. If it had been anyone else, I would have thought they were crazy. But David wasn't afraid of anything and, while he was imaginative and eccentric in many ways, he was never naïve and rarely superstitious.

That morning, he said, he had gone to the theater early. He was at the computer, sifting through emails, when he heard the double doors bang open. His breath caught in his throat. It was too early for Nikki to be out of class and, aside from me, no one else had keys to the theater. Heart pounding, skin hot as death, he couldn't understand why he felt so anxious. The air was alive, he said, and even telling me what had happened I could see sweat beading on his arms. The energy in the theater was the nervous fear that filled dressing rooms before a performance: expectant, hesitant, pregnant with anticipation.

A prop sword leaned against the desk. He gripped it tight, his knuckles white, and stepped onto the stage.

It was quiet, the low rumble of the air conditioner the only sound. The house lights were dark and a single lamp rinsed the floor of the set. He marched up to the double doors and propped them open.

The lobby was empty.

He double checked the lock on the front door and, satisfied that it was in place, made his way back down the long hall, convinced that he had misinterpreted a noise from the alley behind the theater. He went back to the computer and replied to an email. The smell of wet earth drifted into the office and he worried the air conditioning was about to go.

There was a sound at the end of the hallway.

He stopped typing and listened. It happened again, a soft scratch against the wall. Rats, he thought, and made a note to call an exterminator.

The scratching grew loud and frenzied, the sound of claws scrambling over the ground. It reminded him of when the cats he had in college would race across the hardwood floors of his apartment, their claws unable to gain traction. He grabbed the sword again, afraid that a giant rat made its way toward him.

He stared into the shadows swirling in the hall, split and punctuated by the dull red lights, expecting to see something the size of his cats racing his way. The scratching continued, the claws slipping, scrambling to regain footing, pulling the thing along through the black.

It pierced into the red and David's chest tightened.

It was much larger than a cat, closer to the size of a human torso. He described it as shadow pulled into shape from its place on the wall, a rustling, rolling black that caved in like an empty coat in the center, long arms like gnarled tree limbs twisting before it, rapidly pawing at the ground to pull it along.

He slammed the door and leaned against it. A thud hit like a fist, its weight rocking him, and the scratching continued at the door. The smell of wet earth clogged his nostrils, the scent of moldy damp cloth riding along with it. David couldn't breathe, couldn't think, could only lean against the door, eyes shut, sword gripped tight to his chest, praying that whatever it was would leave, would drip back into whatever grime filled hole it had crawled from.

The scrambling climbed the door. It hit the ceiling and he could hear it scratch and paw and fight its way back down the hall from above, slipping back into the black and eventually, thankfully, going silent.

He slid down the door and sat there for an hour, his back pressed against it like a blockade, waiting for Nikki to come and let herself in. He played it off when she did, pretended he had taken a nap in the office, and told himself it was nerves, that the stress of everything was getting to him. He resolved to take a break when the play was done and not to mention the incident to anyone, even me.

Especially me, I suspected, and felt guilty for it. He was telling me now. That was all that mattered.

I ran my finger along his arm. Damp with sweat, I expected it to be hot. Instead it was cool, like leather in the fall. "Jesus, David."

He held up a hand, the same gesture he made when giving direction and an actor began to ask questions. He had always hated to be interrupted, hated to let his mind slip from wherever it was. I was quiet. He sucked a trembling breath and continued.

After the dress rehearsal, he found himself alone in the theater again. Nikki had to leave by ten to pick a friend up from the airport and the rest of the cast wanted to get a good night's sleep before returning early to the theater the next day for one final run through. With opening night less than twenty-four hours away, there was too much to do for David to give in to what he had convinced himself was a hallucination created by lack of sleep and too many energy drinks. He had seen the shape in the hall, he knew he had, but he refused to make the thing real, as though thinking of it as anything more than a hallucination would call it back from wherever it hid.

"Like saying the name of Macbeth," he said.

He asked Vince, our King Duncan, to search the theater with him before locking up, not wanting to be surprised by a homeless man looking for a place to nap, and then triple-checked the locks on the front door after Vince left. He propped open the double doors, turned the house lights on, and placed a Paul Simon CD into the theater's sound system. He went back to the office, locked the door, and, certain the sword was by his desk, poured over the list of pre-sold tickets, comps, and reservations. He gathered up everything he could do at home and shoved it into his messenger bag, leaving exactly fifteen minutes worth of work before he could leave the theater. He took deep breaths, partly to stay calm, and partly to check for the scent of dirt and mold.

When he finished, he powered down the computer, threw his bag over one shoulder, and grabbed the sword. He threw the door open, feeling ridiculous for standing with the prop held out like he had challenged a knight to a duel. The shadows beyond his yellow lamp seemed thinner than they had that morning, weaker against the red glow. Grabbing the remote control for the sound system, he didn't kill the CD until he was at the open doors to the lobby, afraid to hear the scratching, scrambling claws racing toward him, confident in his assumption that if he did not give the idea of the thing credence it wouldn't bother him.

It hit him as the music vanished and silence rushed in to flood the theater that it had needed no thought of it to bring it crawling from the dark that morning.

Rather than use the light board backstage, he closed the double doors to the house and flipped the breakers for that section of the theater off. An electric hum that he didn't realize he had been listening to whined down to nothing and vanished. The front door was ten feet from him, the light to the lobby right there at the door, the streetlight outside shining down on the entranceway, illuminating the cracked pavement and oil splattered fast food bags stuffed against the gutter. Cars zoomed by and he felt safe in the arms of the city and her bustling nightlife. He marched to the door, unlocked it, and flipped the lobby light off.

It had been hiding there, wrapped in the light like a strait-jacket that ripped away with the flipping of that switch, its black shape devouring the light from outside.

It flapped like fabric in the wind, the rustling of linen echoing in the lobby as it reached for him. He fell against the wall, grasped for the light switch, but it was in the way. The height of a man on his knees, the mangled shape of sheets twisted in the wash, headless, not the form of a person but moving still like someone racing on hobbled feet, its center whipping like a flag, something like an arm but knotted and brittle grasping for his face. He closed his eyes and turned away as the smell of earth and mold and stale water filled him. It brushed his forehead, the touch like soggy wool, rotted to almost nothing, pressed against his skin. It was fever warm, thick with illness, and he cried out.

Falling to all fours, desperate to break contact with it, he scrambled to the entrance, his hands slipping on the floor. He shouldered the door and rolled out onto the pavement, was on his feet before he realized he stood, and fought to lock the door behind him.

Through the glass, the lobby was empty.

I realized at some point during the story I had taken my hand away. David gripped it again and took several deep breaths, his jaw trembling. Then he fell against me and cried. In ten years I had seen David cry once, at his father's funeral. I held him until he cried himself out and then held him longer. Words that would make sense of what happened, that would bring comfort or sanity to his ordeal, weren't in my vocabulary. Silent, I brought him a glass of wine and sat with him until sunrise, our eyes glued to the muted television.

Three days later, two shows into the play's run, David was rushed to the hospital. I came as soon as Nikki called but it was too late. Cerebral edema, the doctor said. Fluid leaked into his skull and put pressure on his brain. It was quick and painless, they assured me. When pressed for how, they said it was likely genetic and exacerbated by stress.

When asked why, they had nothing to say.

After his funeral, I opted not to renew our lease. Shakespeare's Scottish tragedy had been our final show and, true to its legend, the theater died when it closed.

On the final day of our lease, I went to the theater to pack up what was left of our things and put them in storage. I didn't realize it until then, but I hadn't spent more than a few minutes inside since his death and never alone, always with a friend or with Nikki or one of the dozens of actors who had performed there while it thrived. I was surprised by how many of them came to pay David respects. Many of them assured me that we had created something special here, that Theatre Obscura had carved out a place in their hearts and would always be with them.

David would have liked that.

In the office, the computer gone and the posters taken down, I felt his loss more than ever. Throwing his things into a box I couldn't help but cry. Pictures of us, cast photos, David's pen cup painted with our crude logo, all of it stabbed me as hard and painfully as if the Scottish Lord mistook me for Duncan. David would never see any of it again, would never write with those pens, would never hang those posters again, and that thought made concrete the loss. It's odd how the absence of someone can be a palpable thing, almost tangible in its heaviness, and it pressed down on me then, sought to crush me into the ground.

In the top drawer of the desk was the leather pouch he had brought back from Scotland. Gripping it in my hand, it felt warm and fleshy, like a recently removed heart.

"Why did this happen now," I had asked a day before he died, my leg healed enough to walk on crutches and help out at the theater. "We've had this place for so long."

"I don't know," he'd said and shook his head. "I really don't. Let's not talk about it, okay? Not here."

Holding the bag of grave dirt in my hand, I shivered. I threw it into a box with spools of blank CD's and extra printer cartridges.

It sat in that box for the years since then, locked away in a storage container in Van Nuys, until the drinking and the pills became too weak to numb me. Now it's on my desk, in front of my monitor as I type, the air around it alive. Expectant.

I don't know what's going to happen, don't know if it will come for me like it did David. But after I write this, I plan to open the bag and pour its contents onto the bed we shared, spread it over the sheets we tangled ourselves in every morning. Wherever David is now, all I can think about is following him. It brushed his forehead and then he died. David was never superstitious, but I am. I never walk under ladders and I never said the name of that play.

"Say it," he teased in the car ride from the airport when he came back.

"No."

"Do it." He tickled my ribs. I knocked his hand away.

"I'm not going to."

"Chicken."

Lying in the dirt stolen from a Scottish cemetery, a picture of us in Rome framed on my nightstand, I'll turn off the lights and this one time whisper into the dark.

"*Macbeth*," I'll say.

Graydon Schlichter came to Tinseltown following a dream, the only person to ever do so, except for everyone else who moved here ever. That dream was to become a professional voice actor, and it was largely deferred for a time, including a brief departure as a litigation attorney. Having left the legal world behind and reclaiming his soul, he now spends his time acting on-camera and off, writing, and of course doing voice recording for audiobooks, videogames, radio spots, internet spots and more. And, as a founding member of Macabre Fantasy Radio Theater, he has great fun blending the stories of H. P. Lovecraft and his contemporaries with the near lost art of classic radio drama. For a sample of his work, take a listen to (almost) any story from the audiobooks of the Hell Comes to Hollywood *series. He swears this story is pure fiction, not based on his work habits or previous projects in any way. And of course, we believe him.*

THIS IS A RECORDING

Graydon Schlichter

"CURSE YOU AIRPLANES!" barked Gary in Jessica's headphones, seemingly at random. Squinting at her computer screen, she replayed the chunk of Gary's audio immediately preceding the self-interruption condemning phantom aeronautics. Phantom, because as she played it again to be sure, there wasn't even a hint of plane noise underneath what had been a perfectly useable segment of narration sans the outburst. Just as she suspected.

Jessica shook her head, pulled out her earbuds, and rubbed her eyes. As she pressed on her closed eyelids, audio waveforms danced across her mind's eye. Ugh. Sometimes she even saw them in her sleep. She called it "dreaming in waveform", which was not a term of affection. But, this story wouldn't edit itself. She put her earbuds back in and clicked play.

Editing. She did not like it, she did not like it Sam I am. But it was part of the job. She and Gary had been working on this anthology for what felt like forever, though in reality it had been less than a year, if only just. *Terror in Tinseltown* was a collection of stories set in and around, where else, Hollywood, California, themed around awful and horrific events occurring there, and some of them were quite good. Aaron, the editor, had a knack for combining pieces from polished veterans, with those of talented newcomers to create a diverse collection that made you laugh in one moment and nauseated you in the next.

The first anthology was an award nominee, and the audiobook that Gary and Jessica had put together was pretty good by all accounts. Good enough that Aaron had approached Gary about producing the sequel before he had collected all the stories that would fill its pages.

But getting the job, in this case, was the easy part. After reading a story, and clearing up any confusion, pronunciations, or other issues, it would be recorded. A story with both male and female characters required Gary and Jessica to each record their parts separately. Then, lucky Jessica got to "zipper it together" combining the narration and characters into a single piece while simultaneously checking for mistakes made while recording.

"I think this might be a typo," Gary's voice interrupted himself again. "Blood could 'scatter' on the wall, I suppose, but it's probably meant to be spatter or splatter or something. I'll record a few variations. In the meantime I'll email Aaron and forward you what he says."

Sigh. Jessica paused the recording, and opened her email looking for the promised forward. It read: *Hmm, I see what you mean. Talked to the author, go with "spatter" to support the CSI vibe of the story. Nice catch. Aaron.*

Jessica deleted Gary's commentary, as well as all the various takes other than the best "spatter" take and continued. But she didn't get far.

"As the detective approached the house, he noticed that despite it allegedly being abandoned there were lights on in a number of windshields," Gary narrated evenly.

"Windshields? What the hell, Gary?" Jessica fumed quietly. Usually mistakes made a certain degree of sense—turning separate words into contractions, swapping the gender on a pronoun, or even replacing one word with another that was both similar sounding and similar meaning. Jessica could take those in stride. But it drove her a little crazy when mistakes like these came out of nowhere making little to no sense.

Choking down her annoyance, she dutifully noted the page number and correct text for the pick-up, "windows", as well as "when" in the audio file it was located. One more thing Gary would need to re-record before she could hand off the story to him. Jessica continued to edit.

The thing about this process was that it was as much art as science. Noting errors and eliminating superfluous takes (and retakes) was actually the easy part, though time-consuming none-the-less. Managing the pacing and performance, deciding whether to cut out a breath here or some mouth noise there, all required finesse to edit cleanly, and an understanding of nuance and subtlety to do so artfully.

And Gary, God love him, was something of a control freak. Although he and Jessica were working together on this project, he was very clear who retained artistic authority.

"On textual or pronunciation questions, we defer to Aaron, but in terms of performance or editing it's my call," he had told her more than once. Gary seemed very concerned about this, bringing it up again and again, often in the absence of a dispute.

Which meant that although Jessica was the first set of eyes and ears on each audio file, she was never the last. This extended to Jessica's performance as well. If Gary wasn't happy with elocution, style, or delivery he would send it back to Jessica to record again, usually grouchy that she had missed the necessity of a re-take.

"Part of the reason you go through it first is to catch this stuff. I get that you aren't perfect, neither am I, but the fine-tuning work is tedious enough without me having to do half your job, too," Gary's tone undercutting his admission of imperfection.

To be fair, Gary was just as hard on himself. Harder even. He hadn't ever made Jessica re-record an entire selection, like his redux recording of *Killer High* from the first anthology. Nor had he ever suggested she was talentless or useless, things he had said about himself when in the deepest throes of his quixotic perfectionism. But that only went so far in making his nit-picking, OCD death grip approach to the project tolerable. Some days it didn't go nearly far enough...

"Good boy," Jessica murmured quietly to herself as Gary caught a mistake in the middle of a sentence and cleanly started that section over, requiring only that she delete the extraneous bit before it. Gary was good about that too, the overwhelming majority of "mistakes" he made while recording he caught and corrected. And, while that made for longer raw files for Jessica to review and edit down, it did mean less time importing and syncing up corrections, which was sometimes the hardest part.

"Shit! Seriously?" Jessica raged after having spent what felt like an hour massaging a series of error-riddled takes into one near-perfect piece of audio, only to discover that Gary had done a retake of that section already and it was just as clean as what she had laboriously constructed, Frankenstein-esque, from the disparate preceding takes.

"Fine, fine, whatever," she grumbled, half-heartedly. She knew better than to go too deep down a rabbit hole like that before checking for a re-take. It just seemed like when she checked there was never a good take waiting for her, and when she didn't there always was. Jessica deleted her hard-won excerpt, deferring to Gary's which was, admittedly more consistent since it was all one take.

Which just made it all the more frustrating. Gary may be a good narrator, and he may be a good producer. Hell, he may be better than Jessica, and maybe he should be in charge. But as a partner? As far as she was concerned, he could die in a fire and go straight to Hell, taking his platitudes and condescension with him.

The throbbing had begun to pulse, just behind her eyes. Jessica glanced at the corner of her monitor, where 2:34 AM was unmistakably displayed. That explained the headache. *How long have I been at this?* she thought. Jessica had gotten into the habit of spending her days off from Norm's, where she waited tables, on creative projects like this one. Lately, Gary had been growing progressively more concerned about timetables and deadlines, which in turn prompted Jessica to work longer and later, whenever she had the time. Which made it difficult for her to keep track of how long she had been editing, or even to stop at any point before her screen started to swim.

"At least I go in late tomorrow...maybe I can finish this before then." Since Gary wouldn't record pick-ups until Jessica had completed her pass on the story, it was an all or nothing proposition to put it in his court. Re-recording never took him long, but progress was progress, and the sooner that the pickups were recorded and inserted, the sooner a story was Gary's problem.

As she worked, Jessica hummed to herself. Her mind wandered a bit, and she began re-writing the lyrics to *Les Miz* on the fly to be more appropriate to her present plight.

How long has it been since I've been on stage or in front of a camera? Jessica couldn't remember the last time she had done any acting at all that wasn't in front of a microphone. She used to love performing live and feeling the energy of the audience. Or the nervous energy of being on set with the entire cast and crew poised, waiting for the director to call "Action!"

But that was when she was younger, and to be honest, prettier. Hollywood had never been particularly kind to aging actresses. When Gary first suggested she try her hand at voiceover it seemed like a fun way to earn some extra cash, and maybe make some useful connections. Lately though it amounted to the sum total of her creative output. Things might have gone very differently if she had gotten in good with a casting director, like Roselin Draakvander, whom she'd been hearing a lot about lately. But industry networking was and always had been a mystery to her, so instead here she was doing another project for Gary...

Pausing the recording and looking at the audio file, Jessica was pleasantly surprised to note that she was nearing the end. *Maybe this won't take too long after all*, she thought. But, looking at the spreadsheet she and Gary used to track the overall progress of the project, Jessica's heart sank a bit when she saw how many stories remained that were some variation of "not done". Much of the raw recording had been done, but despite low-flying airplanes, motorcycles in the alley, garbage trucks, barking dogs, and crying babies, most of the time involved in the process was the editing. Whether it was Jessica's editing or Gary's that was more time-consuming remained a hotly contested topic of debate. Never mind the issue of which was more valuable.

"No one will even notice that," Jessica had proclaimed time and time again, in reference to some issue, glitch, or audio artifact that Gary found unacceptable.

"Maybe not, but I can hear it, and it's unprofessional to leave it in," he had told her each time. Sometimes it was a recorded moment that with two, or five, or ten, or twenty minutes, Gary could clean up into something he was happy with. Other issues required that Gary or Jessica re-record, insert, and blend the audio so that it sounded seamless. And in ninety plus percent of the cases, Jessica was pretty sure it wasn't worth even the two-minute level of effort. But since it wasn't her call...

"And I would have gotten away with it too, if it hadn't been for you lousy cops and your dog!" Gary's old man villain voice was just this side of being a cartoon character.

Which seemed just about right. The story had decided to go for a bit of a Scooby-Doo vibe crossed with its crime procedural core. It was, admittedly, an odd choice, but rather fun. And frankly, few enough of the stories in this collection had happy endings, so catching the bad guy was a refreshing change of pace.

Jessica breathed a sigh of relief. One more story reviewed and ready for pickups. Aside from "windshield" there were only a handful of things to fix. Until Gary gets ahold of it anyway. "No point in borrowing trouble from the future," Gary was known to say, and it was good advice in this case.

Save the file, and close the program.

Progress.

3:47 AM.

Unfortunately, her sense of accomplishment did nothing to dull the throbbing ache in her skull. Rising from her chair, and walking swiftly down the hall, Jessica headed to the bathroom for some Advil. Passing the doorway to the kitchen she was assaulted by a truly foul stench which did nothing good for her headache. *When was the last time I took out the trash?* she thought to herself, wondering if she would need to do that too before finally heading to bed.

Flicking on the bathroom light, Jessica opened her medicine cabinet, found the Advil, and popped the cap in one smooth motion. Unfortunately, she had repeated this pattern often enough that she had it down to a fluid art form. Sure enough, as she tilted the bottle into her cupped hand, the last two pills fell out. *Wasn't this bottle new last week?* Turning on the tap, Jessica filled a cup with some water and used it to toss back her pain meds.

As she closed the mirrored cabinet door, there was a flash of something in the reflection behind her. Almost choking on the half-swallowed pills, Jessica spun around finding herself face to face...with the wall. Her small bathroom wasn't even large enough for someone to sneak up on her without bumping into her. There was nothing to be frightened of.

Finally heading to bed, she passed the doorway to the kitchen again, and heard the sound of buzzing flies. "Ugh. Ok, ok, trash now, sleep later."

Scrunching her nose, and holding her breath, Jessica made her way into the dark kitchen, and collected the garbage bag. It felt light considering the smell, but that happened sometimes she supposed. "Quality over quantity," she giggled to herself. *God, I am tired*, she thought, as she took out the trash.

The iPhone on the kitchen table was vibrating when she returned, "Dad mobile" was visible on the screen before the phone gave up and sent the caller to voicemail.

"Dammit," Jessica muttered as she fast-walked to the kitchen and scooped up the phone, her eyes gliding right over the pulled-out chair and the slumped shadow seated there. Before leaving the room, she noticed that the smell hadn't really improved. So while she waited for the tell-tale buzz of a new voicemail, Jessica opened the kitchen window to let it air out overnight.

Realizing that she hadn't yet brushed her teeth, Jessica was on her way back to the bathroom when the voicemail arrived. She played the message.

"Gary, it's your father. I know it's pretty early still where you are, but your mother is worried that we haven't heard from you for a while. You haven't returned our calls or emails, hell you haven't even updated your Facebook in a week. We know you're busy, but please drop us a line. Love you, Good-bye."

That was strange, when had Gary left his phone here? And why was he ignoring his folks? Jessica thought back to the last time she had heard from him, but she was so tired, and her head was throbbing so much that she gave up the exercise and focused on getting to the bathroom and brushing her teeth.

While there, Jessica decided to take something for the pain, but after a few minutes of fruitless searching she gave up. *Where the hell was the Advil?*

Finally, Jessica crawled into bed, exhausted and in agony. She did so not even looking at the time, knowing that her alarm would be rousing her for work much sooner than she would like.

As she slept, she dreamed. Disturbing, violent dreams, too chaotic to distill into something that made sense. The final image, driven from her mind by the incessant harassment of her alarm, was that of Gary sitting at her kitchen table, his face pale, his throat slit from ear to ear, blessedly silent, with not a single word of criticism or complaint.

Eric Miller has worked in Hollywood as a Screenwriter, Head of Production, Producer, Production Manager, and other fun filled, low stress jobs. His screenplay credits include Night Skies, The Shadow Men, Mask Maker *and* Swamp Shark, *as well as the* SyFy Channel *epic* Ice Spiders *which was said by the* Hollywood Reporter *to be "...first rate entertainment..." as well as providing fodder for a monologue and parody skit by late night TV host Craig Ferguson. Miller has a few scripts lurking in development, such as* Dog Soldiers II, *and has done uncredited rewrites on other produced films. He also wrote, produced, shot and directed the comedy horror short film* The Waffle House Incident. Culling the Herd *is his mostly respectful homage to the zombie genre. Mostly.*

CULLING THE HERD

Eric Miller

"WHEN ZOMBIES ARE HUNGRY, bad things happen, Kenny. So rule number one—you gotta keep the fucking things full. You understand?" said Sydney Sherman as he dumped a bucket full of pig brains into the zombie feeding trough.

As the gray and red mush slowly spread out over the tin gutter, the zombies on the other side of the fence slammed into the bars and reached through, grabbing handfuls of gore that they shoved into their ragged mouths and swallowed with violent intensity. They were the rotting personification of hunger.

Moments later, when the feeding was done, a satisfied moan rose from their throats and carried above the din of the barnyard. The satiated creatures stepped back from the barrier and returned to shambling around the dirt floored pen. They looked relatively harmless now.

"You see, kid? Keep them full, and everything is fine for another six hours. Just like a movie crew." The rotund, middle-aged Sydney looked back to see his young charge standing ten feet back, ready to run for the parking lot if the zombies even came close to getting over the fence.

"I—I—understand, Mr. Sherman," said Kenny. "Keep the zombies full. Feed them every six hours." He was in his early 20's, thin, with longish hair and a farmer's tan. He wore faded blue jeans, a new work shirt, and a scared-as-hell look on his face.

"Sydney, kid. Call me Sydney. I know this is your first experience with zombies, but you don't have anything to worry about. Even if they got out—which they can't, thanks to twenty thousand dollars of concrete, rebar, and titanium—the shufflers are slow as hell and totally brainless. No pun intended. Why all the horror fans think they're scary is beyond me."

"What about the fast ones?" Kenny asked.

Sydney nodded to a sturdy metal building a dozen yards away. An imposing metal door covered with locks was in the middle of the structure, and two heavily-armed men sat behind a wall of sandbags twenty feet from it keeping watch.

Close watch.

"Fast zombies are another story. Those are the most dangerous monsters we supply, no bullshit."

"Worse than vampires?"

"Vampires are pussycats as long as you pay them on time. Werewolves you really only have to worry about once a month. And ghosts can't even fucking touch you, so if you get past the rattling chains and 'boos' there's nothing to worry about. But runners? We keep those sons of bitches locked up tight and under heavy guard at all times."

"I guess they are pretty bad."

"You bet your ass they are. The only reason I keep them in stock at all is because Peter Jackson says he's gonna do a fast zombie reboot of *Braindead* next year, and who's got the balls to say no to him? The dude sends fucking Ringwraiths to negotiate his contracts for crying out loud."

Kenny's eyes were round with awe. "Peter Jackson...?"

"So you're a zombie movie fan, then?" Sydney asked.

"I, uh, yeah. I am. I know the job ad said we weren't supposed to be into horror, but—"

"Fuck the job ad, all right? I put that stuff in there to discourage the tourists. Truth is, you *have* to like the fucking things to work with them. I mean, *look* at them. And the *smell*... Anyway, I had you pegged as a fanboy the second you walked into my office. But that's all right. I'm a bit of a horror movie aficionado myself. That's why I started this place."

Kenny smiled and relaxed. "*Braindead* is one of my favorite zombie films. After *Night of the Living Dead*, of course."

"Not a zombie film."

"What?"

"*Night of the Living Dead* is not a zombie film. They were fucking *ghouls*. Flesh eaters."

"Oh," said Kenny. "I didn't know that."

Sydney shook his head sadly. "No one does anymore, kid. No one does."

Kenny looked towards the reinforced building. "Are we going to feed them next? The runners, I mean."

"No offense, but it'll be a while before you get to work with them. Assuming, of course, you survive your probationary period."

"Survive...?" Kenny gulped.

"As in, not get fired. Relax. This place is safer than your bedroom. *If* you follow the rules. And we got plenty of those, thanks to the fucking Feds and the regulators from Sacramento and the Humane Society. Hell, we even got the creature-rights activists videotaping everything they can, making sure we do everything by the book."

Sydney glared down the ranch's long dirt driveway, past the main house, barns, and holding pens to the main highway, where a Prius was parked on the berm next to the faded *Syd Sherman's Monster Ranch* sign. A young woman could be seen pointing a long lensed camera out of the front window of the Toyota, aimed right at Sydney and Kenny.

Kenny squinted, and imagined he could see a pretty face framed by curly blond hair behind the camera. After a moment he turned from the car and looked at his new boss. "Well, it's nice to know people care about the workers, right?"

Sydney chuckled. "They don't give a shit about you, kid. You or me. They just want to make sure we're not *abusing* the monsters in any way. Can you believe that? I got three hundred zombies of all shapes and sizes in here that want nothing more than to chew the living brains out of my head, and they want to make sure *I'm* not hurting *them*? Fucked up world, Kenny. Fucked up world. You ask me, we need some changes at the top."

"I guess so. So what do you want me to do now?"

Sydney tossed the bucket into a work sink filled with similarly soiled containers. "You can clean this mess up to start. Then check the temperature on all the 'fridges—last thing I need is a thousand gallons of pig brains going bad on me."

"No problem, Mr. Sherman."

"Sydney. And after that, you can help me cull the herd a bit."

"Cull the herd?"

"That's right. We got a big shoot tomorrow morning at Universal—we gotta have 150 shufflers there by 6 AM. It's a big studio pic, so we gotta send the good stock. Can't give them anything that's gonna fall apart before the first shot."

"What's the movie?"

"They've turned New York street into Shanghai for the new zombie epic *The Woking Dead*."

"I guess the Chinese really are taking over Hollywood, huh."

"That was a joke, Kenny," said Sydney, shaking his head.

"Oh. Sorry."

Sydney put a fatherly arm around Kenny's shoulder. "Listen, you're gonna have to learn to lighten up if you want to make a career out of working with the living dead. Otherwise the stress will kill you. Among other things."

"Uh, ok. So we *don't* have a shoot at Universal tomorrow?"

Sydney took a deep breath, and let it out slowly. Good help—*willing* help—was hard to find. "We do have a shoot at Universal. That was not a joke. The Pierce Brothers are rolling on *Deadheads-Armageddon* as we speak. $300 million budget, pulling out all the stops. Nothing but the best zombies for those guys. I helped them get their start, you know."

"What do we do with the rotten ones? Do we...put them down?"

"*Hell* no. I can rent those to indie films all day long. The low budget guys like them ripe and falling apart, for some reason. Sick bastards."

Kenny nodded, finally settling in to the job. He ticked off his upcoming tasks on his fingers. "So I clean the feed buckets, check the temps, help you separate the good zombies from the decaying ones—anything else, boss?"

Sydney jerked a thumb back at the main cage. "If you haven't quit by then, you can clean up the zombie shit from the main pen. It really builds up with all the brains we feed them."

"Zombie shit," Kenny chuckled. "That's a good one, Sydney. You really are a funny guy."

"Unfortunately for you, kid, this time it's not a joke."

Kenny pulled his truck into the Park And Ride off of the 14 freeway, and saw there was only one other car there. A shiny new Prius. He parked next to it and started to open the Toyota's passenger door. He paused, taking a second to smell his gore-splattered clothes, then shrugged. He was filthy from the day's work at the Monster Ranch, but there was nothing he could do about it now. So he opened the door and slid in next to the pretty, sweet smelling blond woman inside.

"Tell me you got the keys," Rebecca said from the driver's seat. Her voice was shrill, full of energy and anger. She put the camera down and held out her hand.

"Yes, I got the keys," he sighed. "I told you I would. Don't you trust me?"

"I'll start trusting you when you earn it, Kenny. Now hand them over."

He pulled a huge key ring out of a filthy jeans pocket, a ring with at least fifty keys on it, and she snatched it from his hand. Her eyes lit up as she sorted through the mass of metal.

"These are for *everything...*" she breathed.

"Yes. For every lock on the whole ranch. Now do you trust me?"

"Oh, yes."

She leaned over and hugged him. Kenny hugged back, and when she eased up a bit, he tried to put a quick kiss on her lips. She neatly dodged the kiss, turning her head quickly so his lips brushed her cheek instead.

"Do you know what we can do with these?" she marveled.

"Well, for starters, we won't have to break the gate down to get it open." Kenny said glumly. "We can just open the pen and herd the shufflers straight out to the street."

"No, you idiot," she snapped. "The shufflers can wait. We can let the fast ones out with these! No one has ever managed to free any before. I could be a hero to the entire freedom cause!"

"I don't think that's a very good idea," Kenny said. "Sydney says they are very dangerous, and—"

"*Sydney*? He's got you calling him *Sydney*?

"Well, that's his name. That or Syd."

Rebecca rolled her eyes. "I can't believe you're becoming friends with the enemy."

"He's actually a pretty nice guy. He treats the zombies pretty well from what I've seen, and we even like the same horror movies."

"You and those stupid movies. I've told you before I can't stand those things. Especially since they contribute to the slavery and exploitation of thousands of innocent people."

"They're not really people, Rebecca. They're zombies. They eat people."

"It is not their fault, Kenny! They didn't ask to be whored out to cheap movies by people like Sydney Sherman, and they certainly didn't ask to be turned into flesh eating ghouls!"

Kenny grinned at her. "You said they were ghouls! Did you know that's what George Romero called them in *Night of the Living Dead*?"

"*Enough* about your stupid zombie movies!" She hit him on the arm, pounding each word home. Then she grabbed him and looked angrily into his eyes. "I need to know if you are with me, Kenny. I need to know you share the same desire, the same need, to free these people from their bonds."

"There're not pe—"

"Are. You. With. Me?"

Kenny gazed into her passion-filled eyes, looked at her flushed skin, and goggled at her full lips. She licked them as he stared, leaving a sheen of saliva beckoning to him.

"I—I'm in," he said.

She leaned in to hug him again, and again dodged his puckered lips. "I'm so glad I can count on you, Kenny. I won't forget what you've done for me tonight. For us all. And we're just getting started."

The full moon shined down on the Monster Ranch. The Prius rolled to a quiet stop outside the gate, and Kenny and Rebecca got out and crossed the road. Kenny used one of the keys to open the gate, and the two sneaked down the driveway. As they walked, Rebecca grilled Kenny on the ranch's security.

"What about the alarm system?"

"I shut it down just like you told me to."

"And the armed guards?"

"Sydney says they are too expensive to have around all night, so he just hires them during the day for show. You know, in case some fucking creature-rights activist...never mind."

"And the regular guard?"

"I left a fifth of whiskey in his shack before I left today. I guarantee he's passed out by now."

They stopped in front of the massive, locked door to the fast zombie building. Rebecca searched through the keys for the right ones to the reinforced tumblers.

"You did good, Kenny. Really good. I'm proud of you. Now are you sure you didn't forget anything?"

Kenny searched his small brain for anything he could have forgotten. There was something he just couldn't put his finger on. He tried to remember it, failed, tried again, and when he heard the footstep behind him he smiled and finally got it. Sydney!

"Are those my keys?" the owner of Syd Sherman's Monster Ranch asked.

Rebecca and Kenny whipped around at the voice to see a half-dressed, smiling Sydney standing behind them. The zombie wrangler's smile evaporated when he saw the crazed gleam in Rebecca's eyes and the pistol in her hand.

She pointed the gun at Sydney's face. "Stay right there, slaver."

"You can call me Sydney. But sure. Staying right here."

Kenny hissed at Rebecca. "You brought a gun? I thought you were into non-violence."

"Guns are not violent, Kenny. People like him are. That's why I brought protection." Rebecca sneered.

"Zombies are pretty violent too," Sydney said.

"Shut up."

"I'm not really the threat here, babe."

"I said shut up, oppressor."

"No problem. But you mind telling me your brilliant plan?"

"We are here to free the desperate souls you have locked in this prison."

"Desperate souls...?" Sydney was confused for a second. "Wait, you mean the zombies?"

"Life Interrupted Persons," Rebecca announced grandly.

"Or, *LIPs*," Kenny added sheepishly.

Sydney laughed out loud. "You pay someone to come up with that?"

Rebecca ignored him.

Noises came from within the building. Scraping, shuffling sounds echoed for a few seconds as the creatures inside were awakened by the talking, then suddenly violent banging started as the fast zombies threw themselves against the door in blind rage. Sydney and Kenny took a step back from the entrance as the pounding grew more insistent, but Rebecca seemed to be oblivious to the danger.

"Okay, you're here to let the *LIPs* out. What happens after you do that?" asked Sydney.

"They run away in glorious freedom, never again to be constrained by the likes of you."

"You really haven't thought this through very well, have you?"

"I've dreamed about this night for years."

"Then you missed some very important information. Kenny, could you please tell your girlfriend here what happened on *28 Weekends Later*?"

Kenny blushed. "We're just dating. And I don't think she cares that the script used major plot points from *Day of the Triffids,* Syd."

Sydney gritted his teeth and tried to remain calm. "Not the script, Kenny. The filming. Remember when the fast zombie virus got into the general population?"

"Technically that was a rage virus, not a zombie one."

"That's true, but the point is, one of the asshole producers tried to save money by using unlicensed runners—not using the proper safety protocols, training and equipment that a professional registered movie monster wrangler such as myself would use, mind you—and the zombies got loose."

Kenny nodded as he remembered the story. "The regular press squashed the story. Art Bell and Fangoria were the only ones that talked about it. The fast zombies ate the producer and director, and turned half the crew in minutes."

"They were fast all right," continued Sydney. "They almost had to nuke Pinewood Studios and West London, but the British Army finally got it under control. All those scenes of destruction in the final film are not set dressing. They shot the real aftermath and used it in the movie. Amazing production value. Too bad so many people died to get it."

Rebecca had finally reached her breaking point. "Would somebody please tell me what the goddamn point of all this horror movie mumbo jumbo is!?" she screeched.

"The point is," said Sydney, "you really, really, *really* don't want to fuck around with fast zombies."

"I think he may be right, babe."

"*Don't* call me *babe*! Now enough talk. There are souls inside that are yearning to be free."

"Yearning to eat your face off, maybe."

Rebecca ignored Sydney, and handed the key ring to Kenny.

"Open it up," she said, then turned her attention to the door while he tried to find the right key.

Kenny searched for the correct one, but it was dark and there were dozens to choose from of all shapes and sizes. He tried a few in the first lock, but none fit. He fumbled for another key, but the ravenous banging from inside flustered him further. "Uh, Sydney? Can you give me a hand?" he asked.

"Right. I'm going to help you release a bunch of fast zombies so they can eat me and the rest of Santa Clarita for breakfast. How stupid do you think I am?"

Rebecca cocked the gun and pointed it at Sydney's right eye.

"Oh, *that* stupid. Let me take a look."

Sydney joined Kenny at the door.

He leaned close as he pretended to look for the right key, and whispered desperately to his young worker. "If you do this, kid, everyone in Southern California's gonna be dead by the end of the day."

"But she says they need to be free."

"Why do you listen to her anyway? You seem like a smart guy." Sydney nearly choked on the lie.

"She says if I do this, she'll be my girlfriend. And, well, you know…"

"Jesus, kid. If you want to get laid, I'll send you to Reno for the weekend and you can free as many little zombies as you want. Just don't do this."

"I don't know…"

The door slammed outward, making them jump.

Sydney pleaded with his eyes. "All right. Forget saving the world. Think about this instead. If by some miracle you survive the night and do wind up in her pants, do you really want to spend the rest of your life with a woman who hates horror movies?"

This woke Kenny up. "You're right. But what do we do? She's got a gun."

"I've got four ex-wives, kid. I think I can distract her. You take this and open the shuffler pen." Sydney snapped a single key off the ring and handed it to Kenny.

"But they haven't eaten in hours!"

"That's what I'm counting on."

Sydney gave a big, fake, covering sigh and turned to face Rebecca, the key ring jangling in his hand. As she focused on Sydney, Kenny slinked away and disappeared into the shadows.

"What's taking so long?" Rebecca demanded.

Sydney shrugged. "Funny thing, the staff has been after me for years to change over from these old fashioned keys to an electronic key card system."

"What's funny about that?"

"Well, ironic might be a better word. You see, there's a key card in *Return of the Living Dead 3*. Lets this kid onto his dad's military base where he and his girlfriend run into some fast zombies. Kinda like you and Kenny."

"We're not dating. Now stop stalling and open the door!"

"All right. Fine. I'll open the door. And you can get eaten with everyone else, just like in *Dawn of the Dead*!"

"No more goddamn horror movies!" she bellowed, waving the gun around dangerously.

"Just give me one more. *The Gate*."

"What are you talking about!?"

Sydney pointed behind her. Rebecca looked around and saw Kenny next to the open gate to the shuffler pen. He stepped deftly aside as the slow zombies stumbled out, heading right for her.

"Sorry, babe. But I'm breaking up with you."

"We're not dating!" she screamed.

Attracted by her yelling, the zombies slowly closed in on Rebecca. Sydney and Kenny hunkered down in the sandbagged guard station and quietly watched the scene unfold.

Rebecca pleaded with the approaching shufflers. "Listen. I came here to free you. I'm your friend. Do you understand *friend*?"

The zombies didn't seem to understand, or care. Moaning hungrily, they reached for her. She tried to back away, but ran into the metal door.

"You stay the hell away from me, all of you!"

The ring of zombies tightened. One of them grabbed at her hair, leaving a smear of gore on her blouse as she twisted away.

"How *dare* you!" she roared, and began shooting. Bullets slammed into rotten torsos and limbs, but the undead monsters kept coming.

"Why doesn't she just shoot them in the head?" whispered Kenny. "Everyone knows that's how you stop a zombie. Or she could just walk away. I mean, look at them. A baby could outrun them."

"I know, right? But people always panic around shufflers." Sydney said. "Maybe if she spent more time watching horror movies she'd figure it out, right?"

"No shit," agreed Kenny.

They high fived.

A moment later, Rebecca ran out of bullets. The zombies closed in, and in a last desperate measure she threw the gun at the closest one and screamed her last words: "Fuck you all then!"

"Throwing the gun never works either," noted Sydney.

The creatures clawed at Rebecca with filthy nails and teeth, razoring into her soft flesh and tearing her apart. She screamed louder as blood fountained though the air. The zombies got into a tug of war, one group pulling her head and arms one way, another group dragging her legs the other. Her bones and muscles held up for a moment, then they ripped Rebecca in half with a splash of blood and guts. The screaming stopped, and the zombies piled onto the feast.

"Rest in pieces," Sydney quipped.

Kenny threw up.

"Not like in the movies, huh kid?"

"It's *exactly* like in the movies. That's the problem."

"Well, it had to be done."

"I guess so. You have to report this, right?"

"Yeah, and there'll be a ton of paperwork with the CDC and county health board. But it's better than the alternative, right?"

"What are you going to tell the police?"

"I'm going to tell them that a nut-job creature-rights activist broke into my ranch and tried to let the runners out. And that my quick thinking ranch hand Kenny stopped her and saved the day along with thousands of innocent lives. And if they ask me, I'll tell them I think she got what she deserved."

"Why would you do that for me? After I lied to you and all?"

Sydney sighed and leaned against the sandbags. He watched the zombies finish off Rebecca's corpse, and once sated, shuffle aimlessly around the ranch. "Two things, kid. One, you have excellent taste in horror movies. That's rare these days. Gives me someone to talk to."

Kenny nodded. "What's the other thing?"

Sydney studied a shuffler as it paused to drop a huge load of zombie shit in the middle of the driveway. He sighed and handed Kenny a shovel. "Good help is *really* hard to find."

Eric J. Guignard writes dark and speculative fiction from the outskirts of Los Angeles. His stories and articles may be found in the disreputable publications reserved for back alley bazaars. As an editor, Eric's produced the anthologies, Dark Tales of Lost Civilizations *and* After Death..., *the latter of which won the 2013* Bram Stoker Award®. *Read his novella,* Baggage of Eternal Night *(a finalist for the 2014 International Thriller Writers Award), and watch for many more forthcoming books, including* Chestnut 'Bo *due in 2016. Visit Eric at:* www. ericjguignard.com, *his blog:* ericjguignard.blogspot.com, *or Twitter:* @ericjguignard.

DREAMS OF A LITTLE SUICIDE

Eric J. Guignard

WHAT IS A HEART?

By any definition it is the mechanism of our body that keeps us alive, pumping blood to all the other organs we require to live. If we were a movie, it would be the producer, pushing, pushing, pushing the blood to move, to circulate, to oxygenate. We don't see it, working behind the scenes, toiling without respite, and often we don't even think about it. The heart is a workhorse, and without it we would die.

But cannot the same be said about Love?

After all, are not the heart and the sentiment of love wound so inextricably as to be inseparable? I would declare that it is not only one heart that keeps us alive but two, for we must have the physical heart beating within our chest, but we must also have the heart of another, the love which motivates our cardiac producer to continue laboring with gusto. Otherwise what would life be, but a series of futile motions, a strip of test screen shots that are cut and quickly discarded?

And what would *we* be, but a race of tin men shambling down the brick road of life, mourning the emptiness within our chests? I wonder how long Baum's Tin Man would have lived, had the Wizard not granted him the heart he desired? I wonder how long until the rust that eroded his exterior would have eaten through the mechanisms of his insides as well? Or, I wonder, how long until he took his own axe and cleaved his metal chest in two or severed his head off its bolted neck? You see, the Tin Man *had* a heart once, when he was a mortal woodsman, and in love. But he became a man of tin, without a heart, and his capacity for love was gone...

I say this as barely three months had passed after I met June Haley. In three months, how a life changes! How it grows large and brightens, then dissolves like a shimmering rainbow that fills the air with brilliance, only to vanish once looked upon for too long. Poetic flair aside, life sure is a wicked bitch sometimes.

I hail from Milwaukee, and before my recent arrival on the Pacific Coast I'd never before left that 'Great Place on a Great Lake.' But I'm special. Some call it a deformity and some call it a *difference*, as if it were an amiable conflict of opinion. Whatever you call it, it got the attention of a Metro-Goldwyn-Mayer scout, who invited me to be part of a movie. A movie!

I hopped on a train for California faster than Fatty Arbuckle chasing a 15-year old with a sandwich. I may never have been in a film before, but I sure watched 'em. Every week at the Emerald Theatre, I dressed to the nines and escaped my miserable Wisconsin life to sweep Greta Garbo off her feet, or blast James Cagney in a quick-draw, or dance alongside Fred Astaire and Ginger Rogers.

I was 26 years old and still lived at home with my folks. Where else could I go? People daily whispered I was a freak, a half-man. I couldn't land a job, especially during the Depression. Businessmen were hurling themselves out of windows, they lost all their money during the stock crash. It didn't bother me as

I never had money to begin with. You never realize what you can't live without, until you experience it first…

Anyway, before I left home I told my folks. Of course they didn't want me to go.

"The studios are just going to exploit you," mother said.

"What am I doing here? Making sure the couch still works?" I replied. "I'd rather be exploited by the likes of Errol Flynn and John Barrymore than stared at by the neighbors."

"But you're not Jewish. You'll never survive the movie business," father said.

"That's just ignorant. Buster Keaton isn't Jewish. Neither is Katharine Hepburn or Jean Harlow. Look at them," I said. "Los Angeles is the city where dreams come true. I'm going to be a star!"

So I arrived in Los Angeles in early December, 1939, and from there took a bus to its heart in Culver City. Filming had already begun, but there were problems with recasting actors and the executives said the script's pace was too slow, and most of it was being scrapped in order to start over again under a new director, Victor Fleming.

I'd not read the book by L. Frank Baum, but I was familiar enough with the story and I knew exactly who I'd be playing. Me and a hundred other midgets were gathered from the distant corners of America to populate the land of the Munchkins.

For that, I was paid $125 a week and given board at the Culver Hotel with most of the other actors and actresses. My father, who'd worked the assembly line all his life, never made $125 a week, *and* he had to pay rent.

It was winter in California, and residents wearing short-sleeve shirts said it was cold outside. Meanwhile, back home in Milwaukee, there was a blizzard. In California, people smiled and waved at each other, even to strangers. In Milwaukee, people were born grimacing. In California, I was celebrated. In Milwaukee, I was mocked. Here, I dreamed of things I'd never thought possible. There, I stared at floral print on the walls.

Then, on top of everything else, I met Juniper Haley. If my life in Hollywood came any closer to Heaven, I would have sprouted wings and a halo.

June was a seamstress in the Costume and Wardrobe Department, and I saw her scurrying about on the set, threading a needle here and stitching a scarecrow patch there, ordered around by the head designer, Adrian Adolph Greenberg, or his busybody staff.

She was not a little person like myself, but neither was she tall as most other women. One day on set she fitted me for costume, and as she stood over me the bottom of her bosom touched the top of my head.

"If my chest ever needs to rest I can use you as a shelf," she said.

I thought I should be infuriated by that remark, but it was *funny*. The intent wasn't malicious, as it would have been back home. Plus her fingers ran across my arms and legs and chest as she measured, and I liked that. I replied, "Everyone needs the experience at least once."

She laughed. The sound was musical, like something the orchestral department would have composed for a Judy Garland solo. She said, "I always knew there was something missing from my life. Now I can die fulfilled."

She told me her name. I told her mine.

"So where'd they find you?" she asked.

"Milwaukee, the envy of America."

"I've done some work out there. I remember watching *A Star is Born* at the Emerald Theatre."

"That theatre is right down the street from where I lived!"

"Small world," she said, then placed her open hand against my cheek. "No offense!"

I flushed. "I might be offended if you weren't so fetching."

She flushed in return. "I guess you can make fun, too. I deserve it."

"I'm serious."

"You've got bad eyes then."

I stuttered, and my flush brightened. I always thought myself adroit with words. I wrote poetry back home, expressions—like my emotions—that I never showed to anyone. I wrote about love and lust in my diary, then hid it all under the mattress where other men might keep saucy photo cards. But now I had to voice something which I normally imagined only while lying in the dark: "Maybe I can take you out for dinner tonight...if you don't already have other plans..."

"Me with someone like you?" she asked.

I don't know what was more mortifying—the expression on June's face or the tone of her voice.

"I'm sorry," I blurted. "I shouldn't have said that. I mean, I just meant, well, I don't know anyone else out here—"

"No, no," she said. "It's not that. I just meant you wouldn't want anything to do with me. You're too nice, and I'm dumped from a string of bad relationships. My heart is frozen hard... You'd probably hate me."

"What halfwit would dump someone like you?"

She turned her face from me, and I didn't know if she was going to sob or sigh or walk away. I placed my hand on her forearm.

She turned back, and she looked hopeful. "I'd love to have dinner with you."

So we went out. I had an advance on my first week's wages and took her to a club that served porterhouse steak and souffléd sweet potatoes while the *Artie Shaw Band* played on stage. It was a hit.

The next night we went out again. Then again after that. She opened up to me, and I fell for her hard.

June Haley had traveled all over following the movie industry's shooting stars. She'd worked on *Captains Courageous* in Massachusetts, and *City Lights* in San Francisco, and even *The 39 Steps* in Scotland. Though she was a Hollywood hand, she dreamed of making leading lady. But she could never get onto the big screen, no matter how many filmmakers she took under the sheets and let direct between her legs. Her body was too thin, her limbs too stumpy, her face too round.

But her eyes were flecked by the quiet dreams of magnolia blossoms, and the depth of sweet sea waters, and the eager longing for approval, as if she were a hitchhiker waving her arms along the side of the road, watching all the cars pass by without acknowledgement. You could not see that in her eyes, unless you looked deep. I don't think anyone had, before me.

A week later, Christmas skies rained winter chill outside her apartment though, inside, her bed smoldered hot as a steamer, its covers pushed to the floor in waded lumps. We sighed and lay tangled in each other, our arms and legs loose and caressing. My eyelids were weighted by great comfort, and it seemed the world had at last emerged from the womb of the cosmos.

She whispered to me, "I think you've melted my heart."

"I'll never let it freeze again."

"Of all the men I've met in California, it took one from Wisconsin to renew my faith in romance... Wisconsin, of all places."

"No one should ever treat you less than the best."

"I wish. No one treats you like a lady out here; all you are is a conquest, a statistic. It's like a bartering system: I'll give up a piece of me if you can do me an industry favor. Get me a part, introduce me to someone, bring me to an event."

I understood.

She told me about her last relationship with the film's costume designer, Adrian Adolph Greenberg. He promised to get her an audition with Louis B. Mayer, and so she did whatever Greenberg asked. Then she caught Greenberg diddling with a make-up girl. He blamed June for his own indiscretion, then dumped her, screaming he would ruin her career. A few months later they made up, and he promised things would be different. Things were, only that the next time she caught him fooling around, it was with a lighting boy. He blamed her again, and she crawled away, sobbing.

"I'm not like that," I said.

"I know."

"Dreams really do come true," I added, though I don't know if I spoke to her benefit, or to my own. "But never in the way you expect."

She kissed my forehead, just where Glenda kisses Dorothy. And, like the land of Oz, the next ten weeks were enchanted.

The ten weeks of June.

౿

What is courage?

It is said that courage is the strength to confront difficulty. It's an intangible faculty, and a part of us that has the potential to uplift humanity. If we were a movie, courage would be our cast, the actors who brave formidable roles like ferocious lions that rule as kings of the screens. Sadly, as we all know, not every lion can be a king, and not every lion is courageous, and many actors simply lack the fortitude to persevere in the face of a challenge.

Some, you might say, are even cowardly, and I count myself amongst their number.

By mid-January, filming had picked up on *The Wizard of Oz*, and scheduling rushed forward at a frantic, breakneck speed. We worked like shackled convicts, six days a week, on set from four in the morning until eight at night, always in costume, always in makeup. I got so used to grooming an orange wig and wearing buckled shoes and green newsboy pants, that I nearly forgot what my normal appearance should be.

Victor Fleming said we would be done shooting by March, but I doubted it. Like any great undertaking, there were set-backs that put us behind schedule: the Hays Commission was all over the Studios' backs about moral censorship, causing constant script changes; Margaret Hamilton, as the Wicked Witch of the West, was burned during a scene in which she made her fiery exit; and the Technicolor process to colorize sepia film was such a cumbersome burden that it required sequences to be refilmed over-and-over.

And I didn't mind—I wished to stay part of that production forever. For at nights, June and I managed to steal away to one of our apartments for a few hours of fervor, those passions that flare greatest at midnight.

One evening in February, June ran her fingers over my chest, each tip tingling against my hot skin. "If you could meet the Wizard and ask him for something—anything—what would you wish?"

"Nothing," I said. "There's nothing I need to make me any more content than I am right now."

"Oh c'mon, don't be a stick-in-the-mud. Everyone wants something more."

I thought about it. I knew it would sound hokey when I said it, but I was feeling lighthearted, a warmth that was half passion and half maudlin, although what I said was also true as the bliss I felt in her bed.

"I'd want to make someone happy. Genuinely happy, like a happiness that's life-changing. Not even my folks have ever been happy with me, as if they felt my deformity was their penance for some grave sin. I've never brought any real happiness to anyone, and I want to know what that feels like."

"Well, that'd be a wasted wish," June said. "You make me happier than a warbler on Broadway."

I smiled big and believed her. "Then the Wizard has granted my wish already."

I imagined a great rainbow arching over our bed and knew I'd made it to *the other side*. We were so different, June and I, but I realized that must be what love is: the fulfillment of that which you're lacking. Whereas I was a realist, June was a dreamer. I imagined lying in that bed with her forever, growing old and speaking of wishes, and then I caught myself and wondered if it was not I who was the dreamer after all. I felt giddy. What else could joy be, if not for this moment?

I sensed her waiting, trying to read my thoughts.

"Okay, your turn," I said. "What would you ask of the Wizard?"

Her green eyes glistened like wet emeralds, and a frown sank her ruby lips. She rolled away from me and looked up to the ceiling.

"I'd ask him for second chances."

"A second chance for what?"

"Everything," she said. "I screw everything up."

The rainbow seemed to dim. I placed a hand reassuringly over hers.

She continued. "Whenever something good happens to me, I somehow poison it. If someone offers me their hand, I bite it. I'm self-destructive and I don't know why, as if I don't believe I deserve anything good in my life, so I turn from it. I'm like Dorothy, given the keys to the magical world of Oz, but all she wants to do is run away, back to her little gray Kansas farm. If I were Dorothy, and taken away to Oz, I'd never want to return home."

"But we're already in Oz," I said. "Look around. What could be more wonderful than what we have now? You'll never have to leave this and return where you came from... I know I never will."

She smiled and nestled her head against my shoulder.

But it turned out to be true, what June said, and the rainbow over our bed soon vanished as if a dark twister had come along and sucked it away.

She *did* screw everything up that was good in her life. *Me.* The one thing that brought her happiness, and she left it. She ruined our perfect future! We were meant to be together, like a movie romance set in real life. I gave her my love, my heart, and she reciprocated. I'd never felt like that before—the passion! The ecstasy!—and I knew I never would again...

It was only two weeks after the night we shared our wishes that she wrote me a *Dear John* letter. I'd been floating through the days amidst visions of marriage and children when I found it stuffed inside my wardrobe locker.

> *Darling, I'm sorry, but we can no longer see each other. I thought I had feelings for you, but my emotions were so topsy-turvy. My heart is with another. Please don't let this note get you glum—you're the biggest man I've ever met, and I had a swell time while it lasted.*
> *XOXO Juniper*

I wept, and the tears washed away my make-up, so that my old face reappeared, my miserable and forlorn Milwaukee face. Time muddled after that and shot by, a reel of film that spins too fast on its projector, until suddenly slowing and sticking at all the wrong moments.

It was the beginning of March and production had somehow caught up to schedule. Filming would end soon, as Fleming predicted. There wasn't much time left to win June back... Letter be damned, I sought her every chance I could.

She'd been promoted from working with the Munchkins to become the personal assistant for Ray Bolger, the Scarecrow. Apparently, part of her job duties were to hide whenever I was around. One afternoon while the cast went to lunch, I hid in Bolger's dressing room and waited.

She entered, alone.

"Who is he?" I asked from the shadows.

She startled, then replied, "Please, darling, it doesn't matter. Our lives move forward."

"But why, June? You owe me an explanation."

"Don't torture yourself. There are plenty of other women better suited for you."

No, I thought, *there aren't.* Instead I asked, "It's not Greenberg, is it?"

If June could have slumped at that remark any more, she would have been a puddle.

"I'm sorry," she whispered.

"Don't you see what you're doing, what *he's* doing? He's toxic, he doesn't care about making you happy, not like me."

"Adrian's really a sweet guy, he just slips up sometimes, like we all do. But he makes up for it."

"Did he promise to get you a role again?"

She couldn't look at me.

I kicked at a sitting table, and a glass with a single daffodil crashed to the floor. "Damn it, June! I've seen Greenberg with three other women this past week alone, not to mention the men. Does he offer everyone the same carrot?"

I stomped on the flower.

Bolger flung open the door. Greenberg stood right behind him.

"What're you doing in my room?" Bolger said, then followed with a cry. "My daffodil!"

He was still in costume and sank to patchwork knees, shaking his head in dismay. Pieces of straw that clung to his hair bounced back-and-forth like crazy pigtails. I didn't wonder why he was cast for the brainless role.

"You *little* monkey," Greenberg said, emphasizing the reference to stature just for me. "Time for you to scurry away." He made a series of chittering sounds, which I can only assume were meant to sound like a slow-witted primate.

Bolger stood, then took hold of my shoulders and nearly lifted me off the ground as he shoved me out the room. "You killed my flower!"

"June!" I shouted.

"Stay away from her, munchkin," Greenberg said, his voice cheery as a ringleader. The dressing room door slammed shut.

I was 26, and I was a man, regardless of my height. But I retreated to the washing room and cried like a child. It was *me* who brought her happiness, *me*! That was my wish of the Wizard, and June said it was so. *It wasn't fair!* The Wizard couldn't take wishes back...that wasn't part of the story. So was it my fault? Had I done something wrong or shown myself unworthy?

Or was this just a challenge, a test, like Dorothy tasked to defeat the Wicked Witch before the promise of her wish could be granted? Perhaps hardships must first be endured before a gift can be fully realized? It was as if the great voice of Oz boomed in my ear, commanding me to conquer Greenberg.

I wanted to look at my reflection and scold myself for having been such a sissy, but the mirror was too high. I left the washing room, storming back up the hallway.

Ahead, Bolger was walking away, still clutching the crumpled flower. Greenberg and June stood in front of his dressing room, arguing.

"I don't want you around that deformity," he told her.

"I didn't ask for him to stalk me," she replied.

"It didn't sound like you were telling him to leave, either."

"And who are you, the prince of fidelity?"

Greenberg scowled and raised a warning finger. Before he could speak, I stepped in front of him, hands clenched to fists.

"I told you to stay away," he said to me.

I fired a straight punch at the first target in my range: his crotch.

Greenberg made a sound like a deflating balloon and doubled over, his face turning crimson. Now we were eye-to-eye.

"She's mine," I said. I swung a jab that knocked his nose sideways.

Then I punched him in the eye, the jaw, the temple. I'm not that strong, nor do I claim any skills in boxing, but Greenberg shattered like a man made of china. He dropped to the ground, pouring tears and shouting for help.

June pulled me off. "Let him be!"

I heard voices down the hall, running footsteps.

"Come away with me, June. Leave this place. I'll make you happy. Leave Greenberg and the deceit, and we can be together forever."

"No, I'm not leaving anything except *you*. We're through. Get over it, it was just a fling."

"But you belong to me!"

"I'm not a poodle, I'm not your pet. I don't *belong* to anyone. I'm sorry I ever wasted my time on someone like you."

"You're ruining everything!" I shouted.

June's face seemed to morph with meanness, like a piece of celluloid that catches fire, then crinkles and shrivels black. "What exactly am I ruining? After me, your life will still be the same as it was before. I didn't make anything worse. You'll return home to Wisconsin and still be jobless, still live with your parents, *still be a midget*."

Two security guards dressed like runway showmen arrived and picked me up, one at each of my arms.

Bolger stood behind them. "That's him! That's the dwarf who killed my flower!"

Greenberg sobbed on the floor, and June knelt next to him, comforting.

"No, June!" I shrieked. "Don't go back to Kansas. I have to give you happiness! Me! You'll never be happy without me, the Wizard said so..."

The guards dragged me away.

June yelled, her final words echoing down the MGM halls like gongs in my mind. "You're delusional, little man. I thought you were fun, but you're crazy, you know that? Crazy as a loon!"

My feet were dead weights, and the guards dragged me like a broken prop across the lot. Bolger followed, babbling nonsensical threats. I thought I would cry, scream, but instead all the waterworks stayed inside of me and turned cold and hard.

I was hauled to MGM's gates, then heaved to the sidewalk on Culver Boulevard. One of the guards kicked me in the ass while I fell on my knees. "And don't come back, runt," he said. "Consider yourself blacklisted."

I curled into a ball and laid there on the concrete. Tourists stepped around me, pointing and snapping pictures. They smiled and waved and pretended life was a fine jamboree. Nobody asked if I was all right, nobody cared. I was just another sight to see: *Look! The Egyptian Theatre! Pershing Square! A Jilted Munchkin!*

There was nowhere to go but return home to Milwaukee, beaten, broken, alone. June was right about that, and I knew what awaited me there.

Only she was also partly wrong. Although circumstances might return to how they were, life could never be the same. I remembered thinking about the rich businessmen throwing themselves out of windows after they lost all their money during the stock crash. You never heard of poor people killing themselves because their pockets were empty…it was only those people who tasted the riches and decided they could never continue living again without it.

And that was me.

Granted, I was emotional, furious. I knew, even then, I should have thought the decision through, knew it was the passion of the moment. But I wanted her to see the pain she caused me, the inconsolable agony…

I wanted to die, and I wanted her to be part of my death. I wanted June to know it was her fault.

I snuck back into the studios and returned to set. Creeping backstage, I found a piece of heavy rope used to hoist lighting reflectors. I took it and moved to the back of the lot amongst the constructed forest glen. A set hand had left a wood ladder propped behind the green-roofed shack that was used as the Tin Woodsman's house. I took that too.

The assistant director announced the call to take places, and cast and crew assembled at their positions along the front of the set. I leaned the ladder behind a gnarled, dark oak and crouched beneath. *Seven years bad luck*, mother used to say, but what use was luck now? I looped one end of the rope over the other, again and again and again, until a noose hung completed from my fingers.

Truth be told, it was not the first time I'd contemplated suicide...I'd tied this noose a dozen times before.

"Action!"

They were refilming the scene where Dorothy and the Scarecrow discover the Tin Man. He sang his solo, *If I Only Had a Heart*, and I quietly accompanied the lyrics as I climbed the ladder, up the tree. I moved in shadows, away from the spotlight. But across from me, beyond the actors, I saw the crew's faces outlined by the soft glow of arc lamps, watching each movement of the characters intently. June was amongst them. Though she also watched, her eyes appeared lost, as if she thought of faraway places.

Judy Garland and the others began skipping away from me, singing merrily how they were off to see the wonderful Wizard of Oz...

The noose fit snug. I looped the other end over a thick branch and swung my legs out, so that I sat on one side.

The actors suddenly turned direction and skipped toward me, then past, where I crouched high above. The yellow brick road looked longer than ever, as if there was no end to it. The Scarecrow tripped, and Toto barked. I jumped.

I fell from the tree and felt the rope immediately squeeze around my neck. By reflex I gasped for breath, but it was all wrong...nothing came in, like a door had been slammed shut. My mouth gaped wide and air dried against the roof of my mouth, so I knew it was there...but instead of flowing down to my lungs it all just swirled back out to the world, rejected.

I had an audience, but nobody saw. They were transfixed on Dorothy and company singing gaily away. My final sight was of their backlit faces, and one in particular. June was framed by a glow arching over her head like a sparkling tiara—no, like a *rainbow*—and her lost eyes were crumbling emerald cities.

Suddenly I regretted what I had done. For I realized that she loved me still, no matter what her letter said, no matter what she told me, for Oz can never be taken away. Oz is within us all, and she loved me still, and I gave up on her and everything else, choosing the coward's way out.

June only needed a second chance... That was *her* wish of the Wizard.

My legs kicked higher than a Rockette. Instead of trying to suck in air, I struggled to scream but, like breathing, that too no longer worked. No sounds were made from me, unless someone was near enough to hear the rustling of my fingers clawing at the rope, or my buckled shoes clacking against each other, until I grew still.

Fleming yelled, "Cut!"

And my body slowly turned, suspended from the branch. They had filmed my death and no one even saw. The last thing to go through my mind was Margaret Hamilton's voice: *I'm dying! Dying! Oh, what a world! What a world!*

ᐿ

What is a brain?

By all accounts, it is the control center of our body, the cerebral organ that oversees our other mental and physical capacities. Its size is small, but its command is great. If we were a movie, the brain would be our director, issuing actions, ordering us when to move, when to stop, when to cry, when to laugh.

And, occasionally, it storms off set, leaving you to wonder: *What am I supposed to do next*?

You see, though it *is* our brain—our director—it is not always right. Sometimes, we don't realize the brain has its own flaws, as does everything else. Or, sometimes, we *do* realize the flaws, recognize that the command it's giving is not right for the scene, yet we follow its directions anyway. How else do you explain screaming in anger at the ones you love most? You know it's wrong, it's irrational, yet you do it nonetheless, as if someone else controlled your emotions.

The brain tells us what is real and what is not. But, again, I declare that the brain is not always right! So how do we know when it's mistaken? How do we realize something is not true, if we *think* it to be? The brain says that when we die, our body decomposes. Our mortal remains should lie motionless, unfeeling, the spirit released, the brain *dead*.

But I am moving still, thinking still, loving still.

My brain did not believe in magic, but perhaps the Wizard does not *need* to be believed in, in order to bestow wishes. Perhaps he is not the huckster that Baum made him out to be. Or, perhaps, the real magic was created on set, forged by the thousands of people who believed in a fantasy. After all, what conjures wonder more than a movie to be made in color? And the witches and talking animals and hopes and dreams! It was romance and adventure, and a charm to escape the dull grays of life to start over somewhere new, somewhere enchanting.

My brain was still alive, as was I then, as am I now. I'd been returned to life, and brought back *different*. I was made *powerful*.

I know what a ghost is. I know what a zombie is. I know what a ghoul is, a vampire, a warlock, specter, spook, and kelpie. I am none of those. I thought at first I was simply the result of a wish, like Lazarus rising from his tomb...but I had it all wrong. I am not the wish of a wizard...

I *am* the Wizard.

When I woke for the last time, it was in Hillside Mortuary on Centinela Avenue. I was shocked to rise in unfamiliar surroundings, as if waking from one dream, only to find myself in another. Once that passed, I discovered I'd been slated for burial in the Jewish cemetery. Of course I'm not Jewish, but it didn't matter to Louis B. Mayer and the rest of them at MGM, did it? They thought I was a nobody. A *little* nobody. The studio heads were Jewish, and I suppose they had contracts with Hillside. MGM didn't want bad press so I was an affair that was hushed and rushed nine miles away from the lots and out to the cold metal slab in Hillside's vault.

My folks ended up being right on both accounts. The studios only wanted to exploit me, *and* I didn't survive the movie business, although not being Jewish had nothing to do with it. I doubt MGM even sent notice of my death to them; better for no one to know. Of course, Mother and Father will still think I'm out here drinking champagne from glass slippers, livin' the ritzy life of a glam celebrity like Clark Gable or Tyrone Power. I'd only written home once since I left, and I wondered when anyone would begin to miss me.

And part of me felt saddened by all that befell me, and part of me felt angry.

I was the Wizard of Oz, but I could not undo my past. So Milwaukee no longer mattered. Nor did my folks matter, or Metro-Goldwyn-Mayer, or religion, or movies, or cemeteries. None of that was for me.

Death was not for me.

Only June. Only Love. What else was it that brought me back, but for the last thing I felt? The one thing I feel still? The desire to grant June her second chance.

And yet I still seethed that Greenberg had stolen June from me like a highwayman who carries more riches in his pocket than his victim. It still stuck in my craw that the studios couldn't bother to return my body home to Milwaukee, where my family's burial ground covers one side of Rose Meadows Cemetery. It still agonized me to look upon my life and consider it had been meaningless...even my death—a statement that went unheeded—was meaningless.

I was the Wizard of Oz, and I could change this world into anything I wanted! I wondered briefly what compelled half the witches to become good and the other half evil, and that perhaps each of us has a defining moment to make such a choice. And then the thought vanished in a fiery poof of black smoke. Nothing mattered, but that June belonged to me.

And my insides were still cold and hard, and I remembered them freezing when MGM security threw me onto the sidewalk.

I returned up that same sidewalk, leaving Hillside Mortuary in flames far behind. I was tired of everyone looking down on me...

I was a giant and all the people of Los Angeles the munchkins. They saw me and fled, or fell to their knees in reverence, as they should. I kicked at sleek automobiles that drove across my path, and they flipped over like dried poppies blowing in the wind. The earth shook at my steps, and a great storm followed in my wake, trumpeting thunder and waving lightning's banners.

I took the city and folded it, and stepped across to June's apartment. Crouching down, I spied into her room. She and Greenberg lay in bed, tangled in each other, their arms and legs loose and caressing, as ours once were. I flushed, and steam rose from my skin. Greenberg got up, and put on a robe, and came outside to smoke beneath the bright full moon.

He did not see me at first.

He gazed up to that pale moon, perhaps contemplating his conquests and wondering if the twinkling stars were not next for him to step upon. But things began to fly across the moon, so that it vanished, and the sky turned black and filled with shrieks and the flapping of immense wings.

"Who's a little monkey now," I said, and my voice cracked the streetlamps.

Greenberg turned to me and screamed, and an army of winged monkeys fell upon him. I commanded them to tear him to pieces, and they raked silver claws across his face. His screams died, as did he, and the street outside June's apartment was littered with his scraps.

And my happiness was boundless. It was life-changing, as I wished, and I had so much to share with June.

I looked back into the room, prepared to take her in hand and fly away forever to enchantment. But Greenberg returned from smoking outside. He commented that next week he would try again to get June a role through Mayer, then lay in bed beside her.

I shrieked! The monkeys sat on the street staring at me with ebony eyes, awaiting my next command.

I flew into a rage and ushered a fierce tornado to tear into her apartment. The walls lifted, bursting outward with a roar, and her bed rose through the debris in wild circles. June and Greenberg clung to each other and cried out, until the centrifugal force sent them spinning in opposite directions. Greenberg landed on the ground upside down, his legs stuck comically above him like the stem of an upended flower. I stomped on him as I did Bolger's daffodil. June landed in my arms, and when she saw me her smile flashed brighter than every theatre marquee in the country.

Then she was gone from my arms, back to her bed, in her apartment, with Greenberg, making love.

I wailed and gnashed my teeth and kicked at the monkeys. I tore the roof off June's apartment and plucked her from bed.

"No, June, come with me! You're mine, you're mine forever!"

But I spoke only to my empty hand.

I took June again and again, but she seeped through my fingers like trying to clutch water.

It's not fair, it's not fair, it's not fair! What use were my powers if I could not control the world? I raised mighty walls around June's apartment, but people passed through. I rained fire upon Los Angeles, but it immediately extinguished. I amassed armies of tin soldiers, but there was no one to conquer.

Life became nothing but a mirage, a cruel and fleeting glimpse of what once eluded me...

What *still* eludes me now.

In resignation, I built a great emerald tower that climbed high above the MGM studios and confined myself to contemplate amidst dreaming clouds. I remained there, alone, and wondered as to my purpose. What good was I as the Wizard if I didn't have power to grant wishes—or was I truly delusional as June said? Was I just a small, timid man hiding behind the curtain of reality?

I conjured a small crystal ball and gazed through it, watching June Haley far below. I held the ball to my chest and imagined it as her, the words she repeated to Greenberg instead meant for me.

But perhaps there was more magic in my capabilities than I yet understood. Wasn't it true that the Wizard did not actually grant the Scarecrow the physical brain he wanted? The Wizard bestowed upon him a doctoral degree instead, a simple piece of paper with fancy words, which impressed upon the Scarecrow the belief he was turned smart, when he truly had been genius all along. To the Lion went a medal, and to the Tin Man, a ticking clock. Those also were not the literal realizations of their wishes, but the impetus to achieve the wishes' intent, which in all cases was simply acknowledgment of something the recipients already enjoyed.

So I contemplated the nature of desire: *What we think we want may not be as it seems, and fulfillment may not be in the way we expect, but it often brings to us realization that what we crave most, we already possess.*

And because of that, I knew it was true that my love for June would somehow bring her home. I had only to figure out the faculties I possessed, and how they would assist in getting through to her.

Soon, my pretty...

⌘

What is home?

Ask a dozen people this, and you may get a dozen answers, but I would claim it as simply that place where we *belong*. Dorothy knew it, and she did everything possible to return there. If we were a movie, home would be the world we create, the dream of Hollywood that is imagined and then brought to life, just as a pile of straw transforms into a talking scarecrow. It's not just the background set, that wood and canvas façade we pretend to be as something else, but it's the mythos we commit our lives to exist within. For some, that world is a transient phase, and for others it's a shifting labyrinth. For me, it's a final destination, the palace at the end of a winding brick road.

A palace with thrones for two.

I had resigned myself that I could not have an effect on the world, outside of Oz. I could not free June from her bleak existence, by my own physical efforts, and carry her home. The throne next to me remains empty.

But I am a resolute wizard, and I did discover a way to her, much like pushing from one bubble against another; the film walls may not break to let you through, but their elasticity does not halt your arm either. The walls merely stretch along with your reach and retract as you draw back.

It's an obvious egress, but I did not consider it immediately.

I discovered it the night Greenberg dumped June to marry a wealthy widower. June sobbed in grief and stared at her reflection in the mirror for what could have been years. I looked at her, from the other side of the mirror, and whispered: *It is time.*

I know not if I had her attention, but I whispered of my happiness, here in Oz, and that I waited for her to join. I whispered from the water that ran hot from the faucet, and I whispered through the steam that filled the air. I whispered that she could never be happy without me. I whispered for her to take a razor and pull it across her wrists, and that all the pain, all the loneliness, would melt away when she took her place on the throne next to me. I whispered I could make her wishes come true.

And she did it. June picked up a razor and began to slice through one thin wrist as easy as cutting an apple. But as the blood welled up like blossoming ruby flowers, she shrieked and collapsed, and threw the razor into the corner.

I cursed. She *still* screwed things up...June couldn't even bring herself to leave that dirty, gray world for a wonderful new land with me.

But as I said, it led to discovery, and I realized a way to help her, a way as I had helped myself.

I visit in June's dreams, night after night after night. She may live without me in her physical world but, like bubbles, death and dreams have a permeation to them, and my reach extends to her slumber. We face each other, standing on a yellow brick road. The road runs in every direction, though it leads to only one thing: a gnarled, dark oak with a ladder leaning against it.

It's time, June, time to leave Kansas.

I hold a noose, composed of heavy rope that was once used to hoist lighting reflectors, and I offer it to her.

It's time, June, time to take the noose.

Sometimes she tries to flee and sometimes she tries to hide, but there is nothing around us in which to abscond. The world is a brick road, and it anchors a blue sky filled with a thousand rainbows.

Take your second chance, and let me bring you the happiness I promised.

She does not speak, she never speaks. But if only she would use the noose!

Do it, June, and return to Oz...

I don't know if I affect her in dreams, but I want to believe. Like magic, it requires a certain amount of faith, and I must trust that I'm connecting with June. I must trust that my perseverance has its due effect, night after night after night.

And perhaps it does.

For as I look through my crystal ball and watch the days go by, she grows gaunt and harried. Her eyes begin to twitch, as if she's constantly looking for something from her peripheral vision that isn't there. When she talks, there's a sense of desperation in her voice. Men come and go from her life, though their stays are increasingly shorter and crueler.

The seasons pass, like peoples' fancies, and each one takes a piece of June as it departs. I continue to whisper in her dreams, night after night after night, and I tell her to take the noose.

Dark circles form under her eyes, and hard lines pull at the corners of her mouth. Her hair grows brittle and breaks, and she takes to cutting it short.

She's given up on her Hollywood dream long ago, though she hasn't left the city. She grows old, and stars come and go, and she talks to herself, and she talks to them, when she is alone. But she doesn't speak to an unheeding void, for I am there, and I listen to her, and sometimes she laughs while facing the back of an old alley, and the singsong quality of her voice still reminds me of something the orchestral department would have composed for a Judy Garland solo.

I tell her to take the noose, take the noose, it's time to take the noose.

And sometimes she cries when she sees pretty girls on the arms of older men, and sometimes she smiles when she sees flashes of a movie shimmering from a storefront television set. And one time she saw a little person, as I once was, walking along the street, and she attacked him so viciously that police sent her for a year to the women's prison at Tehachapi.

And I follow her always, holding the noose. I watch her always, holding the noose. I whisper to her night after night after night.

Her body grows weak as a scarecrow, her jaundiced skin yellow as a lion, her movements rusty as a tin man. Had I not followed alongside her over the years, and watched the changes myself, I would never believe the person she has become once travelled the world for movies and flitted with the royalty of cinema. No one else does.

She lays in a hospice bed now, afraid to close her eyes, afraid of the thoughts of suicide that take hold when she sleeps. Winter has come again, and perhaps she thinks back to long ago, to the nights we kept each other warm and made promises that could never be broken. Or perhaps she remembers the time she watched *The Wizard of Oz* in Grauman's Theatre, so proud to have been part of that production. Then, during the scene where Dorothy and the Scarecrow discover the Tin Man, she saw the shadow of a hanging munchkin fall behind the trees, and she screamed so loud that people stampeded out, thinking there was a fire.

But as June once said, 'Our lives move forward,' and her final credits will be rolling soon. She slumbers more frequently, and my visits grow longer. She gazes upon the noose and begins to lift her fingers to it, so close, oh, so close.

I believe that movies should always have a happy ending, and I hope only that the magic still holds, the magic of Hollywood and the magic of love, enough magic to bring us back together. She's waited so long, but I have too.

And I'm waiting still, to give June her second chance to return to this wonderful land of Oz. Our home is here, for us together, and everyone knows...

There's no place like home.

FADE TO BLACK

19653862R00211

Made in the USA
San Bernardino, CA
06 March 2015